D1606795

A MAN WITHOUT SHOES

A MAN

WITHOUT

SHOES

A NOVEL BY JOHN SANFORD

BLACK SPARROW PRESS
SANTA BARBARA: 1982

ISBN 0-87685-544-3 (trade cloth edition)

45

AUTHOR'S INTRODUCTION

IN 1943, I was under contract to Harcourt, Brace & Co. for the publication of three books, the first of which was about to appear as *The People From Heaven*. For the second, I propounded to editor John Woodburn a novel to be called *Johnson, Daniel*, and as I described it to him, its frame would be the standard army questionnaire known as a Soldier's Classification Card. In addition to his name, his place and date of birth, and the extent of his education, the card recorded his civilian occupation, his fluency in foreign languages, if any, his aptitudes and entertainment talents, and his athletic proficiency. To these, I meant to add headings and data of my own that would explore him much more fully, and it was my hope that when the material was assembled and dramatized, it would realize the life and time of one who, though no one in particular, might well be anyone at all. I thought of him, for no reason I now remember, as Daniel Johnson.

The proposal was endorsed by my editor, but the book was slow to take shape, and three years went by before a version was ready for submission. By then, the war having ended, the world had changed and with it I. Originally, I'd intended to write about the experiences of an ordinary American during the first few decades of this century. No definite person (at any rate, none I knew of) had been a pattern for the character I'd had in mind, an unremarkable member of the lower middle class: he was to have been no great shakes, merely one of many and very much the same. But all in whose time it came were affected by that war, not just for its duration but forever, and in the course of being created, Dan too had changed. Only an imagining to begin with, he seemed to have grown beyond my inventing, and I hardly knew him as the man I'd fancied three years before. The main spread of his development was political, and while he never did a signal deed or spoke in smoking words, what force he possessed was outward, and in his effort to transcend himself, to the extent that he succeeded, he no longer struck me as ordinary.

There'd been a time when my publisher might've been indifferent to the leftward swerve the book had taken, but in 1946, for most of the reputable imprints, left was quite the wrong direction. Along with a letter rejecting it, the manuscript came back to me with a rare violation of the editorial canon: the pages were pencilled with comment, the mildest of which was "Straighten up and fly right." Hard weather was on the way, but there were still a few independent spirits around, and after a time I managed to place the book with Reynal & Hitchcock. There, even when Curtice Hitchcock was killed in a car-crash, I was assured that

> Eugene (Reynal) is returning to the firm after five years' absence with the Army and State Department, and we go on where Curtice left off. Please don't for a moment think that there will be any change in house policy. We plan to go on in Curtice's liberal tradition.

Within a year, sad to say, that liberal tradition was a dwindling memory. The best of the editorial staff—Albert Erskine, Frank Taylor, and Harry Ford—had either resigned or been fired, and many of the choices they'd made for publication were under reconsideration or already in disfavor. Among the latter was *Johnson, Daniel*—or, as then retitled, *A*

Man Without Shoes. The new managing editor told me straight out that Reynal & Hitchcock would not sponsor the book even though it had been contracted for, and he demanded a return of the advance. It gave me small satisfaction to refuse, for once again I was out in the cold. But now, in 1947, it was a new kind of cold altogether: McCarthyism, it was called, and hard weather was no longer on the way; it was here.

For *A Man Without Shoes,* the sixteen seasons of the next four years were all of them winter. During that period, the book was submitted to some thirty publishers, and thirty-some times it was declined. No rejection, however, was predicated on the political cast of the book: the grounds given, though they varied in detail, were always literary, always they smelled of the lamp. No one seemed to notice that Dan Johnson was a hot defender of Sacco and Vanzetti, or, if aware, no one seemed to mind. For all I could find, it was perfectly acceptable for a writer, through his characters, to deplore the many evils in American history; publishers and editors were superior to political prejudice, and never would they turn down a book that went against the grain. See, they appeared to say, see how warmly we welcome a lament for the plunder of a continent, see how we anguish over the skinned Indian, the freed and still unequal slave, see how we too march with Tom Mooney, Gene Debs, Joe Hill, with all the insulted and injured of the American earth! Their quarrel with the book, I was asked to believe, was the quarrel of the scholarly: I'd failed to meet the bluestocking criterion.

Well, maybe so, maybe so. But all the same, under the words they used were traces of the words they'd erased, and what those vestiges said was this: "Straighten up and fly right." By the end of 1950, it was clear that I'd have to lay the book to rest or publish it myself. I simply couldn't bury what I thought was still alive, wherefore I took the other course and sought out a printer—not any printer, but a particular printer. His name was Saul Marks, and I'd known him for ten or a dozen years, ever since the days of a Los Angeles magazine called *The Clipper*.

Published as *Black & White* for its first few issues, the periodical was composed and run off by Saul more or less monthly over the course of about two years. A short life, but a worthy one, for many an honorable name graced the pages. Theodore Dreiser appeared more than once, and so did Agnes Smedley and Dalton Trumbo. Other contributors were Carey McWilliams, Cedric Belfrage, and John Howard Lawson. Guy Endore's correspondence from Mexico was printed whenever received, and there were poems by Genevieve Taggard, Edouard Roditi, and Ring Lardner Jr. Only the final issue, which came out just before Pearl Harbor, wasn't the work of Saul, and the difference is apparent at a glance. He seemed to sign each page; his touch is hard to miss.

I'd been one of the editors of *The Clipper*, and on occasion I'd carried copy to Saul's shop and then hung about to watch him compose type or handle his prized old German press. Always I saw the same great care, whether he was designing a cover for *The Clipper*, a newspaper notice, a museum brochure, or a volume for the Huntington Library—always that fine sense of arrangement, that judgment of spacing, color, ornament. At his death thirty years later, he'd long been accepted as the leading typographer and letterpress printer in North America—but I feel as I've always felt, that he raised a craft to the level of an art.

He never told me why he agreed to print *A Man Without Shoes*. It may have been the book's history, the book itself, or his own restive nature, but whatever it was, he fell in with my proposal, and, aided by his wife Lillian, he began to fashion words from melted bars of lead. He called his shop after Christophe Plantin, a French printer and bookbinder of the 16th century, and when he permitted me the use of the name, I became, for a single publication, the Plantin Press. And that was all he allowed me, except the privilege of observing with my mouth shut. Every choice was his, the type-face, the size of the page, the quality of the paper, the binding, the jacket. He'd stand for no interference, but I wasn't minded to interfere: from where I stood, silent and well out of his way, all he did had virtue.

When the work was completed, early in 1951, I thoughtlessly directed that the entire edition be delivered to my home. It was as if a cord of wood had been stacked in the hallway, and after a while, sales having hardly diminished it, it began to overwhelm me, and I had it moved into storage. There it has remained since the time of publication, so in a sense the book *was* buried after all.

Until now—

John Sanford

John Sanford: a list of publications

Novels and other fiction

The Water Wheel (1933)
The Old Man's Place (1935)
Seventy Times Seven (1939)
The People from Heaven (1943)
A Man Without Shoes (1951, 1982)
The Land that Touches Mine (1953)
Every Island Fled Away (1964)
The $300 Man (1967)
Adirondack Stories (1976)

Interpretations of American History

A More Goodly Country (1975)
View from this Wilderness (1977)
To Feed Their Hopes (1980)
The Winters of that Country (forthcoming)
A Very Good Land to Fall With (in work)

A MAN

WITHOUT

SHOES

A *NOVEL* BY JOHN SANFORD

Los Angeles : THE PLANTIN PRESS : 1951

IN MEMORY OF

SARAH AND HARRIS FRIEDMAN

"The people are a powerful source of power."

A MAN WITHOUT SHOES

PART ONE

FATHER'S NAME

LATE one night in the fall of 1908, a man emerged from a livery stable near Coenties Slip and walked west toward Bowling Green. He was a hack-driver, and all day he had operated a Pope-Hartford landaulet from a cab-rank at the Vesey Street exit of the Astor House. Between calls, he had idled with other drivers along the hotel wall, watching traffic change for the changing hour: the drays and runabouts of morning, the victorias of noon, the electric broughams of evening, and then, in the gaslit dark, the drays again, their Belgians plodding the cobblestones on muffled horn.

A wind off the Bay, damp and salt and faintly iodine, struck the man as he passed the Custom House and headed for home, a cold-water flat on the third floor of a tenement in a narrow street running uptown from Battery Place. There were distant stations on the wind, and there were strange flavors, and the man deep-breathed as if to know them by knowing the migratory air, but the far came no nearer, and the nameless remained unnamed, and he spoke a soft prayer, saying, "Ah, God, to see it all! To see it all some day!"

He entered a vestibule between two store-fronts, and as he mounted a brass-knuckled flight of steps, a door opened above, and

I

light lacquered the spindles of the stairway. A woman's voice made a mild question of his name, and he replied by churning chimes from a pocketful of coins. On the second landing, there was a long embrace, after which, giving the woman a purse, the man locked the door behind them and went to a map of the United States that papered much of one entire wall: with a ruler and a red crayon, he drew a line from the island of Manhattan to the town of Passaic. Then he joined the woman at the table, where she sat counting money and making entries in a ledger, and absently filling a pipe, he stared at the great colored chart tacked to the plaster.

Long before, the five boroughs of New York had been overrun by a slick of red wax, and from this always-growing trespass, there now were paths to Port Jervis and Princeton, along the Sound to the Saugatuck, down the Jersey coast to Barnegat, and, longest of all, to Saratoga Springs. In time, the man thought, there would be lines to every name in the nation; in time, he thought, the record of his trips would be the nation itself; in time, he thought.... And pipe-smoke, blue from the bowl and gray from the stem, fought a skirmish in the air. A pen stumbled over paper. Money met money and spoke civilly of silver. The map blurred under the man's gaze, and he made scenes in his mind and heard unspoken speech.

[*Suppose.* . . .

[*Suppose the Astor doorman nodded you off the wall, and while you trotted to the old Pope-H, set the choke, and spun the motor, he slung a satchel at the meter, caught a tip on the fly, and gave your fare a send-off with a salute.*

[*And suppose you said,"Where to, mister?" and the fare said,"Erie Ferry," and you said, "Erie Ferry, it is," and threw down the flag. Suppose all that.*

[*And suppose the fare was a silk-shirt sport, with two-tone shoes and a grip made of crocodile, and suppose the tip he'd flipped the door-man was a cartwheel—and therefore suppose you drove carefully, with no quick stops, no horn-work, no close calls, a nice smooth swing into West Street, and a real pretty waltz around the horses and the backed-up trucks.*

[*And suppose, when you reached the slip, the fare said,"Make it*

*Weehawken," and you said, "Weehawken, it is," and you ran the
Pope-H aboard and got a good place up forward at the gates, and
suppose you switched off the motor and set your hand-brakes, and
then you stepped out and tested a plug, shot a squirt of oil at nothing
in particular, and ragged off the door-handles and the lamps.*

*[Suppose a little more. Suppose at Weehawken you tooled ashore,
saying, "Where to now, mister?" and he said, "Tait's Restaurant."*

*[And suppose you said, "Tait's? What street's that on?" and he said,
"Market Street," and you said, "I'm sorry, mister, but I don't know
any Market Street in Weehawken."*

*[And now suppose he said, "That's all right. The one I'm talking
about is in Frisco."*

[Suppose! Just Suppose!]

For hack-driver Daniel Johnson, that would be The Great Day.

MOTHER'S NAME

THE coins had been stacked and the crushed bills uncrushed,
and the totals they came to had been committed to columns
in the ledger under a date late in the year 1908, but having finished
her task, the woman was no longer interested in the sorted cur-
rency and the writing materials that lay before her, nor was she
concerned for the moment with the man seated opposite her, or
the map on the wall, or any of the furniture that the room contained,
or the federal-confederate smoke at war in the air: her hands were
clasped over a belly bulging with seven-ninths of a child, and it
was the contents of herself that she was trying to see with the
backs and bottoms of her eyes.

*[On a marble-topped table in one of the bedrooms of a Catskill farm-
house, a coal-oil lamp spread a skirt of light around a box of cigars and
a bottle of whisky. In a nearby rocker, a man flinched as a moth rammed
the lampshade, bounced off, and, revolving to recover speed, rammed
it again. The man dabbed at his nostrils as if to find blood, found none,
and smiled. He tufted his mustache and smiled once more.*

*[A woman's voice, muted by fatigue, came from a bed outside the
cast of the lamp. "What kind of cigars you got, Anson?" it said, but*

the man made no reply. He drew deeply on a cold and mangled cigar and exhaled what he thought was smoke. "What kind of cigars did you bring this time?" The man fancied the sound of knuckles on the door, and without rising, he reached for the knob. It was yards from where he sat, but his fingers seemed to feel the chill china, and he went through the motions of opening the door: no one was there. "Godamighty," the woman said.

[The man turned toward the bed, his head wobbling as he peered into the shadow. "You say something, Maggie Azora?" he said.

["The cigars," the woman said. "What's the brand?"

["Best brand money can buy," the man said.

["Bring me that box!"

[The man built a flimsy look of surprise. "You smoke?" he said.

["Bring me the box, you boozing old bull!" The man transported it to the bedside with dangerous whiskied care. The woman took it, held it so that some light reached its label, and let it fall to the floor. "My God," she said, "was that the only kind you could get?"

["Dollar a box," the man said.

["But the name—Apollo Panetela!"

["Fifty in a box," the man said.

["But Apollo's a boy's name, Anse! A boy's!"

[The man squinted down at the woman from a height of many miles. "Didn't we have a boy this time?" he said.

[Slowly, in affectionate contempt, the woman shook her head. "Come down here, you drunken old punkinhead," she said, and he let himself sag to his knees. "Why do you have to get bug-eyed every time I'm confined?"

["Celebration," he said.

["Celebration of what?"

["I don't know. Just celebration."

["I don't mind you getting soused once a year," the woman said, "but why can't you stay away from cigars? Specially when we have girls. Just once, Anse, just once don't let's call a girl after a cigar."

["The name's Apollo," he said.

["Can't that be her middle name?"

["Apollo's the name. Apollo Panetela."

["People'll laugh at her."

[*"Apollo,"* the man said. *"Polly for short."*]

[*"Please, Anse!"* the woman said. *"Please!"*]

[*"Feel like a kiss,"* the man said, *and he leaned toward her, but the image fuzzed and went away, and his face touched the pillow, and he was asleep.*]

[*The woman turned to another face, a very small one almost hidden by a hood of blankets. "Apollo Varner," she whispered. "Your name is Apollo Varner."*]

"What're you smiling at, Polly?" the hack-driver said.

"I was thinking of names," she said.

"You hit on one yet?"

"I think so. I think I have a fine one."

"What is it?"

"I won't tell you."

"Hell, I got a right to know the name of my own kid!"

"I won't tell you, Dan."

DATE OF BIRTH

ON FEBRUARY 11th, 1909, night began to curl back from the most easterly square yard of the Florida Keys at 6:45. Within an instant, it was day for the Okefinokee Swamp and Bob Anderson's Fort Sumter, and it was day too for Cape Hatteras and the mouth of the Rappahannock, for the rip-rap from Seabright to Sandy Hook, and for the lighthouse cliff at Montauk Point. And now the wet grass at Saratoga became a groundswell of broken glass, and the white markers for the dead turned lilac, and through the raveling mist of Valley Forge, light split to splinters on a brass muzzle-loader still trained on Philadelphia, and it was day over Yorktown on the York, and Jamestown on the James, and Resaca on the Union flood of Georgia, and it was the Union sun that spoke over Mobile Bay, and at Spotsylvania's Bloody Angle, and in the Peach Orchard of Gettysburg. Now the silver ice of Antietam Creek was changed to gold, and day, not John Brown, raided Harper's Ferry, and day, not Jackson, shuttled through the passes of the Massanutten, and now the Piedmont began to warm, and the Cumberland, and all the highland between Chattanooga and Syracuse, and light came to the Western Reserve, and Island Number Ten, and Shiloh, and it was day down the Michigan mitten and the Wabash, and the ironclads of morning ran the hairpin bend before Vicksburg. And now it was bright from Bemidji to the Alamo, and now the Panhandle showed, and the Cherokee Strip, and now the Yellowstone yellowed, and the bald Big Horns where Custer fell. And now the snow shone on the Absarokas and the Shoshone country and the Teton Range, and from Ogden, where the ceremonial spike was hammered down, the sun ran west like a train on fire. And now lakes of sun were made on salt and sand, and here and there morning and morning air went through the open windows of a whitened skull. And now it was February 11th, 1909, for the American earth.

[*Late in the afternoon of that day, two old men sat at a window of a hospital in the Presidio. They were facing west, and beyond a cemetery, beyond the Fort Scott Reservation, beyond Mile Rocks Light, the sun was hull-down in the Pacific.*

[*"I'm thinking," one of the old men said.*

[*"What're you thinking?" the other one said.*

[*"I'm thinking: if Old Abe'd lived, he would've been an even hundred years old tomorrow."*

[*"Well, he didn't live; he got killed."*

[*"Yes, but I was just thinking."*]

Two hours before the day ended, a woman awoke in a cold-water flat near Bowling Green and groped in the darkness for her husband's arm. "Dan," she said. "Dan!"

"You all right, Polly?" the man said.

The woman's grasp tightened as her child began to rip its way out of the nest of her body. "The doctor," she said. "I'm...," but the rest wandered away in a scream.

COLOR

ABOVE the head of the bed, there were two gas-jets, and their light was a small show of hands in the night. The woman lay with one arm crooked, as if holding a bouquet, and on it a sleeping child was cradled. "He's beautiful, Dan," she said.

The man, leaning over the footrail, peered down at the open end of the bundle. "Well, anyways," he said, "he's white."

[*A white man began his first living day in a diaper and spent his dead last in a shroud, a cotton start and a cotton finish, but because no white could be whiter than white flesh, it was he who was white, not the cotton. Though provably less white than snow, clouds, calcimine, and porcelain, it was he who was white, and no other thing of the earth or the sky. Affected by the season and the velocity of the wind, by age and diet and so little as a blocked excretion of bile, he changed color almost from hour to hour: angered, he reddened to salmon; afraid, he paled to the shade of cooked pork; cold, he looked blue; and old, he was the ash of fire long extinguished. But it was he who was white.*]

"How can you talk like that?" the woman said.

"Damned if I know," the hack-driver said. "He ain't really white at all."

NATIONALITY

"I NEVER tried to trace my ancestors," the hack-driver said, "but I'm mortal sure I had some."

[*His son was an American.*]

GIVEN NAME

THE BED was in a leaning tower of morning sunlight, and the man and the woman lay facing each other, watching their child suck breakfast.

"What'll we call him?" the man said.

A milk-wet mouth came away from a milky nipple and yawned, and then, drawing again, it began to eat air. Small legs kicked as if kicking off shoes, and the small mouth opened wide, now to protest. The woman fed her nipple back into the working face, and at once the movement of the child's feet dwindled, and the pumping mouth settled into rhythm.

"Let's call him Daniel," the woman said.

The hack-driver jacked himself up on his elbow. "What the hell kind of a name is Daniel?" he said.

"A good kind. It's yours."

"But why saddle the kid with it? Daniel! Some day his friends'll ask him who he's named after, and he'll say his old man, and they'll want to know what his old man does for a living, and then the kid'll have to say, 'The poor slob, he rides around in a hack.' The *kid* ain't going to be a hack-driver. Why curse him with a hack-driver's name?"

"Anybody's name could be Daniel—a judge's, even."

"Call this piece of cheese Daniel, and all he'll ever be able to do is read a meter. The name queered me, and it'll queer him too. A moniker is a dangerous thing: it can make you or break you. Take Willie, for instance—if your name is Willie, you can stop struggling, because you're going to be a jockey. Or Max—every lawyer in the world is Max this or Max that, and they're all shysters. Or Mamie—did you ever know a Mamie that wasn't a whoor?"

"Fine language," the woman said.

"Hack-driver's language."

"You're not in a hack now, but you ought to be. It's getting late."

"It's only seven, and, besides, I like to watch."

"You've been watching all month," the woman said. "There's nothing you don't know."

"That practicly goes for the kid too. Damn if he ain't giving a good imitation of me."

"Keep your voice down. The window is open."

"Let it be open. The neighbors know we didn't buy the kid at Greenhut's."

"Go dress. You're getting to be disgusting."

"Polly," the man said, and the woman lowered her eyes to watch her son's mouth run down in milk-made sleep.

"What do you want?"

"Did the doctor say when I could be really disgusting?" As the mouth worked its last slow contractions in space, the woman rose and placed the child in a crib near the window. "Did you ask him, Polly?"

The woman drew a green shade through a leaning tower of sunlight.

*   *   *

"Well," the hack-driver said, "what'll we call him?"

"I told you," the woman said.

The man savored the word. "Daniel," he said. "Daniel."

"Daniel Johnson—a good name," the woman said. "It's good because it's common. It doesn't ask for favors, and it won't get any. If the boy wants something special, he'll have to *be* special."

"He mightn't thank us. He might say we should've made it easier."

"What name would you make it easier with?"

"I was thinking of Grover, maybe, or Theodore."

"Would Theodore get him what Daniel wouldn't?"

"Hard to say. It might."

"Then let's not use it," the woman said, and she moved closer to the man. "Let's start the boy off with nothing and see how far he gets. I've got my heart set on that, Dan—seeing how far he gets on nothing."

The man looked at her for a moment. "I don't get tired of you," he said. "I get tired of lots of things, but I don't get tired of you. There's no meanness in you. *I'm* mean, maybe, but not you."

"Dan," the woman said, and the word and the words that followed were barely more than meaning given to exhaled air, "it didn't hurt me before."

*   *   *

"Do we call him Daniel?" the woman said.

"The way I feel right now," the man said, "you could call him Polly."

"Do we call him Daniel?"

The man laughed, "We call him Daniel," he said.

BIRTHPLACE

"ON YOUR LEFT, FOLKS, IN THE RIVER ON YOUR LEFT IS BEDLOE'S ISLAND, AND ON THE ISLAND STANDS THAT GRAND OLD LADY, THE STATUE OF LIBERTY. SHE TIPS THE BEAM AT TWO HUNDRED AND TWENNY-FIVE TONS, SHE'S A HUNDRED AND ELEVEN FOOT HIGH WITH HER SHOES OFF, AND EVERY POUND AND OUNCE OF HER IS FEMALE

WOMAN. HER HAND, DID YOU SAY? HER HAND IS SIXTEEN FOOT
FIVE INCHES LONG, AND HER POINTING-FINGER IS EIGHT FOOT EVEN.
WHAT'S THAT, FOLKS—HER MOUTH? NOW, I KNEW YOU'D BE CU-
RIOUS ABOUT THAT, SO I WENT AND MEASURED IT MYSELF. IT'S
ONE SOLID YARD FROM CORNER TO CORNER, AND A TRIFLE MORE
WHEN SHE SMILES. THAT'S AN ALMIGHTY BIG KISSER, FOLKS: IT'LL
TAKE A LOT OF MAN TO BLOCK IT OFF. . . ." On the drop-seat be-
tween the steering-wheel and the meter of the Pope-Hartford sat
Polly Johnson, and in her lap she held her sleeping son Daniel.
The Johnson household was out for an airing. "Know what I'm
doing?" the hack-driver said.

"Yes," the woman said. "You're wasting a good Saturday afternoon."

"I'm pliking you're a rube that wants to do the town in a couple
of hours."

"What's pliking?"

"Mean to say you never heard of pliking? Pliking is playing
like: it's a mixture of the words. If I plike you're a rube, for instance,
that means I'm making believe you're. . . . Ah, you're kidding.
You know about pliking."

"I don't," the woman said. "And the reason is, you probably
made up the word yourself."

"Suppose I did," the hack-driver said. "What of it?"

"Did you make it up when you were a kid, Dan?"

"It was 'way back. I don't remember any more."

"What did you use to plike?" the woman said.

"Oh, everything, I guess."

"But especially what?"

"Well, I used to plike whatever I wasn't. Being poor, I'd plike
I was rich, and being little, I'd plike I was grown up. I had one
thing, though, that I'd plike all the time." The cab was moving up
lower Broadway now, and in the week-end suspension of sound,
even the small voice of rubber on asphalt was alien. Buildings
stared at each other over slender streets, and doorways now and
then clucked their revolving tongues at trolley-cars. The wedges of
sunlight in the crisscross cracks of the city were misty with set-

tling dust. "You'll think I was foolish: I used to plike I was a horse."

"What's foolish about that?"

"But I pliked I was a rider too—at the same time. I was a horse and rider, both. I rode, and I got rid. Don't that sound foolish?"

"Not to me," the woman said.

"ON YOUR RIGHT, FOLKS, IS WALL STREET, A LITTLE ALLEY AS CROOKED AS A DOG'S HIND LEG. FOR THE CONVENIENCE OF SUCKERS, IT RUNS FROM THE EAST RIVER TO THE TRINITY CHURCH GRAVEYARD: YOU CAN PUT YOUR MONEY IN THE MIDDLE AND BE DEAD AT EITHER END. WALL STREET, FOLKS. . . ."

"You very seldom talk about when you were a boy," the woman said. "Why is that, Dan?"

"I don't know. Because I hate to get laughed at, I suppose."

"I don't laugh at you."

The hack-driver glanced at her, and then, after a moment, he said, "That's the truth, Polly, but I've never been able to figure why. BEYOND CITY HALL PARK, FOLKS, THE APPROACH TO BROOK-LYN BRIDGE, ONE OF THE WONDERS OF THE MODREN WORLD! IT SPANS A SWEET, CLEAR, MOUNTAIN STREAM ALIVE WITH RUBBER TROUT, AND ALONG THE WOODED BANKS ARE THE VINE-CLAD DWELL-INGS OF AMERICA'S WORKING-CLASS, FREE FROM WORRY, FREE FROM CARE, FREE AS GOD'S AMERICAN AIR. BROOKLYN BRIDGE, FOLKS. YOU'RE FREE TO WALK ACROSS IT ANY TIME OF THE DAY OR NIGHT, AND IF YOU DON'T LIKE WHAT YOU SEE, YOU'RE FREE TO JUMP OFF. BROOKLYN BRIDGE, FOLKS. . . ."

The woman said, "What did you want to do most when you were a boy?"

"Just what I'm doing now," the hack-driver said.

"You wanted to be married, and have a child, and drive a hack? Tell that to Sweeney, Dan."

"I mean it."

"The map in the parlor says otherwise."

"A BLOCK DOWN FRANKLIN STREET, FOLKS, AND YOU'RE AT THE TOMBS. ONCE YOU GET IN, YOU NEVER GET OUT, SO KEEP YOUR NOSE TO THE GRINDSTONE, TURN THE OTHER CHEEK, BOW YOUR HEAD,

GET DOWN ON YOUR KNEES, CRAWL ON YOUR BELLY, AND SAY 'UN-CLE.' REMEMBER, FOLKS, ONCE YOU GET IN, YOU NEVER GET OUT! The map? I just keep that for fun."

"The best fun you ever had," the woman said.

"Wrong. The best fun I ever had was making this kid."

"Some day, you'll have the whole country covered with red crayon."

"Polly," the hack-driver said, "what kind of a tip do you think I'd get for driving a sport to Frisco?"

"You should've been a traveling-salesman."

"Too much selling. With my itch, I should've studied for an engine-driver. That's the life—riding a ten-wheeler's ear at seventy on the outside rail! I used to plike it. I was engineer and engine. I stuck the corner of my eye out of the little window in the cab, and I yanked the cord and made two longs, a short, and a long for hicks chewing straw at the crossings (toooot-toooot! toot-toooot!), and I galloped like the side-rods, and I blew myself up and fussed like the steam-chests (ch-ch-ch! ch-ch-ch! ch-ch-ch!). Oh, I was some pliker when I was a kid! ON YOUR LEFT, FOLKS, THE BROADWAY CENTRAL HOTEL, WHERE NED STOKES SHOT JIM FISK OVER THAT HEART'S DESIRE—JOSIE MANSFIELD!"

"You're some pliker right now," the woman said.

"I'm a pliker from a long line of plikers."

"I wonder if your son'll be a pliker too."

"If you get your wish," the hack-driver said, "he'll have to plike like all hell."

"If I get my wish?" the woman said.

"Ain't you the one that wants to see how far he'll get on nothing? THE FLATIRON BUILDING, FOLKS, THE FLATIRON BUILDING AND WINDY CORNER, WHERE SPORTS WITH HIGH-BUTTON TWO-TONE SHOES GATHER TO SEE THE SIGHTS—ABOVE THE KNEE. WATCH THE UNSUSPECTING LADIES, AND YOU'LL GET A FLASH OF THE THINGS THAT MAKE YOUNG MEN OLD AND OLD MEN YOUNG. PRAY FOR WIND, FOLKS, PRAY FOR WIND!"

"What did you ever get married for, Dan?"

"I got tired of standing on Windy Corner," the hack-driver

said, and he laughed until his laughter infected his wife, and now the cab was across Fifth Avenue and heading up Broadway, and it was hailed by a man standing on the curb, but the hack-driver cocked his cap, saying, "Walk, you fat son-of-a-bitch! WELL, FOLKS, HERE SHE IS—BROADWAY, THE BULLYVARD OF YOUR DREAMS, OTHERWISE KNOWN AS EDISON ALLEY! THIS MILE, FOLKS, THESE TWENNY COUNT-'EM BLOCKS, THIS IS THE GENUINE ARTICLE, THE REAL REAL THING: THE REST IS HAYSTACK, COWPATH, SEWER, AND SWAMP! I GIVE YOU BROADWAY, FOLKS, AND WITH IT I GIVE THE MET., MOUQUIN'S, AND LILY RUSSELL (AH, BEAUTIFUL, BEAUTIFUL!); I GIVE WHITE DIAMONDS AND BLACK LACE DRAWERS, I GIVE TERRAPIN AND CHAMPAGNE, I GIVE THE FOUR-IN-HAND (O, TO BE A HORSE AND HAVE A HANSOM BEHIND!) AND ROSEBEN RUNNING SEVEN FURLONGS IN 1:22 FLAT UNDER 126 POUNDS. . . . BUT STAY, FOLKS, AND HEAR ME OUT. THERE'S ANOTHER SIDE TO THE STREET, THE SHADY SIDE: THE SIDE FOR TOUTS, TARTS, DIPS, GULLS, GYPS, SHILLS, VAGS, HAMS, STOOLS, AND STIFFS; THE SIDE FOR HAS-BEENS AND NEVER-WILL-BES; THE SIDE FOR DISBARRED LAWYERS, TENORS WITH WHISKY WHISPERS, AND EX-PUGS PIMPING FOR COFFEE-AND; THE SIDE FOR THE NICKEL-ODEON, THE FLEA-CIRCUS, THE HASH-HOUSE, AND THE NOSE-CANDIED GUNMAN; THE SIDE FOR BUTT-SNIPERS, RUMMIES, AND BUMS WITH OSTRICH-PLUMES AND THE CLAP. AH, BEAUTIFUL, BEAUTIFUL . . . ! You want to know how far this kid'll get on nothing? Well, I'll tell you—no place! I started out with nothing myself, and all the further I ever got was thirty bucks a week for driving sports to hell-and-gone and back, and being an ordinary guy, that's all the further I'll get if I live to be a hundred and drive four million miles! Four million miles! Why, Christ, it's only a coupla hundred thousand to the moon! You think this kid's any different? You think he's any better? You think he's another Abe Lincoln?"

"Yes," the woman said.

*　　　*　　　*

Near Grant's Tomb, she asked the hack-driver to stop, and when he did so, she began to unbutton her shirtwaist. "While I nurse him," she said, "you can look at the sights."

"I like this one," the hack-driver said.

"You've seen it before."

"You know something? Women are funny. The way they handle themselves."

"Have you studied many?"

"Three-four thousand," he said, "and they all act like there's parts of their body that don't belong to them. When you lift that thing to stick it in the kid's mouth, it's like it ain't attached to you."

"It's attached, all right," the woman said. "You can take my word for it."

"Save some for me, honey."

"Turn around and look at the sights!"

"I'll put the flag down. The kid gets four bits worth, and no more."

The flat and flickering Hudson was brass in the sunlight and pewter in the shadow of the Palisades. Ferries dragged their petticoats from bank to bank, and tugs went by with the hidden energy of ducks, and the paddle-wheels of the *Clermont* trod water as she skidded in toward the Night Line docks. The sun was going down in a mackerel sky over the Schooley, and New Jersey was a palpitating dazzle. The afternoon was moving west.

"Ah, Jesus!" the hack-driver said. "To see it all! To see it all some day!"

OCCUPATION

FOR many months, the child ate, bubbled, dribbled, cheesed, puked, cried, sneezed, yawned, jabbed at nothing, smiled at little, urinated, stooled, slept, woke up famished, ate again, bashed a rattle on the ribs of his crib, sucked his thumb, played with his feet, frowned, and bloated himself with thought, and in the end he produced a sound that the hack-driver swore was "Cab!"

RELIGION

"DAN," the woman said, "don't you think he ought to be baptized?"

"The hell with it," the hack-driver said. "I bet he's socking wet right now."

PRISON RECORD, IF ANY

"NOT YET, DAN," the woman said. "I don't think he's asleep."
"Ah, he's been dead to the world for an hour."

"What if he's just lying there? He'd see us."

"But, Polly, he's only five months old."

"I'd feel the same way if he was a cat."

"Hang something on the crib, then."

The woman rose from the bed, took off her nightgown, and draped it over the railing of the crib. Then she lay down again, and when her husband touched her, she turned to him.

In the faint light coming from the courtyard, a small hand rose, its fingers groping and striving, and silhouetted itself on the nightgown, but the man and woman did not see it, nor did they see the hand close finally on the flimsy screen, hold it tightly for a while, and relax—and then the hand fell, and the child was asleep.

"I'd've felt as if somebody was watching us," the woman whispered.

MEDICAL HISTORY

FROM the darkened bedroom, a wavering wail drifted into the parlor. The woman looked up from a sewing-basket, listened, and said, "Dan, I think he's sick."

"He's all right," the hack-driver said. "Leave him alone."

"He's never acted like this. He wouldn't nurse before."

"The kid's a weasel. He just wants you to pick him up and rock him. He found out he's got a voice, but why should we let him find out we can hear it? All kids are weasels."

The woman said, "I want you to go up to the corner and phone the doctor."

"Doctor! Who says we need a doctor? You're frazzling yourself over nothing, Polly. The kid's probably got a bellyache."

"I don't know what he's got, but he's got something, and he's going to have a doctor."

The hack-driver took his cap from a wall-rack. "If you say doctor, it's doctor," he said. "But first, give me a kiss."

"When you come back," the woman said.

"Now."

"All right. Now."

Half an hour later, the child was laid bridging and boxing on a quilt covering the kitchen table, and the doctor began his examination. He searched a crying mouth, he rolled back small eyelids, and gently he tapped a blown-out chest and a deflated belly—but he said nothing. He took a roman-numbered watch from a secret pocket at his belt, he two-fingered the child's pulse, and he timed it for thirty seconds—but he said nothing. He snapped the spinal-fluid of a thermometer down to 98, pressed the bulb deep into the child's rectum, and then glanced about the room, his eyes pausing at the doorway, through which were visible a buckhorn hatrack, a Pluto Water calendar, and a map of the United States—but he said nothing. Turning again to the child, he withdrew the thermometer and rotated it until its core became visible, but only after cleansing the instrument in alcohol did he look up at the disquieted parents. "He's constipated," he said.

EDUCATION

THE hack-driver entered the flat, saying, "I'm home, Polly," and as he passed into the bedroom, his foot struck a small piece of furniture standing just within the door. "Hey," he said, "what's this?"

"What's what?" the woman said, emerging from the kitchen with a milk-bottle.

"This thing here with the hole in it."

The woman squirted a drop of milk on her wrist. "What does it look like?"

"If you want to know, a toilet on wheels."

"That's exactly what it is."

"I'll be damned. How does it work?" 23 67 .2754*

Elbowing her husband out of the way, the woman went to the bed, undiapered the child, and sat him over the open manhole of the toy-toilet. Then she turned down a flap to keep him in place, and while he laid about him with a dented tin cup, she fed him from the tilted bottle.

"Quite an invention," the hack-driver said. "What's supposed to happen now?"

"He's supposed to have a movement."

"Does he know that?"

"Certainly he knows it," the woman said.

"He don't look like he knows a horse-collar from wild honey."

"He knows a lot more than you think. Go wash your hands and get ready for supper."

"What do you call that contraption?"

"A potty-chair," the woman said.

"Good God!" the hack-driver said. "A name like that could bind him like cheese. It'd bind *me*."

"Oh, go wash your hands. You look as if you're wearing gloves."

"Polly," the hack-driver said, "when you were a little girl, and you had to do something, what did you use to say?"

"I said, 'I have to make Number One.'"

"I said, 'I have to pee.'"

"One of the girls at school was very elegant. She always said, 'I have to make A Wish.'"

"Sometimes I didn't say a word," the hack-driver said. "I just peed."

"This is fine talk, Dan."

"What did you use to say when you had to do the other thing?"

"I'm going to make a prediction," the woman said. "This child's first word is going to be a dirty one."

"Potty-chair! Could anything be dirtier than that?"

The woman handed him the empty bottle, saying, "Put this in the kitchen," and then she lifted the child from under the chair-flap.

"Any luck?" the hack-driver said.

"No."

"I guess he didn't get the idea." 20 53 .273

The woman placed the child in the crib, and after rediapering him, she took the bottle from the hack-driver's hand and left the room. He remained where he was, watching his son.

"Danny," he said. "Little Danny-boy."

The child's face suddenly rouged itself, his body became rigid, and a look of great thoughtfulness invaded his eyes. Then, as suddenly as the tension had begun, it was gone, and the child resumed his aimless kicking and punching. The hack-driver reached out, hefted the diaper, and smiled.

"You weasel," he said. "Oh, Polly . . . !"

LANGUAGES

THE woman, on a stool near a sewing-table, slid a wooden darning-egg into a small stocking and began to mend an abrasion in the knee. Crawling at her feet, her son pushed a toy engine, stepped-on and sprung, along a pair of lines in the design of the rug. The hack-driver stood with his back to the map, his attention fixed on a guest seated in a chair cocked against a wall: the guest was his wife's brother, Webster Varner. A cigar trapped in the man's teeth had packed the room with smoke, a filler for all but the hot pillar of air above the hanging gas-jet.

"Well, Web . . . ," the hack-driver said.

"Well, what?" Varner said, and taking the cigar from his mouth, he blew on the red coal and blustered it up to orange. "What do you want to know?"

"Everything you've done since the last time you were here."

"All that for a meal and a nickel stogie?"

"The whole turkey-shoot," the hack-driver said.

"I wouldn't tell it all to the Pope if I was a monk."

"Leave out the part with garters."

"There wouldn't be much left," the woman said. "Web, when're you going to light on something and stay there?"

"I lit thirty years ago," Varner said, "and the thing I lit on was moving."

"You're more Dan's brother than mine," the woman said. "If God told my husband he could have one wish, I think he'd say, 'Lord, make me the cow-catcher on a locomotive!'"

"A man moves even when he thinks he's standing still," Varner said. "He's on a trolley-car that goes around the sun once a year."

"He doesn't have to run up and down the aisle, though," the woman said. "He can take a seat."

"I've got an itchy behind," Varner said.

"Me, I itch all over," the hack-driver said, "but not being my own master any more, I ain't allowed to scratch."

"Listen to that," the woman said. "Remember what Mom always said, Web? 'A man's a creature on a long tether.'"

"But the point is, he's tethered," the hack-driver said.

"It's an imaginary rope, Dan," the woman said. "If you want free, all you have to do is walk away."

"Well," Varner said, "where should I start?"

"The beginning's as good a place as any," the hack-driver said.

Varner huffed up a noose of smoke that rolled inside-out and outside-in, struck the map, and unbraided. "I bummed clear to the Coast this time," he said.

The hack-driver's gaze had followed the smoke-ring, and when it disintegrated, he found himself staring at the crayon sunburst on the right edge of the chart. The discoloration seemed to invite touch, but he placed a finger on it only to see his hand sweep slowly in a course that embraced all between the two oceans. "Clear to the Coast," he heard himself say.

"It's a big country," Varner said. "Godamighty, but it's a big country!"

"How'd you go?" the hack-driver said.

"Right smack through the middle," Varner said. "The first half was easy: from here to Omaha, you can raise a ride while you lie under a tree. But out beyond, there's damn few trees and damn few rides, and if Nebraska's any criterion, damn few human beings. A stateful of hard-shells—the kind that can't see a man on the road, but somehow manage to run over every cat and dog. It wasn't the walking, though, that bothered me in Nebraska: it was what I had to walk on. One stretch, I remember, ran forty-five miles without a dip or a bend. The old straight-and-narrow, it was, and it only made me want to go crooked with a splash. I stuck it out as far as Grand Island. From there, I took to the rods and rode the U. P. to Julesburg. . . ."

"Julesburg," the hack-driver said, and he looked at a black dot in the northeastern corner of Colorado.

". . . And Denver," Varner said. "I'd thought to stay there for a while, but Denver's a town that doesn't hold you: you find yourself washing your hands all the time. A week of it, and I was heading for Golden, where you start climbing the Rockies like a window-cleaner for two of the steepest thousand feet God ever built slantindicular. When you get to Bill Cody's grave up top, you can lean off Lookout Mountain and spit in the South Platte."

The hack-driver took up a stub of crayon suspended from a nail, and almost unconsciously he raised it toward the mountain states, and then almost consciously he let it fall.

"That's where my walking-days really began," Varner said. "I pointed myself west and just marched, and if I hadn't, I'd be there yet. Morning, noon, and night, I plodded along, and where I fell down for the third time, that's where I slept. There was damn near nothing up there but sky. Houses forty miles apart, and in between a one-way nick in a side-hill. It wasn't a road: it was a toe-hold. The summit of Berthoud Pass lies at eleven thousand feet, and I made it one night in a hailstorm that bounced like a cow you-knowing on a flat rock."

"Hail can kill you," the hack-driver said.

"I bleed at a mile," Varner said, "and from Berthoud to Steamboat Springs, there's hardly a yard that isn't higher. When I say bleed, I mean you drip and dribble, and you're always dabbing at your nose, and on the back of your hand, you've always got a fresh slash of red: you bleed all the time. And drink!—man, you're like a drain in a sink up there. The only trouble is, there's mighty little water you can reach without a drill."

"Steamboat Springs," the hack-driver said. "Jesus, what a name!"

The child was still playing train, still tirelessly moving a battered piece of tin over some division without end, and the woman, although at work now on a different stocking, still held the same focus of eyes and fingers, and the hack-driver still stood staring at the map, but the sheet of paper seemed to have become transpar-

ent, as if its two-way terrain of words and lines for places and
things were a window giving on the Union.

"That stretch of country was bad as you'd ever want," Varner
said, "but from Sunbeam, Colorado, to Vernal, Utah, I hit a hundred miles of something that died a million years before time. I
never did find out how hot it was, but it was hot enough to make
the world flutter like a flag—the brush, the sand, the sky, the faraway mountains, your own hands, and your heart. At the west end
of Sunbeam, there was a big sign warning you not to try those
hundred miles on foot, and not being a fool, I sat me down and
slow-fried in the shade till a man came along in a Benz and promised to take me all the way to Vernal. He had his wife and kid up
front with him, so I piled in back with the duffel, and we were off.
Half a day out and a good fifty miles from anything wet enough to
drink, his left front shoe almost blew clear of the rim. It took us
hours to fix it, pretty near the whole afternoon. The tools got so
hot we had to wrap them in rags, and we worked in five-minute
shifts, because only a fireman could've lasted longer, but in the
end, after using all the patches we had and then a boot to cover
them, we got the tire pumped up, and it held. I was about to
climb in again when the guy shook his head, saying he was sorry,
but he had his family to think of, and he'd have to lighten the load.
Thanks for the help, he said, and a lot of other guff, but what it
came to was that I was staying, and he was going. I had a tire-tool
in my hand, and I remember getting set for a swing, but to this
day I can't tell you why I didn't lay a hole in the guy's roof. Some
people are easy; some are hard. All I did was fling the hunk of iron
through his windshield, that and this: I said, 'Mister, many's the
one I've called a son-of-a-bitch, but you're the first pissin' man
that ever really came from the back end of a dog . . . !' I'm sorry,
Polly, I ought to watch my language with the kid around, but that
dirty dingo could've shot me in the lung and done me less damage.
Helping with that blowout had cooked me for walking, and when
the Benz rolled away, I put myself to bed right in the road. I slept
for sixteen hours, and by the time I woke up, the sun had gotten
to me, and I was all through standing up. I managed to crawl over to

a clump of sage, but I could've saved my sweat; nothing would've run over me, because nothing came along for two solid days, only some birds, big black bald-headed bastards that sailed around waiting for me to die—and I was beginning to die. I heard bees swarming in my head, and there was falling water a yard from my face, and a million voices were murmuring words I couldn't understand—and then all the sounds came together in the sound of a motor. The people told me later that when they reached me, I was sitting there licking a hot rock like it was an ice-cream cone."

The child was on the woman's lap now, entertaining his eyes among the spools of color in the sewing-basket. The woman was watching the hack-driver, who was watching something that only he seemed to see. 20 אא .297

"From Vernal," Varner said, "the going was better for a way, and I kept to the road through Provo to Salt Lake and out beyond for about one more day. That brought me to something that looked like the burnt-out bottom of the pot, what an ocean might be if you boiled it away to salt and silt. Nothing on two feet could've crossed it on foot: anyone who tried would've wound up as a few buttons and a belt-buckle in the dust. I hit the rods again, riding Western Pacific iron over the whole of Nevada and down the Feather River Gorge to Oroville. From there, it was only a whoop and a holler to San Francisco Bay, and I made that standing on the lower jaw of a ferry, sniffing the spray for a whiff of Japan."

"Frisco," the hack-driver said. "What's it like, Web?"

"Like itself," Varner said. "It's the only city I've ever been in that isn't like some other city. It's different, from the ground it's built on to the air that gets a washing for eight thousand miles before you use it. Christ, it's a town to live in and never die in. It gives you the feeling that you're so all-alive when you're living that you just couldn't be all-dead if you died. Clothes feel good on you in Frisco, the only place in the world where they do, and your skin stays cool, and fruit is cold, like it was early morning all day long, and even the street-names are like cracked ice: Crocker, Sutter, Sutro, Sansome, Drumm, and Daggett. You're always ready for a steak (God help a panhandler in Frisco!), and you always

feel like walking, and smokes taste good, every one you light, and
you sleep 'way down deep in sleep, and it's all you can do to keep
your hands off the women that pass you by, and sometimes you
don't. You feel like you're charged. Your blood's got seltzer in it,
and you climb thirty-degree grades with your heart working the
way it did before you grew short hair, and from the top of one of
the hills, you look around and down at the bay, and you breathe
as if breathing was all inhale—as if, like the bay, you'd never fill.
You stand there with your back to the Pacific, and east of you, for
three hundred years and three thousand miles, is America—and
all at once you know it's all yours!"

The hack-driver said, "There's an eatery in Frisco called Tait's.
Did you ever run onto it?"

"Sure," Varner said. "It's one of the best. Where'd you hear
about it?"

"Oh, I must've read something some place."

"I ate there two-three times. A guy stood me."

"They say it's like Rector's."

"I was hanging around Graney's one afternoon, watching some
sports shoot pool," Varner said. "It was a two-handed game, and
it broke up when one of the players was called away. The other
said he had some time to kill and wanted to know if I cared to take
a cue. I didn't have enough change on me to buy my way into a
pay-toilet, but I said sure. He said how about a dollar a point to
make it interesting, and I said sure. He broke, and I ran 49 balls
on him before phrigging up an easy little bank-shot with a scratch.
I beat him 100-14 in four innings. He must've thought I was De
Oro in disguise, but he had sand, and he wanted to go on, so I beat
him for drinks, for supper at Tait's, for my room-rent at the hotel,
for a fling at the garters (apologies to my sister Polly), and for a
hundred bucks in cash—and with an eye to the future, I beat him
for breakfast the next day and a jaunt to the track."

"The track?" the hack-driver said. "*What* track?"

"Some aviator was in town to fly his airship at a place called
Tanforan. He did, too."

"You saw that?" the hack-driver said. "Hell, I only read about it. The guy had his picture in the papers. Down below, it said, 'Louis Paulhan flying upside-down at Tanforan.'"

"It was something to see," Varner said.

The woman rose, saying, "I'm going to put the boy to bed."

The hack-driver was unaware that she had spoken. He said, "'Louis Paulhan flying upside-down at Tanforan . . . !'"

"Want to kiss your nephew good night, Web?" the woman said.

"Hand him over," Varner said.

"I guess those're the prettiest words in the language," the hack-driver said. "Paulhan at Tanforan!"

"Instead of playing with your husband all evening," Varner said, "I should've played with this kid," and taking the boy in his arms, he kissed him a long slow kiss on the cheek. "He smells good, but that's all I know about him except his name. Does he talk?"

"No," the woman said. "Not yet."

"Not even a word?"

"Nothing, not even 'mama.'"

"Danny," Varner said, "you're a very nice boy, but you ought to say something for your old bum of an uncle."

The child looked up at him, and at once his mouth formed and gave voice to three syllables. "Tan-for-an," he said.

SEX

"LET me pour you some more coffee, Miss Morey," the woman said. "I've had two cups," Miss Morey said.

"My husband claims you don't really get the taste till you've had three."

"Make my third a small one."

"I'll warm it first," the woman said, and taking up the pot, she went into the kitchen.

Miss Morey looked down at Danny, who was standing nearby and staring at her. She smiled, and rising from the table, she went to the map to ponder the meaning of its crayon overlay. The boy followed her, still staring, and once more she smiled before idling away across the room, her skirt making a sound like scattered

leaves. The boy listened, wondering if the magic cloth were trying
to speak to him, and then, seeing arms extended, he entered them,
and Miss Morey breathed his fruit-odor and kissed his fruit-face,
and hugging him, she swung into the cycle of a waltz: her skirt
whispered again, no longer like leaves, but like voices now, and
the boy heard and dimly understood them all. [*Miss Morey wore
sandalwood, and her jabot and collar, dried in the sun, had some rem-
nant of the sun starched and ironed into the fabric, but there was no
word known for the aroma that covered her piled hair like a veil, nor
for the self-scented garment of her body: she was a schoolteacher,
and she owned, as no one else could ever own, the schoolteacher's in-
comparable fragrance.*] The boy kissed her.

Polly Johnson returned from the kitchen with the coffee-pot,
and as she poured, she said, "Some day you'll teach him, Miss
Morey—some day soon."

HEROES

FOOTFALLS on the stairs brought the boy back from sleep, and
he heard the latch uncatch, and then for a moment, although
his mother was in the other room, he heard nothing. The quiet was
broken by the single word "Dan!" escaping rather than spoken,
and now, through the partly-open bedroom door, the boy saw the
hack-driver, his shirt sown with blood and his nose hidden under
a blood-logged bandage.

[*Like a soldier, you thought, like a soldier in the stories Mom read
you out of* A Boy's History of America.]

"Ask anybody if I wasn't minding my own business," the hack-
driver said. "Along about quitting-time this afternoon, I pulled up
at the Astor House, thinking maybe I'd take one more call and go
home. I seen a guy watching me, and pretty soon he come over to
the cab and said, 'If you can spare a minute, friend, I'd like to talk
at you.' I gave him the up-and-down, and he looked okay, so I
said, 'Pick a subject.'"

[*The one you liked best was about Gentleman Johnny Burgoyne.
They called him that because he was always polite to people, even if
they were old. A Revolution came along, and the King of English made*

him put on a red coat and go far across the sea to assinate Americans.]

"He said, 'What do you say we talk about the Union?' and I said, 'Mister, it's one hell of a country,' and he said, 'I mean the Union of Drivers and Drovers.' I said, 'Oh, that kind of a Union,' and he said, 'Yes, friend, that kind, and being an independent, you'll join up if you're half as smart as you give out.'"

[*When he got to America, he saw it was in the wilderness, filled with quick sand and different animals, and his soldiers tried to tell him, "Be careful, Gentleman Johnny Burgoyne, it is dangerous to assinate Americans in the woods," but he only stood up proudly and said, "I found my way in here, and I will found my way out." Then he drank a bottle of atoxicating liquor, and he was in a stupor.*]

"I said, 'What's smart about coughing up dues?' and he said, 'You'll make more money in the long run.' I laughed, saying, 'If you know anything about hacking, mister, there's more money in the short run.' He didn't laugh. He only said, 'Ain't it kind of late in the day for cheap wit?' I said, 'You sound cranky, mister, so lean off of that door and drag your drawers away from here.' He said, 'Supposing I drag 'em to a nice quiet empty lot.' Well, now, you know me, Polly."

"Yes, I know you," the woman said.

[*It was exciting when the Great British soldiers marched away in the wilderness. They all had fine red coats, and they played horns and music, and they roared laughter about what they would do to the Americans, who only had rags. But before long, Burgoyne was in a surroundment of trees and ambushes, and the war started. A lot of people got shot, and guns went off, and they made a deafening sound so that nobody could hear, and when a British got killed, he groaned out loud. It was a terrible fight, and Burgoyne had to drink another bottle of atoxicating liquor.*]

"We went a ways down Vesey Street, looking for a place to square off, and all of a sudden this gazabo busted out laughing fit to split. It wasn't a yellow kind of a laugh: he could make a fist, all right. It was more like he was just enjoying himself, and finally he said, 'Make all the bum jokes you want, friend, only listen to me with your good ear.' I said, 'Mister, I happen to have two,' and he said,

'They must be plugged, then,' and I said, 'Say something with your face, and I'll hear you perfectly.'"

[*The Americans said, "You are still in a surroundment, Gentleman Johnny Burgoyne, and you must throw up a sponge." Burgoyne roared proudly, "That is an insultment. I will never throw up a sponge to a lot of rabble-taggle rebels." They said, "Well, you will have to, because you are in a surroundment of American milisher," and he roared proudly, "I do not care if it rains milisher!"*]

"He said, 'Did you ever wonder how the rich stay rich?' and I said, 'No, only how they ever got rich in the first place,' and he said, 'They hang together, that's how, and if us poor slobs did the same, we wouldn't stay poor.' I said, 'You ain't trying to tell me Andy Carnegie belongs to a Union, are you?'"

[*The war started all over again. The Great British shot guns till all the Americans put on bandages, and then our tillery shot grapes, and everybody was dead. "Will the surroundment stand?" That was a question.*]

"He said, 'What else? You don't think he keeps his spondulix account of he has a big muscle, do you? The Police Force is his Union, and the Army, and the public-school system, and the churches, and the Press.' I said, 'That's a faceful, mister.' He said, 'Chew on it,' and I said, 'I'm chewing, but it won't go down,' and he said, 'What you need, friend, is a new set of plates.'"

[*The Americans had sharp shooters, and the sharpest shooter of all was Daniel Morgan. People said, "Morgan can throw an apple in the air and peel it before it will come down." He saw a Great British soldier in the battle, and he said, "That brave man is General Frazer. I honor and amire him, but he must die. I will stand behind this ambush and do my duty." A minute later, Frazer was mordally wounded.*]

"I said, 'It really comes to this, don't it? You're against guys like Carnegie because they're rich.' He looked at me for a couple of seconds without saying anything, and I thought I had him, but in the end he shook his head and said, 'I'm not against the rich. I'm just in favor of the poor.'"

[*The war got terrible, and everybody put on bandages. The Great British cried, "Hurrah, we are winning!" and the Americans cried,*

"No. Hurrah, we are winning!" Some of the Redcoats were sleeping in a farm, and they were crying because they were thirsty, so a lady went out with a barrel to fill it with water. The Americans amired her and did not shoot. That showed they were patriotic.]

"I said, 'That's a sweet saying, friend. Let me know when you guys have your next meeting.'"

[*The war went on and on, but there was still a surroundment in Saratoga, and Burgoyne said sadly, "Well, I guess I will have to throw up a sponge. These d—n Americans are too smart for a gentleman." Then he drank a bottle of atoxicating liquor, and he was in a stupor, and the Americans marched in, playing* Yankee Doodle.]

"Then we stuck out our hands and shook," the hack-driver said, "and that's about all."

"The bandage," the woman said.

"The bandage? Oh, I got that at a drug-store."

"You just walked in and asked for a bandage."

"That's right, and they gave it to me, and I paid for it."

"What was the matter? Was your nose cold?"

"Who said anything about my nose being cold?"

"You must've had a reason for covering it up."

"God damn it!" the hack-driver said. "It was bleeding!"

"You must be joking. You're a great joker."

"Well, if you really want to know the rest, me and this Union guy started back towards my cab, and I said, 'Say, ain't we forgetting something?' and he said, 'Not as I know of. . . .'"

The woman sliced in. "And then you said, 'Why, sure we are. We came down here to find out who was the better man,' and he said, 'By God, so we did,' so the two of you jackasses went up an alley and beat the life out of each other."

"That's about the size of it," the hack-driver said. "But I notice you're not asking who won."

The woman smiled. "All right," she said, "who won?"

[*When soldiers get bloody, they put on bandages, so if a man has a bandage, he's a soldier even if he's your own father, and if he's your own father, then he's the best soldier in the whole world: he wins all the fights.*]

The hack-driver glanced at the bedroom door, but the boy did not see this, nor did he hear his father's whispered answer: he was asleep.

HEARING AND VISION

SEATED on a chair that raised him chin-high to the table, the boy gazed at the world through vapor ascending from a bowl of mush.

"It's good for you, Danny," the woman said. The boy prodded the gray gum with the convex of his spoon. "It'll make you big, like your Uncle Web." The boy's hand paused. "Will you eat if I read you the letter again?" the woman said, and when the boy nodded, she said, "Say it."

"I will eat all the oatmeal," the boy said.

The woman opened a typewritten sheet. "'My dear little nephew Daniel....'"

"The whole letter," the boy said.

"'Cochabamba, Bolivia. January 24, 1914. My dear little nephew Daniel....'"

"The next word is 'soon,'" the boy said.

"If you know it all by heart, what's the good of reading it to you?"

"I like to hear it."

Soon you will be five years old, and I am writing from far-off South America to wish you a happy birthday, also to send you a present, which I enclose in a separate package. It may get there late, but I hope you like it all the same. It's an old Spanish peso (silver) from the reign of King Ferdinand VII. You can use it as a pocket-piece. I made a wish on it, and— who can tell?—it may bring you good luck.

When I see you again, I'll fill you full of stories about Bolivia. In this letter, I can only say it's a strange place, very different from anything you ever heard of. But I happen to like places that are strange, and best of all I like strange people. Maybe when you grow up, you'll be like me, traveling around the world and making places on a map come to life.

There are Indians here in Bolivia, and many of them work for the same company that I do. One of them has a little boy I call Danny, although that is not his name. He'd be just like you if he didn't have darker skin and black hair. His father is a great hunter, and all the Indians love him because he kills bad animals. On my last vacation, we went on a hunting-trip together, far away from here in the jungle, and he killed a big crocodile with his rifle. When we came home and showed the skin to the other Indians, there was a great celebration, and everyone sang songs and danced all night.

Well, little boy, that's about all for your birthday letter, except that I want you to be good all the time and think of me once in a while.

There was no mush left in the bowl, but the boy, his vision blurred by a stare, still spooned at it and fed himself its fading taste.

The woman said, "Did you like the letter, Danny?" but the boy said nothing. "Do you ever think of your Uncle Web?"

A word came to the boy's mind, and his mind spoke it [*Tanforan*], and then the word went from his mind to his mouth, and his mouth spoke it. "Tanforan," he said. "Where's Tanforan?"

MANUAL ABILITY

THE hack-driver let a newspaper wilt down to his lap, and slowly lifting his head, he appeared to be contemplating a brown water-stain on the parlor wall. In fact, however, the mottled plaster, like all else in the funnel of his sight, went unseen. The woman watched him for a moment, waiting.

"Polly," he said, "what hand does the kid favor—right or left?"

"What makes you ask?" the woman said.

He shrugged. "It just occurred to me."

"You ought to pay a little more attention, and then you'd know."

"Oh, Danny!" the hack-driver said, and his son appeared in the bedroom doorway. "Danny-boy, see that little ole baseball in your toy-box? Well, I want you to pitch it to me. A spitter, like Matty throws." The boy picked up the ball with his right hand, transferred it to his left, made a hocus-pocus over it, and threw it. "A daisy, son. Thanks." The boy returned to the bedroom.

"Aren't you going to correct him?" the woman said.

"Who mentioned anything about correcting?"

"Why all the fuss, then?"

"I told you. I was just curious."

"You're an odd one, Dan," the woman said. "You were *hoping* he was left-handed."

"Making everybody right-handed is a dumb rule," the hack-driver said. "What's odd about wanting my kid to thumb his nose at the world if he feels like?"

"He can thumb his nose till it blisters," the woman said. "The odd thing is that you think he can only do it with his left hand."

CLUBS, ORGANIZATIONS

"Do you know what this building is?" the woman said. "No," the boy said.

"It's a library."

"What's a liberry?"

"A place where they store books so that people like you can borrow them—and that's the wonderful thing about a book. You can borrow it and return it and still have it: you always keep what you learn."

"What kind of books do they have in this liberry?"

"All kinds. Every kind you can think of."

"Books with pictures?"

"Hundreds of them—and books with words too."

"I don't like that kind. I'll never like books with words."

"Why not, son?"

"I don't want to tell."

"I wish you would, though."

The boy looked down at the sidewalk, and finding a flattened cud of gum, he scraped at it with the edge of a shoe. He spoke softly, saying, "I can't read."

The woman laughed. "Well, there'll always be books with pictures," she said. "Would you like to go in and borrow some?"

The boy said, "Yes."

And then, taking him by the hand, the woman walked him through a door that was not an entrance, but an exit—a door that led from a very small room out into the world.

[*Pictures of ships: the* Santa Maria, *the* Mayflower, *the* Constitution, *the* Savannah, *the* Merrimac, *and the* Oregon; *ships curled like old shoes, ships all sail and heeling like crescent moons; ships in coats of mail, hedgehogs with guns for hair; clippers, sidewinders, submarines, and a box of cheese on a raft; yachts, mail-packets, junks, four-masted barkentines, and tugs; colliers, lightships, square-riggers, and the sunken* Maine; *the* General Slocum, *burned to a hull in Hell Gate, the* Titanic, *forever on her maiden voyage, and the one with the mountain name, the* Kearsarge.

[*Pictures of trains: the* John Stevens, *a barrel on a flatcar; the* Tom Thumb *losing a match-race with a gray horse; the* De Witt Clinton *running thirty miles an hour for the Mohawk & Hudson; the* Governor Paine, *burning wood cut in* 1849, *covering a mile of Vermont Central iron in forty-three seconds; the* Empire State Express, *a high-riding* 4-4-0, *hitting* 112.5 *between Rochester and Buffalo in '93; the yard-goat and the mogul-mallet, the caboose and the double-header; the snowsheds, and the track-pans, and the long long glides of spiked-down right-of-way, and, above all, the names—the Bangor & Aroostook, the Florida East Coast, the Central of Georgia, the Great Northern, the Burlington, the Rock Island, the Nickel Plate, the Monon, the Wabash, and the Big Four.*

[*Pictures of Indians: red men by Remington, red men in black Stetsons, red men on red pennies, red men painted like pinto horses, red men running from village to village, crying, "Come, come to see the people from Heaven!"* ("*The Indians came back at nightfall, and at sight of what had befallen us, and our state of suffering and melancholy destitution, sat down among us, and from the sorrow and pity they felt, they all began to lament so earnestly that they might have been heard at a distance, and continued so doing more than half an hour. It was strange to see these men, wild and untaught, howling like brutes over our misfortunes. De Vaca asked the Indians to take his men into their houses, and the Indians signified that it would give them delight.");* red men fighting a four-century, rear-guard action, starving on the plains where Cody for a day's sport bagged three thousand buffalo, and dying finally wherever the white man came to live, *but leaving behind them an imperishable legacy of names, Minneconjou and Susquehanna, Cherokee and Nez Perce, Winnebago and Sac ("Christians get drunk! Christians beat men! Christians tell lies! Me no Christian!"), Ojibway and Cheyenne, Ponca and Lakota, Chickasaw and Arapahoe, Yankton and Brule ("Do you want schools on the Wallowa Reservation?" "No, we do not want schools on the Wallowa Reservation." "Why do you not want schools?" "They will teach us to have churches.")—and the Nadouessioux, the Sioux for short, or, better, The Enemies.*

[*Pictures of war: Lincoln in Little Mac's tent at the Headquarters of the Army of the Potomac, and behind him, on a flag-covered table, his stovepipe; twelve cannoneers around a ten-inch smoothbore on the stern deck of the* Miami; *a big-nosed eight-wheeler of the U. S. Military R. R.; soldiers resting near stacked carbines; soldiers dying, but not yet fallen down; soldiers dead, and fat in death, at such places as Murfreesboro and Chancellorsville, at Seven Pines and Antietam, and at the one with the name that would be among the last names to live with the mind—Chickamauga.*]

*   *   *

"What books did you borrow today?" the woman said.

"Books about battles," the boy said.

"Battles in the Revolution?"

"No, not battles in the Revolution."

"The War of 1812? The Mexican War?"

The boy shook his head. "No," he said.

"The Spanish-American War, then?"

"I don't like any of those battles. I like the ones with the names!"

"What names do you mean?" the woman said.

"The names you read to me. You know."

"Don't you remember them?"

"I'll always remember them."

"Then why don't you say them?"

"I don't like to."

"Why not, son?"

"I like to hear them."

"The Wilderness," the woman said, and the boy stood very still. "Spotsylvania Court House," she said, and she watched him fill his lungs and hold them full. And then, almost whispering it, she said, "Chickamauga."

VACCINATIONS

A BENCH near the sea-wall in Battery Park held the hack-driver and his son. They had spent much of the morning in the green glassed-in gloom of the Aquarium, and the boy was tired, and now and again his eyes wobbled to a close and shut out sight of the bright and wind-broken water of the Bay, and once, as he dozed, his father leaned over and kissed his sun-struck hair.

On another bench a short way up the walk sat a gray-haired man, and before him, with his hands on his hips, stood a boy in a sailor-suit. "Tell me your name," the man was saying.

"I don't want to tell you my name," the boy said.

"Why not?"

"I don't know you."

"If you tell me your name, and I tell you mine, we'll know each other."

"I don't want to know each other."

"How about shaking hands, then?"

"I don't want to shake hands."

("That's a mean boy," Danny said.)

"Suit yourself," the man said, and taking a paper bag from his pocket, he untwisted its neck and offered an assortment of candy to the boy.

"I don't have to suit myself," the boy said.

The man reached into the bag and brought out a jawbreaker striped like an Italian flag. "Here's a jim-dandy," he said.

"I don't like jim-dandies," the boy said.

("He's terrible mean," Danny said.)

The man exhibited another selection: a piece of taffy with a pea-
nut-butter heart. "They call this a Mary Jane," he said.

("I love Mary Janes," Danny said.)

"Mary Janes stink," the boy said.

"You're hard to please," the man said, and he dumped a gush
of penny-candy into his lap: jujubes, chocolate buds, marshmallow bananas, and wax-gum. "Take your pick."

"I don't want to take my pick," the boy said. "I don't like you.
I hate you."

The man's smile suddenly shrank. Grasping a handful of candy
and holding it overhead, he said, "Get the hell out of here, you
stuckup little pissabed!"

The boy retreated, and from a safe distance, he raised the pistol
of his fist, took aim, and fired. "Oink!" he said as loudly as the letters allowed, and then he ran away.

The man let his hand fall and relax, and over the walk rolled a
motley of candy. He stared at it, and he sat staring until three pairs
of shoes stopped before him, one belonging to the boy, another to a
woman, and the third to The Law.

("A pleeceman!" Danny said.)

"Is this the guy, kiddo?" the policeman said.

"That's him," the boy said.

"Mister," the policeman said, "what did you do to this kid?"

"I did nothing to him," the man said.

"His governess reported you was molesting him."

"That's nonsense. I simply offered him some candy. He didn't
want any, and he ran off."

"That cheap stuff would've spoiled his stomach," the governess
said.

"Get up when a lady's talking," the policeman said. The man
rose, treading pellets of candy. "So just because he didn't want
none of that junk, you went and molested him."

"I just finished saying that I did *not* molest him."

"Then maybe you tried to entice him."

"You're going a little too far, officer."

"Well, you must've did something!"

The governess said, "He called the boy a foul name."

"I did no such thing," the man said.

"You did too call me a foul name!" the boy said. "You called me a pissabed!"

"The idea!" the governess said.

"It was a *good* idea," the hack-driver said. "I saw the whole thing, and the kid deserved it. He's a stinker from Stinkville."

"How dare you!" the governess said.

"Ah, go back uptown where you belong," the hack-driver said.

The policeman said, "Well, move along."

After the three pairs of shoes had gone, the gray-haired man approached the hack-driver's bench, saying, "I have you to thank for. . . ."

"The next time I see you in this park," the hack-driver said, "I'm going to break your God damn ass!"

The man turned and walked quickly away.

"You said a foul word," Danny said. "You could be arrested."

"He's a foul guy."

"What did he do that was foul?"

"There goes a fire-boat," the hack-driver said. "Those shiny things are where the water comes out when they're fighting a fire."

"Why're you going to break his ass?" Danny said.

"He's bad, that's why. When a strange man tries to give a boy candy, it's a bad thing."

"But *why*?"

"It just is," the hack-driver said.

SELF-CONTROL

EVEN when first built, in 1870, Public School 10A, a four-story brick and brownstone, had worn a look of alarm, but now, long since flanked by taller buildings, the expression was one of horror, as if imperceptibly through the years its neighbors had expanded, and the day were at last foreseeable when they would compress and belittle it to a gasket of talc between them.

Polly Johnson and Danny had paused before it at the curb, and the boy watched other children converge on the doorway at a pace that slackened as confinement loomed. They postponed entering in many and violent ways: by lingering to hammer one more dent in the railing along the wall, by doing balancing-acts with lunch-boxes and books, by making sudden lunges at nothing visible, like bugs, or simply by halting near the gutter and trying for distance with spit. Within, a bell rang.

On either side of the hallway, there were cases of varnished golden oak, holding displays of wampum and pottery, sprays of labeled and long-dead leaves, specimens of child-art, and illumin-ated mottoes now fungose with dust. The Principal's office was at the end of the corridor, and Polly Johnson, hand-in-hand with her son, walked toward it through school-sound: chalk on blackboards, singsong rote and giggling, desks banging, and, from somewhere above, a harmonica giving a key.

"You're a week late with your boy, Mrs. Johnson," the Principal said, and looking beyond her, he studied a sepia engraving of the purchase of Manhattan by the Dutch.

"He had a cold, Dr. Delahaye," the woman said, "but a week isn't very long, and I'm sure he can make up the work."

The Principal leaned forward a little, peering at the familiar picture as if it had revealed some new detail. "What work?" he said.

"The work he missed by being sick."

The Principal eyed the woman for a moment, and then he smiled. "He hasn't missed any work," he said. "But will he ever be able to make up the lost play?"

[*There were sand-boxes on the floor, and the sand was strewn with tin shells, and buckets, and tiny spades; there were trains, and tracks for trains, and there were trays of modeling-clay, gray and green and rust and blue; there were slates on easels, and rainbows of chalk; there were armies—soldiers, cannon, horses—of painted lead; there were orange fish in a submarine forest, and a yellow bird sang from a bam-boo cage; there was a plaster bust of Washington, and there was an American flag, and there was a teacher—and the teacher was Miss Morey, Miss Morey!*]

Danny stood motionless and marveling in a vast toyshop without price-tags, and he reached with his eyes for all things in motion
and all things at jumbled rest. On the floor around his left shoe,
a pool of pale amber water grew. 17 87 .304

FAMILY BACKGROUND

SUPPER-SMELLS, sucked under the kitchen door, swirled about
Danny and drifted past him through the open windows of the
parlor, and he watched lights come on as the sky above the courtyard petered out. Clotheslines were fractures in the saffron after-
glow, and telephone-poles were papal crosses against calcimined
brick. A cat's head-lamps moved along the main street of a fence,
a sink drank and gargled, a child coughed, and, somewhere, a feeble doorbell twittered.

[*A woman sitting near an unlit window across the way had long
been listening for a different bell: a bell on a box fixed to the molding
at the floor; a bell that, ringing, would bring her to her feet and take
her to the vulcanized-rubber connections of a wall-telephone. The
instrument—bell-box, receiver, and transmitter—had been installed
three years before. Never yet had it been used.*]

In one of the areas below Danny, a boy was tugging at a kite-
cord snagged on a fire-escape. From a packing-case in the adjoining area, another boy watched him, wielding a clothespin as if it
were a cigar. He exhaled no-smoke and tapped off no-ash, and
then he said, "My name is Waldo Fitch, and I'm smoking to spoil
my wind."

The other boy bent a double wind of cord around his palm and
yanked hard; the cord snapped. Considering the shank dangling
overhead and then the loops still binding his hand, he made a de-
duction. "It must've broke," he said, and now, climbing a sway-
backed sawhorse, he transferred his attention to Waldo. "My name
is Ralph Cooke, and you're blowing smoke in our yard!"

"I'm eleven, going on twelve," Waldo said, and he flourished
his wooden weed. "Watch me stunt my growth."

"I'm thirteen, going on fourteen," Ralph said, "and you're a
crap-head."

[*The air, the earth, and the sea were filled with wire, in single strands, in mats and meshes, in carpets and twisted ropes, and nations were lashed down and continents shackled with it, all to make a room in a flat in a downtown tenement accessible to any voice in any language at any time, but no mouth had ever fashioned the twelve-letter three-digit combination of Bowling Green 757.*]

"There's a fighter name of Leach Cross, and he's a dentist," Waldo said. "He fixes my father's teeth in Harlem, and when I go along, he shows me all the punches, so if you call me a crap-head again, I'll hit you in the solo plexus."

Ralph appraised the younger boy, and then he said, "If you wasn't such a kid, I'd knock you down and cockalize you."

"You and what army?" Waldo said.

"But taking avantage of a kid is a sin, and when you're thirteen years of old, you get held responcivil."

"Why do you have to be thirteen years of old?"

"Because any younger, you're still a kid. It stands to reason."

"Kids can make sins," Waldo said. "I'm sinning right now with all this smoking and rooning my health."

"There's two kinds of people can't sin—kids and loonies."

"Who told you about the loonies?"

"I found out by myself," Ralph said. He produced a stick of chalk that almost at once became a rival of Waldo's cigar: a cigarette. "I happen to know a loony lady."

[*There were other objects in the room—an iron bedstead, a chair, a small table, a gas-range encrusted with boiled-over meals, a few pieces of crockery, and a mirror blotched where its backing of mercury had peeled—but they were things accepted without thought and almost an assumption, like air, and, in use or idle, they in no way arrested the mind. But the virgin telephone (Bowling Green 757) came at the woman like a train running toward her in a dream.*]

Wonderment wrinkled Waldo's mouth as if he were about to kiss with it, and when he spoke, it was with awe and entreaty. "A loony lady!" he said. "What does she do? Tell me, Ralphie! What does she do?"

Ralph fitted an imaginary holder to his imaginary cigarette and squinted down an infinite slope of disdain. "What's it worth to you?" he said.

Reverence tottered and collapsed."Worth!" Waldo said."Why, I wouldn't even pay you in bottle-caps!"

"Then you can go fish," Ralph said.

"Then you never seen any loony lady."

"Say that again, and I'll mobilize you."

"Mobilize, cockalize—and I'm still smoking a cigar," Waldo said. "I'll make a bargain: you tell me about the loony lady, and you get five puffs."

"All right," Ralph said. "What do you want to know?"

"First off, what does she look like?"

"Like a lady. What do you think?"

"She ought to phone at the mouth. Otherwise, how can you tell she's loony?"

"Well, for instant, she stands around all the time looking in the mirrow."

"So do I stand around looking in the mirrow."

"But she makes faces at herself," Ralph said.

"Who can't?" Waldo said, and he inhaled his cheeks, and his features shrank as if painted on a punctured balloon."There's got to be something else beside making faces."

[*Who was she, and what was her name, her weight, her height, her complexion? How old was she, where were her parents, if living, who were her friends, and did she have a husband, a lover, or only some guy named Arthur brought in out of the rain? Was she stout, skinny, strung out, or dumpy, and what was the exact color of her eyes, her flesh, her politics, and her liver? Did she wear false teeth, transformations, corn-pads, and other jewelry, and were there flakes of dandruff on her shirtwaist, sweat-stains on her shields, hard black hairs in wens on her chin or nose? How much money did she have in the bank, under a floorboard, in a coffee-can, in the toe of a sock? Did she believe that Christ was God's only begotten son, or did she worship different and less respectable plaster-casts? Was her heart in the right place or on the right side? Was she afraid of dark rooms, heights, crowds, and hell? What foods did she favor, and were dogs friendly to*

her flavor and her outstretched hand? Who was she, and what was
her name, and who knew she was alive and, knowing it, would spend
a nickel to say, "Bowling Green 757? What hath God wrought?"]

"It's about time I got a couple of puffs," Ralph said.

"Nothing doing," Waldo said. "We made a bargain."

"You sure want your powder flesh."

"I only want all I got coming to me."

"You could see it for yourself, if you wanted, but first you got
to pay off."

"You show me the loony lady," Waldo said, "or I break the
contrack!"

Ralph drew deeply on the chalk cigarette to deaden his anger,
and emitting smoke in such volume that he had to fan it away, he
pointed his chin across the yard."That's her window," he said.
"The one next to the fire-excape."

"But it's dark!" Waldo said.

"What do you want me to do—go up and lighten the light?"

Waldo manufactured an outsize sneer, a distortion so vast that
it altered his voice."You never seen a loony lady in your whole
life!" he said."You just made up all that stuff so's you could weasel me out of my clear Havana cigar! But you got stung, because
the contrack is busted!"

Ralph pitched a fist that hit Waldo flush on the nose. The boy
clapped both hands to his face and sank from sight, baying like a
dog. Peering over the fence after him, Ralph said,"Leach Cross!"

[*The woman rose from her chair at the dark window next to the*
fire-escape, and, putting on a hat, she went downstairs to the street.
At the corner, there was a drug-store; in the drug-store, there was a
booth; in the booth, there was a telephone. Fitting her ear and mouth
to the apparatus, she said when spoken to, "Bowling Green 757"—
and then she listened for what only others could hear.]

Through the dark window next to the fire-escape came the sound
of a bell. It rang seven times, and then it was still, and in the area
below, as its last aftersound died away, Ralph Cooke began to
make a drawing on the fence. His chalk cigarette was merely chalk
now.

Polly Johnson came from the kitchen, struck a match, and made gaslight for the parlor. "You'd better wash your hands, Danny," she said. "It's almost time for supper." The boy said nothing as he went to the sink, opened a tap, and watched water pool in his palms and leak away. As the woman spread a cloth on the table, she said, "Why do you always stare at that window over there?"

"What window?" the boy said.

"The one across the yard. Is it because you think the woman is crazy?"

"I don't know."

"She really isn't. She's just lonely."

"I look and look," the boy said, "but I don't know why."

SCARS, BIRTHMARKS, ETC.

THE hack-driver entered the flat, tossed his cap at the hatrack like a quoit, and headed for the kitchen, saying, "What's to eat?" The way was blocked by his son, who stood before him drying his hands on a dish-towel; on the boy's cheek ran several ragged scratches, and his left eye was a slit between two purple puffs. "Holy Smoke!" the hack-driver said. "What happened to your queer little puss?"

"I got in a fight at school," the boy said.

"Ah, a pugilist! Tell us all about it—how it started and who finally carried the other kid away."

"I had a pretty thing that I made in school, and I was bringing it home to show Mom, and I was walking along amiring it, and we bumped shoulders—a boy that's in my class—and the thing fell down in the street and got spoiled."

"So far, it's all in your favor. Who made the next move?"

"He did. He said why didn't I look where I was going."

"And you?"

"I said why didn't *he* look where *he* was going."

"And him?"

"He said, 'Oh, a hard guy!' "

"And you?"

"I said, 'From Hardville,' like you told me."

"We're off!" the hack-driver said. "What happened now?"

"He said for me to get out of his way or he'd spit in my eye."

"Did you dare him?"

"I triple-dared him."

"What did he do?"

"He spit in my eye."

"Why, the dirty son-of-a . . . !"

"Daniel!" Polly Johnson said.

"So he spit in your eye!" the hack-driver said.

"He spit in both eyes," the boy said.

"The hell, he did! What did *you* do?"

"I spit back."

"That's more like it."

"But I missed," the boy said. "I didn't have enough spit."

The hack-driver sat down and rocked himself. "Well, get on with it," he said. "You didn't grow them welts from being spit on."

"He stepped on the thing that I made, and it got all crushed."

"And then you hit him?"

"No," the boy said.

"You didn't hit him for spitting in your eye, and you didn't hit him for stepping on the thing. What *did* you do, for Chrisake?"

"I picked up the thing that I made, and it was all crushed."

"We covered that," the hack-driver said. "But what did you *do?* What did you *say?*"

"I said, 'You crushed my thing.' "

"Hooray for you! Is that all you could think of?"

"That's all," the boy said.

"Well, then, what did *he* do?"

"He didn't do anything. He *said* something, though. He said, 'Get outa my way, or I'll do the same to you as I done to the thing.' "

"Now, of course, you hit him."

"No," the boy said.

"Would you please tell me why not?"

"Because *he* hit *me*."

"But naturally you hit him back."

"I couldn't hit him naturally."

"What do you mean you couldn't hit him naturally?"

"I was laying on the ground."

"He knocked you down with one punch?"

"Yes," the boy said.

"Why didn't you duck, like I showed you?"

"I did duck. That's how he hit me."

"Well, you didn't have to *stay* on the ground. You could've got up."

"Oh, I got up, all right. I got up in a jiffy."

"That's better. And then, finally, you hit him."

"Nope. He knocked me down again."

"I'm sick," the hack-driver said, and he put his head back and glared at the stained ceiling.

"I got up again, though," Danny said.

The rocker moved a little and stopped again. "And then he hit you a third time, and there you were on the ground, like before," the hack-driver said.

"No, *sir!*" the boy said.

The hack-driver sat upright, and once more his rocking was spirited. "Don't tell me *you* got around to hitting *him!*"

"I won't," the boy said. "He hit me again, but this time I didn't fall down."

The hack-driver groaned. "We're winning!" he said. "We're winning!"

"I wasn't winning," the boy said. "I was losing."

"That's news, I suppose! I know damn well you was losing. You was lost in a cloud of knuckles!"

The boy said, "He hit me a whole lot, in the mouth, in the nose, in the belly, but I never fell down again, not once. I learned how to make him stop knocking me down."

The hack-driver felt the muscles of his jaw harden and shrink, and his eyeballs stung him, and his nostrils prickled. "Give us a kiss, son," he said. "Now, tell us the rest of it."

"He hit me and hit me and hit me, but he couldn't make me fall down any more."

"Didn't you hit him once, Danny-boy? Not even *once?*"

"I couldn't tell. I was crying."

"Crying! What the hell for?"

"He was hurting me."

"You should've hurt him right back."

"There was one time when I heard him say 'Ow!' "

"Ah! That shows you hit him a beaut!"

"No, I think he just skinned himself on my head."

"I guess if your head would've stood up, you could've skinned him alive."

"Maybe, but right after that, the man come along and grabbed his arm."

"The man! *What* man? And what did he grab his arm for?"

"The boy was going to hit me again, and the man stopped him."

"He should've butted out, the God damn buttinsky! You just made the kid say 'Ow!' The tide was turning."

"He grabbed the boy's arm and made him open his fist."

"Oh, Jesus, don't say there was a rock in it!"

"Not a rock, but he had a ring made out of a horseshoe-nail."

"The mishrable yellow-belly sneak!"

"The man made him take it off."

"I'd like to meet that man some time," the hack-driver said. "I owe him a beer."

"Then the man made us start to fight again."

"And you was boiling mad, and you knocked the kid on his ass!"

"I was boiling mad, all right, but I didn't knock him on his ass."

"You should've wiped the street with him!"

"I tried to, but I couldn't."

"Why not? You had the right on your side."

"Maybe, but he was a better fighter."

The hack-driver said, "Even without the ring?"

"Yes," the boy said, "even without the ring."

"Once he quit cutting you to pieces with it, you should've sailed in and crowned him."

"Oh, I only got cut after he took the ring off."

The hack-driver rose and stamped back and forth across the

parlor. "Damn it all to smack!" he said. "When're one of us Johnsons going to win a fight?"

From the doorway of the kitchen, his wife said, "We'll win our
share, never fear."

POLITICAL AFFILIATION

ANDREW BURCH, one of the teachers at P. S. 10A, was a sick
man. He had a pulse of 74, a blood-pressure of 145, fair vision, clear lungs, good digestion, functioning kidneys, no malig-
nancies, and only the barest trace of sugar, but he was a sick man:
he thought of death. He thought of death always, and because he
lived as if life were a condemned building, in his fancy he was con-
stantly dropping dead, dying violently in a catastrophe, being in-
curably infected through a cut or a bruise, wasting away with a
phrase (a lingering illness), or merely aging. It was this last form
of death that he contemplated most: it was the least preventable.

In a moment, now, he would open a notebook and call his class
to order.

There had been many classes, he thought, more than he cared
to remember, and there had been many lecture-rooms, many note-
books, and many and varied faces, but all faces had fused into one
face that was none he could recognize, and all places and all things
had become no place and nothing. He did not see now, as he had
seen at the beginning, the blood-burnished skin of the young, the
tile-shine of their teeth, and their fresh eyes that were like limoges.
He did not see now, nor would he ever see again, that there were
some who came day after day in their one suit and their only pair
of shoes, that there were some who ate during the lunch-hour and
some who watched and watered at the mouth until the last crumbs
were eaten or brushed away. He did not see now the weak and the
strong, the dirty and the clean, and the shy and the brash, nor
could he any longer distinguish between the agony of ignorance
and the composure of knowledge. He did not see that the good
outnumbered the evil all the rest to one, and among the forty-two
children before him on this day, six across and seven deep, there
was none to whom he could turn with love: all were evil.

He had once been only twenty years older than the oldest of his pupils; now the difference between them was doubled: by a subjective and one-sided mathematics, their age had remained constant while his had changed. They had come to him in nonage, and so they had gone away; only he had felt the shifting of the first sand-grain that betokened the avalanche. "I am forty years old," he had told himself once, and from then had he known that his time was running out. Forty had too soon become forty-one, forty-two, forty-three, forty-four—and the first sand-grain had clearly multiplied to more than he could count. And then it had been forty-five, forty-six, and forty-seven, each always for an always-dwindling year, and then forty-eight, and forty-nine, and now fifty—and the fifty was going like the rest. Fifty-one might come, but with tumbling rock, and fifty-two, but with the earth on the move, the whole earth . . . !

There were death-ornaments in the room. Behind the last row of desks hung a painting of a battle-scene in which a mounted general and his mounted staff viewed the progress of some anonymous and distant slaughter. To the left and right of this were a pair of Audubon prints, one of a turkey-buzzard, the bird with an appetite for death, and the other of a duck-hawk, death itself on the wing. On a shelf opposite the window-wall stood a Lincoln death-mask, a clay replica of clay, and displayed in a frame between the two front blackboards was the best historical essay of the preceding class, its own self-composed epitaph. The author of the last paper chosen for this distinction had returned as a visitor, and unconscious of all but his creation, he was standing below it now and reading its familiar yet ever-fresh lines:

WASHINGTON THE MAN WITH THE

DETERMINE FACE

The report come in by messeger. George Washington was alected to the first president of the Untied States. He won by a big majority, so I went to see him. When I got to the house, I met a butler.

I said "Could I see Mr. Washington?"

He said "Who was I?"

I said "I was a freind."

He said "I am sorry to interrup you, but Mr. Washington axpect you."

I followed the butler in the liberry, and there was a man in a three corner hat with a determine face.

"I persume you are Mr. Daniel Johnson" the elagent man said with the determine face.

I said "Yes I am Mr. Washington" because I knew right away who it was.

He said "Why did you come here in the liberry?"

I said swiftly "I come here in the liberry to congradualate you for being such a good president. Also to quiz your early life. But that is not my business if you will not tell me."

He said "I was glad to be alected."

I said "I would like to know about your early life" I quizzed again.

"I was born on 1732" he ansered thinking hard.

I quizzed him "When you were born did you have a good education?"

"The best there was" he said "and that is more than I can say for my teacher" he laughed.

I said "Did you think you would be alected?"

"That is a personel question" he ansered smilling.

After I was all done quizzing he said "Would I like to dine with him?"

I ansered swiftly "No I have to get home."

He said "Then my butler will open the door when you go."

"Good by Mr. Washington" I called.

"Good by Mr. Johnson" he said gravly.

When the butler opened the door I saw with amazmnt that he was a slave.

The bell rang.

"You may go now, Johnson," Burch said, and he turned back the cover of his notebook.

HEIGHT, WEIGHT, REACH

FROM the stringpiece of a Hudson River dock, a quintet of boys watched the passing water-traffic with bulging eyes. The stiff muck of all-day suckers had stifled speech for a time, but little by little tooth and sinew had broken down the almost indestructible candy, and dog-sounds gave way now to words.

Roger Lynch gulped, swallowed, looked enviously at his companions, and said, "I wish I'd've bought another one."

"You shouldn't've et so fast," Dewey Myers said.

Paul Stagg said, "I chew a all-day sucker till it just dreens down my neck."

"I wait till I can bend it," Morton Peck said, "and then I kind of stow it in my gooms. That way, I still got some left tomorrow."

Daniel Johnson said, "What I do depends on if I'm thinking."

"What're you thinking about right this second?" Morton said.

"Right this second, I'm thinking about Nothing."

"He's thinking about nothing," Morton said to the other three and, with an inclusive glance, to certain fancied onlookers.

"Nothing is one of my favorite things to think," Danny said. "Like at night, when the stars come out."

"Nothing is nothing, even at night."

"I mean, in between the stars—that's where Nothing is."

"You're damn right. There's nothing in the sky for a million-trillion miles."

"But how about after that?" Danny said.

"That's as far as nothing goes. That's the end."

"If Nothing ends," Danny said, "Something begins."

Morton appealed to the huge crowd that had gathered to hear the dispute. "When is he going to say something with brains in it?" he said.

"I always say things with brains."

"On my opinion, you're a peanut-head."

"I'm not suppose to use bad language," Danny said, "but if you call me that again, I will have to break your ass."

"Listen," Morton said. "I seen Red Nolan make it come right out of your ears."

"That was Red Nolan. That ain't you."

"He done it once, and he can done it again."

"Maybe, but that still ain't you, Morty."

"You guys make me sick," Roger said. "Always fighting."

"Who ast you to stick your two cents in?" Morton said.

"Nobody. I just stuck 'em in."

"Well, stuck 'em out again!"

"Why didn't you get that hard with Danny?"

"I didn't feel like, that's why!"

"Ah, let him alone, Morty," Paul said. "He's got goggles on."

"He's got goggles on because he don't want to fight," Morton said. "He wants to stick his two cents in, but he don't want to take the consenquences. He don't need goggles. I seen him once when he left 'em home, and he could see as good as anybody."

"That's a lie!" Roger said.

Morton looked first at the countless thousands of his audience and then at Roger. "S-a-y t-h-a-t a-g-a-i-n!" he said.

"Say what again?"

"That I'm a liar."

"I never said it in the first place. I only said what you said was a lie."

"Don't that make me out a liar?"

"Not particulary," Roger said.

"That's different, then," Morton said.

Roger turned away for a glance at the river. When he turned back, one side of his face bulged like a sack of rocks. His friends studied the tumescence, but it remained fixed. Dewey reached out and touched it with a fingertip, saying, "I thought you said you wished you had another all-day sucker." Roger sign-spoke the impossibility of talk. "I bet if we'd've gave you one, you'd've et it."

Roger tried to say something, but with the words came a viscous dribble skeined with color; he sucked back quickly, and it vanished.

"This'd be a good time to see if he's goosy," Paul said.

Roger was again vocal. "There goes a transalanic boat!" he said.

"It's camelflagged!" Dewey said. "That means it's painted so's you can't see it."

"If you can't see it," Morton said, "how do you know it's there?"

Dewey explained. "You know it's there because you're on it, and you know you're on it because you can't cross the ocean without a transalanic boat."

His doubt removed, Morton said, "Oh."

"That camelflag is wonderful stuff," Danny said, "but supposing the man that was camelflagging the boat got some of it on his pants."

"He'd clean it off," Paul said.

"But what would he clean? He wouldn't be able to see what he was cleaning."

"I got it figured out," Paul said. "If he got the camelflag on his leg, the leg would get invisible, but he could still see the other one, and he would know the invisible leg was right next to it."

"I never would've been able to think that up, Paul," Danny said. "You're a pretty good thinker. But what if the guy only had one leg to start with?"

"If I had time, I could figure that out too."

Roger said, "My cousin has a leg that got shot off in the French Army."

"Why didn't he get it shot off in the American?" Morton said.

"Because the American ain't fighting."

"Look. The American Army can fight better when it ain't fighting than the French Army can fight when it *is* fighting."

"All I know is, my cousin got so mad when the Huns sunk the *Lusitania* that he went and enlisted in the French."

Danny said, "The *Lusitania* had guns on." Four faces slowly turned to him. "The Germans said they was going to fire torpedoes on any transalanic boat with guns on. That was fair warning."

"Fair!" Morton said. "What's fair about the Huns laying in the bottom of the ocean and firing torpedoes?"

"The *Lusitania* had no right with guns on," Danny said.

"You know what I think?" Roger said. "Danny's for the Huns."

"Well, I ain't for the Allies," Danny said.

"If you ain't for the Allies," Morton said, "then you got to be for the Huns. You got to be for *some*body."

"I'm in the middle."

"You *can't* be in the middle. How can you be in the middle?"

"I can be in the middle by not being on the sides. I don't like the side of the Germans because they ravitch girls and cut off their hair, and I don't like the side of the Great British because they impressed American seamen, and we had a Revolution."

Roger said, "My cousin told me the Huns was so thirsty they drank blood."

"The Great British are thirsty too," Danny said. "They drink more blood than anybody in the world. That's how they got the name of Redcoats."

"I don't care about thirsty or not," Morton said. "Four of our fathers come from the Great British Islands, so we have to be for the Great British."

"I'm for the Great British because they speak English," Dewey said.

"I wouldn't be for anybody that didn't speak American," Danny said. "Pew on the Great British!"

Roger, Morton, Paul, and Dewey looked at each other, and then they rose from the stringpiece. There was a moment's silence while one of them elected himself spokesman. "You *got* to be for the Great British!" Morton said.

"You got to take the oath of alliance!" Roger said.

"You got to do whatever we tell you!" Paul said.

"Or else the four of us'll kick the shit out of you!" Dewey said.

"Pew on all of you!" Danny said.

*   *   *

Half an hour later, Polly Johnson was swabbing Danny's head with arnica. "What I can't understand," she said, "is why you were for the Germans."

"I wasn't for the Germans," Danny said, "and I wasn't for the Great British. I was just against those four guys telling me what I had to do."

DANGEROUS THOUGHTS

"THIS one's for you, Danny," Polly Johnson said, and she handed the boy a letter. "It's from Uncle Web."

"Ah, the globe-trotter!" the hack-driver said. "Where's he now?"

Danny examined the cancellation. "A place called C. Z.," he said.

"C. Z.—where in hell is C. Z.?"

"Maybe it's the City of Zanzibar," Danny said, and he slit the envelope and removed a letter, a postcard, a photograph, and a pamphlet. "Look what he sent."

"Read the letter first," his mother said.

Putting the other enclosures aside, the boy opened a folded page. "Up at the top, it says, 'June 17, 1917,' and right under, it says, 'Coco Solo, C. Z.' There's that C. Z. again."

"Canal Zone," the woman said. "Read."

Danny said, "I will now read the letter."

Dear nephew Daniel, the note you sent to Rancagua, Chile, was four months old when it finally caught up with me. As you can see, I'm not in Chile any more, so the note went all the way down there for nothing. Or maybe I shouldn't say nothing, because after all it did have a wonderful boat-ride.

"A wonderful boat-ride," the hack-driver said. "All tied up in a mail-sack and buried in some ratty hold."

The woman said, "If that was the only way you could go to Chile—all tied up in a sack—you'd go."

"Read on," the hack-driver said. "Sure, I'd go."

You're probably wondering what I'm doing here in the Canal Zone. Well, Danny-boy, take a look at my picture. Old Webster Varner is now a Chief Yeoman in Uncle Sam's Navy.

"In the Navy!" the hack-driver said. "Now, what do you know about that?"

His wife took up the photograph. "He looks good in uniform," she said.

"Let's see," the hack-driver said, and the photograph was passed to him. "The same aimless slob."

Even your father has likely heard by this time that our country is at war.

"As Danny used to say," the hack-driver said, "that's an insultment!"

No matter what you've read in books, war is not a noble thing. You blow your enemy's brains out, and they load you down with medals, but it's murder all the same. I suppose you're asking yourself what I'm doing in the Navy if I don't believe in killing—and I'm going to tell you. A lot of funny things have happened in that wonderful land of ours since the Revolution—damn funny things. Somehow or other, a pack of crooks have managed to gobble up everything in sight —by force, by trickery, by just being there first—and it's gotten so's the average man nowadays is lucky if he dies with enough in the bank to cover a forty-dollar funeral.

"That's God's own truth," the hack-driver said. "A guy has to save up to die."

But it won't always be like that, Danny. The day will come when us poor stiffs—me, you, your old man, and the rest—snatch back what belongs to us. We won't always be owned lock, stock, and barrel by Wall Street, and you can take my word for it—or rather the word of a better man than I'll ever be, Eugene V. Debs. There's a great one, kid, and the older he gets the greater he grows.

"You want to know something, Polly?" the hack-driver said. "That brother of yours is a Socialist."

"You must be joking," the woman said.

But that isn't what I started out to say. I joined the Navy because it's *my* Navy, even if the crooks don't think so, and it's *my* country more than it ever was theirs, even if they'd only laugh if they heard me say it, and it'd be the loveliest place on earth if only it was free in fact, the way it is on paper. And that's why I'm in the Navy—to make the paper things come to life, to fight for freedom wherever it isn't. Democracy is contagious.

The boy looked up. "What's democracy, pop?" he said.

"A thing we're supposed to have here in America," the hack-driver said. "Only the crooks went and grabbed it off for themselves."

"What do they want with it?"

"Nothing special. They just didn't want *us* to have it."

"Didn't they leave us any at all?"

"Oh, some. About three bags full."

"I never seen a bag around here."

"It's a thing you can't exactly see."

"Then it must be camelflagged, like a transalanic boat!"

"Write that to your Uncle Web—he'll like it. I like it myself."

"You still haven't explained what democracy is," the woman said.

"It's an idea, son, like 'All men are created equals.' You know where that comes from?"

"The Decoration of Independence," the boy said.

The hack-driver looked at his wife. "You know," he said, "this kid might get somewhere on nothing, after all."

"He might," the woman said, "but it happened to be the Gettysburg Address."

"It happened to be both," the boy said.

The hack-driver laughed, saying, "Read us more, boy."

I send you several things in this letter. I've already mentioned the snapshot, and the postcard is simply a map of North and South America—or is it? Look at it carefully and see if you can learn how I swam in two oceans on the same day.

The boy took up the card. At first glance, as his uncle had written, it appeared to be only a map, but held at an angle, it revealed the surrounding waters as faces, one of a man and one of a woman, with mouths joined at the Isthmus. "I know!" the boy said. "The Alanic and Pacific Ocean kissed Panama so hard that it broke in half and made the Canal!"

"That wasn't a kiss," the hack-driver said. "It was a bite."

The pamphlet is something for the future. Put it away till you're thirteen or fourteen, and then take it out and study it. It was gotten up by the Government, and the Navy issues it to every man in the service. It deals with the prevention of certain sicknesses that men get when they. . . .

"I'll put it away for you, Danny," the woman said.

"How will I know when I get to be thirteen?"

"I'll remind you."

FAVORITE SPORT

THE woman brought cups and a coffee-pot from the kitchen, and setting them among the strewn paraphernalia of homework, she said, "Danny, be a good one and run up to the corner for a bottle of cream." The boy rose, went to the hatrack, and put on his cap. "Hurry those fat little legs of yours," she said, and as the door began to close, she fired three more words at the narrowing crack. "But don't fall!"

["*Hurrah!*" *the crowd was cheering.* "*Hurrah for Christy Mathewson, the Big Six! He is the Big Six because he is the best pitcher! Look at Matty with the baseball! Hurrah because he will win the game!*"

["*What is the score?*" *said Christy Mathewson.*

[*The catcher told him the score. "The score is three balls and two strikes, and you are now down in the hole."*

["*Well, I will climb up, then," Matty said.*

["*Hurrah!" the crowd was cheering. "Matty said he will climb up out of the hole! Oh, if only the hole is not too big! Do not be afraid, Matty will climb up! Hurrah!" the crowd was cheering.*

[*The catcher was serious. He said, "I will now go in back of the plate, and you will have to pitch the ball."*

[*Matty said, "I will pitch with all my might."*

["*Hurrah!" the crowd was cheering. "Matty will pitch with all his might!"*

[*The catcher croushed down in back of the plate, and the batter croushed and swang his bat very mean because he was going to hit the ball. Matty wound himself up and croushed. There was no noise on the Polo Ground. Everybody was too excited.*

[*They said, "He will throw a spit-ball! That means he will spit on the ball! Throw the ball! We are too excited!"*

[*Matty stood up on one foot. The other foot was on his shoulder. He threw the ball. . . .*]

A bottle of cream spun end-over-end through the air and smashed against a hydrant knee-high from the sidewalk.

["*Strike three, and you're out!" said the empire. "Matty has win the contest!"*

["*Hurrah!" the crowd was cheering.*]

When the boy entered the parlor, empty-handed and late, the room seemed so actively silent that he paused near the door and lowered his head to weather the storm, but after many seconds of waiting, he risked a raising of his eyes and saw that his entrance had gone unnoticed, and even on joining his father and mother at the table, he knew that for them only two people were present.

The hack-driver sat looking at the map, and for once its legend of numbers and lines, its symbols and shapes and colors, detained his mind not at all, and his gaze moved in a smooth and idle journey over what had shrunk to a mere drawing called the United States. His wife, staring at the upper half of a window, saw nothing in the darkening sky.

"I wonder if you know why I'm doing it, Polly," the hack-driver said. "I wonder if *I* do, even. All I'm sure about is, there ain't a thing in the world I wouldn't sooner do than die, not a thing—and still I ride around in the old Pope-H day after day, and every minute I'm asking myself, 'Should I go or stay? Should I go or stay?' I couldn't tell you a single place I drove to, or if I paid the fares instead of the people paying me, but I can tell you what I was thinking, all right, because it was always the same: 'Should I go or stay?'"

"And you finally decided to go?" the woman said.

"I'm no red-white-and-blue hero, Polly. I'm only an ordinary guy, but like all the rest, I'm quite a ways from being a chump, and I know there's damn little in this patriotism-business for me and my kind. Web has it down cold: we're not out to make the world safe for anything but Wall Street. The big words are what we hire street-cleaners to sweep away. All the ordinary guy is going to get is shot at."

"They can't *make* you go, Dan."

"No, but they can clap you in prison, and that's even worse. Who wants to sit around in the jug while everybody else is taking a chance? How could I show my face to myself if I done that?"

"Are you going, then, because you're ashamed *not* to go?"

"I'm going for twenny reasons," the hack-driver said, "and not one of 'em's worth a snicket. Mostly, I guess, it's a matter of being afraid—afraid to claim exemption, afraid to enlist, afraid to get drafted, afraid to dodge, afraid to be killed. More than anything, though, I'm going because I've got to prove that I ain't afraid at all."

"Going where, Pop?" Danny said.

"To France," the hack-driver said.

"You will have to go on a transalanic boat."

"I was thinking of swimming, only them uniforms shrink so fast they'd choke me before I got to Sandy Hook."

"What uniforms, Pop?"

"The uniforms of the United States Army."

The boy rose, wide-eyed and open-mouthed.

"Yes, sir," the hack-driver said. "The United States Army."

"Then you'll be like George Washington!" the boy said, and he came to a salute. "George Washington, the man with the determine face!"

"In a way, son, in a way," the hack-driver said, and he went to the window and looked out at the darkness for a long time—until the hand on his throat let go.

TRAVEL

THE woman and the boy sat in one of the open-end day-coaches of a Jersey Central local as it rocked across the Raritan River bridge south of Perth Amboy. Below them, the tan silted water was iced-coffee, floating here and there a muddy frozen block of itself, and on the hills beyond and the branches of barren trees lay skiffs of gray snow that merged with the soiled towel of the sky.

"What's the next station?" the boy said.

They had taken a ferry to the west shore of the Hudson, and there, through the dock-arcade, the woman had led the boy to the train-shed and shown him the ten-wheeled camel-back that would haul them on their journey, and for many moments, mute before this softly-breathing wonderwork, he had gaped at its separate cabs, its steam-chests and fat sand-domes, and its poised rods and perforated drivers, and it was these last that his mind had retained through a world of track and other trains, tanks and gantries, and frozen fields and thawing rivers, and now, his face flattened against a window, he was between the Amboys.

"The next station is Jamesburg," the woman said.

"And after Jamesburg?"

"Prospect Plains,and then Hightstown.That's where we get off."

"Is that the end of the railroad?"

"No, but we change trains there. This one doesn't go where we want to go."

"I thought trains always go where you want to go. What's the good of a train that goes where you *don't* want to go?"

"There are other people on the train, and it goes where *they* want to go—to Philadelphia."

"Where do *we* want to go?" the boy said.

"A little place called Pemberton."

*   *   *

"PEMBERTON! ALL OUT FOR PEMBERTON!"

The hack-driver was waiting for them on the platform, and the boy looked at spiral puttees, a brass-buttoned overcoat, and a hat like a paper boat, and he looked long, for his father and mother had lashed themselves together with arms and become one at the face, and the train was only a last car drawing back surprised when they came apart and turned to their son.

"Danny!" the hack-driver said. "Danny-*boy!* I'm so glad to see you I could take a bite right out of your apple-face!"

"If you bite my face," the boy said, "I will bite your face, because you are George Washington, the man with the determine face."

"A hard guy. Been in any more fights?"

"Five. I lost four, but I finely won."

"Hurray for the Johnsons!"

"Us Johnsons finely won."

"*You're* the one with the determine face," the hack-driver said. "How'd you like to push it against a bowl of soup?"

*   *   *

After eating, the Johnson family walked out along a dirt road winding with Rancocas Creek as it gargled under a broken vault of ice. A few days of warmer weather had run off most of the snow, but a sudden freeze had once again set the crumpled earth like stucco, and hoofprints and tire-tracks, stone-hard now, stumbling-blocked the way. Among grooves in the fields crawled paper-stiff leaves of last-year's corn, and now and then, from dead weeds near the rail-fences, pheasant opened and whistled away.

"How do you know, Dan?" the woman said.

"In the Army, you never know anything," the hack-driver said. "You go along week after week, sleeping, eating, drilling, kidding with the guys—and then some morning you turn out, and you're in a different world. All of a sudden everybody's just a little bit quieter, and it seems like whatever you say sort of hangs in the air, like your breath on a winter's day. I'll bet there isn't a man at Camp Dix doesn't know some outfit's due to move."

"Maybe it won't be yours," the woman said.

"Well, whichever, as soon as I got the feeling, I put in for an overnight pass. The best I could finagle was a noon-to-six, and I had to lie my life away to get that. Nobody was getting nothing. The M. P. at the depot said the only soldier on the up-train today was laid out in a box. Ah, the hell with the war! How're *you?* You working hard?"

"Not very, Dan, and I feel fine."

"I've seen you look better in bed."

The woman smiled. "Ten years ago, maybe."

"The older you get, the more I like you. I'll like you when you're eighty. After that, I might give you a full night's sleep."

The woman watched her son for a moment. He was down off the road now, in a grove of pines at the creek-bank, and his feet were deep in needles that hissed as he plodded through them, hunting for cones to kick into the water. "I thought of leaving him home," she said. "I thought you might want to go somewhere, and he'd be in the way—and then I thought you might be angry."

"I wouldn't've been so angry, Polly."

"Wouldn't you?" she said.

"I'd've met you at the train, and I'd've fed you, and then I'd've hired an iron bed in some cold room, and when we got up there, you know what I'd've done? I'd've knocked your teeth out, one by one. I don't know how many teeth you've got left, but I'd've made them last till my pass expired."

"I guess it's lucky I brought apple-face."

The hack-driver put his arm around the woman. "It isn't that I like the kid any better than you," he said. "It's just that I don't have much use for one of those last drowning pieces."

"Nor I. It would've made me ashamed."

"I'm crazy about you, Polly. You'll be a cute one all your life, even at eighty—and I changed my mind about letting you alone after that. Then I'm *really* going to annoy you."

"I'm crazy about you too, Dan. Probably because you're such a fool."

"Would you care to kiss a fool, Polly?"

The boy climbed the bank to the road and came to a halt, saying, "Shame! Shame! Everybody knows your name!"

"Meet Mr. and Mrs. George Washington," the hack-driver said. "The people with the determine face!"

MILITARY TRAINING

As she entered the flat, the woman said, "Any mail today?" and her son indicated a letter lying on the parlor table. She set down an armful of paper sacks and began to slit the flap of the envelope, but she paused to say, "Or would you rather eat first?"

"First the letter," the boy said, and reaching up under the new chandelier, he pressed the black nipple of a light-switch.

His mother smoothed several sheets of Y. M. C. A. stationery, saying, "It's from Somewhere In France, as usual, and it's dated August 22nd, 1918. Here's what he writes."

> This letter will be in three parts. The first is for Dan-boy, the Battling Bulldog of Battery Park. The second is for the Old Lady, sometimes called Polly and once in a great while Apollo, after a dollar cigar (dollar a box). The third part is for the both of you.
>
> Here goes the first part. Danny, old kiddo, your father's been a soldier for close onto a year now, and if you want the God's honest truth, I'm sick and tired of it, and I get sicker and tireder by the hour. I only wish to hell I was back in N. Y. C., driving the old Pope-H around and stinking up the town.

"He uses pretty bad language," the boy said.

"Do you, ever?" the woman said.

"Oh, once in a while, same as the other guys."

"Is that all you can learn from them?"

"I didn't learn any bad language from them. I learned it from Pop."

"And I suppose they learned it from you."
"That's right," the boy said.
"That's fine."

I want you to be a good boy at school and not get in
trouble, but that don't mean you shouldn't fight if you get attacked, just so you keep your chin close to your chest, or else
you'll be laying down counting stars, and of course never shut
your eyes when you swing, and don't get your tongue between
your teeth unless you want to eat a tongue sandwich without
mustard.

Where was I? Oh, I was telling you to be good in school,
and I meant it. Learn what you can because what you miss today is gone forever, and you don't want to grow up a crafty old
geezer that only cares about how much did he rake in last week.
Earning isn't learning, son, and money won't make you smart.
It sure won't make you dumb, either, but let's not go into
that. Just you listen to Mom. She's the one is got the brains
in this family, even if she is getting on in years, but don't tell
her I said so because girls are kind of touchy about their age.
Where was I?

"He never knows where he is," the boy said. "He's always get-
ting lost."
"He couldn't find his way to the corner," the woman said. "A
fine hack-driver, he is."
"He's the best hack-driver in the world!"
"Do you mean to say you like him?"
"I like him even when he don't know where he is!"
"Just between you and me, I do too."

I was saying you should listen to the old wreck, but now
I'm going to take my life in my hands by telling you that you
don't necessarily have to get led around by the ear. You're no
diaper-boy any more, almost ten years old, and you've got a
head to think with, and besides we brung you up to know the

difference between right and wrong (I mean as far as we knew it ourselves), so if it's time for you to get a few hard knocks, go on out and meet them halfway. You only find out if you can fly by flapping your wings, and you're flying just dandy if you ain't laying sprauled out some place on your phiz.

One thing more, Danny-boy. Don't laugh at me if I spelt some words wrong. I try real hard, but not being the wiz that Mom is, I'd hate for you to laugh at only a poor slob of a hack-driver.

"He's the best hack-driver in the world," the boy said, "and any-body that laughs at him gets peed on!"
"Where did you learn that one?"
"From the best hack-driver in the world!"
"I ask foolish questions."

Here's the second part of the letter, and it's for my dear beloved wife Polly. That bum of a brother of yours, I guess he knows the time of day as good as any man, but he sure made a skull when he wrote once that democracy was conta-geous. There's mighty little of it that this soldier in the in-fantry can see. Our officers are a pack of rah-rahs that think this war is being fought for their especial benefit, which it damn well is, and about the greatest risk they run is an ink-well exploding on them in some chataeu. Also I never heard of servants in an army, but everybody from a shavetail up (a general is shaved all over) they all got guys from the ranks to shine their shoes, dish up their grub, and practicly wipe. . . .

"What did you stop for?" the boy said.
"That was the end of the sentence," the woman said.
"You can't just *wipe*. You have to wipe *something*."
"You're right, Danny. I told a little lie."
"Bad language again?"
"Yes."
"Maybe you could read the bad parts fast."

"I know a better way," the woman said. "I'll read the bad parts to myself."

[*practicly wipe their behinds.*]

The woman glanced at her son. "Well, I read that one," she said. "I hope it's the last."
"I been trying to guess what you left out, and I think I got it."
"Keep it to yourself."

And just open your moosh to complain, and all they give you to defend yourself against a carload of spuds is a skinny little peeling-knife. Servants in the U. S. Army! That's a new one on me. My C. O., the one that I'm elected to blow his nose for, he hasn't drew a sober breadth since he went off the. . . .

"More bad language?" the boy said.
"A few words," the woman said.

[*since he went off the titty.*]

"Did you do it?" the boy said.
"I did it."
"He's giving us a lot of trouble."
"He's still the best hack-driver, though."

But in some ways he's pretty regular, like for instance he don't censor my letters. Matter of fact, he don't censor anybody else's because it hasn't been proved yet that he can read. They say his adjutant caught him *talking* American once, but in the Army it's a good thing not to believe all you hear in the latrine. So far as I'm concerned, the Capt. only speaks one word fluently, and that's a word in French meaning lay down on your back madamoselle.

The woman said, "I shouldn't've read that."

"I wonder what the word is," the boy said. "It's probally 'bar-leyvoo.'"

"Pro07ally," the woman said. "Now comes a whole sentence that I have to leave out."

[*They give him a medal the other day, no doubt for keeping the rain off of all the girls in the Argonne salient.*]

The boy said, "You're smiling."

"Am I?" the woman said. "How can you tell?"

"It shows on your face."

"I hope that's all that shows."

About grub, Polly, you know I never could write you a reference to Mr. Delmonico, but after eating the crap they hand out over here, I'd give a month's pay for one of your appetizing soggy little pies. An Army cook, every time he lays a hand on food, he's guilty of feloneous assault with intent to kill. When he ain't maiming a good side of beef, he's on a can-opening bender, which means you could sometimes go for a week on goldfish and beans. We would like that stuff better if they made it in slightly smaller cans and left it there. Then we could swallow them whole and only get the pleasant taste of tin.

Polly darling, do you remember the things we talked about that day in Pemberton? About whether I'd've been glad if you didn't bring. . . .

The woman said, "There's a long part coming now that you can't hear."

"What'll I do while you're reading it?"

"Make believe we're still down there in Pemberton. Walk along the bank and kick pine-cones into the creek. Plike it's a year ago."

[*About whether I'd've been glad if you didn't bring apple-face? Remember that? It sure would've been nice to get that over-night pass. That way, I could've seen Danny, also you and me*]

could've been together like we never could in some damn rented
bed, knowing we managed those couple of hours by sneaking away
from the kid. I never would've felt right about that. He's just a
little slob of a kid, but sometimes when I only look at him I have
such a hard time breathing I feel like I'm up to my neck in sand.
I love that little boy, Polly, and the reason is not that he's got a
soft round face, or because it feels good to run your hand the
wrong way of his hair, or because it's so much fun to watch him
when he don't know he's being watched, or even because I'm his
father. The reason is because he came out of your body, and that's
the thing I love best in this world.

[*The walk we took that day, I've thought about it so many*
times that when I start to go back over all of our years, I only
see you like you were on one particular afternoon.]

"I'm all done kicking things in the river," the boy said.
"There's only a little bit more," the woman said.
"I guess that's the longest piece of bad language in the United
States."
"I have to admit I'm enjoying it, though."

[*Red in the face with cold, dressed in two-three kinds of brown,*
like the woods and the fields were, and not terribly pretty maybe
to anyone but me—and in my eyes you weren't as if we'd been
married ten years, but that same afternoon (although it's true
we went to bed together twice without a license), and we were lay-
ing naked next to each other in the dark, and you were saying
Dan, Dan.]

The woman turned a page, saying, "Well, that was the end of
the bad language. Here's the rest."

And now a word for the family. A word to end words, you
might say, just like this is a war to end wars—sure, in a pig's
fat ass. . . .

"You read a real dirty one out loud!" the boy said.

"He fooled me!" the woman said. "He told us this part was for the family, and like an idiot, I took him at his word!"

"He's a good joker."

"The best there is."

There'll be more wars, just like there'll be more words. Now, where was I . . . ?

"He's lost again," the boy said.

HONORABLE DISCHARGE

AT MADISON SQUARE, the Broadway and Fifth Avenue sidewalks were packed with people. The bunting on Victory Arch stood stiff in the wind, as if the Arch were making headway, and a blizzard of torn paper whirled along the thoroughfare, and whistles made rippling graphs of sound, and bells spoke the single word of their tongue, and horns blabbed, and marching boots struck asphalt under ticker-tape drifts. A returned contingent of the A.E.F. was on parade.

Opposite Park & Tilford's, in the 26th Street slice of morning sunlight, were Polly Johnson and Danny, the latter wearing the uniform of a Boy Pioneer. He had not yet been admitted to the organization, but on its assurance of membership when he reached the age of twelve, he had entered into negotiations with one Ormond Hoyt (recently dismissed for conduct inconsistent with the tradition of the Frontier, to wit, dropping a paper sack of water on the head of his Chief Woodsman) for the purchase of his uniform.

["*Give you fifty cents for the whole business," you said.*

["*Fifty cents!" Ormie said. "Why, I coughed up two bucks for the coat and pants alone!"*

["*I can't afford that, so I guess I'll invest my money in a catcher's mitt.*"

["*You can't get any mitt for any fifty cents.*"

["*The man said I could have it if I gave him fifty cents down. Then I'll only owe him a nickel a week for two years.*"

["*By then, all the mitt you'll have is the thumb.*"]

["*Not if I don't use it.*"]

["*What's the good of something you don't use?*"]

["*You mean, like a Pioneer uniform?*" *you said.*]

["*That's different," he said. "That's so different, it ain't even the same.*"]

["*I wonder if the man still has that mitt.*"]

["*Tell you what, Danny. Cough up ninety cents, and I'll throw in the staff.*"]

["*I thought the staff went with the uniform.*"]

["*The uniform is only what you wear," he said. "Pants, leggins, shirt, and hat. You don't wear the staff. Where can you wear the staff?*"]

["*In my hand, and that makes it part of the uniform. You got to throw in something else.*"]

["*You're a regalar Sherlock, Danny.*"]

["*A catcher's mitt will stop these insultments.*"]

["*Wait," he said. "Cough up that ole ninety cents, and I'll leave my Talent Badges on the shirt. The ones for Pottery, Horsemanship, and Tree Indentification.*"]

["*They were on the shirt when you bought it off of Ralphie Cooke,*" *you said. "I suppose you'll let the sweat-band stay on the hat.*"]

["*I got to," he said. "It's part of the hat.*"]

["*And so's the Talent Badges part of the shirt. You ain't giving nothing away when you throw in Talent Badges.*"]

["*We been friends a long time, Danny, or I wouldn't do this. You pony up ninety cents, and you can have the whistle. That's fair as fair.*"]

["*What would I do with a whistle?*" *you said.*]

["*Well, supposing you was up in Van Cortlandt Park, and you got attacked by a boa-constructor, or a bear, or even a wild animal. You'd blow on the whistle, and all the Pioneers would come and save you with their Pioneer pocket-knives.*"]

["*Have you got one of those?*"]

["*Sure. How do you think I save people's lives?*"]

["*How about throwing it in, then? You don't have to save people any more.*"]

[*"Okay. For the ninety cents, I'll throw it in."*

[*"Ninety!" you said. "Who said anything about ninety?"*

[*"I did!" he said. "I been saying it all along!"*

[*"Well, I only said fifty, and fifty buys a mitt."*

[*"Ah, show the color of your money."*

[*You gave him two quarters, and then, loading yourself down with the things you'd bought, you started for the door. On the landing outside, you stopped and looked back, and you said, "Come over here a minute, will you, Ormie?"*

[*"It's too late to back out, if that's what you want."*

[*"I just want you to stick your hand in my pocket."*

[*"Why should I?" he said.*

[*"Stick it in, and you'll see."*

[*His hand came out with another quarter, two dimes, and five pennies. "What's this for?" he said.*

[*"I don't want to gyp you," you said. "Mom told me I could pay a dollar for the uniform, and I only gave you fifty cents." Then you went downstairs, and for three or four steps you thought of the pleasure your mother would have when you told her what you'd done.*

[*Only for three or four steps, though, because all of a sudden Ormie called down, "Stung! Stung! Did you ever get stung! I paid thirty cents for all that crap and a lot more you never even seen!"*

[*And then there was a loud laugh, and a door slammed.*]

With the high-borne colors of a regiment and the dipped trophies of the enemy, a dead-spot of silence marched up the Avenue, and heads were bared and hearts covered, and paper about to be flung was held. Danny Johnson's arm snapped up to give the Pioneer salute ("left hand to brow, as if scouting"), and his hat fell off. Long after the swimming flags had passed, the boy was still at salute, honoring gun-limber and caisson, ambulance and horse, and file after file of smiling infantry—and then suddenly his mother had him by the shoulder as if he were under arrest, and she was pointing his face at the sidecar of an approaching motorcycle.

"I wish it was full of water," the hack-driver said as he rolled by. "I need a bath."

*   *   *

Bathed, fed, and dressed now in one of his old whipcord suits, the hack-driver sat sock-footed in his rocker and smoked a cigar. Admiring their hero were his wife and son. "The nearest I come to a medal," he said, "I faded a Croy de Gear on the transport home. I lost it back the next night, though."

The boy said, "You wrote you was bringing me the Kaiser on a dog-chain."

"I lost him too. The bones must've been loaded."

"He would've been a good thing to have."

"I see you're a Boy Scout of America."

"That's for sissies. I'm a Boy Pioneer."

"What's the difference?"

"The Boy Scouts do a good turn every day. We don't."

"You've got to do something."

"I suppose so, only I'm not really a Boy Pioneer yet. I just bought the uniform off of Ormie Hoyt."

"Ah, you're prepared."

"No, that's the Boy Scouts. They're always prepared."

"And the Boy Pioneers are always caught short. That's a fine outfit you're getting into."

"How about taking that uniform off and getting ready for school?" the woman said. "You missed the whole morning." She watched the boy go into the bedroom, and then she turned to her husband. "Well, Dan, you're home."

"Glad or sorry?" he said.

"Too glad ever to make a joke of it," she said. "It was a bad year, and looking back now, I seem to have spent it waiting for something to explode."

"Well, it's over, honey, so take a breath and relax."

"I can't, Dan, not just yet," she said.

He looked at her for a moment, and slowly his face worked into a smile. "Why, Polly!" he said, and he rose and went toward her.

The boy came from the bedroom, saying "I'm going," but with his hand on the doorknob, he paused to study a mother-and-father kiss.

"I thought you were going," the hack-driver said.

"I'm going," the boy said, and he closed the door behind him. He was astride the banister, ready to slide to the floor below, when he realized that he had forgotten to take his cap.

Through the transom, he heard his mother say, "I've got to make up for that day in Pemberton."

He no longer wanted the cap. He let himself slide.

PROPERTY, IF ANY

"THE lucky stiff is in Cuba now," the hack-driver said, tapping a letter from an envelope. "How does he do it? How in hell does he do it?"

"Do what?" the woman said.

"Cover so much territory," the hack-driver said, and crumpling the envelope, he tossed it through the window into the courtyard.

"He's round," the woman said. "He rolls."

"I wanted that Cubic stamp," Danny said, and he went to the window and peered down.

"Me, I hope my heart out, and maybe after seven years, some slob'll come along and say, 'Drive me to Asbury Park.' *Asbury Park!*"

"I've never been to Asbury, Dan. What's it like?"

"Like a thousand other seaside dumps."

"Then why're you so crazy to see all those dumps?"

"You just don't understand, honey."

"Do you?" she said.

The hack-driver ignored the question. "I'm about to read a letter from my dear brother-in-law," he said, "and when I finish, I'll have a bellyful of bile. 'U. S. Naval Station, Guan-something, Cuba, October 28, 1919. Dear Stick-in-the-mud.' That's a good start for a lousy day. They're all lousy, but this one's going to be worse. I'll probably jump into the Pope-H and go right through the floor. If I don't watch out, I'll have a pushmobile. And I've simply got to do something about that back seat—the fares are squawking about their piles. What a car! What a way to make a living! What a life!"

The woman leaned over the back of his chair and looked at him upside-down. "Is it really so terrible?" she said.

"Well, not at the moment."

"All the time kissing," the boy said.

"Butt out, stinker."

Well, I'm nearing the end of my hitch, and then for a little sight-seeing. . . .

"I wish I had that Cubic stamp." the boy said.

"A little sight-seeing!" the hack-driver said. "Why, that dog has seen more than God, and he's seen it twice!"

I've got my eye on a place called Russia. It's about as easy to get into as Heaven, but I'll manage it somehow, even if I have to tunnel under from hell. They say something big is going on there, but old Web Varner won't believe it till he can touch it. Imagine a country where the people own every-thing—banks, mines, railroads, the air they breathe, the ground they walk on, and themselves! No fat-ass crooks to figure out a man's life so close that at the end all the poor pruned-down bastard can show for it is three cigar-store coupons and a cold ham-hock.

The hack-driver said, "Did I once say he was a Socialist? I take it back: he's a Bullshevik."

The woman said, "He started when he was ten years old. I re-member he heard a speech in the street one day, and he rushed home to tell us that we, not Vanderbilt, really owned the New York Central. Pop said, 'Maybe, son, but I'd hate to see Vanderbilt's face when we broke the news.' By the way, it's Bolshevik, not Bullshevik."

"Who cares about the spelling? It's the meaning that counts."

"Do you know what Bolshevism is?"

"It's the people owning the means of production," the hack-driver said. "And don't look so surprised."

"I didn't mean to," the woman said.

"There's Morty and Roger," Danny said. "I hope they don't see that stamp."

"Yes, ma'am," the hack-driver said. "Don't look so God damn surprised."

America was once a tidal-wave of words, and in 1775 words were as hot as a pistol, and we set the world on fire with them, but we got scared of ourselves, and we let the fire go out (in fact, we *put* it out), and our words are cold now, and so is America. We were going to make history for the next thousand years. Hell, we made it for exactly twelve, and then we wet our powder with the Constitution.

The woman said, "Well, *his* powder isn't wet."

"I'm going down and get that Cubic stamp," the boy said.

For a moment, the hack-driver sat still, listening to step-sounds ebbing, and then he said, "I love all the Varners."

I may ship straight from Havana, in which case we won't be seeing each other for quite a while. I haven't spent a button since joining the Navy, and I had some bucks in the bank before I went in. The last time Polly wrote me, Dan, she kind of indicated that you just about had your snoot above water, so what with the kid growing up and all, and you and the cab falling apart, I'm enclosing a little check on the Corn Exchange in the hope it'll tide you over till. . . .

The hack-driver and the woman dashed to the window. In the courtyard below, Morty Peck was disputing possession of the envelope with Danny Johnson, the Battling Bulldog of Battery Park. Leaning over the back fence, Goggly Roger Lynch was egging Morty on.

"I found it," Morty said, "and it's mine!"

"Finders keepers, losers weepers," Roger said.

"Give it back," Danny said, "or I'll wet your powder. That means I'll knock you down in the water."

"You and who else?" Roger said.

"My uncle sent that emvelope, so it belongs to me," Danny said.

"Your uncle!" Morty said. "You never had an uncle, and if you did, he'd be an aunt!"

"The time has come for me to wet your powder," Danny said, and forthwith he delivered two blows. The first struck Morty's left eye, and the second his right eye, and they resulted in his full surrender of the envelope and immediate retreat across the fence.

From up above, the hack-driver said, "That was a neat one-two, son. I never done better myself."

"He bent the stamp a little, but I can straighten it," Danny said, and he began to peel it from the envelope.

"Watch out how you do that. You'll tear it."

"I'm being careful. You got to be careful with stamps."

"Maybe you ought to soak it in hot water."

"No, I got it off," the boy said, and he started for the courtyard door, tossing away the envelope as he went.

The woman nudged the hack-driver. "Do you want that envelope for anything?" she said.

"Jesus, I forgot!" he said. "Hey, Danny, bring that hunk of paper up too, will you?"

"Big Dan and Little Dan," the woman said. "My two damn fools."

NAME OF BANK

THE POPE-HARTFORD drifted up Fifth Avenue on the late-afternoon tide. It contained no paying passengers: no silk-shirt sports, no tarts in ostrich-plumes, no shysters named Max, no jockeys or gamblers, no member of any board of directors, no obscure citizen merely in a hurry—none of these rode the worn waffles of cab's upholstery. Instead, the interior was crammed to the roof with boxes, bundles, pots and pans, blankets, books, rolled-up clothing, and the aggregate drabness of bright trinkets acquired one by one through the years. On a bucket between the hack-driver and his wife, who occupied the drop-seat under the meter, sat Danny their son—the Johnson family, on the move for the first time since becoming a family, was heading for its new home, a flat in Harlem near the corner of 121st Street and Park Avenue.

In front of the Public Library, the cab was held up for a moment by the upheld hand of a traffic policeman.

"Look at the lions," the boy said.

When the cab passed the policeman, he appraised it without expression—up, down, and across—and turned away.

"Cossack," the hack-driver said. "All cops are Cossacks at heart."

"Why do they have lions on the liberry?" the boy said.

"To scratch matches on. I should've scratched one on that cop's chin."

"What in the world have you got against that cop?" the woman said.

"Didn't you see the way he looked at me? It was on the tip of his tongue to say, 'Take that wreck offa the Avenoo!'"

"What was on the tip of yours?"

"I'd've said, 'What for?' and he'd've said, 'I'm going to run you in!'"

"You wouldn't've been frightened, of course."

"Not me," the hack-driver said. "I'd've told him just where he got off. I'd've said, 'Start running,' and we'd've been on our way. He'd've said, 'A fresh egg, eh?' and I'd've said, 'Just laid.' He'd've said, 'Pull over to the curb and produce your license!' I'd've looked at him contemptibly, and I'd've flipped open my wallet and shown him my picture, saying, 'Reckonize me, Inspector?' and he'd've curled. They all curl when you call 'em Inspector. He'd've said, 'Seems like I seen this mugg before,' and I'd've said, cool as a cuke, 'I'm Dago Frank.' 'I thought you was familiar,' he'd've said, and then I'd've said, 'They took that snap of me just before I went to the Chair in 1914.' By now, he'd've been wishing to Christ he never tangled with me."

The woman said, "Wouldn't I have said anything while all that was going on?"

"What could you do that would've curled him better than I was curling him?"

"Oh, something like, 'What're you two game-cocks sore about?'"

"How would that've helped?"

"He might've calmed down and said, 'Lady, I was only point-ing out to your husband that this old car might break down and block traffic,' and hearing him talk like that, you might've calmed down too, at least long enough to say, 'Officer, I have a Constitu-tional right to drive where I please, but if it's a favor you want, consider it granted.'"

"Where would that've got us?"

"The two of you would've been friends."

"Who wants to be friends with a cop?"

"*I* could've said something," Danny said, "and you would've won the argument, and you would not've had to be friends. He would never've said another word after what I would've said."

"That sounds more like my speed," the hack-driver said. "What would you've said, son?"

"I would've looked right in his eye and said sneering, 'I don't like pleecemen,' and he would've got mad and said sneering, 'What do you mean—you don't like pleecemen? You *got* to like pleece-men!' and then I'd've said sneering, 'I don't like pleecemen be-cause they're a servant of the ruling-class!' That would've won the argument."

"Then you should've said it. What were you ascared of?"

"I was ascared he'd ask me what I meant. Uncle Web told me once, but I forgot."

"The ruling-class is anybody with five bucks in the bank."

"How much do *we* have in the bank?"

"Just about that, give or take a quarter."

"Then why ain't *we* the ruling-class?"

"We don't have any servant."

"What about that pleeceman?" the boy said. "If a highway-robber went in the bank and tried to steal, wouldn't the pleece-man stop him?"

"If he was the guy back there, more likely he'd say, 'Hurry up, but only take the small change.'"

"How would the robber know which money to take?"

"It's right there on the books. In one column, it says, 'Daniel

Johnson—$5.40,' and in the next column, it says, 'Rock D. Johne-feller—$1,000,000.'"

"But supposing the robber said, 'Why should I only steal five bucks off of Daniel Johnson? I could get a million off of Rock D. Johnefeller.'"

"The guy I just argued with would say, 'Take Johnson's money. He's only a poor slob, so what could he do about it?'"

"But supposing the robber said, 'I come in here to fill up this satchel with money, and if I only take Johnson's money, it will not fill up this satchel. It will only fill up if I put in some of Johnefeller's money, so I am going to do it.' What would the pleeceman say then?"

"He'd say, 'Johnefeller's money is dynamite. Put it in that satchel, and it'll blow up in your face. Why not be sensible? If Johnson's money won't fill up that satchel, there's a lot of other poor slobs in here that only have five bucks too. All of 'em put together couldn't squawk as loud as one Johnefeller, so take their money and be sensible.'"

"Would the robber be sensible?" Danny said.

"The only one that ever wasn't is still in jail."

"What happens to a robber that's sensible?"

"He gets to be president of the bank."

"What's the good of that?"

"What's the *good*?" the hack-driver said. "He can take off his mask!"

*　　*　　*

The last box and bundle had been carried upstairs, the last rag of clothing had been accounted for, and the last lost mate of the last shoe had been found. The bed-rails had been joined and the mattresses imposed, the map had been tacked over a tear in the wallpaper, and a thirty-watt bulb had been turned on to take the place of the sunken sun. Through floor and ceiling, new voices had been heard and new odors endured, and finally there came a long and sunday-vacant moment when the Johnsons, all three, had looked about them at surroundings different for the first time in a dozen years, and in that moment each had known in a private yet com-

municatory way, that fewer years remained of life: each in that moment had grown older, because each had become aware of the past.

"We ain't getting anywheres, Polly," the hack-driver said.

Twenty-four blocks down Park Avenue, the *Buffalo Express*
poured from a tunnel in Manhattan rock, the pound of its triple
trucks changing to a cannonade as ballast gave way to elevated rail.
Rolling at a mile a minute, the train passed the Johnson flat in
pulsant thunder that swamped speech and drummed the world—
and then the last car was gone, and with it the sound and the
trembling.

"We ain't getting anywheres!"

PART TWO

LET US HAVE PEACE

ON A LAWN between the Claremont Mansion and Grant's tomb, four boys lay outflung in the summer morning like wounded. A fifth boy, a Negro, stood near the curb, listening, but not speaking, glancing at the others but not demanding, close by but apart: he was with them, but they were not with him.

"...If I was maroomed on a desert," Monroe Squire was saying, "all I'd want to eat is ten million ice-cream combs."

"What flavor?" Harry Keogh said, and raising his head, he trained his muzzle on a dandelion and fired chain-shots of licorice-juice across the intervening grass.

"Pistache," Monroe said, and he came up part way from supine to watch the Fort Lee ferry *Tenafly* come into dock. She reversed engines, and a boom of green milk exploded from her stern. "If that boat was pistache, I'd eat it right down till it sunk."

Gilbert Spence turned to Daniel Johnson. "What's your favorite thing?" he said.

[*Food*] the colored boy said, but only he heard the word.

A low-slung tug, the *Rose MacNamara*, slouched past up-river, lifting a boiling wake like a bustle, and over the churn played a gray and white acrobat, a gull.

"I'm hungry," Danny said.

*   *   *

Perlman's Candy Store was a ten-foot hole in an old taxpayer under the 125th Street Viaduct. Sunlight came through its smeared

81

window in a steep slant of spinning dust and floating lint, and it broke on metal and glass into tinsel stars. Behind the soda-fountain, a man in a black mohair skullcap was preparing four banana-splits, and five pairs of eyes—four from across the sticky marble and one from the doorway—were watching him. Half a banana, cut the long way, lay in each of the four banana-curved dishes, and riding it were three scoops of ice-cream—vanilla, chocolate, and strawberry. Perlman dipped a ladle into a jar and excavated a dripping load of marshmallow, and this he poured over the knobs of ice-cream. Another ladle dredging another jar came up with crushed pineapple to stud the marshmallow, and a third ladleful sprinkled the now mobile muck with walnuts. A final touch was added: a maraschino cherry was rammed into each of the middle mounds.

"Ten cents apiece," Perlman said.

Four dimes went slowly across the counter. Perlman scraped them into his hand, and turning to a cash-register, he pressed a key: the machine flung its tongue out, and the coins vanished. Four spoons sank through ice-cream and struck submerged bananas. Four mouths were stoked. In the doorway, an empty mouth tried to savor an imagined taste, but the taste remained in the mind, and the mouth watered.

"I always eat slow," Monroe said. "That makes it get bigger."

Harry said, "Three scoops is three scoops, and it wouldn't be four even if you took all day."

"If you finish before I finish," Monroe said, "then it stands to reason I got more than you, because I got some left, and you ain't."

"How can you have more than you have?" Gilbert said. "That's dumb."

"Whatever I had left over at the end would be extra."

"If we get done faster," Harry said, "it won't be account of we got less, but account of you slowed down to crow over us."

"He better not crow," Gilbert said, "or we'll take what he's got left and pour it down his pants."

"If he crows one single crow," Harry said, "it'll be the last crow he ever crows."

"What's your policy, Danny?" Gilbert said. "Do you eat fast, or do you make squish-squash like Monny?"

"I eat without a policy," Danny said.

"You got to have a policy!" Gilbert said.

[*The colored boy was eating your ice-cream with his eyes, and in a minute your plate would be empty. You knew how to fill it again, though. All you had to do was take that other dime out of your pocket and plank it down on the counter, saying, "A banana-split for Drag-ass Baxter." But you knew something else—that three guys would turn and gawk at you with their pusses full of gunk, and finally one of them'd say, "Why, Mr. Jesus Johnson!"*]

"I say you got to have a policy!" Gilbert said.

"I don't got to have nothing!" Danny said. "I can eat fast, and I can eat slow, and if I want, I don't have to eat at all! And that's what I feel like right now—not eating! If anybody here wants to try and make me, stand up and say so!"

He climbed down from his stool and walked toward the door, followed briefly by a triple stare that ended on the now ownerless sundae. "No akey!" Monroe said, reaching for the dish.

Harry caught his arm. "We divvy," he said.

"Sure, we divvy," Gilbert said. "Half for little ole Harry and half for little ole Gil."

"What about me?" Monroe said.

"You had more than we did to start with," Harry said. "You told us so yourself."

Danny waited at the corner for the colored boy to overtake him. "Here," he said, taking his hand from his pocket. In his palm lay a crumb-dusted maraschino cherry.

THE UNION FOREVER! HURRAH, BOYS, HURRAH!

ON the morrow, Graduation Exercises would be held in the auditorium of Public School 604, and parents in pairs would fill the hall, each pair to fix on the fuzz of one special head, on the nap of one special face, on the blue serge suit holding one special thirteen-year-old life—but one such pair would be proud beyond the pride of all the rest, for one special mouth, made by them during some long-gone and almost forgotten night, would speak to their still unsubdued expectations. It would give voice to Part VIII of the program:

WHAT I WANT TO BE WHEN I GROW UP
A paper to be read by a member of the graduating-class of May, 1922.

The identity of this member was not yet known. Three of the seven eligible papers remained to be heard by the judges—the eighth-term English class in which the competition had been held, and its teacher, Miss Anita Campbell. Soon now, by volume of applause, the award would be made.

"Seymour Wolf," Miss Campbell said.

The boy rose and went toward the front of the room. He avoided a foot put out to trip him, turned his head to blurt derision, and tripped over another foot further down the aisle. He faced the class, saying, "My composition is called, 'What I Will Want To Be When I Will Grown Up.'"

"A sheeny," someone said.

Miss Campbell's pencil was a long yellow finger indicating Darcy Burke. "Up!" she said, and Darcy was up. "And out!" she said, and Darcy was out.

Seymour said, "I will now read."

When I heard about this contest, I said that is a contest I will go in and write on paper. So I went to Mt. Morris Park and I climb up to the top of the mount where the osbervation-tower is, and I sat down and thought out what I will write in the paper. I thought and thought in the sunshine on the grass, and at last I made up my mind. I will write that I will want to be a soldier. . . .

"A Yiddische soldier," someone said.

Once more, Miss Campbell's pencil picked off a victim, this time a boy who had been left back, one Leonard Griffin, and as he reached the door, she said, "I'll see you next term, Leonard."

"Not me, you wouldn't," Leonard said.

"You'll never get a diploma, then."

"I don't want any diploma. I'm going to get working-papers."

"If you ever learn which way is up, you'll make a fine elevator-operator. Good luck, Leonard."

Seymour said, "I will now read again."

My hero will be a genral that had the same name as me, Wolf, only he spelt it with an *e* on the end, Wolfe. This Wolfe with an *e* on the end, he was a soldier of the English when he was only fifteen years of old, and he wanted to get permoted, so he was very industerious, trying hard all the time. . . .

"Seymour," Miss Campbell said, and then she paused, and into the void she dropped a manufactured cough. "Is your paper very long?"

"Oh, no," Seymour said. "Only eight more pages."

"Are they just as good?" she said, and *good* was given very gently.

"They're even better," the boy said.

"Come here," she said, and when he came, she put her hand on his arm. Their eyes touched too, but only for the communicating instant when his said [*Please*] and hers said [*No*]. The boy went up the aisle to his desk.

Miss Campbell's pencil moved to the next name on her list, the last but one. "Daniel Johnson," she said.

He took his place before the class, saying, "My paper is in comversation."

"Ah, you've written it in play-form."

"No, in comversation."

"That's how plays are written—in dialogue."

"Mine isn't dialogue. It's comversation."

"Is there any difference?"

"Yes, ma'am, but I don't know what it is. Well, I guess I will begin."

In this comversation, I am suppose to be two different people, and I am arguing with myself which thing I will be when I grow up—a train-dispatcher or president. The one that has the best argument will win, and I will be the thing in that argument.

I said, "I think I will go out for being president."

I replied, "No, I think I will go out for being train-dispatcher."

I quizzed, "What is so wonderfully about that?"

I answered, "I will get to see all the trains."

I stated, "If I'm president, I can *ride* on them."

I said, "But I will tell them where to go. I will have all kinds of switches marked Bufflo, Rockchester, and Georgia, and when a train comes along, I will make it go on the Lehigh & Valley Railroad."

I retorted, "I suppose that's fun—pushing switches all day."

I sneered, "Better fun than laying in the White House."

I explained, "I will be running the United States, and you will only be running trains."

I scoffed, "Nobody runs the United States. They run by themself."

I asked, "What would happen if I make up my mind I wouldn't pass any laws, and all I'm going to do is shoot marbels?"

I snapped, "Nothing. That's what we got a vice-president for."

I cried, "But supposing he felt like shooting marbels too? What's empossible about that?"

I thundered, "The thing that's empossible is for a train dispatcher to sneak out. There would be a wreck on the train."

I jeered, "But supposing you *can't* stay in. Supposing you absolutely *have* to go out."

I repeated, "If I am a train-dispatcher, and I absolutely have to go out, then I absolutely have to stay in. . . ."

He broke off when he saw Miss Campbell glance at a watch pinned face-down over her heart.

"How does it turn out?" she said.

"I comvince myself," the boy said.

"Of what?"

"That I ought to try for president."

"Well, son, you have a noble ambition."

"Oh, that isn't my ambition. My ambition is to be a train-dispatcher."

"I thought you said you convinced yourself otherwise."

"I did, but it wasn't my ambition."

"Only a few minutes are left, Danny," the teacher said, "and there's one more paper to be heard."

"I'm sorry if my paper is rotten. My pop read it, and that's what he said."

"I don't think it was rotten. Very few things ever are." Danny sat down, and his place was taken by a Negro boy named Julian Pollard, "Read, Julian."

Julian said, "My paper starts off like this."

Honored mother, teachers, friends, and my father that got killed in France. . . .

"Stealing a chicken," someone said.

"Up!" Miss Campbell said, pointing her pencil at Harry Keogh. "Read the motto of your class and get out."

Under an enlarged photograph of Abraham Lincoln hung a framed sampler, reading: ALL MEN ARE CREATED EQUAL.

"'All men are created equal,'" Harry said.

"Now, out!"

Harry gathered his school-supplies—a pen, a penwiper, a bottle of ink, and a gnawed ruler—and left the room.

Julian said, "I'll start all over."

Honored mother, teachers, friends, and my father that got killed in France, I am going to write down in this paper the thing I would most want to be when I grow up: I would want to be a lawyer. When you are a lawyer, you can go in the court and argue for justice. There is a lot of people that want justice, and when you are a lawyer, you can help the people get it. Poor people want justice all the time, but they have not got the money to pay for it, and somebody else gets the justice. So when I was a lawyer, I would try to get the poor people justice free of charge.

I do not think I could be a more honorable thing than a lawyer if I was a honest lawyer, and that is what I would always try very hard, to be honest. It is not easy. Some people think it is, but that is because they are not poor. They have all kinds of things that they want, and so they do not have to be unhonest to get them, although they sometimes are. But if you are poor, then you are like to get in trouble. I feel sorry for the poor people that live in poverish without justice, so that is why I want to be a lawyer when I grow up. . . .

The bell rang, and the school-year was over.

"That was a fine paper, Julian," Miss Campbell said. "A very fine paper."

The door opened, and Dr. Page, the Principal, entered the room. With him, through the widening and then narrowing crack, came the sound of hoarded shouts released: *No more pencils, no more books, no more teachers' sassy looks!*

"Have you chosen a boy for Part VIII, Miss Campbell?" the Principal said.

"We've just heard the last paper, Doctor."

"I didn't get to finish it," Julian said.

"Oh, I'm sorry, Julian," the teacher said. "Do you mind waiting, Doctor?"

"Not at all," the Principal said. "Proceed."

Julian said, "This is the rest of my paper."

That is what I *want* to be, but it is not what I am *going* to be. I am going to be something else, and I know it, so I think I should write that down too. I am going to rack up balls in a pool-parlor, and I am going to shine shoes under a elevator-station on Eighth Avenue, and I am going to be a janitor, and a waiter, and a Red Cap, and a Pullman porter. I am not going to be a lawyer helping poor people get justice in the court. I am going to be a poor people myself. I am black, so I am going to be a dishwasher, and a window-cleaner, and a price-fighter, and a garbage-collector.

That is what I am going to be, but I am not going to like it. I am not going to laugh about wanting to be something with honor and only get told, "A lawyer, boy? What's a matter with your head? Don't you know your place, boy?" I am not going to say, "Yessuh," and grin like Aunt Jemima. I am going to be mad. I am going to get in trouble. There is a sign in our classroom that says all men are created equal. It don't say anything about only being equal if you are white, so I am going to try and be equal, and they are not going to let me be equal, and I am going to get in trouble about that, and I know it. That is all I have to write in this paper.

The boy stood where he was for a moment, rolling the composition into a scroll, but it was a club that he held when he walked to his seat and sat down. Dr. Page unbuttoned his Prince Albert as if he were about to take it off, but the motions were automatic, and he buttoned it again, still automatically, as if he had just put it on. Miss Campbell did nothing but follow the Negro boy with her eyes.

And then she spoke, saying, "I shall now call the names of the seven contestants, and the one receiving the most applause will represent you tomorrow at the Exercises. Esteban Lopez [*scattered support*], Duane Madison [*strong backing in his own precinct*], Samuel Shapiro [*the solid candidate of at least a quarter of the class, among them a boy named Edward Friedman, who said, "Yay for Sammy!"*], Herbert Ortman [*the choice of the cultured and the thoughtful; support weak to light*], Seymour Wolf [*one vote, his own*], Daniel Johnson [*silence*], and Julian Pollard [*continued silence*]."

Miss Campbell rose now, and again she said, "Julian Pollard," and still there was no response. Burying her pencil in a billow of palmer-method hair, she began to clap her hands, bringing them together time after time, until her cheeks trembled and her breasts swung, until the pencil worked free from her shaken hair, until the class, little by little and then all, caught her passion—and then there were no hands in the room that were not naming Julian Pollard the winner of the competition, none but those owned by Julian himself and Dr. Page.

The Principal stilled the class with a gesture. "Tomorrow's program is overlong, Miss Campbell," he said. "I think, therefore, that we shall go directly from Part VII, the presentation of diplomas, to Part IX, the singing of the National Anthem, and so conclude the Exercises. I wish you all a pleasant vacation." He went to the door, and through the widening and then narrowing crack, no sound entered now but the walking-away retch of a pair of shoes.

Miss Campbell made her way slowly up the aisle to Julian Pollard's desk. The boy sat still, looking down at his composition— no club now, but once more merely a tube of paper—and he did not move until the teacher touched the persian-lamb of his head. He came to his feet then, and the contact broke.

"Julian," Miss Campbell said. "I've lived in this room for fifteen years, longer than you've been on earth. I don't sleep here, and I don't eat here, but this is my home, and this is where I like my friends to come and see me. I've had many visitors, many friends, in these fifteen years, but this is the first time that anyone, friend or otherwise, has come into my house and spit on the floor. Worse than that," and she glanced at the picture of Lincoln, "far worse, the greatest man who ever lived has been spat upon too. I want to apologize for Dr. Page, Julian. I want to apologize because my house is so dirty today."

The boy's face was upraised now.

"If you'll let me," the teacher said, "I'd like to kiss you."

THE BLACK & WHITE POLISHING COMPANY

"Pop," Danny said, "I made up my mind about what I want for graduation."

"Name it, and maybe you'll get part of it."

"I want two dollars and thirty cents."

"What for—to study up to be a train-dispatcher?"

"When're you going to stop picking on him for that composition?" the woman said. "You promised him a present. Either make good or back out."

"I'm no welsher," the hack-driver said. "What do you want the two bucks for, son?"

"Two-thirty," the boy said. "I'm thinking of starting up a shoe-shine parlor."

"What kind of a shoe-shine parlor could you get for two dollars and something?"

"The open-air kind."

"Open-air! You mean, where you get down on your knees in the street?"

"I wouldn't have to kneel on the sidewalk. There's a leather cushion goes with the outfit."

"And I suppose there's a sign too, saying, 'I don't have to do this for a living. I like it.'"

"No, the sign only says, 'Shoe-shine—10c.' That goes with the outfit too."

"So far, the outfit is a sign and a cushion."

"You get a shoe-box and a foot-rest and a sign and a cushion, and you get two bottles of Kwik-Kleen Shu-Kreem and two cans of Kwik-Kleen Waxola, and you get four brushes and five flannel rags. That's the outfit, and Hank Johns says it's as good as new."

"Who the hell is Hank Johns?"

"He owns the outfit."

"I take it he's retiring to live off his profits."

"He has no profits. He's busted."

"That's a fine business you're buying."

"I'm not buying the business, only the outfit."

"He must be some shoe-shiner, this Hank Johns."

"He's a crack, but he lets too many guys practice on his outfit."

"One of them good-natured slobs, eh? No wonder his prat is out."

"He lets me practice every afternoon."

"What does he do—go to the races?"

"No, he just waits for me to get done practicing."

"The next question scares the life out of me. What happens when you get done practicing?"

"I fork over the money I took in."

"Why? You earned it, didn't you?"

"I know, but I was only practicing."

"Son," the hack-driver said, "you ain't quite ready to go in business yet."

"Why not?" the woman said.

"He'll get gypped blind, bald-headed, and naked—and besides, he ain't going down on his knees like a nigger for every son-of-a-bitch with a dime."

"Negro," the woman said.

"Negro, nigger—what's the diff?"

"Negro!" the woman said.

"All right, Negro," the hack-driver said, "but it's still a colored business."

"There's no law saying whites can't shine shoes."

"You don't see 'em doing it, though."

"Do you know why?" the woman said.

"Sure, I know why. Because they're no good at it."

"But why are they no good at it?"

"Because the colored people are better at it, that's why."

"Why are they better at it?"

"Because they do it more."

"Ah!" the woman said. "And why do they do it more?"

"What do you mean—*ah?*" the hack-driver said. "They do it more because they're better at it."

"Dan," the woman said, "would you mind if I called you a dunce?"

"Not at all. I'd like it."

"Well, you're a dunce!" she said.

The boy thought ["*I am going to try and be equal, but they are not going to let me be equal, and I am going to get in trouble about that.*"], and then he said, "The colored people do it more because they have to," and as he stared at the place in the air where his words seemed to be hanging, he felt his mother's fingers lightly brush his face.

She put her voice out with care, as if it were fragile. "Why do they have to?" she said.

He thought ["*I am black, so I am going to be a dishwasher, and a window-cleaner, and a price-fighter.*"], and he said, "Because people won't let them be anything better."

"What people?" the woman said.

"The white people."

The woman glanced at her husband, but joy changed to pity when she read the words written in his eyes [*My own kid knew, and I didn't.*], and turning again to Danny, she said, "Get me the bank." When the boy handed her a miniature cupboard of inlaid wood— sent from Ecuador by Uncle Web—she sprang a secret panel in the base and dumped a pile of coins on the table. Making a stack of nine quarters topped by a nickel, she set it before her son and said, "You're in business."

"Wait a minute," the hack-driver said. "He ain't proved he can handle that kind of money."

"Test him," the woman said.

"Damn if I don't," the hack-driver said. "Danny, if you gave a guy a ten-cent shine, and he handed you a dollar-bill, how much would he have left?"

The boy said, "Eighty-five cents."

The hack-driver sought clemency for his idiot son from an imaginary guest occupying the fourth chair at the table. He said, "What can you expect, Mr. Nobody? He's the only child of a dunce and a dame named after a cigar."

The woman said, "Danny, ten from a hundred leaves what?"

"Ninety," the boy said.

"Then why did you just tell us the man would have eighty-five?"
"I figured him for a five-cent tip."

Now the woman turned to the imaginary guest. "Mr. Nobody," she said, "my old man got stung."

"Hold your horses," the hack-driver said. "The kid ain't passed the whole test yet. Danny, supposing you gave the guy a ten-cent shine, and he handed you a twenny-dollar-bill. How much would he have left?"

"Nineteen dollars and eighty-five cents."

"Wrong! He wouldn't have *nothing* left!"

"Why wouldn't he?" the boy said.

"Because you'd stick the bill in your pocket and run like hell on fire!" The hack-driver reached out and shook hands with Mr. Nobody. "Who's stung now?"

The woman glared at him until his glee toppled, and he lay about himself in ruins, and then, abandoning the wreck, she said to her son, "He didn't mean that. He was only talking for the benefit of Mr. Nobody."

* * *

For some hours now, Danny's shoe-shine outfit, neatly arranged alongside one of the downtown kiosks of the 125th Street subway-station, had been ready for the transaction of business, but as yet no one had placed a foot on the box and requested the proprietor to kneel on the cushion for a dime's worth of labor. In contrast, a colored boy with a rival enterprise only a yard distant had served a succession of patrons, both white and black, throughout the morning, and Danny had noted his trade with envy and his skill, particularly his closing flourish—the playing of *Yankee Doodle* on the finish-rag—with admiration.

[*You wished that Gil and Harry and Monroe would go some place else, instead of parading up and down in front of you and getting off killing remarks. They weren't helping you any.*

[*"Say, guys," Monroe said, "I'm thinking of getting a shine. Know any good bootblacks?"*

[*Gil said, "I heard of one down Lenox a ways that can make your shoes say, 'Hot dog, man!'"*

["*I got a job off of him the other day,*" Harry said, "*and I'm here to tell you he's the bootblackingest bootblack that ever bootblacked.*"

["*You got to watch some of these beginners,*" Monroe said. "*They could roon a pair of wing-tips in one shine.*"

["*Some of 'em couldn't shine an apple with spit,*" Harry said.

["*I know one that couldn't even shine a thing that was shiny,*" Gil said.

[Monroe said, "*Nobody can touch my shoes unless he can play* My Country Tears Of Thee."

["*Danny couldn't even play that on a victrola,*" Harry said.]

"Your name Danny?" the colored boy said.

Danny smiled.

*   *   *

They were friends at the end of the first day, partners at the end of the first week, and still friends at the end of the first month. They called themselves *The Black & White Polishing Company—Tudor (Tootsie) Powell and Daniel Johnson, owners,* and they divided the profits as follows: two-thirds to the senior member of the firm and one-third to the junior. This had been a fair arrangement at the outset, and it was still fair now at midsummer, even though Danny had begun to snap out an occasional bar of music with his shoe-rags: he knew little that Tootsie had not taught him, and he could do nothing that Tootsie could not do better.

"Getcha shine!" Danny was saying. 19 99 .318

Nearby, Tootsie was crouched over a pair of oxfords, and with the job nearly over and payment in sight, his hand was sweeping a brush in a yard-long arc. Now he tapped a few drops of water on a toe-cap, and flirting the dust from a rag, he began to ride it up into the realm of song.

"Getcha shine!" Danny was saying.

A man in riding-breeches set a boot on Danny's box and said, "Touch 'em up."

Danny surveyed the expanse of muddied leather and said, "A riding-boot is a quarter."

"A quarter!" the man said. "Your sign says a dime!"

"*Yankee Doodle went uptown, riding on a pony.*"

"A riding-boot and a shoe is two different things," Danny said. "*Stuck a feather in his hat and called it macaroni.*"

"I'll shop around," the man said, and stepping down from Danny's box, he moved on to Tootsie's, now free.

Tootsie made a frowning inspection of the boots, squinted at the sky, where his eyes added an invisible column of figures, and brought the total down to earth. "Fifty cents," he said.

"What!" the man said. "That boy over there'll do the job for a quarter!"

"No, he won't," Tootsie said.

"I'll show you," the man said, and he returned to Danny's box.

"Fifty cents," Danny said.

"Damn it, you said a quarter before!"

"A quarter a boot."

"We're partners," Tootsie said.

*   *   *

"*And called it macaroni.*"

Snap! And Tootsie had finished his last shine of a late-August day. "Ten cents," he said to his customer.

"Ten cents *what*," the man said.

"Ten cents for the shine," Tootsie said.

"Ten cents for the shine *what*," the man said.

"Just ten cents for the shine."

"Now you don't get a cent, you fresh little nigger bastard!"

Tootsie rose. "You don't have any right to talk like that," he said. "I gave you a shine, and I only asked you to pay for it."

"To pay for it *what*," the man said.

"He don't have to say 'Please' to you," Danny said.

The man strode over to Danny and looked down at him, saying, "You want to get into this?"

"I *am* in it. He's my partner."

"Get him to say 'Please,' or you're out a dime."

"I wouldn't get him to do that if you owed us seventeen dollars!"

"Then say it yourself, nigger-lover!"

"Nobody has to say 'Please!'" Danny said.

The man sowed a backhander along Danny's jawbone, and, driven against the wall of the kiosk, the boy struck his head on the heavy glass. As he sagged to the sidewalk, the man went away.

[*Tootsie was going away too. Everything was going away. It was all tipping and sliding away downhill. But now it was tipping back. And now it was all straight again. And it stayed straight.*]

Tootsie was on his knees, holding him up with an arm under his shoulders. "You all right, Danny-boy?" he was saying.

"Nobody has to say 'Please' to nobody," Danny said, and he wiped away a teardrop of blood wept by his mouth.

* * *

In the Johnson parlor, *The Black & White Polishing Company* sat full and staring before an empty milk-bottle, two empty glasses, two fudged-up plates, and the remaining third of a layer-cake. Chocolate dyed the corners of a white mouth, and there was chocolate on a chocolate cheek.

"More cake, partners?" Mrs. Johnson said.

The boys looked at each other and grinned. Their teeth were tiles in chocolate stucco.

"I'll give you a slice to take home, Tootsie," the woman said.

"Next year, the party'll be at my house," the colored boy said.

* * *

After supper that evening, the woman brought her old ledger to the table, and turning to a section reserved for her son, she added and verified a long list of entries. Then, reaching down alongside her chair, she lifted a bulging flour-sack from a basket and poured pounds of coins over an outspread newspaper, and these she began to sort and stack while her son watched her above a chin-rest of crossed arms. From time to time, he glanced at his father, but the man sat sideways to the circle of the table, and gazing at the map, he was tangent to all that the circle contained.

"Write what I tell you, son," the woman said, "and we'll see what we have." The boy took up a pencil and drew a dollar-sign in the blank space of an ad. "Ten stacks of twenty quarters: write fifty dollars. One stack of thirty halves: write fifteen dollars. Nine stacks of twenty-five dimes: that's twenty-two and a half. Two stacks of twenty nickels: two dollars. One stack of fifty pennies: fifty cents. And seventy cents in loose change. What do you get?"

The boy added. "Ninety dollars and seventy cents," he said.

The woman turned the ledger to him and put her finger on a sum. "Ninety dollars and seventy cents," she said.

"I didn't know I made that much. That was a pretty good business."

"And to think it all started with a graduation-present."

"That didn't start it; *I* started it. The present didn't make the money; *I* made the money."

"But without the present, you couldn't've bought the outfit."

"I know," the boy said, "but without me, the outfit would still only be an outfit. *It* didn't get down and shine the shoes; *I* shone the shoes."

"What would you've shined them with if you had no outfit?"

"I guess I wouldn't've done any shining."

"And if you did no shining," the woman said, "you'd have no ninety dollars and seventy cents."

"That's what I been saying! If I didn't do any shining, there would still be only the graduation-present here on the table—two dollars and thirty cents. It was the shining turned that into ninety dollars and seventy cents. It was the shining turned a mishrable little two dollars and thirty cents into something that's eighty-eight dollars and forty cents bigger—and I done the shining!"

"I'm not trying to take away from your work," the woman said. "You did better than anyone would've expected. But somebody made the work possible, and the profits as well. That somebody was your father: he put you in business."

[*Did that mean he owned the whole business, or only the amount of the graduation-present? Did you owe him the ninety bucks, or the difference between the two bucks and the ninety, or only the two bucks—or nothing?*]

"Where did he get the money to put me in business?"

"He earned it," the woman said. "He worked for it with *his* outfit—the cab."

"Where did he get the money for his outfit?"

"He borrowed it from the bank."

"How much did he pay back?"

"What he borrowed, plus interest."

"Did he pay the bank all he made with the outfit?"

"No, only what he'd borrowed."

Danny counted out nine quarters and a nickel, added a few pennies for interest, and put the coins aside. "I will do the same thing as Pop done with the bank," he said.

His mother came to her feet, and saying nothing, she held the maw of the sack against the table-edge and raked the stacks into it one by one. She left for last the little pile that Danny had sequestered, and when this too had vanished, she knotted the sack and let it fall clanking in front of the boy. Then, holding her hands in quarantine, as if contaminated, she walked out of the room.

"She's mad at me," Danny said to his father. "What did I do?"

The hack-driver tapped a clot of ash from his pipe-bowl. "You and Mom was talking about some money I borrowed to buy the Pope-H," he said. "You know when that was? Nineteen-o-eight. That makes it a year older than you, kid."

"A year older than a kid is still a kid."

"For a car, it's a goat—and it runs like one. Falls all over its beard."

"Can't you fix it?"

"You can't fix a thing that's old except by making it young, which even God ain't done yet. You can give it a coat of paint and a new set of shoes, but inside it'll still be the same wheezy works that ran a half a million miles."

"I guess you'll have to buy a new outfit."

"I been thinking the very identical thing. I got my eye on a Pierce-Arrow."

"That's the kind with lamps on the mudguards."

"It's a 1920 model, but it's as good as new, because it's broke in. A Pierce-Arrow, you don't break it in till you've drove it a couple of years."

"A Locomobile is got the best hubcaps."

"I told the man I'd take her for a whirl some time, and he said, 'You better hurry. I expect to move this job in a week.' I said, 'What's the best you'll give me on the Pope-H?' and he said, 'Four hundred bucks—and grab it before they drag me back to the asylum.'"

"A Stutz goes the speediest."

"I said, 'Four hundred from a price of seven hundred is three hundred, and I only got two hundred. Where in hell am I going to raise that extra century?' He said, 'Try the bank,' and I said, 'I ain't loaning no money off no bank,' and he said, 'Mister, if you need this Pierce-A as bad as you say, you'll get the dough some place, even if it's your father-in-law.'"

The hack-driver rose suddenly, and shaking his head, he went into the bedroom and closed the door behind him. The boy sat where he was for a moment, idly poking at the lumpy sack of coins. He heard his mother's voice through the transom, but the words were blurred and lost. His father's, in reply, were not. "I couldn't do it!" the man said. "So help me God, I couldn't do it!" The boy thought [*It was like you were a tight suit of clothes around yourself. It was like your skin was a crowd.*].

He went to the bedroom door and knocked.

"Come in," his mother said.

The hack-driver was seated on the bed, facing away. "What is it, kid?" the man said.

Danny offered him the sack.

[*All of a sudden, your clothes weren't tight any more.*]

WHAT'S YOUR NAME IN AMERICAN?

DANNY's first lecture at De Witt Clinton High School had not yet begun, but the class had gathered, and filling every seat in the room and all the sitting-space afforded by the lockers along the walls, it awaited the ringing of the bell and the resurrection of the instructor, Dr. Jesse Knox. It was one minute before nine, and Doc Knox, three hundred pounds of pneumatic flesh, slumbered at his desk.

The bell rang.

The instructor came to life, but it was a life that he seemed to live chiefly in his mouth, a valve-like hole in a mass of distended fat; the rest of his body, a gasbag dressed in blue serge, remained dead. "The first of you sprats to draw a picture of a fat man," he said, "the first one even to use the word 'fat,' in my presence—I promise to throw him out in the hall without bothering to open the door. I don't like people to make fun of me. I'll go further: I don't like people. I've given this course twice a year for twelve years, and I always start with the same warning, but every term some fool from Missouri puts me to the test. I don't like people to make fun of me!"

"Fat slob," someone said.

An expanding expanse like smoke rolled up one of the aisles and then rolled back, dragging a suit that contained a boy. Only because the boy managed to open the door for himself did he make his exit without breaking wood, and then Doc Knox resumed his seat, and his body was dead again.

"The subject of this course is Political Science," he said, "and the worst way to learn it is to believe the trash in your textbooks. The *real* meaning of the Bill of Rights you'll have to absorb from me, and the *real* effect of the Constitution, and the *real* difference between Jefferson and Hamilton—from *me*, not from the books. Listen to *me*, and you'll know the truth. If you're ready, we'll start." His eyes made steppingstones of the upturned faces. "You, there," he said to Danny. "What's your name in American . . . ?"

A MAN'S AMBITION MUST BE SMALL

AT A TABLE in the Clinton lunchroom overlooking the Hudson, Danny sat before two sandwiches, an apple, a pint-bottle of milk, and a chocolate bar. The boy bit a chunk from one of the sandwiches, and sucking a rod of milk up a straw, he stared through a window at warehouses, docks, water, sky, and the United States. Clouds sailed west below clouds standing still, and with them, under sealed orders, sailed a cargo of rain. The boy watched them for

a moment, wondering where the rain would fall, and for no reason
that he knew, the name *Juniata* accosted his mind. He bit another
half-moon from the sandwich, drowned it in another draw of milk,
and turned absently to a scribbled-on section of plaster wall. Tangled trails of graphite became words.

"Poor Alice she gave away two hundred dolars worth before she found out she could sell it."

"What're you doing?" a voice said.
Alongside Danny stood an older boy, his jacket unbuttoned to
display, pinned to a point of his vest, the black-and-red enamel of
a Dotey Squad badge.
"I'm reading what it says on the wall," Danny said.
"Stand up when you're talking to the Squad," the monitor said.
The neighborhood became an island of quiet: a dozen boys had
stopped eating, stopped talking, and stopped moving.
"I'm not standing up just because you tell me to," Danny said.
"If you want to talk to me, you can sit down, but I'm eating, and
you have no right to inarup me."
"Point out what you were reading."
Danny gestured with his scalloped slabs of bread. "That thing
there," he said.
"'Poor Alice,'" the monitor read, "'she gave away two hun-
dred. . . .' That's smutty."
"What's that mean—smutty?"
"If you read the posters on the bulletin-boards, you'd know
there was an Anti-Smut Campaign going on. A smutty thing is a
dirty thing. It's smutty."
"Instead of getting up all those posters," Danny said, "they
ought to wash the walls."
"You admit, then, that what you read was smutty."
"Sure, but I had to read it first to find out."
"You should've known it was smutty *before* you read it. It was
written on a wall, and anything on a wall is smutty."
"How about the things written on the bulletin-board?" Danny
said. "That's on a wall."

"You're a wise guy," the monitor said.

"I was born in Wiseville."

"Well, wise guy, I'm running you in!"

"You don't say. When're you going to do that?"

"Right now, and I don't want any more argument!"

"You can't run me in right now," Danny said.

"I can't!" the monitor said. "Why can't I?"

"Because I didn't finish my lunch."

From nearby tables, a laugh went aloft. The monitor whirled, but the laughter was dead and gone, and mouths innocent and guilty were chewing again—some on food and some (the guilty) on air.

"That's tough—you didn't finish your lunch!" the monitor said. "Come on down the Squad Room!"

"I'm finishing my lunch!" Danny said.

"You're *not* finishing your lunch!"

"Oh, no?" Danny said. "What's this, then?" He snatched up his second sandwich and the bottle of milk, and he bit and sucked, bit and sucked, until his face bulged and sprang a leak.

"Say, you're finishing your lunch!" the monitor said.

Danny gulped, and the mouthful started on its way, and then he gulped again, kicking the food when it was down, and it stayed down. "That's what I told you," he said, and he continued eating.

He ate the last discoverable crumb, and he drank from the straw until the bottle was empty of milk and full of derision. He folded his sandwich-wrappers down to the smallest possible square, and, ambling, deposited them in a distant trash-basket. He made a second trip with the milk-bottle and a third with the straw. Then he re-strapped his books, tightened his tie, and, while he peeled the tin-foil from the chocolate bar, looked about for forgotten nothings.

He faced the monitor now, saying, "What're we waiting for?" and he nipped off a piece of candy.

*   *   *

Tried, convicted, and denied an appeal, Danny had been sentenced to ten hours in the Squad Room, to be served in equal daily instalments immediately after dismissal from school. This was the fifth and final day of his confinement, and he was listening for the bell that would make him once more a free man.

In the corridor, a clock wound up and pitched five strikes, and the fifth touched off the gong. The door opened at once, and the Squad Master, Aaron Dotey, entered the room. "Johnson," he said, "your time is up." The boy rose. " I haven't dismissed you yet." The boy sat down. " Your time is up, and your offense has been paid for. But the Dotey Squad is never interested in punishment as such; it is concerned with reform. No boy ever leaves here without being asked the question that I ask you now: 'What have you learned from your experience?'"

[*You weren't hurting anybody. You were just sitting there and eating your lunch, and then accidently you went and read that Alice thing on the wall, but nobody would listen to you when you tried to explain, and you got punished just like you were the one that wrote it. What could you learn from that?*]

" I'm waiting," the Squad Master said.

[*Talk about justice. Where was the justice in convicting you for starting to read something and not knowing how it was going to turn out? Justice! If that was the kind of justice people got in the court, no wonder they needed lawyers like Julie Pollard.*]

"Johnson," the Squad Master said, "I asked you what you've learned from your experience!"

" I learned a lot," Danny said.

"That's fine. That's just what we like to hear."

"Only you didn't teach it to me."

SOME DAY YOU'LL TEACH HIM

RAIN fell lightly, as if sprayed, and it fell fine, filling the crevices of clothes and smearing, when palmed, into a pellicle of water. Mounds of shopworn snow melted under the persistent fall, and the curbs along the gutters were awash. With his hands buried in his pockets and his books held in a headlock, Danny walked east on 59th Street, stooping slightly before the westbound wind. He passed the College of Physicians and Surgeons and the Roosevelt Hospital, and reaching Ninth Avenue, where the trolley-cracks were creeks, he paused to hunt for a ford. A truck went by with a bone in its teeth, and the boy was splashed with slush from his knees down. A woman standing near him was splashed too, and Danny tipped his cap when he saw that she was Miss Forrest, his section-officer at De Witt Clinton. [*Miss Juno Forrest!*]

"Hello, Johnson," she said.

"Hello, Miss Forrest."

"Do you live in this part of town?"

"No, ma'am. I'm going over to Madison Avenue and take the uptown car."

"You'll be soaked by the time you get home."

"I never get wet in this mackinaw. Except my pants."

"Here's a chance to cross," the teacher said.

"Could I help you?" Danny said. "You might slip and fall down."

The woman smiled. "May I take your arm?"

[*Miss Juno Forrest!*]

Guiding her from high point to high point over the uneven cobblestones, Danny was twice forced to wade deep in the gray water-ice underfoot.

"Thank you," the teacher said when they reached the sidewalk. "You ought to be wearing rubbers."

"I oil my shoes every winter," Danny said. "Could I carry your books?"

"You have your own."

"I could easily carry yours too."

"Thanks, but I'll manage."

"Do you live near here, Miss Forrest?"

"I have a flat on 58th Street."

"We live in a flat too."

"Everybody lives in a flat."

"Only some people call it an apartment. My father says it's an apartment if the house has an elevator, and it's a flat if it's a walk-up. Ours is a flat."

"What does your father do, Daniel?"

"He drives a cab."

"Are you going to follow in his footsteps?"

"I can't," the boy said, and he laughed. "He never walks."

They rounded Columbus Circle and continued east along Central Park South. There were still a few sooty dabs of snow on the park lawns, and over the soft ground grackle rocked like little hobbyhorses, while sparrows feinted at sparrows among the leafless trees. Winter had gone, and rain was spring-cleaning the earth.

"How old are you?" the teacher said.

"Going on fifteen," Danny said, and he gave her a brief glance.

"Say it," she said.

"How old are you?"

"Going on thirty-five."

"How many children have you and Mr. Forrest got?"

"None—and I haven't got a Mr. Forrest."

"Oh," Danny said.

"Why do you say, 'Oh'?"

"I don't know. I just said it."

"I'm what you call an old maid."

"I don't call you that," Danny said. [*Miss Forrest, you called her, Miss Juno Forrest!*]

"People don't call an old maid an old maid. They think it."

"I don't even think it." [*You thought of a forest with one 'r,' and you thought of the sound of it, and you thought how the sound was like the word: the sound a forest made was forest, forest.*]

At the Seventh Avenue corner, the teacher said, "I live down the street. Would you like to visit with me and have a cup of tea?"

"Yes," Danny said.

The doors of the house were plate-glass set in iron frames, and from the dim day the teacher and the boy entered a dimmer hall. The elevator-operator wore braid and letter-carrier gray.

In the car, Danny removed his cap. "I thought you lived in a flat," he said.

"That's what it is," the woman said. "Wait and see."

*　　*　　*

A few tea-leaves, tea-logged and cold, lay stranded on sugar sand. The boy, his elbow on the window-sill, sat looking out at the dwindle of Central Park, an oblong spinning out to nothing in the creeping barrage of dark. The teacher was in profile to the last light, her face half silver and half blue.

"...I don't know why I tell you all this," she was saying. "Maybe it's because I want you to know that teachers are human beings too. You see us for six hours a day, but there are eighteen more to the twenty-four, and we don't stop breathing when you're dismissed. You leave school and go home, and after a certain number of hours, you return—and there's your teacher, your old-maid teacher, sitting just where she was when you left her, and she looks the same, and she's dressed the same (a different shirtwaist, a different brooch, but no matter), and it's as if she hadn't moved, hadn't lived, since the day before. But she *had* moved, and she *had* lived! When the door closed on the last of you, she'd turned to the window and stared out at the rain, listening to the sounds of the school dying down for the day, and then she too had gone home (a three-room flat, a three-room apartment, three cubic holes in a hole called a house), and there, sitting, standing, or wandering from hole to hole, she'd passed the afternoon, and now it was evening, and now it was night, and there'd been nothing to take her mind off a clock ticking away another day lost, and now it was time for sleep, and taking a few pins from her hair, she'd begun to brush it, to brush it. . . ."

[*The sound a forest makes is forest, forest.*]

The boy rose. "I have to go home now," he said.

The woman rose too, and she stood near him in the dark, and he thought of Miss Morey, and he remembered the scent of sandalwood, of sun-dried cloth, of hair so fragrant that it flavored the air, and he remembered a kiss that over the years was still so flavored, and he heard Miss Forrest say, "Will you come and visit with me again some time?"

And he said, "Yes, I will, Miss Forrest."

FINDERS KEEPERS, LOSERS WEEPERS

WALKING home from school on a spring afternoon, Danny entered Central Park at the Maine Monument, turned north to The Green, and crossed the grass on a diagonal toward The Mall. Here and there on the broad flow of lawn, there were pairs and larger conspiracies of children, some huddled, some in athletic formation, and some pursued and in pursuit. A short distance ahead of Danny, and moving in the same direction, a man strolled over the sward, idly cranking a cane as he went. At length, hanging the cane from the V of his vest, he drew a handkerchief from his hip-pocket, and as he did so, a wallet fell to the ground. Unaware of the loss, he polished his glasses, replaced the handkerchief, and continued on his way. Danny picked up the wallet and followed him. [*A loser was somebody that lost something, and a finder was somebody that found it—but how could you be a finder if you knew who the loser was?*] The cane became a golf-club, and just before reaching The Mall, the man drove a dandelion off its own tee, and then, lighting a cigar, he headed for the East Drive along a winding walk. [*Wasn't a finder supposed to help a loser?*] The man paused (giving Danny pause) at a patent-leather perambulator. He peered under the hood, said something to the nursemaid (who looked quickly away, smoothing her starched skirt), and shrugged, and hooking his neck with the crook of his cane, he led himself off. [*Supposed. Why was anybody supposed to help anybody else? If he couldn't look out for himself, why should you do his work? Who the hell was he?*] Scratching the small of his back with the curve of the cane, the man went downhill to the Boat Pond and stopped to watch toys in a water-waltz. Two sloops, one leading the other by the length of a bowsprit, were running head-on for the stone embankment, and as the man fended them off with the cane, a pair of boys raced up, came to a spraddle-legged halt, and stood glaring at him. One of them said, "Whatsy idea rooning our race for the Inanational Cup Race?" [*You heard a lot about honesty being the best policy, but they didn't tell you for who. If the man that had the Pierce-A would've told Pop the transmission was filled with sawdust, honesty would've been the best policy for Pop, all right, but how about the man with the Pierce-A? It was the same with the wallet. If you gave it back, honesty would be the best policy for the guy with the cane, but it would be the rottenest policy in the world for you, because he'd have the wallet, and you wouldn't. What was the matter with honesty? Why was it only good for one side?*] At the far end of the pond, the man turned unexpectedly to make a purchase from a candy-hawker—a nickel's worth of jelly-beans—and Danny was abreast of him before he could slacken speed. He leaned over the candy-stand, hunting for merchandise that was not on display: time. Would the man pay for the jelly-beans with a coin, or would he reach for his hip-pocket? The man paid with a coin. Flipping one of the colored beads into the air, he caught it in his mouth and moved away up a path climbing out of the pond-basin. Danny bought a marshmallow banana and dogged him. [*If you were honest, they told you, you'd have a clean conscience, and you'd be able to sleep at night, but when Pop went around to get his money back on the Pierce-A, they said the man couldn't be disturbed, and if he couldn't be disturbed, it stood to reason he was sleeping—so it looked like you could sleep with a dirty conscience too.*] They passed Cleopatra's Needle and the Metropolitan Museum. They crossed Transverse No. 3, where a boy on skates collided with the man, spun off, teetered, slithered, skittered, lost his balance, and fell. They entered upon the gravel walk rimming the Reservoir. [*Oh, you'd sleep if you kept the wallet, never fear, and the chances were you'd sleep better than if you gave it back: you wouldn't be worried about whether you'd been dumb.*] A flock of mallards rode at anchor near the water's edge. The man plunked a pebble among them, and three ducks turned up their skirts and dove. When they popped to the surface again, they had their hands on their hips, and they were abusive. [*The man with the cane might be Rock D. Johnefeller, and everybody knew that he never went out of the house with less than ten thousand dollars. If you gave him back the wallet, you'd have a nice clean conscience, and you'd sleep fine—till you started dreaming about the ten-cent reward!*] The man placed one hand behind his back, and with the other, the one holding the cane, he ran nobody through the body. He carefully wiped no-blood from the blade, flirted his dry fingers to dry them, and then, making a scabbard of his fist, he sheathed the weapon. It became a cane again almost at once. [*If you brought the wallet home, Mom would crack you in the jaw, and if you gave it back, Pop would do the same, so it was a crack in the jaw either way—except that one way you'd have the wallet. But that was a load of crap, and you knew it. Pop was as honest as Mom, and he'd crack you for keeping the wallet just like she would— only he wouldn't crack you for holding onto it between 67th Street and 90th, and she damn well would!*] The man balanced the cane on a fingertip. The man twirled the cane as he led a Fife & Drum Corps. The man speared imaginary scraps of paper and thrust them into an imaginary sack. The man was a polo-player whipping a mallet, a sniper sighting along a carbine, a batsman falling away from a duster, and a man walking with a cane. [*The guys'd laugh till they split. "Danny, the little tin Jesus of Harlem!" "Danny, the Alger-boy!" "Danny, the rail-splitter!" "Danny, the Wanny, the Wick-Stick-Stanny!" "Danny, you could've bought a million ice-cream combs!"*] Near the northern end of the Reservoir, the man was not fired on from ambush, but the cane became a crutch, and leaving no trail of blood behind him, he limped off the gravel path and made his painlessly painful way toward the 96th Street gate.

"Hey, mister," Danny said. [*"Danny! Danny! Oh, you damn Danny Merriwell!"*] The man stopped limping and stopped. "Here, this belongs to you."

The man patted the back of his pants. "I'll be jugged!" he said, and the wallet changed hands. "You're an honest kid."

"Oh, not so very."

"What do you mean—not so very?"

"All I did was give back your wallet."

"And that's not so very?"

Danny said, "Are you Rock D. Johnefeller?"

"Never heard of the bum," the man said, "but I'm going to give you a buck for being not so very."

"I don't want your buck, mister."

"You sound like you belong to the Boy Shouts."

"The Boy Pioneers. But I don't belong any more."

"It isn't every day I meet somebody that's not so very, so I'm going to give you *two* bucks."

"Keep your money."

The man said, "You know, there's a limit to what being not so very is worth."

"I don't think it's worth a cent," Danny said.

"Over here now, it's worth *three* bucks."

"Buy yourself a new cane."

The man shook the wallet. "Do you know how much folding-money I have in this? Take a guess."

"What for? I'm not out for a reward, so I wouldn't care if you had a million."

"I never heard of anybody refusing a reward."

"Why should anybody *get* one?"

"For being honest. Like you."

"I'm not so very."

The man studied Danny for a moment. "What makes you say that, kid?"

"Do you know where you dropped that wallet?" Danny said. "Two miles back, on The Green."

The man chalked the tip of his cane and executed a massé, and then, overhead, he shifted a counter on a wire. "So that's why you say you're not so very," he said.

"Yes," the boy said.

"Well, *I* say you're *very* very—and I'm going to give you *five* bucks!" The man riffled his money and brought five singles from the wallet. "Now, what the hell do you think of that?"

"I think I'm not going to take the money," Danny said, and he walked away. 12 84 .324

He walked quite rapidly at first, and then only rapidly, and then not a bit rapidly, and then rather slowly, and then almost lingeringly, and finally not at all. He looked back. The man was watching him, bills in hand and smiling.

"What do you think now, kid?" the man said.

"Now I'm not so sure."

The man made a wad of the bills and tossed it. [*Do you, or don't you? Do you, or don't you?*] Danny caught the money on the fly.

"Thanks, mister," the boy said.

"You're welcome," the man said. "And remember what I told you: you're *very* very."

Approaching the gate, Danny saw an old woman sitting on a camp-chair near the wall. On her lap was a basket loaded with pretzels.

"Pretzels, two cents," she said.

[*You never should've taken the money, and now that you had it, you didn't want it. You ought to give it away, all of it.*]

"Pretzels, two cents," the old woman said.

Danny dropped something into her basket and marched off up Fifth Avenue. The old woman stared after him and then stared down at the basket. She picked up the something and smoothed it out: it was a one-dollar-bill. She stared after Danny again. He was marching uptown, whistling *Yankee Doodle*.

HARRIET MUST BE HOME BY SIX O'CLOCK

FROM the front window of their flat, Mr. and Mrs. Daniel Johnson watched their son, who had just appeared on the sidewalk below in the company of Miss Harriet Bryant, and from the front window of a flat in the adjoining building, Mr. and Mrs. Howard Bryant watched their daughter. Harriet and Danny started off up the street, turned a corner, and were gone: it was 1:01 o'clock on a spring Sunday afternoon, and they were having their first date.

The itinerary that Danny had planned included: a ride across town on the 125th Street trolley (ten cents); a ride on the Broadway subway to Van Cortlandt Park (ten cents); a walk in the park for Nature-study and the witnessing of sporting-exhibitions of any kind (free); a ride back to 125th Street on the Broadway subway (ten cents); a walk across 125th Street for sodas at Huyler's (twenty cents); and, lastly, a walk home (free). For the realization of this plan, Mr. and Mrs. Howard Bryant had agreed on a time-limit of five hours.

At 1:10, hardly a moment after boarding the trolley and making his first expenditure of the day, Danny felt a minor but persistent physical discomfort somewhere between his navel and his backbone. He tried to subdue it in conversation with Harriet. "I always look at the ads," he said, "but they're all pretty foolish."

"I like the pictures," Harriet said.

"'My thing is the best thing,' they say."

"My favorite is the one where a man is smoking, and the smoke goes up and makes a lady's face."

"Take the ads for tires," Danny said. "They all say, 'This is the best tire in the whole world.' But they can't all be the best. One of them is got to be the worst."

"My next favorite is the kind that shows people before and after they take things. In the 'before' part, the person is always fat or old or sick or tired. In the 'after' part, he runs around with lightning coming out of him."

"The dumbest of all is where men're having a tug-of-war with a pair of pants instead of a rope."

"In the ads about silverware," Harriet said, "there's always a bride and groon. I like that."

"Either the men can't pull very hard," Danny said, "or else the pants're made out of iron."

The trolley crossed St. Nicholas Avenue at 1:22, and Danny was reminded of the slight discomfort by the discomfort itself. It did not seem to have grown worse since first noticed, but it had grown no better, and Danny wondered briefly whether it would come or go.

"All out for Broadway!" the conductor said.

At 1:36, Danny and Harriet caught a train for Van Cortlandt Park, and at 1:40, he realized that the pain had come to stay—indeed, to increase.

"I'm never going to get married," Harriet said, "but if I ever get married, my husband is going to smoke a cigar like the man in the ad."

"Why aren't you going to get married?" Danny said.

"Because all men're beasts."

"What's that mean—all men're beasts?"

"I don't know. I heard my mother say it."

By the time 168th Street was reached, the pain had revealed itself to be a pressure, and by Dyckman Street, the pressure had become traceable to two definite centers: two small balloons seemed to have found their way into the boy's body, and while not yet full, clearly they were being inflated. It was 1:59.

"Are you ever going to get married?" Harriet said.

"I never thought about it," Danny said.

"Well, think now."

Danny began to think at 2:06, and he thought until 2:12, at which time the train crossed Spuyten Duyvil Creek, but during those six minutes his thoughts had been concerned only with the two balloons that he contained: they were growing, they were growing!

"Did you think yet?" Harriet said.

"I been thinking all the time, but I can't make up my mind."

"What takes you so long?"

"I can't remember if all ladies are beasts too."

As the train drew out of 238th Street, which it did at 2:21, Danny put his hand behind him as if to straighten his jacket. His real purpose, however, was to verify with his fingers what his mind had imagined: that the balloons had begun to bulge from his back. They had not.

"My mother never said anything about that," Harriet said.

"Van Cortn Park!" the conductor said. "All out!"

It was 2:26 when they left the train. At 2:27, they passed a door near the ticket-seller's window: on the door hung a blue and white sign reading MEN. At 2:29, they were in the park and walking across the grass toward the Parade Ground, and walking with them, uninvited, was a small brown dog. A tree changed the dog's course as a leash would have changed it, and after making a thorough reconnaissance with its nose, it set itself up alongside the trunk and hosed it down. But Danny and Harriet had gone by, and it was 2:32, and the boy was thinking of home. [*You'd bust before you got there!*]

"Of course," Harriet said, "if I ever met anybody that wasn't a beast. . . ."

"I'm not a beast," Danny said, "but sometimes I wish I was."
[*What did you say that for? Were you crazy?*]

At 2:41, they crossed the outfield of a pick-up ball-game just as
a long fly was driven over a diamond marked off with folded coats.
There were basemen, but no fielders, and the ball, falling safe far
behind short, rolled among some bushes.

[*If you got it, you'd be in the bushes too!*] Danny started to run,
saying, "I'll get it!"

"I'll help!" Harriet said, and she ran too.

Danny stopped. "Ah, they'll find it themselves."

Harriet stopped. "I don't like baseball."

[*It was worse now. You shouldn't've run.*]

Between 2:50 and 3:35, Danny and Harriet wandered through
the wooded park—over knolls and rock, along the bank of a lake,
on trails among the shrubbery—and Harriet identified nine trees
(linden, ash, maple, elm, birch, beech, walnut, sycamore, and pop-
lar), eight birds (sparrow, starling, pigeon, robin, warbler, shrike,
jay, and flicker), and four animals (dog, horse, squirrel, and chip-
munk). [*What were you going to do? What were you going to* DO?]
From 3:35 to 4:15, Danny and Harriet watched a ball-game between the Edgecomb Rockets (colored) and the Mosholu Giants
(white). The score in the fourth inning, when they first came upon
the scene, had been 27-5 in favor of the Giants; when they left, at
the end of the sixth inning, the score was 39-31 in favor of the Rockets, and a boy near Danny was singsonging, "The sky is pink. The
Giants stink." [*You couldn't wait a minute, not another single minute!*]
At 4:24, they passed the clock over the ticket-seller's window at the
Van Cortlandt Park station, and two seconds later, they passed a
blue and white sign reading MEN. At 4:26, their train pulled out for
downtown. [*A terrible thing was going to happen, and the more you
thought about it, the more terrible it was going to be—and the sooner
it was going to happen. You had to talk. You had to move your feet.
You had to swallow, blink, bite your nails, curl your toes, and count
the chung-gum squashes on the floor. You had to read the ads, every
word, every letter, every number. You can teach a parrot to say children
cry for it (225th Street) everybody drives a used railway mail-clerk in*]

*six easy payments (207th Street) not even your best four out of five get
that schoolgirl toasted amazement in the big blue package marked
Jesus Saves (181st Street) for heartburn headache hernia colds corns
rectal soreness morning-mouth periodic pain look for this signature
(168th Street) the sky is pink the Giants stink all men are pink beasts
strrrike shrike shriek shroke clupeco-shrunk (145th Street) tooth-decay
tattletale gray buy this buy that buy mine buy the best (125th Street)*
THE BEST!]

It was 5:16 on a spring Sunday afternoon.

"Let's take the car!" Danny said.

"I thought we were going to walk," Harriet said.

"The car's faster!"

"We've still got lots of time."

"Maybe Huyler's'll be closed!"

"We could go to a druk-store."

"Druk-store sodas are no good!"

"We could get ice-cream combs."

"Sodas are better! Let's take the car!"

They took the car, reaching Huyler's at 5:31.

"What'll it be?" the soda-clerk said.

"Chocolate soda, chocolate cream," Harriet said.

"Two!" Danny said.

"Two what?" the clerk said.

"Two chocolate sodas!"

"What kind of cream you want?"

"Chocolate!"

"Why'n't you say so?"

"I did say so! I said,'Two!'"

"How should I know what 'two' means?"

"Two means two! It don't mean six!"

"You're kind of fresh, ain't you?"

"I ain't stale!"

"Lucky for you this is Huyler's."

"If it's Huyler's, jerk two sodas!"

"Take your time, cull. Take your time."

[*What'll people say? What'll Mr. Huyler do?*]

Harriet had barely penetrated the foam of her soda when Danny finished his, and blobs of unmelted ice-cream were cold-burning the lining of his stomach. He pressed his legs together and jigged his revolving chair, and as Harriet big-eyed him over a spoonful, he gave her a spasm of a smile and began to beat a rhythm with his fingers and feet.

They left Huyler's at 5:51 and drew up before Harriet's house at 5:59.

"G'bye!" Danny said, and he fled.

Traveling at high speed, he passed through the parlor of the Johnson flat at 6:00. His father and mother looked at each other and then at the banged-shut door of the bathroom, and faintly through the panels they heard a long sighed-out "Ooooooooh!" When Danny emerged, it was 6:05.

"Why did you wait so long?" his mother said.

"I had to be polite," the boy said. "What've we got for supper?"

THAT'S TELLING HIM, KID

"YOU'LL know the truth if you listen to me," Doc Knox had said during the first lecture in Political Science, and now, during the last, he was saying, "A slew of you numbskulls are wondering, after twenty weeks of this course, what it's had to do with *The Star-Spangled Banner*. Most of you won't ever know, because most of you came here without brains, and after sitting here without imagination, you're about to leave here without names. Not yet old enough to vote, you've already been forgotten, as if you'd lived for seventy years with no more to your credit than wearing a hole in the top of a chiffonier with a gold-plated collar-button. With three exceptions, you're the people who'll some day be retired, after fifty years of service as night-watchmen, with a testimonial and a brass clock that won't run. You're the people whose contributions to Truth will be such astounding feats as balancing thirty thousand matches on the neck of a bottle, rolling six hundred miles of string into a ball, and saving two tons of cigar-store coupons to win a vacuum-cleaner. You're the streetcar-conductors of tomorrow, the waiters, the clerks, the hack-drivers, the barbers—the people who grow old without having aged, the people who eat everything and taste nothing, who look without seeing, who talk without words, who live without rhyme and die without reason. It was not to hear my own voice that I said at the beginning, 'I don't like people.'"

[*What was so terrible about being a hack-driver?*]

"I like the truth, though," Doc Knox was saying, "and therefore all year I've spoken only to the three of you who will some day know what it is: William Eliot, Saul Benjamin, and Martin Kennedy. The other thirty-five I now gratefully face for the last time are the dummies of The Great Ventriloquist. The words that seem to come from your mouths are those of The Eternal Faker whose hand is under your suit, and you move, but your motion is wired. Is it speech when a conductor says, 'Fares, please?' Is it action to drive a hack from Murray Hill to Washington Arch . . . ?"

Danny raised his hand.

"What do you want?" Doc Knox said.

"My father is a hack-driver."

"Well, what about it?"

"You have no right to talk about him."

"I'm not talking about your father. I never met the gentleman."

"You were being sneering about hack-drivers."

"I was talking about hack-drivers in general."

"I don't know about general hack-drivers. I only know about my father."

Doc Knox addressed the class. "Is there anybody here whose father is a clerk?" Three boys showed hands. "Is there anybody whose father is a barber?" One hand went up. "A streetcar-conductor?" One. "Now, is there anybody who thought I meant his father in particular?" Danny's hand was alone. "That makes you the only one the shoe fits."

"I don't care what the class thinks," Danny said. "I don't even care what *you* think. I only care what *I* think, and I think it isn't right for teachers to go around insulting people and calling them dummies and telling them they'll wind up being a hack-driver, as

if that was the worst thing in the world for anybody to be. It isn't
the best—I know that as good as you do—but no matter what, it
isn't a person's fault if that's all he can do for a living. My father
never went to college like you did, so he turned out to be a hack-
driver, but that's no reason to make fun of him. Maybe if he'd've
went to college, he'd've turned out to be a better teacher than you
did. At least, maybe he wouldn't go around saying, 'I don't like
people. I like the truth.' The truth, the truth—that's all you ever
talk about, but you didn't really teach us the truth. We found out
about the Consatution is built up on property, not democracy, and
the Spanish-American War was on account of the sugar-planta-
tions, not the starved Cubans, but that isn't what anybody means
by the truth. It don't do any good to know about the sugar-plan-
tations if you don't like the starved Cubans...."

THE GROWING PAIN

DANNY carried no books home today: there were no books to
be carried. The last examination of his freshman year had
been taken, the last sundae had been downed at Ward's Drug
Store, and the next to the last summer goodbye had been said, and
he walked east on 59th Street, lugging nothing in his hands but
his hands: he traveled light, and he was all spring and sponge,
flight and feather, push and piston, and there seemed to be no re-
sistance in the air. He crossed to the parkside beyond Columbus
Circle, but he scaled the wall only with his eyes. Hair hung down
over the faces of trees, and now and then a breeze came to comb it.
[*The sound a forest makes is forest, forest.*]
He remembered the cup of tea and the biscuits, the window and
the rain, the teacher's voice and the teacher's words, and the darkness of the room, and he remembered a sound that he had heard
only in his mind, the brushing of hair, and he thought he could
hear the name Juno Forrest, Juno Forrest. The iron-framed doors
were open, and the dim hall grew dimmer as it deepened, and
standing before the gilt grille, the boy listened to the elevator wob-
ble down its slots, and he breathed the cool stale air of the shaft,

but when the car neared the ground-floor, he turned suddenly to the stairway and walked up to the seventh landing. He rang the bell of Apartment 8F. [*The sound a forest makes is forest.*] There was no answer. He seated himself on the steps leading to the roof, and in the silent gloom, in the windowless room, he closed his eyes, and then he was in a room within a room, and there to think was to feel thoughts grow, and they grew, and he desired the growth to be without end.

And then someone else was in the room and close by, but the voice of the someone seemed far away and sifted by distance. "Danny," it was saying. "Danny."

He opened his eyes to see Miss Forrest at the foot of the flight. She held her purse in one hand and her key-ring in the other. "Hello," he said. "Hello, Miss Forrest."

"What're you doing here?" she said.

"I was waiting for you."

"Were you? Why?"

"You said to come and see you again."

"I'm glad you remembered."

"I thought we could have another talk."

"What would we talk about?"

"I don't know. We had a good talk last time."

The woman shook her head. "We really didn't, Danny," she said.

"It was good when you were telling me about being a teacher, and about teachers being human."

"You knew that all along, didn't you?"

"I guess so, but now I think everybody is human."

"This is getting to be a good talk too, isn't it?"

"That's what I came here for."

"I know," the woman said, "but I don't think we ought to have any more talks."

"But why, Miss Forrest? I like to talk to you better than anyone else."

"I feel the same way, Danny."

"Then why can't we have any more talks?"

"I didn't say we can't," the woman said, and the key-ring fell, and she picked it up. "I said we oughtn't to."

"I wish...," Danny said, but he knew that wishing was futile.

A FAKE AND A PHONY

DANNY and Tootsie had finished work for the day, and with their shoe-shine boxes slung, they were walking home across 125th Street in the late-afternoon sun, their block-long purple shadows outflung before them.

"Danny," Tootsie said after covering some distance in silence, "what's your philosophy?"

[*What the hell did that mean?*] "My philosophy?" he said.

"That's right. What's your philosophy?"

[*Was it something like a scout-oath, or what?*] "Well, I'll tell you, Tootsie. My philosophy is.... What I mean to say.... I been thinking about my philosophy for a long time and I finally figured it out."

"That's good," Tootsie said, "but what is it?"

"It's this: do good by your fellow-man." Danny kicked an empty matchbox a few cracks along the sidewalk, and then Tootsie took it over and made a goal when he hit a hydrant with it. "Do good by your fellow-man," Danny said again. "That's my philosophy. Whenever I feel like doing a thing, I first ask myself if it's going to do good by my fellow-man. If it is, then I do it. If it isn't, then I don't." He ran a finger between his throat and collar, using the gesture to cast a quick glance at the colored boy; he learned little, for Tootsie continued to stare straight ahead up his shadow. "There's nothing so noble as the simple word of 'friend,' so if my fellow-man comes to me in his hour of need, I will do good by him. I will not be a fair-weather friend; I will be a friend in deed. I will share my portion with him when his fortune is at a low ebb, and I will not charge him interest, and I will turn the other cheek even if he does not do good by me. That's my philosophy...."

They were crossing Fifth Avenue, and now Tootsie's way lay north. They paused for a moment at the curb, their shadows still making two long stains running east. 12 67 .307

"See you tomorrow," Tootsie said.

"See you," Danny said, and he watched Tootsie move off. [*Jesus Christ, what must he be thinking of you?*]

THE STAMP ACT

THE regular weekly meeting of the Mt. Morris Philatelic Society was in progress. The founder and first president, a boy named Perry Floyd, was chairman as well, and equipped with a tack-hammer and a block of wood, he was guiding the disposal of such items as the agenda contained: 1) a reading of the Society pledge by Albert Hughes, vice-president; 2) a reading of the minutes of the previous meeting by Maxwell Gage, secretary; 3) a financial statement by Carl Eames, treasurer; 4) the collection of dues by the same; and 5) a report called "News of the Stamp-World," delivered by the chairman himself. After the next routine item—6) new members—the meeting would be thrown open to 7) selling and swapping.

Officers and rank-and-file alike had begun to crackle packets, open stamp-books, and arrange displays for the trading-session, but Chairman Floyd brought them to order with his tack-hammer.

"Item 6," he said. "New members."

Danny Johnson raised his hand, and the Chair recognized him. "I got two people that want to join our Society," he said.

"What's their name?" the Chair said.

"Julian Pollard and Tudor Powell."

"I never heard of them. Who are they?"

"Friends of mine."

"What's their qualification?"

"I went to school with Julian, P. S. 604. He was smart, and a thing he was specially good in was geography, so he ought to be able to learn about stamps. The other one, Tudor, is my partner. I'm in business with him."

"What business?"

"The shoe-shine business."

"The shoe-shine business! What kind of a qualification is that?"

"By being in it with him, I found out he was very honest and would never cheat anybody, and that's a pretty good qualification."

"Does he know anything about stamps?"

"I don't think so, but he could learn, just like Julian."

"Have these guys got enough money to pay the initiation-fee?"

"My partner has, and if Julian's short, I'll loan him the fifty cents."

"Well, I don't see any objection," the Chair said. "All those in favor of the new members, raise your right hand." The vote for admission was unanimous. "They're elected. Tell them to come to the next meeting."

"They're waiting downstairs," Danny said. "They could come to this one."

"If they pay the initiation-fee."

Danny went to a window and called down into the dark street. "Come on up! You got elected!"

"Item 7," the Chair said. "Selling and swapping."

The room, the parlor of the Floyd flat, at once became a market-place for peddlers of stamps in sets, stamps in blocks, uncancelled stamps, hand-cancelled covers, internal revenues, commemorative issues, Latin-Americans, Africans, British Colonials, and grab-bag specials. Being both customer and merchant, each boy hunted for bargains while barking his wares. Examinations were made under glass, the Stamp Bible was consulted, argument and haggle began, and money and merchandise changed hands. More stamps appeared, choicer ones now, and silver coins supplanted copper.

The doorbell rang.

"I'll open," Danny said, but no one heard him. He went to the hall and let the new members into the flat. "You got elected unanimously," he said, and congratulating them, he led them toward the parlor.

For a moment, none of the tradesmen noticed the trio, and they stood between the shirred portieres, watching the loud and gymnastic making of deals. Turning from the crowd at length, one of the boys, in the act of secreting a coin, stopped and stared. Another boy happened to glance at the doorway, glanced off, doubled back quickly, and froze. And now a third and a fourth and a fifth all singly stared, and now a sixth and a seventh, and in the end, the eyes of the entire Society were holding a meeting among the curtains. It was a very quiet meeting. 22 88 .310

"Fellows," Danny said, "these're the new members—Julie Pollard and Tootsie Powell...."

The founder and first president cut across him. "But they're *niggers!*" he said.

Words, launched, were coming down the ways of Danny's mouth, and he heard himself say, "Tootsie stands for Tudor...," but the filler was draining from his smile, and his face was left with the smile's empty form, a cramp.

"No niggers can belong to this Society!" the founder and first president said.

"No niggers *want* to belong!" Julian said, and he pitched the black boulder of his fist at Perry Floyd's face. The founder and first president came apart harelipped as he fell, and lying in a snow of stamps, he bled over the rectangular flakes. Julian looked at him for a moment, and then he left the flat, followed by Tootsie and Danny.

"So we got unanimously elected!" Julian said when they reached the street. "Looks to me, Negroes ain't allowed to collect stamps!"

"I never thought to say you were colored," Danny said. "I figured the guys were regular."

"Have to be white to belong to a little ole stamp-club!"

"Well, anyway, you had the fun of belting that stinker in the moosh."

"Don't do me no good to be belting people in the moosh! That's the way I'm going to get in trouble! I'll hear the word 'nigger' some day, and I'll have a bottle in my hand, and some day I'll have a knife, and God damn it, some day I'll have a gun!"

"Not everybody's like that pissy Perry Floyd."

"Whole damn club is pissy Perrys! Whole damn world!"

"That isn't fair," Danny said. "There's me, and there's lots of other people you don't have to get mad at."

"Like to meet up some time."

"You met Miss Campbell. She was nice to colored people."

"Met Doc Page too, and he was a white-meat bastard! Would've read my paper if it was the other way 'round. But if you're black, it's never the other way 'round. Be black, and you're suppose to be ass-frontways—only I don't turn my back for nobody, and that's how I'm going to get in trouble!"

Tootsie said, "Who you been listening at, Julie?"

"It wasn't you, Mr. Kneel-down!"

"I don't aim to always shine shoes."

"No? How *you* going to get your yaller Stutz?"

"I don't aim at a yaller Stutz," Tootsie said.

"You just don't *aim*," Julian said. "You're black, Tootsie, and you're being aimed *at*."

"Maybe, but I ain't *aiming* to be aimed at, and you are. You're so sure you're going to get in trouble account of being black that you won't rest till you do. They'll be caving your head in, and you'll be getting a fat comfort out of saying, 'I told me so.'"

"Could was, but I still ain't shining no shoes."

"I'll quit that when I get what I want out of it: a box of money."

"And I still ain't waiting on no tables, like your old man."

"A box of money," Tootsie said. "I'm going to college."

"You in college right now—Kneel-down College!"

"Have to kneel down to get what I'm after, but I don't mind because I ain't kneeling down to people—only to money. Everybody does that, and there's lots do it standing up."

"You got it all doped out—all except how to unkink your hair."

"I'm black, and I want to *stay* black."

"You can kiss off that college-stuff, then."

"I'll get to college," Tootsie said.

"If they let you, Mr. Kink-head. I want to be a lawyer, but they ain't letting *me*."

"People sitting around figuring how to stop Julie Pollard being a lawyer?"

"Not any more. They all done figuring."

"Who's 'they'?"

"State of New God damn York."

"They didn't figure too good, because there's forty Negro law-yers in Harlem alone."

"And seven hundred Pullman porters that wanted to be, but ain't! They rake in your cush in law-school, they sell you booky-books, and they even give you a crack at the exams—and then they flunk you and say, 'Tough titty. Try again next year.' Next year! What do you do for meat-eating till *next year?* Does the State feed you till *next year?* In a pig's brown! You go out and get you a job being a elevator-boy, or you rack 'em up, or you pimp for some poor ole black bum, or you bust in a Western Union and get shot in the entrals. 'Try again next year, nigger.'"

"What happens if a white man flunks?"

"White man don't flunk."

"Now, that's a lot of crap," Tootsie said.

"What I care about a white man flunks? Phrig him! He can look out for himself."

"No better than you can. If a man's poor, he's poor—and he can be poor in any color."

"White man can do something else."

"Suppose he don't want to. Suppose he wants to be a lawyer or nothing, like you."

"I say, phrig him!"

"We're going awful slow," Tootsie said, "If you say phrig *him*, why shouldn't he say phrig *you?*"

"Let him. I still ain't kissing his peach."

"Poor people don't have to kiss each other's peach."

"Tootsie," Danny said after a long, attentive silence, "where do you get all that stuff you're saying?"

"Mostly from my father."

"He sounds like he's a smart man."

"All waiters're smart. There's nobody in the world that's as smart as a waiter on a table."

"We got some pie left from supper," Danny said. "Come on up my house, and *I'll* be a waiter on a table."

Not long afterward, three boys full sat in the downpour of the Johnson chandelier, their milk-mustaches still glistening.

FROM WANDERING ON A FOREIGN STRAND

"I NEVER saw action in the war," Uncle Web was saying, "but all the same, I was seriously wounded at the Peace Conference: they were only out to divvy the world a new way, so as soon as I got my discharge, I made a beeline for Russia. All the further I got was Brussels: every God damn road was blocked by some God damn counterrevolutionary army—the British, the French, the White Guards, the Finns, the Poles, even the Germans. The *Germans*—and only a little way back, they were our worst enemies! All Philip Nolan said was, 'I wish I may never hear of the United States again!' I go him one better. I say, 'I wish I may never hear of *any* country again!' I hope the whole globe catches fire from Russia and burns to the ground, and then, if there's any flag left to fly over the ruins, it'll be the red one!" He put a match to a dead cigar, and it came to life. "What've you been scribbling there?" he said to his nephew.

Danny let a pencil fall. "Nothing," he said.

The hack-driver reached across the table and drew a sheet of paper from under the boy's hand. "What's this mean?" he said. "'Tanforan, Tanforan.'"

"I don't know," the boy said.

"Over and over again—'Tanforan.'"

"I was just writing it. I don't know why."

CHAMPEEN OF THE WORLD

THERE was a knock on the door of the Powell flat, and Tootsie's father said, "See who that is, Tudor."

"It's probably my uncle," Danny said.

When Tootsie opened the door, he found Webster Varner standing in the hallway. "Hello, Mr. Varner," he said. "Come on in."

"Hello, Tootsie," Varner said. "How be you?" After being introduced, he said, "I told Danny I'd call for him if I was in the neighborhood. Nice place you have, Mr. Powell."

"Nice as some, Mr. Varner," Powell said.

"Well, Danny," Varner said, "how about that chocolate sody?"

"I'm ready, unc," Danny said.

"Want to join us, Tootsie?"

"If he won't be in the way," Powell said.

"Not at all. Glad to have him."

Tootsie ran for his jacket and cap.

"Mind if I look at your books?" Varner said.

"That's what they're for," Powell said.

There were many books in the Powell parlor—in cases, on the Dutch shelf, on the mantelpiece, in a china-closet, propped on tables, and stacked in corners. Few of them were new, and many were coverless, but all that Danny's uncle happened to pick up and open were name-plated *Ex Libris: Raymond Powell* and filled with marginal notes.

"Interested in economics, I see," Varner said.

"Mighty little else to be interested in," Powell said.

"Veblen," Varner said as he passed a row of volumes, "Morgan, George, Kropotkin, Marx. . . ."

"And Lenin," Powell said.

"I don't see him, but I'm sure he's around."

"If Marx is around, Lenin's around."

"And Trotsky," Varner said, "but I don't see him, either."

"You won't," Powell said. "I threw him out."

"Threw him out! How's that?"

"Threw him out like I threw out Kautsky."

"Now, what the hell'd you do that for?"

"Trotsky can't stay in the same room with Lenin."

Danny said, "Tootsie's ready, unc."

"Be with you in a minute," Varner said, and he turned back to Tootsie's father. "Just what did you mean—Trotsky can't stay in the same room with Lenin . . . ?"

*　　　*　　　*

"Sorry I'm late," Danny said when he joined his partner at the 125th Street subway-station in the morning. "I slept and slept."

"Did you finally get that soda?" Tootsie said.

"Listen. You know what time that argument was over? Two o'clock!"

"I'm glad I went to bed."

"I snoozed off on the couch, and I got woke up four different times. I never heard such terrible noise."

"Politics is a loud business," Tootsie said. "*Here y'are! Getcha shine!* Who won?"

"Nobody," Danny said.

"Before I went to bed, I seem to remember my father had your uncle over a barrel."

"And after you went to bed, my uncle had your father over a barrel."

"My father usually wins an argument."

"Nobody won. Somebody was always over a barrel."

"When my father gets a man over a barrel, he stays there."

"Well, they kept on changing places this time."

"I should've stayed up. I never saw my father over a barrel in an argument yet."

"It was the worst argument that was ever argued," Danny said. "*Getcha Shine! Ten cents!* They'd go along for a while, just the best of friends, and one of 'em would be asking questions, and the other'd be giving answers, and then all of a sudden—pow! One of 'em would figure he had the other in a hole, and he'd jump up, waving his arms and hollering and stamping and making sounds like he was tearing something in his neck, and finally he'd point at me, saying, 'Did you hear that? Did you hear that?' like the whole argument depended on me hearing a couple of little ole words. And then, before I ever got a chance to talk, the one that gave the bum answer would be laying over a barrel with his tongue hanging out. *Shine 'em up like new! One dime!* You'd think he was a goner for sure, but next thing you knew, there they were, the best of friends again, and the one that just got trimmed was asking the questions and reading pieces out of books, and the one that handed out the trimming was answering and listening and answering, and finally he'd answer the wrong answer, and—blooie! *He* was over a barrel. It was like a price-fight."

"What was the argument about?" Tootsie said.

"Russia."

"That's my father's favorite argument."

"My uncle was for somebody named Trotsky."

"Trotsky! Then he must've *lost* the argument!"

"I just told you it was a standoff."

"It couldn't've been. Wasn't my father for Lenin?"

"Yes, but that don't mean he had to win."

"If you're for Lenin, you've got to win—if the other side is for Trotsky."

"Who's this Lenin—the champeen?"

"He's the champeen over Trotsky."

"Who says so?"

"My father says so."

"My uncle says different."

"Then your uncle is wrong."

"Why is my uncle always wrong? Suppose I said your father was wrong."

"*Getcha shine!* Not about Lenin. He couldn't be."

"My uncle says Trotsky stands for a revolution all over the world, and your father says Lenin only stands for a revolution in one country. A revolution all over the world is a better revolution than a revolution only in one country, so Trotsky is got to be better than Lenin."

"A revolution all over the world is better if you can get it, but you can't."

"Why not?" Danny said.

"Because there's some people that don't want it."

"My uncle says if they don't want it, then they don't know what's good for them, and you got to stuff it down their neck."

"Can't stuff a revolution down anybody's neck! That's crazy!"

"How do you get a revolution, then?"

"You wait till the people ask for it, like a shoe-shine. A man don't want a shoe-shine, then he don't *get* a shoe-shine. You can't knock him down and polish 'em up. You wait till he asks you."

"If people want a revolution, who do they ask?"

"Nobody particular. They just stand up and say, 'The hell with this form of government. It's only for the rich men and the capitalists. We want a new form of government.'"

"My uncle says the people won't do that for a long time, and the capitalists will go in Russia and crush Socialism."

"My father says the way to stop that is to make Socialism so strong that the capitalists will get crushed if they try to do any crushing in Russia. That's what Lenin says too."

"*Shine, mister!*" Danny said.

E PLURIBUS UNUM

THE Congressional Limited fired itself from a cave in the Palisades and skimmed over the Hackensack Meadows toward Manhattan Transfer. Powered by a box-electric with diamond trolleys genuflecting to the overhead live-wire, the red train took a banked bend at fifty-five and shook off a posse of dust riding hard on the heels of the observation. Their feet cocked on its brass railing, Danny Johnson and his Uncle Web watched northern New Jersey recede. Square miles of cattail went away, and reed-stockaded creeks, and sudden shys of track, and scow-skeletons in black mud, and the rolling-stock of the nearby Lackawan'.

"Manhattan Transfer! Manhattan Transfer!"

The electric was cut loose, and it cruised, making way for a black short-stacked Pacific, a chunky cakewalking muscle-bound buck, and then there were two croaked and dismal longs, and once more the train was rolling. It crossed the Passaic, paused at Newark, and took the outside rail for the straight line through Princeton Junction. At eighty, overtaken hauls seemed hobbled, and northgoing varnish was sucked from sight in seconds: near things flashed past fused and fragmentary, and only the distant remained with the eye. The Pacific grew sideburns of steam, and gray hair flowed back over the cars and track.

"Trenton! Philadelphia the next!"

The Delaware [*Among the pebbles on its floor, among broken glass and tin cans and castoff tires, in the silt and the slag and the sunken slough of a century and a half, lay a button from a buff and blue uniform, a lead ball for a flintlock, and a few now stone bones—relics of the Christmas night that saw, eight miles above this crossing, a hand-*

ful of ragamuffins catch some red-coated bastards by surprise.] and the Schuylkill, and it was Philadelphia.

"Wilmington the next!"

Below Chester, the tracks bisected an arc that once was a fence for the Penns and the Baltimores, with monuments at every mile and a coat-of-arms at every fifth [*They were gone now, the posts and the bench marks, and the men who had made them (a Mr. Mason, it might've been, and a Mr. Nixon or Dixon or some such name) were all but forgotten—except in the South.*], and beyond that line lay the Brandywine, and it was Wilmington.

"Ballamore the next!"

From Elkton, head of Elk, and on down the great Chesapeake explosion into Maryland, the man who had spoken the first word spoken by the boy spoke other words, some new and others known, but all with the federal flavor of *Tanforan* and *Chickamauga*. One of these was *Susquehanna*, and there were *Chincoteague* and *Choptank, Conowingo* and *Monocacy*, and *McConnellsburg* and the rolling distant thunder of *Cumberland*, and now it was Baltimore.

"Washington the next!"

From Laurel on the Patuxent, the Pacific loafed, and gantries left behind seemed to be coming on, and track veered slowly off the main to pace the train, and a face seen was no longer erased by speed, and now relays of power were passed, and a goggled engineer waved at Danny from his cab, and it was Washington.

"Last stop! Change for Richmond and points south!"

　　　　*　　　*　　　*

They passed the Willard, crossed over at the Treasury, and followed the high iron railing around the White House grounds. It had rained the night before, and the lawns, still damp, were smeared with sunlight, and the chocolate earth sent up its scent in the warming morning air.

"Getcha shine!"

Near the main gate stood a black bootblack.

Danny touched his uncle's arm, saying, "We ought to get a shine before we go in a place like the White House," and receiving assent, he set his foot on the shoe-box and said. "Well, how's business?"

"Couldn't be worse if folks went barefoot," the bootblack said.

"This ought to be a good stand."

"Ought-to-be ain't is."

"How long you been in the game?"

"This my third aministration."

"You mind if I tell you something?"

"Can't say till you tell it."

"You *brush* the cream dry. That's wrong. You ought to *fan* it dry."

"What's the diffence?"

"Brush it, and you only brush it off. Fan it, and it sinks in."

"Why I want it to sink in?"

"It makes a better base for the wax."

"Who been telling you all that?"

"My partner."

"What he know about shoe-shine?"

"He's a shoe-shiner," Danny said. "And so am I."

The colored boy broke work in the middle of a rag-sashay, and he stared up smiling. The smile was brief, however, and it was going away when he said, "White folks don't shine shoes," and gone when he said, "They only wear 'em."

"They shine 'em where I come from."

"That ain't Washinton."

"I live in Harlem."

The bootblack's eyes no longer attended his hands: the hands whacked wax on felt-for shoes, and the eyes looked up at eyes looking down. "Heard about that place," he said. "It where I want to go when I die."

"Why wait? My partner lives there, and he's still alive."

"Partner ain't colored."

"Guess again," Danny said.

The bootblack rose now, his finish-rag dragging on the ground, and he gazed beyond Danny at a white house striped with the black ribs of the railing. "You in partners with a colored boy?" he said.

"Sure," Danny said. "How much I owe you?"

"You mean, he *work* for you."

"No, *I* kind of work for *him*."

"That couldn't happen even if it happened."

"He gets the most out of the partnership because he's a better shoe-shiner. How much I owe?"

"You lyin'," the colored boy said, "but we all square."

"That's mighty nice of you," Danny said.

"We square, but you lyin' your head off."

"Why do you keep on saying that?"

"You lyin' hard as iron."

"I'm *not* lying—and I'll prove it by showing you a trick! Put your foot on that box!"

With Danny kneeling before him, the bootblack was almost surprised into compliance, but in the end he said, "You lyin', boy."

Danny caught his foot and drew it up to the stand, and then, whipping the wrinkles from a rag, he said, "I'm going to play you a tune. Take your pick: *Yankee Doodle* or *Dixie*.

"Never heard that *Yankee Doodle*.

"You pick *Dixie*, then?"

"Pick *Yankee Doodle*."

"I thought you never heard it."

"Heard the other."

"Here goes," Danny said, and he brought the rag sawing down over a broken old shoe, and Yankee Doodle went uptown, riding a flitch of flannel, and in a flogged-out rhythm, he stuck a feather in his hat and called it macaroni, and then Danny reprised the last line, and his uncle joined in, and again, and the gate-guard joined, and once more, and the colored boy called it macaroni too.

Danny rose, tossed the bootblack his rag, and said, "You'll have 'em standing in line," and then he followed his uncle through the outer portals of the White House. A little way beyond, he turned to wave a goodbye, and the colored boy, his face wedged between two bars of the fence, waved back with the rag.

"You the lyin'est liar," he was saying.

*   *   *

"Well," Uncle Web said, "how do you like Washington?"

"It's all right, I guess," Danny said, "but I wouldn't want to live here. It's a cemetery. It's dead."

"A cemetery isn't dead. Only the people."

"You look at a nice thing, and right away they tell you who died there."

"People die everywhere," Uncle Web said.

"But in Washington, they make a fuss about it."

"And the bigger the stiff, the bigger the fuss."

"Why should that be?" Danny said. "Take the Washington Monument. It's five hundred and fifty-five feet high, but it'll never make George Washington that high. He's still the same size he always was, maybe even a little smaller."

"Take Ford's Theatre. Is Lincoln smaller?"

"The Monument was built long after Washington died. He never saw it, and the men that piled up all those stones never saw him, so the whole thing is only a tombstone, five hundred and fifty-five feet high, for a six-foot dead man. But Ford's was built for living people, and Lincoln was living when he sat down in that box, and he was living when Booth sneaked up in back of him and fired that bullet in his brain, and he was still living when they carried him out to the house across the street. He wasn't ever going to see the theatre again, but he'd seen it once, and that was enough to make it different than a stack of stones. They can do anything they like to Ford's, they can turn it into a museum or build more stories on it till it gets to be as high as the Monument, but it'll never be only a tombstone."

"Tell me something, Danny," the man said, and now the boy was looking away. "Would you feel as you do about this town if the place was called Lincoln, D. C. ?"

"No," the boy said. [*You'd only loved your own father like that, not even God or Jesus Christ or the United States, only your own father, and always, for as long as you could remember, you'd hated the man with the derringer and the dagger: it'd been your own father's head that he broke open with that ball, and your own father's eyes that he closed once and for all, and your own father's body that they carried away to the Petersen bedroom, and your own father's blood that soaked the pillows, and your own father that so many people stood watching the whole night long, and your own good father that died in the early morning. You loved one, and you hated the other, and you always would —all your life!*]

* * *

A guide had conducted a party through the rooms at Mt. Vernon, saying, "This was Washington's bed-warmer. . . .This was Washington's study. . . .This was the quill with which he. . . .This was his favorite chair. . . .This was the window at which. . . . In this room, the Father of our country breathed his . . . ," and now the party was touring the grounds. "These were the slave-quarters," the guide said.

A woman said, "The what-quarters?"

"The slave-quarters," the guide said.

"I didn't know Washington had slaves."

"All gentlemen had slaves in those days."

Danny said, "That's what made them gentlemen."

The guide turned away. "This tree was planted by . . . ," he said.

The woman said, "Washington would've been a gentleman even without his slaves."

"Sure," Danny said. "He'd've been like Lincoln."

* * *

"All aboard for Ballamore, Philadelphia, and New York!"

From camp-chairs on the rear platform, Danny and his uncle watched a few stragglers hasten past along the ramp, and soon the buffer, the gates, and the train-shed seemed to drift away, and the trucks of the northbound Congressional began to spin out twin filaments of track, and looking backward in space, the boy looked backward in time as well, and what he saw was another train, a train of seven cars wreathed in black bunting, and in one of these he saw a piece of freight, not a mail-sack or a suitcase or a stenciled crate, but a mahogany box containing a dead passenger, and before the high domes of the locomotive he saw seventeen hundred miles of union earth, the same miles traversed by that passenger four years earlier, but they lay in reverse now, and the last was the first, and the first was the last, and the farms passed, and the ties and towns and telegraph-poles, began with the end and ended with the beginning, and the book of creeks and culverts, of stones and stakes, of seventeen hundred consecrated miles, read from right to left, and the boy saw seven million faces deployed along the ballast from the District of Columbia to the State of Illinois, and there were fires in the night, and the slow-spoken gloom of artillery, and tolling bells, and the heavy farewells of rain-soaked flags, and he saw famous men driven from famous birthplaces to points along the right-of-way, and he saw unknowns who had walked for a week to watch for a moment, and then the funeral-train was gone.

"Ballamore! Ballamore the next!"

CONCERNING SOME DIRTY LINEN

THE Johnson family was nearing the end of a Sunday cold-cut supper. The coffeepot had been brought to the table, and the cinnamon of cinnamon-buns, a scent like that of carnations, rose to mingle with coffee steam. Mrs. Johnson poured. Mr. Johnson smoked. Danny Johnson thought.

"What's on your brain, son?" the hack-driver said.

"Tootsie wants to rent a store next year."

"The trouble with a store, you got to pay rent."

"That's what I told him, but he said we could handle more business and make more money."

"For the landlord," the hack-driver said.

"I told him that too, and he said the landlord wouldn't get all the extra money, and I said he'd get some, and he said some wasn't all. I said some was too much if it was rent, and he said the landlord had to get something for building the building."

"He gets a tablet in the Hall of Fame."

"I said what more did he want than the building, and he said the building was no good unless it was rented, and I said who told him to build it."

"That should've curled him."

"It didn't. He don't curl so easy. He said why should we kick about rent if we made more money with the store than we would've made without the store. I saw I had to crush him, so I said because we had to get down on our knees to make the money to pay the rent. He wasn't crushed at all. He said there was no use biting our nose to spite our knees, and he laughed."

"A bitter laugh," the hack-driver said.

"I said we'd never get rich kneeling for some fat landlord, and all he did was laugh some more."

"He laughs too much. He'll cry yet."

"He didn't when I was around. He only said I was the second-best shoe-shiner in Harlem, but I was a long way from being the second-best thinker."

"Which you took laying down."

"I took it standing up. I said I always thought I was a thinker and a half, and you know what he said to that? He said I was just a Bolsheviki."

"He's a fine one to talk. His father could start a revolution in the College of Cardinals."

"I brang that up. I said if anybody was a Bolsheviki, it was his old man, and he said that didn't mean he could tell the landlord to go to hell for his rent."

"I suppose you crushed him again," the hack-driver said.

"I tried. I said I thought the Bolsheviki didn't believe in landlords."

"But, like you say, he don't crush easy."

"He don't crush at all. He said it didn't make any difference whether you believe in landlords or not. As long as you had them, you either paid rent or you slept in the park."

"That left him open like a door! In Russia, the *landlords* sleep in the park!"

"I brang that up too, but I'm sorry I did."

"Why? How'd he get around it?"

"He said this wasn't Russia."

"What kind of an answer was that?"

"I don't know, but it must've been good."

"What was good about it?" the hack-driver said.

"It crushed *me*," Danny said.

* * *

There was no sugar-sack of coins to be emptied and counted that evening: the boy's share of profits for the second year of his partnership had been entered week by week in a little blue bankbook issued by the Corn Exchange. This lay before him on the table now, its pages partly open, and being only a symbol for cash, itself only a symbol, it seemed as lifeless to him as the paper moth it resembled.

"A hundred and thirty bucks," the hack-driver said. "That's a real stand of alfalfa."

"I must've shone a thousand pairs of shoes," the boy said.

"What're you going to do with all this mazuma?"

"I don't know. Save it, I guess."

"I thought kids wanted all kinds of stuff. Fish-rods. Duds. Things."

"I never go fishing, and I got enough clothes."

"But not enough money!" the hack-driver said. "Not enough money!"

His wife said, "Wait a minute, now."

"Wait, hell! There's a selfish streak in this kid that runs from his scalp to his crotch, and it's stiff enough to hold him together if he breaks his back! He stuck that dough in the bank to stop me from loaning it! I'm wise to him, and I'll be buggered if I like it!"

"How do you know why he banked the money?"

"Ask him!"

"Is Pop right, Danny?"

"Yes," the boy said.

The hack-driver bounced his pipe on the table, flinging coals and ash over the oilcloth, and rising, he looked down at his son and said, "You little piece of cheese!"

The woman herded the dottle into a cupped hand. "If he's a little piece," she said, "then we must be big pieces."

"What kind of crap is that, Polly? Did we *teach* him to be a stinker?"

"No, but I guess we didn't teach him *not* to be."

"We never taught him not to kill, either, but that wouldn't make us responsible if he did. All I know is, all of a sudden I can't stand the sight of my own flesh and blood. I never claimed to be much, but, Christ, nobody can say I'm small about money. People like us've got to know the value of a buck, but I always thought it was a hundred cents, not a hundred and four, like our cheesy son thinks. A buck ain't a buck to him. It's a buck plus interest—and that's something he picked up outside of this big beautiful palace of three rooms and a watercloset."

"I don't blame anybody but myself," the boy said. "I been thinking I was selfish for a long time, and now I'm sure of it."

His mother laughed. "Sit down, Dan," she said to her husband. "I think we can save something out of this wreck."

"I'd sooner stand," the hack-driver said. "If I get mad again, I won't have to jump up. I can holler from here."

"Danny," the woman said, "the hardest thing in the world is to get a person to admit he's wrong. Once he does that, the rest is easy. With you, there's no trouble at all. You realize you've been selfish, and all that remains is to stop."

"And if you can't stop by yourself," the hack-driver said, "I can always help with a paste in the mouth."

"He won't do any pasting," the woman said.

"I know it," the boy said. "He's talking big for Mr. Nobody."

"He won't do any pasting for a very simple reason: the only one who can cure selfishness is the person who's selfish. It can't be done from the outside."

"I've tried to do it from the inside," the boy said, "but it doesn't do any good. You can't get over a thing just by telling yourself it's wrong. Remember that night last summer when we counted the money I made? Well, when I finally went and handed it over, you started to cry, and Pop gave me a wonderful look, like I was the best boy in the world—but I didn't feel that way the next day, and I never felt that way again. I guess if it's hard to admit you're wrong, it's even harder to do anything about it."

"I remember that night very well," the woman said. "You began by wanting to keep the money for yourself, by being selfish, but as soon as you gave it to Pop, that changed—*you* changed."

"I don't see how I could've. If I started out being selfish, that's what I really was, and I didn't get to be different just because I felt sorry."

The woman spoke over her shoulder to her husband, saying, "You can sit down now, Dan. I don't think you're going to get mad any more." She studied the boy for a moment and said, "Never eat your heart out for being human, son. Anybody on earth would've felt as you did—anybody would've hated to give up what he'd worked so hard for. The world being what it is, you only felt what all people would've felt, and I don't want you to blame yourself for it—especially when you came up with the right thing in the end."

The boy said, "You mean if I gave Pop this money now, after first wanting to keep it for myself, I wouldn't be selfish?"

"It's what you do in the end that counts, not what you feel in the beginning."

Danny moved the bankbook across the table until it touched his father's hand. "It's yours," he said.

The hack-driver broke the contact. "Feelings don't count with your mother," he said, "but they count with me. I want to know what kind you'll have tomorrow."

"I don't know," the boy said.

"What kind do you think?"

"I think maybe I'll have a good kind."

"Last year it was a lousy kind."

"I know," the boy said, "but I'm older now."

*   *   *

The woman came from the kitchen with a tray of food. "I thought you men might like a snack before you went to bed. A *shack*, my mother used to say."

"*Shack*," the hack-driver said. "Where'd she get that pronounciation?"

"She had a lot of funny ones. *Fresh* was always *frush*, and *cherry* was always *churry*, and *spinach* was always *spinit*, and her heart, as she described it, *thobbed and thobbed*."

Danny helped himself to a wedge of cake brought home from a party at Tootsie's that afternoon. "I used to say *dicktective*."

The hack-driver said, "I was twenty years finding out about the *pot* in *depot*."

"My mother used to call Web a *runnygate*," the woman said. "And he was going to wind up bad because he did too much *sky-gacking*."

"What's *sky-gacking?*" Danny said.

"Stargazing. You're a sky-gacker yourself."

"I guess I'm going to wind up bad."

"Well, you're getting off with a headstart," the hack-driver said. "You're broke."

"A person doesn't have to wind up bad because he sets out poor," the woman said. "Look at Lincoln."

"You look. I'm busy watching everybody else that was born in a log-cabin, because they're going to die there too. Me, I had poverty when I was a kid, and I never got cured."

"But you're not winding up bad," the woman said.

"No?" the hack-driver said. "What do you call this?" He took his eyes on a sight-seeing tour of the room, pausing here and there at points of interest: an oak sideboard tattooed with circular soaks of ink; a buckhorn hatrack; four stuttering chairs left from a silent set of six; an engraving of *The Horse Fair*, now foxed; a row of giltless books; a waffled couch that for ten years had served as a boy's bed; and a map of the United States. "I suppose this is good," he said.

"Rich and good don't mean the same thing."

"They do if you're poor," the hack-driver said, and he laughed without laughter. "Remember what you said, Polly? 'Let's start the kid off with nothing and see how far he gets. I got my heart set on seeing how far he gets with nothing.' Well, you're going to have your wish."

"I still want it," the woman said.

"And after fifteen years, I still ask why."

"A person can't be honest if he has money."

"You mean you wanted me to be broke all my life so's this bed-wetter could be another Washington?"

"Washington wasn't so honest," Danny said. "He told the truth about the cherry-tree because he got caught with his pants down. A person isn't really honest unless he tells the truth with his pants up."

"And if you're rich," the woman said, "your pants're always down."

"That's what has me up a stump," the hack-driver said. "Why can't a rich man be honest? There ain't no law against it. Every millionaire can't be a crook, and every poor slob can't be a Boy Pioneer. I don't see what money's got to do with it."

"Do you, Danny?" the woman said.

The boy said, "The two times I had money, I turned out to be a weasel."

The woman looked at her husband and then at the occupant of the fourth chair, Mr. Nobody. "My old man thinks you can be rich but honest," she said.

"Leave Mr. Nobody out of it," the hack-driver said. "There's no such thing as money in the world he lives in. He don't pay no rent, he don't eat, he never gets sick, and he's tax-exempt. Where I sit, it's different. I work for a living, and all I got to show for it is a wife that's still kind of cute, a son that's honest but goofy, and two bucks worth of furniture—but day in and day out I have to listen to how sinful it is to be rich. Christ, let me be a sinner for a change! I'm tired of seeing how far I can get with nothing! I know the answer by heart—nowheres!"

"You got further than you'll ever know, you fool, and Danny'll get even further."

"When I was his age," the hack-driver said, "I could take apart any machine ever put together, and I could stick it all back and make it factory-new, and I could even add a little something that the factory never thought of. I used to look forward to making a mark with that knack, but all that happened to me was an assful of bunions, and it'll happen to anybody unless he's another Abe Lincoln. I've got all kinds of respect for Danny, but I have to say that Abe's still safe, and what sank me is going to sink my son: money. He's going to need it for his own kids some day, and he's going to need it for a couple of broken-down parents, just like I did, and he's going to have to go out and pick it where it grows—in somebody else's backyard. He's going to have to work for the future and the past at the same time, one pulling him ahead and the other pulling him back, and he'll be stopped cold, like I was. I ain't sore at nobody for that. I'm only reading it like it's wrote."

" I'm starting to get mighty sore at *money*," Danny said.

NO COPPISH

THIRTY-ODD heads were bowed over thirty-odd papers, on each of which a representation of a paramecium was taking shape. The model that thirty-odd hands were engaged in copying was printed on a chart hanging from the blackboard of the Biology Lab., and thirty-odd boys (from Aaronson to Zachary) were drawing thirty-odd pictures, all of them different. The one that Danny Johnson was endeavoring to grow hair on resembled the island of Manhattan: it was long, like the strip of land, and narrowing toward some protozoan Spuyten Duyvil; its nucleus, dark and almost square, was Central Park; and like the docks in the rivers, its cilia stood on end.

The three-o'clock bell rang, a monitor collected the papers for Dr. McElroy, and the class was dismissed. When Danny left the building, he headed not for 59th Street with the converging run of boys, but for the quiet brownstone block to the south, a block of five-story walk-ups trimmed at the street-level with brass piping that curved into and out of each vestibule. Halfway between Tenth and Ninth Avenues, he stopped to wait for Miss Juno Forrest.

The sky was chalked like the window of a vacant store, and a damp east wind opened sheets of newspaper, turned the pages, and flung them away west along the gutter. There was snow in the air, an early-winter snow, and when it fell, it would fall as transient slush. Danny watched a boy coming toward him from Ninth Avenue. The boy was flogging each section of the brass rail with the bones of a broken umbrella, and skipping the one that Danny was leaning against, he resumed his musicmaking on the section beyond. Danny turned to watch him go, and from Tenth Avenue, her head down in the wind, came Miss Forrest.

"Hello," Danny said, and he joined her.

"Hello," she said. "I didn't think you'd be here."

"Oh, I'm always here. Even when you're not."

"I thought you'd find it too cold today."

"I like the cold."

"What's that paper sticking out of your book?"

"This?" Danny said, touching a green throwaway. "A guy gave it to me in the lunch room. Mig DeLuca, his name is. An Italian. There's going to be a meeting where two of his people are the speakers."

"Do you remember their names?"

"One is called Sacco. I forget the other."

"Vanzetti?" the teacher said.

"Something like that."

"You couldn't've read the paper very carefully. Sacco and Vanzetti are in jail in Massachusetts. The meeting is probably being held for their benefit."

"What're they in jail for?" Danny said.

"They killed somebody and stole a lot of money."

"Why is the meeting for their benefit, then?"

"Some people don't believe they're guilty. They say they didn't have a fair trial."

"Are you one of those people?"

"No," the teacher said. "Are you?"

"I never heard of Sacco and Vanzetti before, but I know Mig DeLuca, and he wouldn't be for anybody that stole."

"Sacco and Vanzetti are anarchists."

"What's an anarchist?"

"A person who doesn't believe in government."

"What *does* he believe in?"

"In being *without* a government."

"Without a *particular* government?" Danny said.

"Without *all* government—good or bad, democratic or autocratic."

"Why doesn't an anarchist want any government?"

"He thinks people can govern themselves."

"That isn't such a terrible thing to think."

"No one has a right to think what's wrong."

"I thought you had a right to think anything."

"Not if you think it with a gun in your hand. These two Italians stood for the abolition of government, but when they went out to kill and steal, they proved that they needed government more than anybody else, and the Court sent them to jail."

"For doing bad things or for being anarchists?"

"I don't believe that's very important."

"I do. I think it's the *only* thing that's important. I think you have to know if the Court hated bad things, or if it only hated anarchists, like you do."

"What difference would that make?"

"I'm not sure, but I think it would make the difference between justice and unjustice."

"That sounds very farfetched to me."

"Maybe it is," Danny said. "I better go to that meeting and find out."

They were nearing the teacher's house now, and now they were standing on the sidewalk before the glass doors, and now they looked at each other for a moment, and now they said, "Good afternoon," and turned away, the woman to the gray building and the boy to the gray street, and now the first of the snow began to fall.

WHEN CLINTON WAS THE GOVERNOR

IN the gutters, black mounds of snow melted under the spring sun, some of them crumbling to reveal their white cores, but Danny, waiting for Miss Forrest in the hothouse air, felt grown by it, felt expanded instead of shrunk, and absorbing warmth among the ruins of winter, he knew (without knowing why) that it was a day to be remembered, and for remembrance he put away images of sparrows on the swarthy sherbet, of a cat lionizing itself, of a dog ambushing its own tail, of people who came from houses as if from hiding, and he would remember too that it was a day when sound seemed to live long and travel far.

[*It was a day when Mig DeLuca had said,"It's a hell of a day for my people to be in jail. We have their pictures on the wall in my house, and every night my father drinks a glass of wine to them, and my mother bows her head and cries, and when I go to bed, sometimes I cry too, because I know that drinking wine and bowing the head and writing letters to the Governor will not save my people.*"]

And now Miss Forrest was saying, "Come down to earth, Danny."

IN EIGHTEEN TWENTY-FOUR

"IT was a hundred years ago," Danny said.

"What was?" Miss Forrest said.

"When Clinton was the Governor."

"A long time—a hundred years."

"It isn't so long, now that they're over. Sometimes a day is long, but that's only while it's going on. When tomorrow comes, the thing we called today never seems long or short: it's just gone."

"It's only the young who have no past."

"You're young," Danny said.

The woman laughed. "Nothing looks old on a day like this, not even a teacher." 10 75 .325

A day of hot sun and sparkle. A day of shimmer over asphalt and clouds like laundry on a line. A day of slow-motion, of objects barely avoiding obstacles, as sticks pass stones in a stream.

"I don't mean you're as young as I am," Danny said. "But a person can be older than me and still be young."

"How old are your parents?" the teacher said.

"About the same age as you, I guess."

"Do you think *they're* young?"

"Not specially," the boy said.

"Then why do you say *I* am?"

"Because you're not related to me—but don't ask me to explain that. I couldn't."

"Maybe I make you feel older," the teacher said.

Danny looked at her. "I never would've thought of that," he said.

DO YOU KNOW DR. DAHLGREN?

"QUITE well," Miss Forrest said. "Why?"

"He owns a camp in the Adirondack Mountains," Danny said, "and every summer he picks ten boys from Clinton to go up there and be waiters on the table, and he pays them a hundred dollars a season, and they're allowed to keep the tips they get from the councillors and the parents. The camp is called Camp Clintonia, and it's on Schroon Lake in the Adirondack Mountains." The teacher took the boy's arm as they crossed Broadway, but she did not release it when they reached the curb. "I've got a chance to be one of the waiters. I'm pretty good in Doc Dahlgren's subject—you got to have 85 or better to be eligible—and now all I need is a letter of recommendation from somebody on the Faculty."

"If you get the job, you'll be away all summer," the teacher said. "From your family."

"It'll only be two months."

"Two months is a long time."

"Remember what we were talking about?" Danny said. "A time is never long when it's over."

"I know, but it takes a long time to be over," the teacher said. "What would you want me to say in the letter?"

The boy shrugged. "I never got recommended before," he said.

"I'll do what I can," the teacher said. "but on one condition— that you write to your folks at least once a week. They'll miss you."

"That's an easy condition, but I'll write because *I* miss *them*. It's the person that does the missing that ought to write."

After a little way, the teacher said, "Yes," but she spoke the word softly, and she thought it went unheard.

THIS SIDE OF CARD IS FOR ADDRESS

ON the rear car of a North Creek local, Danny stood with his elbows in the angles of the collapsible gate and watched the city of Albany slide away on a treadmill of track and ties. ["*I'm sorry I didn't get to see you yesterday, like I promised, but I had a lot*

*of things to do, and when I got finished, it was too late, and then when
I tried to phone you this morning from Grand Central, I couldn't find
your name in the book. So I will just have to write what I would've
told you if I saw you—that I hope you have as good of a vacation as
you got for me. I'm only away for four hours, but I miss you already.
I guess two months is longer than I thought. . . ."*] And now Albany
(with the State Building, the Day Line docks, the people and trees
and trolley-cars, and a penny postal lying in a mailbox at the D & H
depot) was gone.

WAITERS ARE THE SMARTEST PEOPLE

T HE lake at dawn was slick under a fleece of mist, but now and
then a trout briefly puckered the surface, or a kingfisher plung-
ed, and these were the first moves of the day, and then came a wind,
woolgathering, and squirrels stuttered in the copper beeches, and
and the bills of woodpeckers uttered Morse, and now a bugle-call
answered itself from across the lake, and now boys' voices were on
the warming air, a multiple sound with a single tone, as from a
swarm of birds, and the day began.

[*"Say, Al,"* you said, *"could I talk to you for a minute?"*]

[*He said, "Councillors are called Mister at Clintonia."*]

[*"Okay,"* you said. *"I'd like to talk to you for a minute, Mr.
Nicholson."*]

[*"Get it over with, Johnson. I'm in a hurry."*]

[*"It's about the Mess Hall rules. Breakfast is served from eight to
nine, and the guys at your table never show up till eight-fifty."*]

[*"What about it?"*]

[*"Well, coming in that late, they don't get done till ten, and us
waiters kind of count on the time between meals."*]

[*"I didn't think waiters counted."*]

[*"It's the only chance we have for hikes and fishing—things like
that."*]

[*"Things like that,"* he said. *"Answer me something, will you? Do
you pay the camp, or does the camp pay you?"*]

[*"The camp pays me, but it pays you too, so we ought to be on the
same side."*]

["*Whatever side you're on, I'm on the opposite. I'm a councillor, and you're a waiter, and I'll thank you to keep your place!*"]

["*If I knew you felt that way, I wouldn't've spoke to you, but as long as I did, I might as well finish: come in earlier for breakfast, or you'll still be waiting for it when supper rolls around. I can stall too, you know.*"]

["*We start that game tomorrow,*" *he said.* "*Look for me at one minute to nine.*"]

The lake caught whispers of wind, and sun-sequins flashed, and leaves clapped hands, and shadows shortened toward shadowless noon.

[*The kid said,* "*I want to use the handball court.*"]

["*Wait till we finish our game,*" *you said.*]

["*Waiting is only for waiters.*"]

["*But you're all alone. You got nobody to play with.*"]

["*I'm going to practice for the tournament, and I want the court.*"]

["*The waiters have a right to use it too.*"]

["*Not when a camper's around. Ask Dr. Dahlgren.*"]

["*Look,*" *you said.* "*This is a challenge-game.*"]

["*I'm only going to ask you three times more, and then I'm going to tell Dr. Dahlgren.*"]

["*Why do you have to be such a stinker?*"]

["*Now I'm not even going to ask three more times.*"]

["*Ah, Christ,*" *you said,* "*take the court and break your ass!*"]

Bats whacked balls, and balls whacked mitts, and there were thrashing arms and running feet, and reels unwound and whined, and keels gave passing patterns to the water, impermanent waves, and shadows grew slowly eastward.

["*I been looking for you, Jerry,*" *you said.* "*I wanted to tell you about that tray of dishes I busted yesterday. They fined me a buck for it.*"]

["*That's tough,*" *he said,* "*but why tell me?*"]

["*I tripped on your foot.*"]

["*You should've kept your eyes open.*"]

["*You should've kept your hoof out of the aisle.*"]

["*Where do you expect me to put it?*"]

[*"Under the table, where it belongs."*

[*"I'll put it wherever I feel like," he said.*

[*"Do that," you said, "but next time I find it in the aisle, I'm going to reach down and snap it right off your leg."*

[*"Say, you're talking to a camper!"*]

The sun was low now, and shade sprang from pebbles, and blades of grass were shorter than their own silhouettes, and thrushes played flourishes on flutes, and fireflies flew on and off, and against the trees on the far shore a single light came on. 25 72 .285

[*It was your turn to wait on the waiters, and when you got to the dessert, you slapped a tray down on the bakery-counter, saying, "Ten big portions for the proletariat."*

[*The bake-chef shoved a pie-tin at you, and he said, "Cut it ten ways."*

[*"Half a pie for ten working-stiffs!" you said. "Nix on that!"*

[*"Nix is nix," he said.*

[*"Why, I could eat half a pie singlehanded! I could eat the tin and all!"*

[*"Don't eat the tin," he said.*

[*"Why do campers get seconds when waiters don't even get firsts?" you said.*

[*He laughed, saying, "You ain't organized."*]

In a circus of brightened faces, a campfire burned on the beach, and songs were sung to the calisthenic flames, and now and then, when a figure passed between the light and the lake, a giant shadow strode over the water, and after a time the fire-hour ended, and the faces withdrew, leaving only a stadium of stones to ring the embers.

*　　*　　*

"That bake-chef was only trying to be funny," Danny said, "but when you come right down to it, a Waiters' Union wouldn't be such a bad idea."

In a pine-grove near the boathouse, the ten waiters of Camp Clintonia were bedded down in needles.

"My father don't like unions," Vic Sabin said.

"When we signed up with Doc Dahlgren," Danny said, "he

told us we'd get treated like regular campers, but if that's what this is, all I can say is I'm losing weight on it."

"My father says if you want to stay out of trouble, stay out of unions."

"If you ask me, your father sounds like a Boss," Danny said. "Doc promised we could use the camp facilities just like anybody else, but as far as I can see, that only holds good for the toilets. We start to play handball, and we're right in the middle of a champeenship game, and any snot-nose Junior can kick us off. We're out in a rowboat, and even a Midget can holler he wants it, and we got to come in. We get docked a quarter for every busted two-cent plate, no matter who busts it, and we don't sit down to eat till every regular camper is full as a banana. Christ!"

"How about the rest of it?" Earl Sultan said. "How about that hundred bucks we was supposed to get at the end of the summer? When we took the job, Doc never said nothing about we had to pay our own railroad-fare, and now all of a sudden we get charged fourteen smackers to ride to work!"

Pete Swann said, "The minute that train pulled out of Grand Central, we couldn't possibly make more than eighty-six bucks apiece, but that don't get my ass out nearly as much as being stuck for our laundry-bill. Two bucks a week times eight: there's another sixteen we can pull the chain on!"

"Fourteen and sixteen is thirty," Marty Solomon said, "but the way things're going, we won't even make the seventy that's left. Breakage is good for a buck and a half a week. Figure fifteen for the season."

"That leaves fifty-five," Joe Geiger said, "but peel off the price of bus-rides to Pottersville in the camp bus, and wear and tear on our uniforms. That's good for another sawbuck."

"It's only forty-five now," Ed Oliver said.

"It ain't over yet," Solly Fishman said. "Take a buck off for the camp paper."

"Take off another for the camp show," Stan Vogel said, "and two more for insurance."

"And two more for meals on the train," Wally Willard said.

"Thirty-nine bucks!" Danny said. "But you ca[n] odds it'll get less and less. When Doc signed us on, well we'd land in New York without a cent."

"What about tips?" Vic Sabin said.

"Tips!" Danny said.

"*What* tips?" Marty Solomon said.

"There ain't no such word," Ed Oliver said.

"Tips!" Danny said. "I'm bowlegged from waiting on parents and guests, and I swear to God I ain't collected a nickel from them in four weeks!"

"That's funny," Vic Sabin said. "I'm in fifteen bills so far, and I'm going to triple that before I'm done."

"No wonder you don't want a union," Danny said. "You might have to cough up some of that dough for dues."

"Damn right," Earl Sultan said. "I think we ought to get up a committee."

"But supposing Doc tells the committee to cop itself a walk," Vic Sabin said.

"It'll cop a long one, then," Danny said. "We'll go out on strike, all the way to Pottersville, and while we're eating sodas at Griswold's, the whole damn camp can starve. I say we ought to stand up on our rights!"

"I'm in favor," Pete Swann said.

"Second the motion," Joe Geiger said.

"All those for having a union, say 'aye,'" Danny said, and there were ten 'ayes,' nine strong and one weak. "The Waiters' Union of Camp Clintonia is formed. Now we get up a committee."

"I nominate Danny Johnson," Vic Sabin said.

"I second the motion," Wally Willard said.

"I move nominations be closed," Vic Sabin said.

*   *   *

"Dr. Dahlgren," Danny said, "the Waiters' Union elected me to be a committee to talk to you about some of the camp rules."

"When was the union formed?" Dr. Dahlgren said.

"A few minutes ago. The rules us waiters don't like are the ones that take away the money you promised us before we came up here.

We all expected to make a hundred dollars salary and whatever we collected in tips. Only one of us has got any tips so far, but that isn't your fault, and we don't blame you for it: you can't help it if the parents're a bunch of cheapskates. But you made the rules, and it's the rules that take away our salary little by little, and we can't afford it."

"Who suggested that the waiters form a union?"

"I did. The way we figure, none of us can make more than thirty-nine dollars out of the hundred you promised, and we don't think that's fair. For instance, it isn't fair to charge us for our railroad-tickets after saying we'd be treated like regular campers, and there's other things that aren't fair, either, like charging us for dishes that the campers break, and for laundry, and for rides in the camp bus. All those things add up to a lot of money, to sixty-one dollars and maybe more, and it isn't fair."

Dr. Dahlgren took a ledger from a shelf above his desk, opened it at one of the projecting tabs, and totaled a few figures, "You've earned forty-six dollars so far, Johnson," he said, "and the charges against you come to forty. . . ."

"Forty!" Danny said. "What for?"

"Forty," Dr. Dahlgren said, and taking two bills from a tin box in his top drawer, he laid them on the ledger and turned it to face Danny. "Sign there," he said, pointing.

Danny signed *D. Johnson* near the man's fingernail.

"Now, put that money in your pocket," the man said.

Danny stored the bills in a wallet of imitation alligator.

The man referred to his wrist-watch and then looked at Danny. "You have exactly one hour in which to pack your things and get off the grounds," he said. "You're fired."

"Do you know what you are, Dr. Dahlgren?" Danny said. "You're a crook."

"Get out of here, you dirty little bastard!"

* * *

". . .We had it arranged that when I got done talking to Doc Dahlgren, I should meet the waiters back in the pine-grove and tell them what happened. I went straight down there and give them my report, and then I said all those in favor of going out on strike should raise their right hand. Only one hand went up, and it was mine."

"The stinken finks!" the hack-driver said. "What did you do…?"

*   *   *

"…What *could* I do, Miss Forrest? I packed my stuff and got out."

In the teacher's parlor, the window was open wide, and the blind, drawn to within an inch of the sill, hung still. Through the slit, a sliver of green park could be seen, with a figure or two lying in the greener shade, and a few cars, snarling over the soft asphalt, could be heard.

"Did Dr. Dahlgren give you a return-ticket?"

"I asked him, but he only called me a bastard again."

"How did you get back to the city?"

"I went out on the road and got hitches."

"It was nice of you to write to me so often."

"I was hoping you'd answer, but after a while I realized you must've went away somewhere."

"I was at a hotel on Lake George."

"Why, that's right near Pottersville! You should've let me know, and I would've come to see you on my days off."

"Your letters told me what you were doing."

"My letters? But you didn't get those till you got home."

"I had them forwarded."

"I never knew you could do that. What did you think when you got the one about me being kicked out for an anarchist? I wrote it from Saratoga."

"It came yesterday. Just before I checked out of the hotel."

"I hope *you* weren't kicked out for an anarchist."

"I was tired of the place."

"It's lucky I happened to drop around this afternoon," the boy said. "I wouldn't've known you were home."

"It's very lucky," the teacher said, and she turned away to stare at the bright and quivering strip of park. "What do you plan to do for the rest of the summer … ?"

*   *   *

"...Well, being as how I'm such an anarchist, Mig, I thought I'd look you up and see if I could do something to help Mr. Sacco and Mr. Vanzetti."

"You know what a mimeograph-machine is?" Mig said.

"I never even heard of one."

"You've heard of a crank, though."

"Sure," Danny said, and he grinned."A crank is an anarchist."

"You're going to turn one for a couple of wops."

A COUPLE OF WOPS

TACKED on the wall above the mimeograph-machines were two faces in rotogravure, the faces of Nicola Sacco and Bartolomeo Vanzetti, both of them smiling down at Danny as he wound one of the stencil-drums and ground out a growing stack of throwaways. The apparatus clicked and clinked and clanked, but its sounds were almost smothered by the pounding of presses that filled an acre of loft. Ink had stained the boy's hands and apron, and his head, where he had swabbed off sweat, wore black swipes, but he knew they were there, and occasionally, when he glanced along the table at Mig DeLuca, he winked a blackened eye. Always, however, his gaze would return to the two faces before him, and always it would momentarily fall to a third one, plastered below the others in a slash of paste, and always then the rollers of his machine would suddenly seem to say *thayer thayer webster thayer*.

At five o'clock in the afternoon, Mig DeLuca said,"Okay, Mr. Anarchist, you can quit now."

Danny said, "No coppish," and kept on cranking.

Mig approached him with a newspaper-clipping and said,"Listen to this, kid."

I could see the best man, intelligent, education, they been arrested and sent to prison and died in prison for years and years without getting them out, and Debs, one of the great men in his country, he is in prison, still away in prison, because he is a socialist. He wanted the laboring class to have better conditions and better living, more education, give a push his son if he could have a chance some day, but they put him in prison. Why? Because the capitalist class, they know, they are against that.

"Vanzetti?" Danny said.
And Mig said, "Sacco."

I love people who labor and work and see better conditions every day develop, makes no more war. We no want fight by the gun, and we don't want to destroy young men. The mother been suffering for building the young man. Some day need a little more bread, so when the time the mother get some bread or profit out of that boy, the Rockefellers, Morgans, and some of the peoples, high class, they send to war. Why? What is war? The war is not shoots like Abraham Lincoln's and Abe Jefferson, to fight for the free country, for the better education, to give chance to any other peoples, not the white people but the black and the others, because they believe and know they are mens like the rest, but they are war for the great millionaire. No war for the civilization of men. They are war for business, million dollars come on the side. What right we have to kill each other? I been work for the Irish, I have been working with the German fellow, with the French, many other peoples. I love them people just as I could love my wife, and my people for that did receive me. Why should I go kill them men? What he done to me? He never done anything, so I don't believe in no war. I want to destroy those guns. . . .

Mig broke off reading, and Danny did not have to turn to learn why. Instead, he studied the trio of likenesses on the wall, and after a moment, over the running-down presses, he heard his friend say, "I'd sooner be a shoemaker or a fish-peddler in prison than have a face like yours and be a Judge and a free man. I'd sooner die looking alive than live looking dead, and, oh Jesus, if I could only speak their wonderful wonderful words . . . !"

A SHORT WALK ON A FALL AFTERNOON

"You weren't at the usual place yesterday," Miss Forrest said.

"I had to go right uptown," Danny said. "There was a birth-day-party."

"Whose?" the teacher said.

"Somebody that lives next door."

"Do I know the boy?"

"It was a girl. Harriet Bryant."

The teacher said, "Oh," and then said nothing, and they reached her house after a long silent block.

"Did you read the pamphlet I gave you the other day?" Danny said as they stood for a moment in the backslapping wind.

"I did, and I found it pretty one-sided."

"Why was it one-sided?"

"It looks at the case from only one point of view."

"How many point of views does it have to have?"

"To be convincing, it should've been impartial."

"The man that wrote it was just the opposite."

"I know he was, and that's why what he wrote was unconvincing."

"Well, if I had to be convinced, it would've convinced me."

"Possibly, but *I'm* the one who had to be convinced, and I wasn't. The pamphlet was prejudiced."

"But, Miss Forrest, *you're* prejudiced. How could the pamphlet convince you unless *it* was prejudiced?"

"Was it a nice party?" the teacher said.

"It was all right, I guess," the boy said.

DEPENDS ON WHAT BOOKS YOU READ

Danny and Mig DeLuca walked along Central Park past the side-streets of Yorkville. Overhead there was a flurry of stars and underfoot a new and almost untrodden snow, a winter coat that seemed to have been grown by the ground.

"You ever hear of Tom Mooney?" Mig said. "The Mooney case?"

"No," Danny said. "Is it a case I ought to know about?"

Mig shaved a hackle of snow from the back of a bench. "In 1916," he said, "before we got in the war, there was a Preparedness Day parade in San Francisco. In the middle of the crowd, a bomb went off and killed ten people. The police arrested Tom Mooney and Warren Billings, saying they'd fixed the bomb to go off at a certain time and left it in a satchel on the sidewalk. Mooney and Billings said the whole thing was a frame-up to give Labor a black eye for not wanting America to get mixed up in the war." Mig spat, and his spit sank into the snow. "Who do you think was telling the truth . . . ?"

*   *   *

Mounds of snow, soiled public linen, lay along the gutters, but the damp air was turning cold, and soon more snow would fall and the city would put on a clean shirt over its dirty underwear.

Mig said, "If you were standing on the gallows with a rope around your neck, do you think you'd say, 'This is the happiest moment of my life'?"

"Not if I was innocent," Danny said. "And I guess not even if I was guilty. I won't ever be happy to die."

"There's a place in Chicago called Haymarket Square," Mig said. "In 1886, some workers were holding a meeting there to complain about the police beating and shooting strikers at the factory where they made the McCormick harvester. The meeting was about to break up when along came the police to make it break up faster. The workers had a few pistols, though (they were tough in those days), and the police got a dose of their own medicine. While the battle was going on, somebody heaved a bomb, and a police-sergeant got blown out from under his hat. A whole bunch of labor-organizers were arrested and tried and sentenced to be hung."

"Did one of them really say that about the happiest moment of his life?"

"His name was Adolf Fischer."

"It was a brave thing," Danny said. "It was so brave that he must've been innocent."

"How do you know that?"

"A man as brave as Fischer would've been brave enough to admit he was guilty."

Mig said, "You're learning, kid."

*　　*　　*

The snows, both new and old, had gone down the drains, and now it was the season of vaporous rains that fell slowly, as if fine-sprayed, and with them on the west wind from the plains came the wet-earth smell of spring. 18 73 .291

Mig said, "Are you against slavery?"

"That's a dumb one," Danny said. "Sure, I am."

"Suppose you were living before the Civil War."

"I'd've been against it any time."

"What about if you were a preacher?"

"Then I'd've been specially against it."

"In a slave-state, though—Missouri, say."

"That wouldn't've stopped me."

"You were a preacher, and you owned a newspaper."

"I'd've written things against slavery. Like *Uncle Tom's Cabin.*"

"Suppose the slave-owners got a mob together, and they broke up your press."

"If I had enough money, I'd've bought me another."

"Suppose the mob came and dumped that one in the Mississippi."

"I'd've fished it out or bought me a third."

"You bought it, and the same thing happened all over again."

"I'd've got so sore I couldn't see straight."

"That's a little too sore, kid."

"Well, anyhow, sore enough to get another press, God damn it!"

"That's better. You're on your fourth press now."

"If my money held out, I'd've bought forty."

"It isn't holding out. You've got that fourth press, and you're printing your paper on it, and you get the tip that the mob is coming again, and you can only save the press if you move it across the river to a free-state—Illinois."

"I'd've moved it, but all the way over in the boat, I'd've wrote another article against slavery."

"You set the press up in a warehouse over there, and you get word that the mob decided to follow you. Now, what?"

"I can't answer that till I know if I would've had any money left by that time."

"You have some. A few bucks, maybe."

"That's enough," Danny said. "I would've bought me a nice long gun."

"All right," Mig said. "So you're in that warehouse with your gun, and the mob is outside, trying to get in and break up the press—the fourth press."

"You know what I'd've done?" Danny said.

"No," Mig said. "That's why I'm asking."

"I'd've plugged the first son-of-a-bitch I could draw a bead on!"

Mig put his arms around Danny and hugged him. "Kid," he said, "if you did all that, you'd've been just like Elijah Lovejoy!"

"Who was Elijah Lovejoy?"

"That preacher we were just supposing. Only he wound up getting shot dead that night, Danny."

*   *   *

Mig and Danny lay on a lawn in Riverside Park, looking up at the sky of a spring afternoon.

"Jesus Christ!" Danny said.

"What're you christing, kid?" Mig said.

"What the hell kind of a country do we live in?"

"A big swell country, kid—rivers, and trees, and mountains, and railroads, and farms, and fine houses. A big swell country."

"Sure, but who owns it all?"

"Don't you know?" Mig said. "The people."

"The people!" Danny said. "The people don't have enough of it to get buried in!"

"They own all of it, from here to Golden Gate."

"You're out of your mind, Mig."

"I didn't say they *had* it, kid. I said they *owned* it."

RIDING ON A PONY

"WELL, Danny," Miss Forrest said when she reached their meeting-place, "it's no more pencils and no more books till next September," and then she looked away along the brownstone street. "I wonder how you'll feel a year from now, when it's no more pencils and no more books for good."

"I wonder too," Danny said.

[*When the bell rang to end the exam, Mr. Holloway came right to your desk, saying, "I'll take your papers, Johnson."*

[*You said, "I have to put them in order."*

[*"Never mind that," he said, "They're in good enough order as they are."*

[*"But you won't be able to understand them."*

[*"Don't worry about what I'll understand. Just hand over those papers."*

[*"I need time to fix them," you said.*

[*"I'm sure you do, but hand them over all the same."*

[*"Please, Mr. Holloway," you said. "I'll only take a second."*

[*"GIVE ME YOUR PAPERS, JOHNSON!" he said.*

[*"I won't!" you said, and you tore them up and stuffed the pieces in your pocket.*]

"Miss Forrest," Danny said, "would you keep on liking me if you knew I did a rotten thing?"

The woman's reply was inexact and late. "I like you a very great deal," she said.

"I cheated on the English final. . . ."

*   *   *

". . . Do you feel bad because you were caught?" Miss Forrest said. "Or because you cheated?"

"I don't know," Danny said. "It's the first time I ever cheated and the first time I ever got caught."

"Mr. Holloway caught you at the end of the exam. How did you feel at the beginning, when you took the pony out of your pocket and slipped it among your papers?"

"I didn't notice any kind of a feeling."

"How did you feel while you were using the pony? How did you feel as you went through question after question, copying down the answers? How did you feel all the way up to one instant before you were caught?"

"I didn't pay much attention to my feelings. I was too busy copying."

"In other words, your 'rotten feeling' came only after you were caught."

"Yes, but that don't mean I had it *because* I was caught. Getting caught might've made me feel rotten about the cheating all the way back to the first question."

"I'm sorry, Danny," the woman said, "but your regret came too late to be genuine."

"How can regret come early?" Danny said. "You'd have to regret a rotten thing before you did it, and that's impossible. You've got to do the thing before you can feel rotten about it, and once you've done it, your regret can come the next minute, or the next year, or just before you die, but no matter when, it can still be honest. You think I only regret being caught, but I regret the cheating too, or I never would've told you about it. Cheating is a mean thing, and people oughtn't to do mean things, but sometimes they *do* do them, not just mean people, but even decent people, and afterwards they feel rotten about it, and I say it's wrong to tell them they're Humpty-Dumpties, and it's too late to make them like they were before. People aren't Humpty-Dumpties! They're people!"

The woman put her hand on the boy's arm, and when he stopped, she put her mouth on his mouth [*and you weren't ashamed, because all at once the people on the street seemed to disappear, leaving only you and Miss Forrest between buildings that were blind, and long after she'd taken her mouth away, you felt it touching you—cool, soft, damp, and moving a little*].

"I'm glad you still like me," he said. . . .

*   *   *

". . . Nothing you can say will do you any good, Johnson," Mr. Holloway said.

"I only want you to listen," Danny said. "It doesn't have to do me any good."

"I gave you a flunk for the term, and I entered the mark on your school-record. That mark will not be changed. Now, what've you got to say?"

"I came here to tell you why I tore up my exam-paper. I tore it up because I had a pony in it. . . ."

"Do you think that's a secret?" Mr. Holloway said. "I saw you take out that pony before the exam was a moment old."

Danny rose, staring. "You saw it before I had a chance to use it?" he said.

"Of course I did. Teachers aren't quite as stupid as you kids seem to think." Danny turned away and started for the door. "Is that all you have to say, Johnson?"

With his hand on the knob, the boy looked back. "It's all I have to say to *you*, Mr. Holloway," he said.

"You stand right there! What do you mean by that remark?"

"When I made up my mind to come and see you, I thought I'd be talking to a human being, but I know now that you're not. You proved it when you said you were wise to the pony from the start: you saw me take it out, and you knew I was going to cheat with it, but instead of stopping me then, you let me go ahead. You didn't care about keeping me from being a cheat, you only cared about catching me at it, and that makes you like a law in a lawbook, Mr. Holloway—you only care about the punishment, not the criminals." He opened the door and went away.

FOR A REDRESS OF GRIEVANCES

ON 34th Street, opposite the Waldorf, Danny stood near the curb outside the pedestrian current. In his hand, he held several sheets of paper fastened to a square of stiff cardboard, from a notched corner of which hung a pencil-stub on a string. "Sign your petition!" he was saying. "Sign your petition!"

[*The Boss said*, "*Why do you want the job?*"

["*I need it*," *you said.*

[*"Is it only the salary you're after?"*

[*"I could get other jobs, and I could get more pay, but I need this job more than I need the money, and I wish to Christ you'd tell me where to hang up my cap."*

[*"Why do you keep saying you need this particular job?"*

[*"I think they're innocent," you said.*

[*"I think so too," he said. "I've thought so for five years."*

[*"And if people are innocent, they oughtn't to be in jail."*

[*"I've thought that for longer than five years."*

[*"Do I get the job?" you said.*

[*"Not yet. What does your father do for a living?"*

[*"He's a cab-driver."*

[*"What do you expect to be?"*

[*"I don't know. I had some ambition up to a week ago, but I got caught cheating on an English exam, and now I'm not so sure any more."*

[*"Aren't you ashamed to make such an admission?"*

[*"No. I'm only ashamed of the cheating."*

[*He said, "Do you think Sacco and Vanzetti would want a cheat to help them go free?"*

[*"Why not?" you said. "A whole slew of cheats locked them up."*]

"Sign here! Sign your petition!"

In front of Hearn's, Danny watched a woman come toward him with several bundles on one arm and trying with the other to prevent a little boy from wandering away into the 14th Street forest of legs. The woman came up to Danny and stopped, saying, "Would you hold these bundles for me?" and when he took them, she drew a handkerchief from her purse and muzzled her son with it. "Blow, honey," she said, and the little boy blew. "Blow harder, honey." The little boy blew harder. "Oh, that's not blowing at all," she said, and the little boy gathered himself together and blew from his shoes. "That's a good boy," she said, and she accepted the bundles from Danny, saying, "Thank you, young man."

"Would you like to sign this petition?" Danny said.

The woman smiled. "I'm afraid not," she said.

"Don't you even want to know what it's for?"

"I never sign petitions," the woman said, and still smiling, she walked away with her bundles and her boy.

[For nine dollars a week, you ran the addressograph-machine, you mailed your own weight in letters twice a day, you stood a trick at the switchboard from noon to one, you sharpened pencils and filled ink-wells, you made the bank-deposits, you took copy to the printer, you shot up to the corner for soda-pop, you went to meetings and put liter-ature on the chairs (a million chairs!), and you folded and filed and carried and phoned and swept and collected and wrapped, and you rode miles and miles on buses and cars, and once, when you had to go downtown with a famous lawyer, he stood you to a frosted chocolate, but mostly it was stacking and sorting and stamping and packing and walking and running—and in your spare time you grabbed some pe-titions and stood around on street-corners.]

"Here y'are! Sign your petition!"

A man came from the Vanderbilt Avenue exit of Grand Central Station, and approaching Danny, he clipped on a pair of eye-glasses, took the petition, and began to read aloud from its pre-amble: "'We, the undersigned, in the interest of justice, do hereby respectfully petition the Supreme Judicial Court of the Common-wealth of Massachusetts to reverse on appeal the convictions of Nicola Sacco and Bartolomeo Vanzetti, as being against the weight of evidence, and, further. . . .'" The man removed his glasses.

"You can sign it with that pencil," Danny said.

"The only thing I'd sign for Sacco and Vanzetti is a death-war-rant," the man said, and scaling the petition into the gutter, he walked on.

[Whenever you rushed copy, you ran into Mig DeLuca, and he al-ways roughed up your hair, saying, "How's the boy-anarchist?" He'd gotten his diploma in June, and he was through with Clinton and working full time now, not on the mimeos any more, but on the hand-press, and he was knocking down a cool twenty-five a week, nice dough for a guy of eighteen. That wop liked you, even after you'd told him about getting flunked for cheating, and you liked him, even after he'd told you, "And I had you spotted as another Lovejoy."]

"Sign your petition here!"

On the little island made for the Maine Monument, Danny was approached by a man who looked neither to the right nor the left,

nor up nor down, nor, indeed, in any direction at all: he seemed
not to see, or even to feel, for two or three people in his path were
jostled aside by his straight-line progress.

"Sign your petition!" Danny said.

The man fumbled for the pencil, scourged and goaded his signature across the page, and continued on his settled course toward some secret bourn.

"You didn't read what it's for," Danny said.

"I sign anything," the man said. "I'm against everything."

[*You were up on the roof with a bunch of the boys, and Tootsie was
unlacing your gloves so that Harry Keogh could try his luck with the
champ, Julie Pollard, who stood there grinning at you. You'd just
sparred three rounds with him, mostly backwards, and you'd hit the
deck in the first and third, but you grinned back as much as your numb
jawbone would let you. Tootsie flipped the gloves to Harry, and then
you leaned against the chimney to watch the next massacre.*

[*"Well, white-trash?" Tootsie said.*

[*"How's biz?" you said. "You still call it the B. & W. Polishing
Company?"*

[*"Sure do. I like that name."*

[*"Save enough for college yet?"*

[*"Enough for the first two years."*

[*"You ought to be glad we broke up."*

[*"Why should I ought to be glad?"*

[*"Your partner turned out to be a crook."*

[*"Who he been crooking from?"*

[*"Little ole Danny got nailed with a pony in an English exam,"
you said.*

[*"What do you know?" he said. "Crooking from hisself!"*

[*You stared at him for a moment, and then you patted his cocoa
face, wobbled his chocolate-drop of a nose, and hugged him tight, saying, "That's right—crooking him hisself!" and you knew that at last
you could get the hell up off your knees.*]

"Sign here! Sign your petition!"

Danny's stand was alongside the south lion of the Public Library. Passers-by had filled two pages with signatures, and a fresh
sheet had just been snapped into place under a rubber band.

A voice said, "Whatcha got there?" The voice belonged to a policeman.

"A petition," Danny said.

"A petition for what?"

"To free Sacco and Vanzetti."

"Them bomb-throwing ginnies up in Boston! Keep moving!"

"What for? I can stand here as long as I like."

"You're blocking the sidewalk, and it's against the law to collect a crowd."

"I don't see any crowd except us and the lion."

"That petition is against the law."

"Where does it say so in the Constitution?"

"How should I know? I don't carry the Constitution around with me."

"Well, I *do*," Danny said, and he took a booklet from his pocket and opened it to an earmarked page. "'Congress shall make no law respecting an establishment of religion,'" he read, "'or prohibiting the free exercise thereof; or abridging the freedom of speech or of the press; or the right of the people peaceably to assemble and *to petition the Government for a redress of grievances.*'" Danny looked up, and the policeman turned away. "Wise guy," he said to the broad blue back.

A woman's face appeared above the paws of the lion. "I was just hoping he'd start something," she said.

"I meet cops like that all over town," Danny said. "I really know Article I by heart."

"May I sign?"

[*Pop took some of the petitions, and in no time at all he got to be the most quarrelsome hack-driver in Manhattan. The minute a fare piled in, he'd open up about the Sacco-Vanzetti case, and if the guy saw eye-to-eye with him, it'd be a nice clean ride, but let the poor slob have doubts, and Pop'd finish the trip driving with his feet while he poured insults over the back seat at the rate of five cents for each additional quarter of a mile. All the same, he brought home a filled petition nearly every day—and he'd've done even better if he hadn't been plugging for a couple of characters named Sacci and Vanzetto.*]

Near the Information Booth in Pennsylvania Station, Danny accosted a man standing in a clump of luggage. "Would you like to sign this petition?" he said.

"Who's it for?" the man said.

"Sacco and Vanzetti."

"Not interested. Not in the least."

Danny turned away to find himself blocked by a porter who had paused to arrange some parcel-checks. "How about signing this petition, mister?" he said.

The porter said, "What petition for who, boy?"

"There's a couple of people in jail that ought to be out."

"What they done to be in jail?"

"Nothing."

"In jail for nothing? Sound like they colored."

"They're white. They're Italians."

"That's colored enough. Where I supposed to sign?"

Danny addressed the older of two women in a line at a Lehigh Valley ticket-window. "Will you sign this petition, ma'am?" he said. "It's for Sacco and Vanzetti."

The younger one said, "I wouldn't sign that, mother."

"No?" the mother said. "Why not?"

"Sacco and Vanzetti are those murderers up in Boston."

"Did you see them commit the crime, my dear?"

"They're guilty. I read about it in the papers."

"What do the papers know?" the mother said, and she reached for the pencil.

A man flicked a cigarette at an urn and missed it. "Bum shot," Danny said. "Want to sign a petition?"

"Who for?" the man said.

"Sacco and Vanzetti."

"What do they want?"

"Justice," Danny said.

The man laughed. "They're too late," he said. "It just pulled out in a private car."

A woman dropped her purse, and Danny helped her round up its fugitive trash. When she offered him a reward of a nickel, he said, "All I'd like is for you to sign this petition."

The purse was snapped shut. "Do I look like a Jew?" she said, and then her mouth was snapped shut too.

A man tapped Danny on the shoulder, saying, "What's this thing you're asking people to sign?"

"A petition to save Sacco and Vanzetti."

"I was standing right there. Why'd you pass me up?"

"Oh, I don't know. I guess I didn't think you'd go for it."

"Why not?" the man said.

"To tell the truth, you looked too rich."

"Don't you like rich people?"

"Not when they don't like Sacco and Vanzetti."

"You sound like a dirty little anarchist yourself."

Danny smiled. "I was right to give you the go-by," he said.

"A dirty little anarchist son-of-a-bitch!"

"Say that again, mister, and you're going to miss a train."

Danny waited for a man who was bowing to a drinking-fountain. The man rose, wiping his mouth, and after a glance at the preamble of the petition, he caught up the pencil and carved his name across three of the ruled spaces, saying, "God damn it! God damn it to hell!"

[*That was the kind! The ones that got sore, the ones that started fishing around for something to give away (pennies, even), the ones that shook hands with you, that had to touch you and sometimes kiss you, the ones that could only cry over their dirty fists and foreign names! They made up for the ones that called you a son-of-a-bitch.*]

He stood at Miss Forrest's window, looking down at the darkening park. "I asked you to sign before you went away on your vacation," he said, "and I asked you again the day you got back. Now for the third and last time, I'm asking you to just write down your name—that's all, to just write down your name on a piece of paper."

The teacher said, "It's much more than a piece of paper and much more than the two words of my name: I have to believe in what that petition is for, and I don't. I've read all the things you've asked me to read, and I've studied the facts of the case as carefully as a juror, but I still believe those two men are guilty of murder.

Believing that, I must also believe they should be punished. How can I sign a petition for the exact opposite?"

"Nobody has a right to be as sure as you are."

"I have the same right to be sure that you have."

"No, you haven't, Miss Forrest. I'm sure that Sacco and Vanzetti are innocent, and you're sure that they're guilty, but I can be sure without costing them their life."

"All the evidence—the identification, the torn cap, the rifling in the gun-barrel and the marks on the bullets, Vanzetti's previous record in the Bridgewater holdup—all that makes it reasonable to believe the men are guilty."

"Then your answer is no, and you won't sign."

"It isn't that I *won't*, Danny. I *can't*."

The boy turned, looked at her for a moment, and said, "I'm sorry to say this to a person that's been such a good friend of mine, that's been my *best* friend, but, Miss Forrest . . . ," and now his gaze was on the petition that he held in his hand, on the two-inch pencil and the soiled string and the worn cardboard backing, ". . . I'll never be able to think of you as a friend any more, not if you let me go away from here today without your signature."

"You're not being fair," the teacher said. "Suppose things were turned around, and I told you we were finished being friends unless you signed a petition saying Sacco and Vanzetti were *guilty*."

"Sacco and Vanzetti are innocent, and there's no other way to look at it, not and still be a friend, and that goes even if the friend is you, Miss Forrest, and I wouldn't wait for you in the street any more, and I wouldn't walk you home, and I wouldn't come up here and talk to you, and I wouldn't write to you if you went away, and I wouldn't think about you like I sometimes do when I'm alone. I'd hate you, the way that Judge hated my friends."

"Let me have the petition, Danny. I'll sign it."

"I wouldn't know you if I saw you anywheres! I wouldn't answer if you spoke to me! I wouldn't ever want to be here with you in the house, just the two of us! I'd hate you, Miss Forrest, and I'd hate all the time I've lived liking you . . . !"

"I'll sign! I'll sign!" the woman said. "What more do you want?"

THE TUESDAY AFTER LABOR DAY

A FEW moments before nine o'clock in the morning, Danny crossed Ninth Avenue under the tracks of the Elevated, heading west for the first day of his last year at De Witt Clinton, and as he passed between buildings so long known that they were no longer seen, he thought of the three years gone as if they were a composite day—a day compounded from a thousand, all different yet all similar, all separate yet all superimposed, and the one, like all, seemed strange. [*You remembered the way the tiles were set in the front hall, the flabby footballs in the Trophy Room, the woven wire in the plate-glass of the stairways. You remembered the Auditorium, the Store, the Gym., and the Chem. Lab., and you remembered many boys, many teachers (Miss Forrest! Miss Forrest!), many books, many pictures in many rooms, many rainy mornings, and many afternoons when the sun bouncing up off the Hudson turned the ceilings to water.*] At the end of the brick wall around the Roosevelt Hospital yard, he cut over on a diagonal toward the main entrance of the school. Waiting for a gap in traffic, he paused at the curb.

"What do you say, kid?" someone said.

Danny turned. "Mig!" he said. "What're *you* doing here?"

"You know what? I did a funny thing when I left the house this morning. I forgot I was all through with Clinton, and by the time I woke up to what I was doing, here I was on the corner. Funny thing."

"You're a dirty wop liar, Mig."

"Now, you know I wouldn't lie to you, kid—but as long as I'm here, I might as well wish you good luck in your last year. . . , Mr. Lovejoy."

"I love all the wops," Danny said. "Good peoples."

[*When school broke that afternoon, you waited for Miss Forrest and walked her home, and then you kept on across town to the office of the Defense Committee, but the Boss was busy, and you couldn't get to him till along about seven, and even then you had to waylay him as he was steamed for the subway.*]

"Give you till I finish this butt," he said.

Danny said, "You know, school started today."

"Don't tell me you want to be book-educated."

"So I'll have to work part time from now on."

"How much time is part time?" the Boss said.

"I can report at four o'clock."

"School only keeps till three."

"I know," Danny said, "but I can't get to work till four."

"It takes you an hour to walk ten blocks?"

"I always do something along the way."

"It sounds like a dirty something."

"No, sir," Danny said. "It isn't dirty."

"Well, whatever it is," the Boss said, "we can't pay any nine bucks a week for a couple of hours a day. Where do you think our dough comes from—Beacon Street?"

"I'm not asking for nine bucks. I'll work for anything you say is fair."

"What do *you* say is fair?"

"Five, and I'll give you all day Saturday."

The Boss tossed his cigarette into the gutter. "You still think they're innocent?" he said.

"Christ," Danny said, "there's more evidence against Judge Thayer!"

"Make it seven-fifty—but don't forget the Saturdays."

LET THE VOICE OF THE PEOPLE BE HEARD

"WHAT do you know about writing letters?" the Boss said. "Same as everybody," Danny said. "I've written a few."

"With a pony, or without? Don't bother answering. Your first assignment is to compose a form letter about The Case. A statement of the facts, down-to-earth and snappy—and a snappy reminder that we're broke. If the thing's any good, we'll run it off on the mimeos and send it to every Italian in the City Directory."

"Suppose it stinks."

"Don't *let* it stink!"

[*You thought and thought, but when you finally fitted a sheet of paper into the typewriter, you had nothing that your own mother could've called an idea, but all at once, out of nowhere, a real good one seemed to clap you on the neck like a hand, and long after the lever had shot the sheet out, you sat there dreaming while you ticked the blank roller of the machine.*]

"I guess you need a pony after all," the Boss said.

"Boss," Danny said, "don't even breathe: I think I got an idea."

"Spring it, kid," the Boss said, and he boosted himself up onto Danny's desk.

"This won't be our first letter asking for money: it'll be our hundredth, and if it's like all the rest, it'll bring in about forty bucks, mostly in stamps. You know why? Because we do the asking, us guys in the office. The asking ought to be done by the people that do the giving."

"You lost me, kid."

"Instead of the usual thing, how would it be if this letter started out with facts and wound up with opinions—not *our* opinions, but the opinions of teachers, waiters, cab-drivers, subway-guards? How would it be, for instance, if we got an Italian shoemaker to say his say about The Case? And how would it be if we got an Italian fish-peddler . . . ?"

"How would it be?" the Boss said. "It'd be sweet as sugar!"

[*You put in a lot of time collecting stuff for that letter, and one day you clipped it all together and turned it in to the Boss, but an hour later, when he came over to talk to you, you were staring up at two pictures on the wall, and you felt low.*]

"It's no good," Danny said.

"What makes you think so?" the Boss said.

"It's eight pages of words, single-spaced."

"What's the matter with words, kid?"

"They won't get anybody out of jail."

"What do you figure we ought to use?"

"Crowbars, battering-rams, and guns."

"You think we ought to shoot it out?"

"I think we ought to do something that'll work."

"If words won't, nothing will," the Boss said. "There's nothing in the world like words. The trick, though, is to pick the good ones."

"Five years of good ones, and Nick and Bart're still in jail. Ten years of good ones, and so is Tom Mooney. Did good words help Parsons, or Spies, or Fischer, or John Brown, or anybody else? There's no such thing as good words!"

"If that was true, kid," the Boss said, "you'd live and die without knowing that so many great men had lived and died before you. It was their words that they were lynched, shot, and beaten to death for, but you can't kill words, kid, and if you try, they'll turn around some day and kill you. You can get rid of an Albert Parsons easily enough, but not this: 'O men of America, let the voice of the people be heard!' And you can hang a John Brown any day of the week, especially if the hangman is a Captain Robert E. Lee, but these words are far more deadly than Brown ever was, and they're still with us: 'Had I so interfered in behalf of the rich, the powerful, the intelligent, the so-called great, or in behalf of any of their friends, either father, mother, brother, sister, wife or children, or any of that class, and suffered and sacrificed what I have in this interference, it would have been all right. Every man in this court would have deemed it an act worthy of reward rather than punishment.'"

"That was a beautiful thing to say," Danny said, "but it would've been even more so if John Brown'd said it and lived. People always say fine things about the rotten things that happen to them, but the rotten things go right on happening."

"This isn't Heaven, kid," the Boss said, "and in case you don't know it, those're people out there in the street, not Christs walking on water. That's all you'll meet in a long lifetime, is people. They don't know everything yet, but if they ever do, they'll learn it from words—and they're learning all the time, whenever somebody gets beat over the head, or tarred and feathered, or castrated, or castor-oiled, and I say to you, kid, God help those with a rope or a blackjack or a gun in their hands on the day when they know enough!" He shook Danny's manuscript. "But they'll never learn anything from this. What were you trying to show—that Sacco and Vanzetti're only supported by assassins? How does it sound when I read it out loud?"

Joe Scarlatti says: "I been in ice-business all time after I come to this contry in 1913. In this contry is much enjustice for Italiani, hitting by police, shooting, deporting, framming up, putting in jails for nothings. And now the two peoples Sacco Vanzetti in jails same way, and now it is sure thing all Italiani be kill or push out of his home if they not at once get pistol and defend themself from capitlist-imperalist brutalism. We must march to the jails and liberate all the politicals."

"And how do you like this?"

Wladek Gajda says: "States of America is land of big chance for poor man, no? Well, me, I am poor man with big chance live in cellar of apartsment-house, a janater. I am open up the mouth to this, I am been told why you no go back where you come? But I am been citisen States of America, pay good money for papers, and I am have right to be on land of big chance, and now I am see I will always live in cellar without I am fight and kill to live right. This why I am say all people must fight and kill to get Mr. Sacco Vanzetti out of cellar which is jail."

"What did you do, kid—write all these yourself? Where are the teachers you were talking about, and the waiters, and the lawyers, and the letter-carriers? All you've got here is a gang of coal-heavers that want to see the color of Wall Street blood this afternoon. This stuff is hot enough to cook on. The opening is okay, and the hat-passing at the end is okay, but everything in between has to come out, every last one of these crank-letters, because that's what they are. In their place, I want what you promised me. I want a letter from a sensible shoemaker. I want a letter from a careful lawyer. . . ."

"I get you, Boss!" Danny said.

[*A week later, you handed him another batch of manuscript, and he made you wait at his desk while he read it.*]

"The letters," the Boss said. "That's all I care a damn about."

Juno Forrest says: "I have been a member of the faculty of DeWitt Clinton High School for several years, and as such I feel that I have been entrusted with a share in the development of American youth. I do not take my responsibility lightly, for I believe that educators, along with parents and the clergy, are bound to do everything in their power to promote good citizenship. All their efforts, however, will be fruitless if those in their charge lack one basic requirement: respect for the law. There can be no such respect if the ordinary rules of justice are not observed by our courts, and it is for this reason, and not because I am morally certain that Sacco and Vanzetti are innocent, that I believe the defendants are entitled to a new trial, a trial conducted in the traditional American way, impartially, fairly, and in an atmosphere free from all suspicion of prejudice and hysteria."

Raymond Powell says: "My grandfather was born a slave in Georgia, and he stayed there when he was freed after the war, thinking he would get his forty acres and a mule. Instead, he got hung. My father was only nine or ten at the time, but he knew enough not to want to die like that, so he came up north to die more slowly, and he did. He was married at twenty, he had six children by the time he was thirty, and he died of consumption before reaching forty. I am the only member of that family still alive. I have a family of my own now, and I don't want it to die by lynching, or consumption, or rheumatic fever, or syphilis. I want it to have a home and food and decent work and a good education. I want it to live, because people have that right just by being people, not only by being white. And more than anything else, I want it to *feel* that it has the right to be on earth—and that is why I am heart and soul against the conviction of Sacco and Vanzetti. I am against it above all because they are innocent, but as a Negro, I am also against it because they are poor. The Negro will only win his rights by siding with the oppressed, and the oppressed are the poor, who are all colors."

Francis X. Russell says: "I'm a building-contractor, and I don't use nothing but ginny-labor. In my book, they're real nice people, steady, moddest, argue a lot but never go hog-wild like the micks. I wouldn't hire a mick on a bet. Only ginnies, and I make it a rule to treat them square, full pay, no kickbacks, and time-and-a-half for overtime—and if they want a union, that's all right by me too, what's it my business? I found out long ago if you treat people good they'll do the same by you, like my ginnies. I never stood over them with a clock and a whip, but I always got a good day's work out of them, and that's all I expect. But this Sacco-Vanzetti thing is starting to bollix up the works. The way I figure, my ginnies kind of hold me partially rasponsible for two of their people being in jail, and maybe I am, who can say? I feel lousy enough about it to always chip in for lawyer-fees and the like, and twice I got up off my butt and spoke at Sacco-Vanzetti meetings, but things are only getting worse, and my ginnies don't like me so much any more. Do I think them two guys are guilty? Well, it's hard to say, not knowing them personally or seen them in action in the court. Man is full of sin and shame, but I think I'd string along with the poor devils, and I'll tell you why. First, I know ginnies, and they're goodhearted people, talking murder but gentle as Jesus. Second, I also know people like this Judge Thayer, and they don't have enough milk in them to change the color of tea. And third, aside from me and the ginnies in Boston being Catholic, I just don't believe the evidence against them."

Daniel Johnson says: "When Sacco and Vanzetti were arrested in 1920, I was only a kid halfway through public school.

I never even heard of their names till four years later, and if it wasn't for meeting an Italian boy, I might've gone along all my life without knowing about their great struggle for justice in a country that's supposed to stand for justice ahead of everything else. I can't vote yet, being only seventeen, but I'm as much of a citizen as I'll ever be, and that means I'm as much of a citizen as any American ever was. I'm no Lincoln, or Jackson, or Jefferson, but sometimes I get to thinking that we come from the same family, like they were my uncles or grandfathers, and I couldn't be prouder of the fine things they did if we really were related by blood, just like I couldn't be more ashamed of the cheap things that Hamilton did, and Buchanan, and Andrew Johnson, and Grant. The way this country started out, everybody thought it was going to be the greatest place on earth, with liberty and justice for all, but we got less and less fine things and more and more cheap things—the Mexican War, the Dred Scott decision, the whole Reconstruction, the Indian Wars, the Pullman Strike—and I feel that every time one of them happened, a white star in our flag turned black. We've got a lot of black stars now, and it can't go on much longer, or we'll run out of white ones, and then it won't be a flag any more, but a rag so dirty that no decent man will wipe his feet on it, let alone take his hat off to it or die for it. It'll belong to the Hamiltons and the Roger Taneys and the Webster Thayers and the rich, and *they* can uncover for it, and *they* can die for the red-black-and-blue, but no decent man will weep when it comes down for the last time —and it *must* come down, because only traitors will be left to defend it."

[*They're still only words, you thought, and then you had to say it, and you said it.*] "They're still only words," he said.

"Maybe," the Boss said, "but, by Christ, they're made out of iron this time!"

[*You felt as if you'd won a medal.*]

GIVE A DOG A BAD NAME

IN FEBRUARY, at the beginning of his eighth term, Danny applied to the head of the Department for permission to surrender his study-periods and schedule a repeat of English 6. The request was granted, but on working out a program, Danny found that only one course in the subject matched his spare time—the one given by Mr. Holloway.

[*You boned up on English like you meant to teach it some day, but weeks went by, and Holloway never called on you once, and you took to volunteering, and still he ignored you, and then finally it dawned on you what the dirty louse was up to: he was going to let you ride the course without a single mark for or against, and you'd pass or flunk on the basis of your showing in the final exam, so that no matter how tough he made it, you'd have no comeback. Ah, the miserable bastard! You tried a few times to trick him into letting you recite, sliding down low in your seat and making believe you'd just as soon be forgotten, all the while hoping he'd think you were unprepared and jump you with, "Johnson, get up and make an ass of yourself," but he was too cagey to fall for that, and then you just gave up and sat it out.*]

Exam-week, and four years of high school with it, would soon be over. The State Regents had been taken earlier, and of the school-finals, only a few moments of the last—English 6—remained. Danny had completed his paper, and while he read it for errors, the master clock in the Principal's office began to run off the closing quarter-hour.

[*You went through your booklet from cover to cover, and except for putting in a comma here and there, you found nothing that you knew enough to change. It'd been one bugger of an exam, harder and sneakier than English 8, and a lot of guys were going to bust it that could've passed any other exam in the Department—and all on account of you. Holloway had taken aim at little ole D.J. and bagged a bunch of poor innocent slobs, and you felt sorry for them—and in a way you felt sorry for that sad son-of-a-bitch of a teacher too, because he hadn't hit the one thing he gave a damn about hitting: you.*]

The bell had not yet rung, but there was no need for Danny to wait for it, and he rose, handed in his booklet, and started for the door.

"Just a minute, Johnson!" Holloway said. "What's your hurry?"

"I'm finished," Danny said, "and I'm taking myself for a walk."

"First, open your coat," Holloway said.

Pens paused, even those held by the time-torn and the desperate.

"Open my coat!" Danny said. "What for?"

"So that you can empty your pockets onto my desk."

"That's searching me! What right've you got to do that?"

"None. That's why you're going to search yourself."

"You let other guys go without showing what they had in their pockets. Why not me?"

"They didn't cheat last year. You did."

"That don't mean I cheated this year! Did you see me cheat?"

"The question is, did you cheat *without* my seeing you? And you're going to answer it by emptying your pockets."

"I'm not supposed to prove I'm innocent! You're supposed to prove I'm guilty!"

"If you're innocent, you ought to be only too glad to prove it yourself."

"That's not how it is in the law," Danny said. "I cheated last year, and you punished me by giving me a flunk, but you can't go on punishing me for the same thing year after year. It isn't fair to say I'll always be a cheat because I cheated once, and it isn't fair to make small of me like this in front of the whole class. If you saw me with a pony this afternoon, you have a right to say so straight out, but you have no right to just sit there and be suspicious!"

"I have a right to flunk you again, though."

"Not for cheating—only for writing a poor paper!" Danny said. "And you'll have to bust your back to make this one out to be poor. I know what I got in there."

Holloway picked up Danny's booklet, and weighing it gravely, he said, "It *feels* pretty poor, Johnson."

"But, God damn it, you haven't even read it!"

"It'll be poor when I get to it," Holloway said. "Unless you empty your pockets. . . ."

[*You turned yourself inside-out. From your chest-pocket, you took the pen-and-pencil set you'd gotten from Pop and Mom on your seventeenth birthday. From your outside pocket on the left came a box of jujubes, two Sweet Caps, and a blotter advertising the Corn Exchange Bank. In the one on the right, you had about a dollar in small change and a book of matches. You looked at Holloway, but he still wasn't satisfied. From the label-pocket of your coat, you brought a pin-seal wallet, the one Gil Spence had given you for teaching him the Charleston, and from the watch-pocket of your pants an Ingersoll Yankee on a fob of foreign coins. There was a red-and-white bandana in your left hip-pocket, and your right was empty except for a little wad of worn newspaper that fell apart when you tried to spread it (the face of a man, it might've been, maybe two men). In the left pocket of your pants, there were a few paper clips, and then you stuck your hand into the right one, the last pocket of all, and for a few seconds you let it stay there. Holloway came up slowly from his chair ("Teachers aren't quite as stupid as you kids seem to think."), and you did your best to smile away the jigging water on your eyes, but it was too late, and they were windows in the rain.*]

"What's in that pocket, Johnson?"

Danny's hand came forth, and it came with the lining. A pinch of dust fell to the floor, a few crumbs and nameless grains, a skein of lint, a match-head, and that was all.

And then the last bell rang.

*　　*　　*

". . . I should've said, 'You can go plumb to hell, you old bastard! I wouldn't empty my pockets for you to save your life, and if you flunk me for standing up for my rights, I'll come back and bat your ears off with a piece of pipe!' Instead, I practically got undressed for him! Jesus Christ, why did I do it? Why was I such a yellow dog? I should've said, 'You mean old devil, you're not sore because you caught me cheating last year; you're sore because you *didn't* catch me *this* year!' I should've said, 'You're like Webster Thayer, another dried-up pimp for the rich! He didn't try Sacco and Vanzetti for murder; he tried them for being Italian radicals!' I should've spit in his face! I should've backed him against the wall and cuffed his plates out! I should've, I should've, but I didn't: I showed him my wallet, my rotten little box of candy, my snotty handkerchief, my guts! Nick and Bart've been in jail for years now, and they've lost everything but their lives, but they're still fighting back, and they'll *always* be fighting back, even after they're dead—but not me, not Danny Johnson! I let a mutt like Holloway bulldoze me into zipping open my heart! I feel sick! Honest to God, I feel sick! I'm no damn good for anything in the world . . . !"

"Please, Danny," Miss Forrest said. "Please . . . !"

THE SPOKEN WORD, THE WRITTEN WORD

"WHEN I left that building a week ago," Danny said, "I swore I'd never set foot in it again."

"You said that before, son," his mother said, "but what we're trying to find out is why."

"I've got my reasons."

"I think, in all fairness, that Pop and I have a right to know them. We gave up something to send you to high school for four years, and in return, the least you can do is tell us why you refuse to go to your own graduation."

A far-off mumble of Pullman trucks grew uptown into the *Commodore Vanderbilt* doing a glissando over a keyboard of ties. "I have important reasons," Danny said. "Important to *me*."

"Important enough to prevent your parents from enjoying a moment they've looked forward to for such a long time? We have no other sons to wait for, Danny. If we don't see you on that plat-form tonight, we'll never see anyone."

"Let him alone, Polly," the hack-driver said, and he put a hand on his son's arm. "It's all right, kid."

"When I left that building," Danny said, "I went across the street and looked back, and I said right out loud, 'So help me God, I'll never go through those doors again!' And I never will."

"But why?" his mother said. "That's what I can't understand."

"Let him alone," the hack-driver said. "Let the kid alone. . . ."

*　　*　　*

. . . Danny stopped in a dark hallway and knocked on a dark door framed in fine lines of gold. The door opened, and Mig DeLuca was a black form on a block of light.

"Mr. Lovejoy!" Mig said. "Come on in, kid!"

"I thought maybe we'd go for a walk."

"I'll walk you. I'll walk your feet off. But first come in and say hello to my people."

On the wall opposite the door hung two photographs, their corners furled over the thumbtacks that held them in place. . . .

*   *   *

. . . It was a warm and motionless evening, and the smoke of cigarettes rose a long straight way before blooming. A tug broke the slick Hudson water, shaking the stripes of light laid down by Jersey, and the river, in the tug's wake, was a rippling flag.

"Miss Forrest," Danny said, "why do you waste so much time on me?"

"It isn't wasted, Dan," the teacher said. . . .

*   *   *

. . . Danny entered the subway-car, found a seat, and stared up at a cornice of ads.

A voice said, "You win any fights lately?"

Danny turned. "Dewey!" he said. "Dewey Meyers!"

"The Battling Bulldog!" Dewey said.

"Jesus, Dewey, how long has it been?"

"God only knows. Years and years, I guess."

[*Remember* P. S. 10A? *Remember Miss Morey and Mr. Burch? Remember Goggly Roger Lynch and them jawbreakers? Remember the Boy Pioneers? Remember the time you and me and Paul Stagg and Morty Peck . . . ? Remember . . . ? Remember . . . ?*]

Dewey almost missed his station, barely managing to force himself through the slamming door. "See you," he said into a window sliding past.

Danny waved, and Dewey's face was gone, and then once more he stared up at the cornice of ads. . . .

*   *   *

. . . Miss Forrest said, "One night a few weeks ago, you asked me why I spend so much time on you."

"I said 'waste.'"

"Waste, then. What I want to know is, why do *you* waste so much time on *me?*"

"Spend," Danny said. "I like you, Miss Forrest. . . ."

*   *   *

". . . TRAIN FOR PHILADELPHIA, WILMINGTON, WASHINGTON, AND POINTS SOUTH—ON TRACK NINE!"

"That's you, Tootsie," Danny said.

[*An hour before, at seven in the morning, you and Pop had called for him in the Pierce-A, and sitting on his straw suitcase, he'd been waiting for you in front of the stoop. His father and mother and sister stood near him, you remembered, and a crowd of neighbors packed the doorway and the steps and spilled over onto the sidewalk, and there were black faces in many of the windows upstairs and across the street, and everybody looked happy because Tootsie was everybody's son that day: every family on the block was sending a boy away to college. You remembered getting out to help with the suitcase, but a couple of kids beat you to it, and very carefully they picked it up, and very carefully they stowed it under the meter (no fare), and then Mrs. Powell kissed Tootsie goodbye, and she wasn't the only woman who began to cry into an apron, and then he hugged his sister and shook hands with his father, and then the two of you climbed in, and Pop honked out a pair of longs, and you were off.*]

"That's me, Danny," Tootsie said.

"Well, shoe-shine boy, you made it."

"All I made is a start."

"That's all you ever needed, Tootsie."

"TRAIN FOR WASHINGTON—ON TRACK NINE!"

"So long, Danny-boy."

"So long, partner. I only hope you get to be President."

They shook hands four-handed, and then Tootsie took up his suitcase and went through the gate, and at the head of the steps he turned to wave, and Danny waved back with a fist. The colored boy started down, and Danny watched a golden word on a red sticker (TUSKEGEE) until it was out of sight. . . .

*   *   *

". . . I've got to go to Boston, kid," the Boss said. "My old lady'll have my toothbrush packed by the time you reach the house. Get it to me at the Grand Central clock by four sharp. You've got an hour."

Danny put on his hat and headed for the door.

"And pick up a toothbrush for yourself," the Boss said. "You're going along."

Danny broke into a run.

[*You saw three hours of New England before the sun went down— fields, woods, hills, rivers, and for a long way the Sound—and then in the dark a farm was a single light, and a town was many lights, and a steamer was a loop of lights, and sometimes all you could see outside was the inside of the car, and somewhere along the line you fell asleep and dreamed of delivering documents, of chasing around corners for coffee, of two faces, two lincoln-tired faces. . . .*]

"Doing anything this morning?" the Boss said.

"Anything you tell me," Danny said.

"I want you to go over to Charlestown."

"Not to see Nick and Bart!"

The Boss shook his head. "To see the prison," he said. "To stand there for a while and look at it, that's all."

[*You stood there and looked, and you knew that never again would you be able to hear of the Mayflower Compact, or Plymouth Rock, or the First Thanksgiving, without thinking of a high and dirty stone wall, and never again, without being surrounded by that wall, would there be a Tea Party, or an Old South Church, or a Bunker Hill. They were all in jail, along with an Italian shoemaker and an Italian fish-peddler, and history belonged to them now, not to the Back Bay windbags who could still come and go.*]

"Did you have any important thoughts?" the Boss said.

"Some," Danny said, "but no walls fell down. . . ."

* * *

. . . On the supper-table, propped against a sugar-bowl, stood a letter from Tootsie. Danny had read it, and phrases were still being played by his mind [*"I'm here to learn one thing: how to be black."*]. "Pop," Danny said, "do you ever feel badly about not being able to send me to college?"

The hack-driver looked up from his plate. "Do you ever feel badly about not being sent?"

"Well, to tell the truth, I sometimes say to myself, 'Why couldn't my old man've been rich?' and then I say, 'Tootsie got to college, and his old man's a waiter on a table.' I kind of switch back and forth. I think, 'It's up to a father to see that his children get a good education,' and then I think, 'How would you like to hear that from your own children?'"

The hack-driver glanced at his wife for a moment, and then he said, "I know what you're thinking—that I'm going to blow up—but I'm not, and I'll tell you why. Our fine little boy ain't said a thing that we didn't say ourselves one morning about eighteen years ago. Remember that morning, Polly?"

"What did you talk about?" Danny said.

The hack-driver put a spoon into his coffee-cup and steered it through many circuits before saying, "It's funny, but we talked about tonight."

"Talked about tonight eighteen years ago?"

"I said, 'The day'll come when he chucks it up to me about being a poor stiff of a hack-driver,' and Mom said, 'I want to see how far he gets on nothing.'" The man's eyes made a cruise of the room and returned to the coffee-cup. "I never meant for things to turn out like this—three rooms in a tenement, and no eats tomorrow if I croak tonight—but all in all, I'm glad that Mom's had her way. You'd only be a stinker if we had money, and as things are, you're an *honest* stinker. I've got no regrets."

[*You'd never forget the way Mom looked at Pop when he said that: her expression was like a kiss on the mouth—and you knew that no matter what you ever did for her, no matter how far you went on nothing, you'd always and only run second to a man who called himself a poor stiff of a hack-driver.*]

"Dan," the woman said, and she spoke to the father, not the son, "*you've* gone far on nothing too. . . ."

* * *

. . . Low slow clouds sailed among the reefs of the city and ripped their hulls, and the first rain of a long dry fall fell hard. Side by side at a window, Danny and the Boss watched the downpour streak the air and tuft the asphalt, and they watched people cower, as if rain struck only the erect, and they watched a truck turn the corner, tread water for a way, and then swerve, sideswiping a sedan parked at the curb. 26 95 .291

"Another lawsuit," the Boss said.

"I'm a witness," Danny said." I'm going down and give in my name."

"What did you witness, Mr. Witness?"

"That woman started to cross in the middle of the street, and the truck-driver had to slam on his brakes so's not to hit her."

"What else did you witness?"

"His wheels locked, and he skidded into that sedan, but it was all the woman's fault, and that's what I'm going down and say."

"You'll be wasting your time, kid. The truck-driver's going to foot the bill."

"But he wasn't responsible. It was an accident."

"You want the law on the subject?" the Boss said." 'Accident is no excuse for trespass to property.'"

"That's a hell of a law!" Danny said." If the guy hadn't hit the floor with his brakes, he'd've killed the woman!"

"That's just what he should've done. He made a bum pick."

"Boss," Danny said, "you're crazy!"

"I wish I was, because 'Accident is full excuse for trespass to the person.'"

Danny stared at him for a moment, and then he said, "You mean if something happens that you have no control over, and you have to make up your mind whether to run over a human being or a dog, you only have to pay damages for the dog?"

"That's a hundred per cent right."

"Well, I think it's a hundred per cent wrong!"

"So do I, and I'm a dog-lover—but that's the law."

"Why don't people do something about it?"

"They're doing the best they know how," the Boss said. "They're trying to be dogs. . . ."

*   *   *

. . . Danny wrote, "I don't know why I've let such a long time go by without answering your letter, but it surely hasn't been a case of out-of-sight out-of-mind, because I talk about you whenever I see the guys, especially Julie Pollard, and I think about you a lot, and last Sunday I looked in on your folks to find out what was new with you. . . ." [*And you went on to tell him about how you put in your spare time at Billy Grupp's gym, watching Julie work out, and you told him about Mig and what Mig was doing (even though the two of them had never met), and you told him about your second trip to Boston, when Thayer denied the Madeiros motion, and what you wound up with was so hard to explain that you didn't explain it at all: you simply wrote it.*] ". . . On the way back, somewhere around New London, I saw a track-crew heading for home on a handcar —up and down, up and down, two men up and two men down— and I thought to myself, 'Christ, that kind of thing could go on forever! If I was aboard, I'd pull up when I ought to push down —just for the hell of it . . . !'"

Tootsie wrote, ". . . Anarchist-stuff. All it'll get you is a broken head. . . ."

Danny wrote, ". . . That'll be all right, just so I break one on the other side. . . ."

Tootsie wrote, ". . . Grow up. The world never comes out even when it loses one good man and one bastard. . . ."

Danny wrote, ". . . Greetings of the season. I wonder what Christmas is like down there in hell. . . ."

Tootsie wrote, ". . . Same as up there in Heaven. The rich prayed and ate, and the poor prayed and watched. . . ."

Danny wrote, ". . . I never believed everybody ate down there. I just didn't know anybody prayed. . . ."

Tootsie wrote, ". . . They pray all the time, boy, and most of 'em wouldn't stop if a nigger was being lynched on the bell-rope. . . ."

Danny wrote, ". . . I'm eighteen years old today. I think I'll celebrate by socking a cop in the nose. . . ."

Tootsie wrote, ". . . You sound like Julie. Always wanting to bust somebody. Always wanting to get what you want by force. . . ."

Danny wrote, ". . . There's no other way to get it. Life is a handcar, and I wish I could run it into a ditch. . . ."

Tootsie wrote, "…Thayer should've sent you up instead of the Italians. He'd've had a lot more reason.…"

Danny wrote, "…Tomorrow's a day of special importance. They come up for sentence.…"

A DAY OF SPECIAL IMPORTANCE : APRIL 9, 1927

"GET the papers, kid," the Boss said.
[*In the office that morning, the whole staff, from the Boss on down to you, had waited for one particular message* (BOSTON CALLING NEW YORK!) *and marked time with its heartbeat and blood. The call had come through just before noon, and when the Boss picked up the receiver, it was as if clocks and pulses had suddenly stopped, and in the dead moment you'd heard him say a single word—the word* "Oh," *spoken very quietly—and the clocks had begun to tick again, and the hearts, and then after a long while he'd taken a coin from his pocket and spun it out over the glass top of his desk, where it dwindled to a waltz and ended in a curtsy.*]

The people in the street seemed unreal, and the more customary their conduct, the more unreal they grew. They walked and spoke as usual, some idly and some with passion, and they gaped at merchandise and turned at will to catch the hang of passing clothes, and they whistled according to their ability, chewed gum and toothpicks, laughed when laughter seized them, and tapped cigarettes in fashionable fashion—actions with little purpose and no meaning, yet the boy observed them from a mood of exile, as if he were a mourner watching children at play. A man spat into the gutter, a woman held her skirts as she crossed a grating, a girl made a chalk-line on a shopwindow, and a policeman held an acrobatic club, but beings and behavior both were seen from another world.

"Read to us, kid," the Boss said.

[*You didn't want to read. You wanted to walk a long long way, through the park and over to the Drive and then up along the river, watching the tugs and the ferries and the wind on the water and the smoke of trains against the Palisades. You didn't want to hear the sound of voices, your own or any other.*]

"Read about Nick and Bart, kid," the Boss said.
Danny said, "I'm not a very good reader. . . ."

. . . Replying to the Clerk's question, whether there was
any reason why sentence should not be passed, the prisoner
Sacco said: ". . . The sentence will be between two class, the
oppressed class and the rich class, and there will be always
collision between one and the other. We fraternize the people
with the books, with the literature. You persecute the people,
tyrannize over them and kill them. We try the education of
the people always. You try to put a path between us and some
other nationality that hates each other. That is why I am here
today on this bench, for having been the oppressed class. Well,
you are the oppressor. You know it, Judge Thayer. You know
all my life, you know why I have been here, and after seven
years that you have been persecuting me and my poor wife,
and you still today sentence us to death. I would like to tell
all my life, but what is the use? . . . I am never been guilty,
never. Not yesterday, nor today, nor forever. . . ."

[*More than ever now, you wished you were down there on the plank
and broken-rock embankment, listening to the water suck at the gaps
and slap the green-haired piles. Long freights would go by. . . .*]

. . . On being asked the same question, the prisoner Vanzetti said: "Yes. What I say is that I am innocent, not only of
the Braintree crime, but also of the Bridgewater crime [Ed.:
prisoner was referring to a prior conviction for holding up a
truck belonging to the White Shoe Company]. . . . That is
what I want to say, and it is not all. Not only am I innocent of
these two crimes, not only in all my life I have never stole,
never killed, never spilled blood, but I have struggled all my
life, since I began to reason, to eliminate crime from the earth.
. . . Not only have I not been trying to steal in Bridgewater,
not only have I not been in Braintree to steal and kill, and
have never steal or kill or spilt blood in all my life, not only

have I struggled hard against crimes, but I have refused myself the commodity or glory of life, the pride of life of a good
position, because in my consideration it is not right to exploit
man. . . ."

[. . . *The Katy, the $oo Line, the Seaboard, the Denver & Rio
Grande, the Hocking Valley—long freights would go by, and you'd
wonder what they contained and where they were going, and you'd
say to yourself what Pop always said when he stared at his old marked-
up map of the United States: that you'd see it all some day . . . !*]

" . . . Not even a dog that kills the chickens would have been
found guilty by American jury with the evidence that the Commonwealth have produced against us. I say that not even a
leprous dog would have his appeal refused two times by the
Supreme Court of Massachusetts—not even a leprous dog. . . .
We have proved that there could not have been another Judge
on the face of the earth more prejudiced and more cruel than
you have been against us. . . . We know, and you know in
your heart, that you have been against us from the very beginning, before you see us. . . . We know that you have spoke
yourself, and have spoke your hostility against us, and your
despisement against us, with friends of yours on the train, at
the University Club of Boston, on the Golf Club of Worces-
ter, Massachusetts. I am sure that if the people who know all
what you say against us would have the civil courage to take
the stand, maybe Your Honor—I am sorry to say this because
you are an old man, and I have an old father—but maybe you
would be beside us in good justice at this time. . . ."

[. . . *You had a father too, not yet old, but aging, and for another
dozen or twenty years, he'd go on dreaming up shapes and colors for
all the things he'd never see with his eyes—and then one day he'd die,
and the dreams would end, and the only signs that they'd ever been
dreamt would be a few smeared lines on a map ready to fall apart. . . .*]

".. .The jury were hating us because we were against the war. . . . We believe more now than ever that the war was wrong, and we are against war more now than ever, and I am glad to be on the doomed scaffold if I can say to mankind, 'Look out. You are in a catacomb of the flower of mankind. For what? All that they say to you, all that they have promised to you, it was a lie, it was an illusion, it was a cheat, it was a fraud, it was a crime. They promised you liberty. Where is liberty? They promised you prosperity. Where is prosperity? They have promised you elevation. Where is the elevation?'"

[. . .They promised you liberty, Pop, but where is liberty? I'll tell you, Pop, if you'd like to know: it's in your hand, and your hand can make a fist, and it's in your mouth, and your mouth can talk, and it's in your feet, and your feet can walk you away. What keeps you, Pop? What holds you back . . . ?]

".. .This is what I say: I would not wish to a dog or to a snake, to the most low and misfortunate creature of the earth, I would not wish to any of them what I have had to suffer for things that I am not guilty of. But my conviction is that I have suffered for things that I am guilty of. I am suffering because I am a radical, and indeed I am a radical. I have suffered because I was an Italian, and indeed I am an Italian. I have suffered more for my family and for my beloved than for myself. But I am so convinced to be right that if you could execute me two times, and if I could be reborn two other times, I would live again to do what I have done already. I have finished. Thank you."

[. . . Nick and Bart had hands too, and they had mouths and feet, but when they shook their fists and said, " Where is liberty?" they didn't start running to find it, and they never would, not even if the gates were open, and the guards were looking the other way. They'd stand their ground, making beautiful words till they were dead, and they meant it when they said that if they had new lives, they'd only speak

*them away as they were speaking these....That wasn't for you,
though, was it, Mr. Lovejoy? No man pursued you, but you wanted
to run, didn't you, Mr. Lovejoy...?*] Through the window, Danny
saw a silent-film of people in the street. Their lips moved, their heels
struck the sidewalk, and their clothing rustled, and they tapped
canes, snapped purses, dropped coins, and whistled for cabs. The
sound for their soundless animation was in the office: weeping.

The Boss took the paper from Danny's hands and scanned the
account, and then he said, "Here's the bitter end, and it's rich."

> ... JUDGE THAYER: "There is only one duty that now de-
> volves upon this court, and that is to pronounce the sentences.
> First, the Court pronounces sentence upon Nicola Sacco. It
> is considered and ordered by the Court that you, Nicola Sac-
> co, suffer the punishment of death by the passage of a current
> of electricity through your body within the week beginning
> on Sunday, the 10th day of July, in the year of our Lord 1927.
> This is the sentence of the law. It is considered and ordered
> by the Court that you, Bartolomeo Vanzetti. . . ."
> MR. VANZETTI: "Wait a minute, please, Your Honor. May I
> speak for a minute with my lawyer, Mr. Thompson?"
> MR. THOMPSON: "I do not know what he wants to say."
> JUDGE THAYER: "I think I should pronounce the sentence....
> Bartolomeo Vanzetti, suffer the punishment of death...."
> MR. SACCO: "You know I am innocent. That is the same
> words I pronounced seven years ago. You condemn two inno-
> cent men."
> JUDGE THAYER: "...by the passage of a current of electricity
> through your body within the week beginning on Sunday, the
> 10th day of July, in the year of our Lord 1927. We will now
> take a recess...."

*   *   *

"... And then he folded up the newspaper," Danny said. "He
did it very carefully, straightening the pages and smoothing out
the creases—and when he was all finished, he just threw it away
and started to flow up and down the aisles like the ocean, like waves

breaking. He was so God damn hell-bent that some of the women actually backed themselves up to the wall to avoid him, and the way he swore was like nothing I ever heard in my life—the most terrible curses, the kind you find in the Bible, and on top of those the dirtiest words ever written on a toilet-wall—but nobody seemed to mind, not even the women, because he was really ranting for all of us. 'I've been struggling with some of you hysterical bastards for years,' he said. 'I've wiped your noses, dried your eyes, and given you pats on the back and shots in the ass—but that's all over, God damn you, and the first of you sniffling ninnies to shed another tear gets down on the floor and laps it up. We're finished with tenderness, and we're finished with love: from here all the way to hell, I want to see hatred! When you come to this dump in the morning, I want you to come hating, and I want you to hate harder all day long and go to bed foaming at the mouth! I want you to hate everything—yourselves, the Commonwealth of Massachusetts, that stale codfish-cake called Webster Thayer, and the whole sonabitching world! If you've got that straight, get up off your fat and try to hate me like I hate you—like I hate everybody on the face of the earth except . . . except Nick and Bart. . . .' And then you know what he did when he said those last four words?"

"What?" Miss Forrest said.

"He began . . . he began . . . began to cry. . . ."

NEITHER SNOW NOR RAIN

Tootsie wrote, ". . .You talk about Thayer as if you actually expected him to break down at the last minute and give his two worst enemies thirty days in the workhouse. Your trouble is, you think of him as a man when he's really a class. Vanzetti knows that, and it's time you knew it too. . . ."

Danny wrote, ". . .You can know a man's class and yet not know all about him. He can come from kings and be a Thayer, and he can come from nobodies and be a Bartolo—so class can't be the only thing that makes people what they are, and if you think so, you're only sizing them up through a crack. . . ."

Tootsie wrote, ". . . By your reasoning, Thayer could've been a Brandeis. What stopped him . . . ? "

Danny wrote, ". . .Who ever knows that? Maybe he didn't have the brains. Maybe he had a weak heart when he was a boy. Maybe he was afraid of the dark, or he was born too soon or too late or in the wrong climate. . . ."

Tootsie wrote, ". . .Wake up, boy. The only thing that stopped him was his class. People don't turn into Thayers by accident. . . ."

Danny wrote, ". . . I can understand being dialectical about a system, but not about people. They're all so damn different that you simply can't make the kind of rules for them that you do. There's got to be something besides class. . . ."

Tootsie wrote, ". . . Dish up the name of it, partner. Maybe it'll stop the next lynching. . . ."

Danny wrote, ". . . Remember one day when we were walking home with our shoe-boxes? You asked me what my philosophy was, and I quick made up some shite about doing good by my fellow-man. I still get red in the face when I think of that—I'm red right now. You didn't fall, though; you were wise to me. I had no philosophy then, not even the Y.M.C.A. crap I tried to palm off on you, and maybe I haven't any even now, but here's an odd thing: if I ever do have, it'll be the same one I tried to fool you with, only I'll really mean it. . . ."

Tootsie wrote, ". . . Here's another odd thing: you *did* fool me. I thought it was pretty fine to like people as much as you did, and I admired you for it. I admire you now for admitting you were a liar, and I'll admire you even more when you finally make the lie come true—but I'll admire you most when you realize that liking people isn't enough, because that'll only make you a half-assed liberal. You've got to like the good in them and hate the bad, and you'll never be able to do that unless you know what's at the bottom of both. The bottomest thing is Property, and a man who has it can't be kind or fair or democratic in the same way as a man without. If he could, I suppose he would, so you see I have as much faith in people as you, but what's the use of faith if the Italians die in the Chair? And they *will* die, Danny, because the Judge

Thayers and the Governor Fullers aren't ready to kiss their Property goodbye. They never will be; they aren't the kissing kind. . . ."

Danny wrote, ". . . Your father being up on things like Socialism and Economics, you learned a lot that I didn't, and, besides, you were a better thinker to begin with. But a guy's got to get the job done with the tools at hand, and to this cheap brain of mine, you've only hit on some of the answer—and I don't want you to jump me if I can't come right out with the rest. All I know is, in this world there's no such thing as a standard man with interchangeable parts. We're made of the same kind of stuff, but we come in different sizes, different shapes, different colors, and different weights, and when you add differences of place, time, health, environment, and brain-power, you've got an assortment that'd make a junk-dealer drool. But being made of the same kind of stuff, we're something more than a hopeless scramble of junk, and what goes on in one of us—in the head, in the heart—can be understood by the others, and therefore a man like Thayer is no stranger to me. He's a human being who happens to be sour and cruel and selfish and small and full of spite, but that describes me just as well, and knowing that I have moments of kindness and generosity and bravery and maybe even of love, I have to believe that he has too, and that in the end, as I would, he'll relent. I'm sure I'm right, Tootsie, and you'll see . . . !"

Tootsie wrote, ". . . All right, I'll see, but I'll have to do my seeing from down here. I expected to spend the summer in N.Y.C., but a job in Montgomery came my way, and I'll be working there till the fall semester begins. I leave tomorrow. Try me care of General Delivery. . . ."

Danny wrote, ". . . The Lowell Commission, appointed by Gov. Fuller to find out if S. & V. had a fair trial, held its opening session on the 1st of July. It'll take a couple of weeks for them just to read the record, and after that they'll have to hear witnesses, so one thing we can be sure of is that the executions scheduled for the 10th will be called off. . . ."

Tootsie wrote, ". . . Say *postponed*. . . ."

Danny wrote, ". . . It's the 10th, and Nick and Bart aren't dying this sunny summer day! I told you, Toots! I told you . . . !"

Tootsie wrote, ". . . I'm glad too, boy. . . ."

Danny wrote, ". . . I came up here with the Boss on the 11th —my third trip. We expected to sit in on the hearings of the Commission, but it's meeting behind closed doors. Even so, we have high hopes. I look at it this way: Fuller never would've appointed the Commission if he didn't mean to commute the sentences. He's a politician, and with an eye on the White House, he needs the support of labor. How would he get that if he let Nick and Bart die in the Chair? Not quite having the guts to come right out and say they were railroaded, he's going to let the Commission pave the way and then grab the credit. You watch. . . ."

Tootsie wrote, ". . . Watch what? You don't seem to realize who's on that Commission. The head of it is Abbott Lowell, president of Harvard, and the others are this Stratton, president of M.I.T., and a writing-guy name of Robert Grant. *You* watch, boy. I haven't got the heart. All three of those babies wear white silk stockings, and none of them means to die on the barricades. Lowell, Stratton, Grant—you ask me, those are just three different ways of spelling Thayer. . . ."

*   *   *

Miss Forrest wrote, ". . . I see where the hearings ended today, and I know you and all the others must be very much on edge while awaiting the decision of the Commission. I trust that it's favorable and that it comes soon, because I miss our evening walks, but you're doing valuable work up there, and nothing should be allowed to interfere with it. My dearest hope is that some day you will be able to say you played a part in obtaining justice for innocent men. I've thought many times of that first talk we had about Sacco and Vanzetti—I remember so very well the green throwaway you had in one of your schoolbooks—and it seems strange to me now that I could ever have had the opinions I then expressed. . . ."

Danny wrote, ". . . I miss them too, Miss Forrest. . . ."

Miss Forrest wrote, ". . . It won't seem so lonely if you write. . . ."

Danny wrote, ". . . It's a little after seven in the evening, and I'm dashing this off in a lunch-wagon just before going back to the State House. The Governor was supposed to announce the Commission's report at five this afternoon, but he didn't show up, and after waiting around for a couple of hours, we rushed out for coffee-and. We're rushing right back in a minute. . . ."

And Danny wrote, ". . . I've written and written, and still I haven't said what I did after the Boss told me to get out and go to bed. I got out, all right, but bed tonight would've been like a grave, so I went for a walk. I walked for a long time, and finally, around two in the morning, I found myself back on Beacon Hill. I don't know what I expected to find there in all those fine old houses that stare at you from rumple-glass windows, like eyes with cataracts—but it wasn't all those lights upstairs and down, as if it was early in the evening. There were lights everywhere, along Beacon and Charles, all around Louisburg Square, and up and down the crooked lanes between the Common and the Embankment, and there were many people in the streets, going slowly and talking quietly and never laughing, and there were policemen in many doorways, and they watched everybody that went by, but very few of us looked very long at them. It was as if we were ashamed —and we *were* ashamed, really, because every part of America is American, and the dirty things that happen in one part make every other part dirty too. Boston belongs to me as much as it belongs to the Bostonians, and the whole history of New England is as much mine as theirs (*more* mine, maybe), and I knew as I walked the streets tonight that I carried more dirt on me than I'd ever be able to wash away. . . ."

THE TIME NOW IS . . . .

SAYING little, they went northward through the lamplit park, across the groundswell of the Green, along the Mall, and over a hunchbacked bridge to the Ramble and the Reservoir, and then, saying nothing at all, they left the park and went westward to the black Hudson below the Drive, and there, on the splintered stringers of a dock, they paused for a while to watch the moving water and the broken candles of light that lay upon it. A gull came from the darkness to perch on a pile, and beyond it, on the far bank, the running legend of an electric-sign ran off to make way for running time.

[THE TIME NOW IS . . . 10:04. *In an hour and fifty-six minutes, seven years of agony would end, as Nick and Bart had always known they would end, in death. The peddler of fish and the shoemaker, the simple and ignorant foreigners that spoke your own language in such a way as to make you the alien, the gentler-than-Jesus wops, the stainless among the stained—they had known the finish from the start. You had known nothing at any time, and even now, with only a hundred and sixteen minutes left of their lives, you still knew nothing because you still had hope. Judge Thayer had said, "Did you see what I did to those anarchistic bastards?" but you still had hope. For what, though? In the name of Christ, for what—a miracle? Yes! You believed in God, then? Yes! Enough to say a prayer? Yes! Then why in hell didn't you say it?*]

They stood very close to each other in the spiced and small-sound night. They heard the same river-rustle, the same city-murmur, and the same muffled cough of West Shore locomotives. They heard the same footsteps in the distance and the dark, the same fragments of speech and laughter, and they were served the same flavors by the same currents of air—the flavor leached by the river out of three hundred miles of New York, the flavor of cut grass, of roofing-tar, of damp ground and dry stone, of burnt gasoline and seven million burning lives. They stood very close together, and each could smell the other's hair.

[THE TIME NOW IS . . . 10:21. *They knew the exact time they were going to die, and they knew the exact place, and they knew that nothing would change that time and place, and they knew too that they would die there and then not by accident but by design—and it was beyond you to stop wondering how you would feel if this were the far end of your own life, and all that remained of you belonged to a piece of machinery called a clock, which, wound, relentlessly told you the rate at which you were dying.* THE TIME NOW IS . . . 10:29.]

He struck a match and touched it to a cigarette, and a milk of smoke flowed into the sphere of light, and then he flicked the flame away, and it shocked itself out on the dock. He drew a few times, looking at the woman's profile as it brightened for the fire and dimmed for the ember, and then she turned full-face to him, and suddenly the spaces they had lived in alone for so long merged, and they stood mouth to mouth, each seeking to absorb and be absorbed.

[THE TIME NOW IS . . . 10:38, *and while you watched, the 8 vanished, and a 9 appeared, and then directly all four digits were gone, and a minute-long parade of letters began, its incandescence emerging from nowhere on the right and marching straight to nowhere on the* *left.* THE TIME NOW IS . . . 10:40.]

"I've always thought you had the most beautiful name in the world," he said, "a name to be whispered, a whisper in itself, a sound I've always been able to hear simply by thinking the words. I'm thinking them now, and they're saying themselves to me, but very softly, and they fade like a breath on a windowpane."

[THE TIME NOW IS . . . 10:51, *and you knew that the time was over when what you wanted so much had to be taken in dreams. There was no need for dreams now, unless this too was a dream, and there was nothing to wait long for, nothing to stop you—except two lives that still had sixty-nine minutes to run. The thought shamed you, and you felt heavy in the heart, because the shame could never now be shaken.*]

Neither of them spoke as they turned from the river to the park and entered upon a dark path among the granite boulders and the trees. They walked with their arms touching, as if manacled, and now and then they pressed closer to touch at the hips and thighs, and once each felt the other tremble and for a moment broke away.

[*You were far downstream now, and the sign was hidden behind rises in the ground, but time was an always-outgoing tide, and once you were aware of it, you could tell its flow with your mind.* THE TIME NOW IS . . . 11:19.]

From the lower end of the Drive, they went eastward to Amsterdam, down Amsterdam (soon Tenth) to the school, and then across town again along a block of brass-railed brownstones (he remembered four years of afternoons, four years of waiting)—and they were on the diagonal orange gash of Broadway.

[THE TIME NOW IS . . . 11:53.]

Not far from the entrance to the teacher's house, a small crowd had collected around a news-stand in front of a cigar-store. On the stacked papers stood a loud-speaker, and from its tin throat came tin words. The gathering listened in silence, and people passing listened too, some lingering to hear more and others moving on without pause. Above heads turned sideways and cocked to catch the crackled broadcast, Dan saw a clock in the window of the store.

[THE TIME NOW IS . . . 11:59.]

The long needle of the second-hand moved into still another sweep, and the final minute for two lives began.

[*You would say one thing now, and you would say it only once, and if it failed, you would never in your life say it again. You would say these words (and you said them): "God Almighty, please do something for Nick and Bart!"*]

But the minute passed, and no marvel, no wonderwork, came in on the all-purpose air; instead, for a choked-off instant, there was a flurry of syncopation. The clock hid behind its hands in the temporary shame of midnight, but the shame on the faces of people was revealed and lasting, and it seemed to impel strangers to touch in kinship, and they touched most tenderly and best who came together in the fire-union of the smoking-ritual.

An old man spoke aloud to none and all, saying, "Well, they burned 'em," and he turned from the news-stand, shaking his head, and again and again as he walked away, he said, "They burned 'em. They burned 'em. . . ."

A passenger climbed out of a cab, stood at the curb as the old man went by, and then came down the walk to the crowd. "Burned who?" he said, and for a moment there was no reply. "Who burned?"

"Sacco and Vanzetti," someone said.

"Who the hell're Sacco and Vanzetti?"

[*Jesus Christ, you thought, when're us Johnsons going to win a fight?—and you knew that if you didn't try to win one now, you'd live in an endless and always-growing disgrace.*]

"Who the hell're Sacco and Vanzetti?"

[*Your left hand made a fist, and you fired it with all the eighteen years of your life, but far more than yourself went along: the crow eaten by Julie Pollard went too, and the long and galling ruination of Nick and Bart, and the grief of the lonely and loving man who died with a bullet behind his eyeball, and the sad defeat ("We ain't getting anywheres!") of your own father. You saw a straw hat reel into the gutter, you saw drops of blood on the sidewalk, you saw feet dribble someone (without a hat) toward the corner—and then you saw only Miss Forrest.]*

The tottering elevator carried them to the eighth floor and left them on the landing, and then, making off with its feeble light, it tottered down, and they reached the woman's door blind in the blackness, and Dan said, "I say your name to myself all the time!" and the woman said, "Say it to *me*, Dan—to *me*!" and he said, "I'm saying it! [*"Juno Forrest!" you were saying, "Juno Forrest!"*] I'm saying it in my mind! I'm thinking it!" and then the woman opened the door, and they entered rooms only a shade less dark than the hallway, and now more than night, now walls, exiled the world, and of the unrequited years, nothing was left but a common desire to end them, and the woman spoke to a faint face in the gloom, saying, "Tell me what else you're thinking, Dan. . . ."

[*You were thinking that you wanted her to be naked (and she made herself naked), and you were thinking that you wanted to be naked too (and naked you were when she helped you), and you were thinking that you wanted to put your hands on her body (and she took them in her own and showed them where to write), and you were thinking that you wanted to do what only your hands had words for (and she drew you down and received you)—and you were thinking that now you were coming to the end of thought, that you were galloping toward it, running away with yourself, and then for a long shuddering moment, you were thinking that you weren't thinking any more. . . .*]

"Tell me what you're thinking, Dan. . . ."

[*"Please excuse me," you were thinking. "Please excuse me, Nick and Bart. . . ."*]

* * *

". . . I can only call you Miss Forrest."

"But why, Dan? Why can't you say Juno?"

"I'd think I was doing something dirty."

"What we just did—was that dirty?"

"A thing can only be dirty if you make it dirty in your mind."

"How is my name dirty, then? I don't understand."

"Please don't be angry at me for this, Miss Forrest, but there was a time when I did dirty things to myself. I was ashamed of them when they were over, but even more I was ashamed of how I'd made believe my hands were you, and how I'd sometimes call them by your name, and how it'd always be your body that I imagined being up against in the dark. I stopped doing the dirty things after a while, but I still punish myself for them, and I do that by never speaking your name and never looking at more of you than your face. I wish I could see you the way you are now, because I know you'd be better than all or anything I was ever able to dream, but I dreamt you naked when I had no right to, and I have to be punished by never seeing you except in my mind. I remember waiting for you in the street and turning away if a wind was blowing, so that I wouldn't see the shape of your legs and the shape of this, and I remember times when you leaned toward me, and your dress opened a little and showed the space between these, and I looked away then too, and I remember summer days when the light was behind you, and I punished myself by closing my eyes—I thought if I punished myself enough, maybe the time would come when I'd make up for the dirty things, but I'm not all square yet, and somehow I think I'll never be."

"What you did to me in your mind wasn't a dirty thing—or if it was, Dan, then no dirtier a thing than I've often done to you, and with less right than you ever had, because I was a woman, and I was doing the thing to a boy. I tried to punish myself too, by telling you to go away, but I told you only once, because I didn't really mean it, and because I knew that some day I'd be punished in a way that I could never punish myself: I'd grow older. What you just did, Dan, I've longed for for a long time, and I'll pay for it when I'm too old to make you want to do it again in your mind."

"You'll never be too old, Miss Forrest."

They turned to each other. . . .

*   *   *

It was still dark when he rose to dress, but in the slit below the drawn shade, a fainter hue than the sapphire of the room was visible. To a face he knew was looking up, he spoke down quietly, almost within his own orbit of sound, saying, " Nick and Bart're only cold meat now, but they can't be colder than I feel inside, because I realize for the first time that I never heard anyone say he'd change places with them and mean it. They died for everybody else, but nobody would've died for them, and when I think of their last minutes, I can imagine how they must've hated to go—and how they must've hated all of us that stayed behind. All their lives, they only wanted to do great things for people, and people let them, right on up to the greatest, but they were men, and they knew what they were losing, and in the end they must've hated all they'd ever loved. I could never blame them for that, not after what you let me do to you tonight—but all the same, I feel cold enough to be dead."

"When will you come back, Dan?"

"Do you want me to come back?"

"I don't want you to go."

"I have to go."

"Shall I look for you this evening?"

"Yes," he said. "As soon as it's dark."

*   *   *

He crossed Central Park South under a litmus-paper sky that the acid of dawn was dyeing red. The stars were guttering, and the moon seemed to have worn thin and become translucent. As yet, on the hosed-down walks and the sprinkled pavement, few people were about for the early-day and dustless air, but there were many birds on the wall of the park, on the backs of benches, and bustling in shallow puddles along the curb. At Fifth Avenue, Dan turned northward through a vault of elms.

Day-beginning sounds filled the stair-shaft of the tenement— sleep-slow voices, water on water, fat frying, and the high-pitched language of crockery. At the door of the Johnson flat, Dan paused for a moment without knowing why but wondering, and then he entered, hung up his hat, and stood staring at himself in the mirror near the rack, still wondering and still unanswered. His father rose from a chair at the window, put aside a newspaper, and approached him, silently offering his hand. The son looked down at it, and he fancied it as saying *I'm sorry, kid. I wish there was something I could* . . . but there fancy dwindled, and he heard no more. He took the hand and shook it briefly, and then he went toward his mother, meaning to embrace her. The action was in being before he realized that it had been designed for Miss Forrest, and he bungled in changing the shape of his mouth and the course and aim of his hands.

After eating, Dan lit a cigarette and sat absently watching the drift of its smoke. He noticed at length that heat from the coffee-pot caused the haze to ascend, and for no reason that he was aware of, he drew the pot toward him, flipped open its lid, and drew a deep breath of coffee vapor—and then suddenly fifteen years rewound and came to a stop, and he saw a small boy standing in fascination before a woman wearing a starched shirtwaist and a magic whispering skirt, and over its rustle he heard words that only now he knew he had remembered: *Some day you'll teach him, Miss Morey.* The years spun back, and Dan looked at his mother. He found her looking at him.

*   *   *

[*The office of the Committee was no longer an office: it was the parlor of Harry Keogh's house the day he was run over by a truck. Mourners had come to make their muted but vast sounds of sympathy, to say their ungovernable say, meaningless for both the living and the dead, and a picture on a wall was all the Keoghs had to prove that they'd ever owned a son. No less gone were the sons of this family here, and it sat empty and empty-handed, staring at likenesses on a wall.*] After a few moments, Dan left very quietly, and then for a long time he walked the gumdropped streets of the city, and if he thought any thoughts as he wandered, they failed to remain with his mind. Wherever he went, he went aimlessly, nothing impelling him and nothing detaining, and he saw faces without seeing people, and he heard voices without hearing words, and he emerged from apathy only when a name, long after being sensed, became insistent: Bowling Green.

By then, he had entered Washington Street from Battery Place and come to a stop before a forty-story butte of steel and stone. Where its marble water-table now rose in a perpendicular from the sidewalk, there once had been three doorways, all of them narrow and all with low lintels, as if built for a smaller breed of men: the left-hand one of these had given into a stationery-store displaying ashen trash and dead flies; the one at the right had led to a dark little shop where all day long a man had sat at the window, licking, pasting, and palming bunches of green-brown leaves, trimming them now and then with a rocker-bladed knife, and then licking, pasting, and palming them more, and always, by evening, the leaves had become cigars; the middle door had been the entrance to a tenement, and in a sudden conceit, Dan supposed going inside, climbing two flights of stairs to a room in a rear flat, and looking down at a bed in which a woman lay, and he supposed the woman to be with child, and the child, now eighteen and a half years old, supposed that he was watching himself being born. [*The stub of a cigarette fell at your feet, and, still in the daydream, you glanced upward, ready to glare at some grinning neighbor, but in the punched face of the building, there were no faces at all, grinning or otherwise, and you knew that the candy-store man was forever gone, along with his wonderful windowful of dusty junk, and the cigar-maker with his sheaves of tobacco torpedoes, and the house, and one particular flat, and the mother in labor, and the fruit of that labor—all were gone.*]

The school was still standing and still a visage in the vise of the taller structures on either side, but their grip seemed to have tightened with the years, and more constricted than ever were the many glass eyes, the brownstone brows, and the red-brick cheeks under their red-paint rouge. No voices came from the classrooms in the late-summer afternoon, no thin and trivial songs, and no high thin laughter, and there were no footfalls in the halls, no called-out names, and no gangs with their skirling "Wee-haw-kee!" Near the doorway stood a single boy dedicated to the task of defacing the wall: with a piece of pale blue chalk, he was filling in alternate oblongs of brick. [*You remembered the day you had come here for the first time, and you remembered the showcases in the corridor, and you*

remembered the Principal's office and the Principal's name, and you
remembered the dazzle of toys on the kindergarten floor, but what you
remembered best, because all the rest so soon gave way, was your
mother. Why were you thinking of her, you wondered, and why with
so paralyzing a pang did you recall the blunder of the kiss?] Many
bricks had been powdered blue, but against the vast expanse that
remained, they achieved only the effect of a stripe, and the project,
once so attractive to the boy, had lost its appeal. He still labored,
but he labored less, and now, aware of being watched, he looked at
Dan and said, "I guess I picked out the wrong color chalk," and
then he walked away.

[*Blunder, you'd called it, but you knew well that none had been made*
and, more, nothing done except by design. Still in the dark room of
your mind, though, was the reason, and if you thought long enough, the
door would open. Did you want it to open? You remembered the day
your father had come home from France (it was opening! it was open-
ing itself!), and the flags and the hooded artillery were dim, and the
crowds, and the ticker-tapeworms; what was still vivid was your moth-
er's haste to send you off to school, and always you would hear her
voice through the open transom, saying, "I've got to make up for that
day in Pemberton." And you remembered the Pemberton day too: the
engines in the Jersey yards, the snowed-on track, the sooty sky, the
brown streams in the white fields, and the long walk on the Rancocas
road—and of all those things, the last by far would come first. And
you remembered the night, a year earlier, when your father had made
up his mind to enlist, but the enlistment had been only a cipher for the
words whispered after the lights were out, for the rasping sheets, and
the sprung springs, and the single gasp. And now, without symbol or
device, you remembered coming into a room and finding your mother
naked, and you remembered her anger when she told you to go away,
and you remembered your own anger—and her surprise. And you re-
membered a time when there had been no anger even though both of you
had been naked: you had bathed with her, and she had let you play at
washing her till you became excited and tried to reach her breast once
more with your mouth. And you remembered a time when you had
touched her at will, with your mouth, with your hands, with all your

*body, and often you had slept between her and your father, and she had
been more yours than his—and then you were back at the beginning,
when she had been yours altogether, a dark and drowsy term like a long
night indoors out of the rain.*] He understood now the meaning of his
recollection that morning of Miss Morey. He knew her to have
been the first of many substitutions attempted by his mind, and he
knew that the series had ended with Miss Forrest, for in her the
aim of them all had been realized: the surrogate had become the
principal.

He glanced about and found himself on the Hudson waterfront
near Pier 13 (the DL&W—the Lackawan'), but all the rest of the afternoon he wandered nameless, unnumbered, and deserted streets.

*   *   *

She opened the door during the doorbell's ring, and in the moment before she stood aside, her figure made a black shadow on the
early-evening sky in a window beyond her. He went past her into
the entry and paused, looking down at his hat as if it had been given
to him by someone else to hold, and then it was taken from him,
and he had empty hands until the woman's body came against him,
and he filled them with it, again and again saying, "Juno, Juno . . . !"

"I wasn't sure you'd come back," the woman said. "I thought
you might be ashamed."

"Of what?" he said.

"The thing we did last night."

"I'm not ashamed of that. I'll never be."

The woman freed herself and moved away, saying, "What did
you do all day, Dan?"

"When I left you," he said, "I went home, but I couldn't stay
there. I couldn't stay at the office, either. I couldn't stay anywhere.
I walked. I wandered around. I didn't care where. The only thing
I wanted was to keep going, and I did, and after a long time I found
myself in front of the house I was born in—at least, in front of
where it used to be, because it's gone now. All the while I was drifting about, I must've been heading for that one particular place without knowing it— and without knowing why. I know now, though."

The woman gazed down at the road-lights in the park, strings
of beads strung wide, and she said, "Do you?"

"I think I went for a last look," he said, "the kind a person takes before he goes in for the night."

"What were you looking for?"

"Myself," he said, "although you'd suppose that would be the one thing you could look at anywhere, the one thing that was always with you. It isn't: a person is scattered all over, wherever he's been, and the pieces don't always go along when he moves away; they stay behind sometimes."

"Is that why you came back here this evening?" the woman said. "To find some more of yourself?"

"To find?" he said. "I don't want to find anything. All day long, I was only trying to lose." He went closer to the woman and contemplated her face in the last light from the saffron hem of the sky. "I wanted to see myself once more the way I was, and I did—and now, before the room gets dark, I want to see you."

Again the woman disengaged herself, this time to move from place to place and eddy among objects that she idly touched in passing, and still in motion, she said, "What happened today that made you decide to call me Juno?"

"I didn't know I'd done that," he said.

"Last night, I was Miss Forrest. Tonight, the first word out of your mouth was Juno. Why?"

"I don't remember calling you Juno, but if I did, it came out naturally."

"Only a few hours ago, using my name would've made you feel as if you were doing something dirty. Why don't you feel dirty now?"

"I don't know, but I think I'd only feel dirty now if I called you Miss Forrest. It'd be like saying . . ."

The woman reached for a lamp-chain, and the day-end glow was gone from the window and the sky. "Like saying what, Dan?" she said.

"Like saying the name of my mother," he said. "I had a lot of peculiar thoughts today. I remembered things I never dreamed were in my mind—things like being jealous of my father as far back as the first time I was able to think, even before, maybe."

The woman said, "Is that one of the parts of yourself that you left behind? Because if you think so, you're wrong: it went with you. It's *still* with you."

"Not any more," he said, "not since last night," and he realized, as soon as the words were in flight, that no other words in the language could possibly overtake them.

"You once asked me how old I was," the woman said, "and I told you that I was old enough to be your mother. From then on, I *was* your mother, but as long as you didn't know it, I was willing to let you do anything with me that you'd've done with any other stranger—but I'm not a stranger any more, Dan; deep down in your mind, I'm what you always wanted me to be." She looked at her hands, at a picture on the wall, at the ceiling, the floor, and then nothing. "But it comes so soon," she said. "It comes so soon, Dan. I'd hoped to have a few years, three or four at the most, and they'd've meant little to you, because you'd still've been a young man when they were over, but they'd've meant a great deal to me, because I'd've been middle-aged. Sooner or later, you'd've realized what you were using me for, or found someone your own age, or simply grown out of me, and I'd not've minded, because I'd've had all the time between now and then, and whatever it amounted to, it would've been enough. But I never thought it'd be only one day, Dan—one day!"

"The way you talk, what I found out today was a bad thing, but I think it was a good thing, and I'm only sorry I didn't find it out long ago, because then I'd've been with you all this time instead of with my mother. As it is, I've never really been with you till just now, when I came in here and called you Juno. For four years before that, whether I knew it or not, I was always somewhere else and always with another person. To me, *that* was the bad thing, and I'm glad it's over and done with tonight instead of next year, because tonight, for the first time, I can be inside of *you*."

The woman shook her head. "Not tonight, next year, or ever," she said.

He responded to a question that had not been asked, saying, "She'll always be only my mother now . . . ," and then he paused. "Why do you say that, Juno? What do you mean?"

"I mean you're going away, and you're not coming back."

"I never said anything about going away."

"I know, Dan, but I did."

He took a moment to understand and another to believe, and he said, "You don't mean I'm going, then; you mean you're putting me out. After four years of being friends and a day of even better, you're putting me out!"

"You put *yourself* out, Dan."

"There couldn't be anything crazier than that on earth! I came back here because there was no other place left that I gave a damn about and no other person that I cared to see—not to say goodbye! If I'd gotten all I wanted in only one night, I'd've told you so this morning, and that would've been the end of it, but I couldn't forget four years in a couple of hours even if I tried! Nobody could—nobody but you! You're the one that's had enough!"

"I've had what a school always gets from a pupil: nothing. You've been graduated, Dan, and now I wish you'd go."

[*In a little while, she'd turn on the light in the bedroom and draw the shade, and then she'd unpin her watch and wind it* (THE TIME NOW IS . . . *a matter of life and death*), *and then she'd stand before a long narrow glass, staring at a staring image in another room, an identical life in an identical world, and then she'd take off her clothes and begin to brush her hair, and the unspoken word "forest" would be heard, and as she moved her arms, her breasts would swing, making no one lustful except herself—and then she'd be lying in bed in the dark, and there'd be no hands to ply her passion but her own.*] He went toward the door.

"Dan . . . !" the woman said.

He felt as if he had been sandbagged to a stop, and there were seconds of silence before he remembered saying, "What?" and letting the door swing shut, he turned.

Apparent to him at once were the origin and extent of the woman's disorder, always inoperable and now past even relief: no less than his mother had become his mother again, Miss Forrest had become Miss Forrest, and he knew late what the teacher had known from the beginning, that their union had ended with his first sight of her bare of the raiment worn in his mother's guise. Adorned as his mother, she had enjoyed an intermission and ripened before ripening eyes, and her day-by-day accumulation of age had gone unseen; stripped to Miss Forrest, she had withered under the sudden weight of time loaded on in mass, and her forty years were evident beyond all chance of change.

"You tell me to get out," he said, "and when I start to go, you stop me, and last night it was all right to do a certain thing, and tonight it's all wrong, a crime, a sin. I'm twisted around. I'm covered with hands, picking and picking at me. I don't know what you want any more. I don't understand you."

The woman looked at him, saying nothing, and in a spasm of dismay that clenched within him like a cold hand, he saw her fumble for the long line of buttons that fastened her dress. He thought of escape, but powerless to inflict so deep an injury on her, he remained to watch her inflict one equally deep on herself, and when the dress parted, he was seized of the sense that she had made an incision in her own body. The few pieces of pink silk that she displayed for him seemed somehow public now, and they had no meaning other than the meaning of laundry. He stood with his back against the door, staring at what he had tried for so long to visualize, and shrunk with regret, he knew at last how much more perfect than the actual had been his dreams.

"You can't go away now, Dan," the woman said. "If you stay, I'll let you do whatever you want to me, the thing we did last night or any other thing you ever thought of, dirty as well as clean. I won't mind so long as you don't go away." [*But you did worse: you stayed where you were, helplessly watching a vast and suicidal error.*] "For God's sake, Dan, don't let me stand here like this!"

"You don't have to stand there," he said, and he thought it strange that he sounded so pitiless when all he felt was pity. "You can go inside and lie down." 26 83 .279

She turned away, and he watched her in anguish, knowing that this last of many views of her would supersede the rest, and that henceforth, whenever he brought her back to mind, he would see her body in silk like flaccid flesh, her legs in sagging stockings, and

her feet in sensible shoes. He shivered a little, and then he followed
her into the bedroom.

*   *   *

When he left the woman, shortly before midnight, he crossed
town to Madison Avenue, and there he boarded a Harlem-bound
trolley, riding the rear platform and looking back over the spun-out
rails. Near 72nd Street, a passenger signaled for a stop, and before
alighting, he thrust a newspaper behind the controller against which
Dan was leaning. Part of a caption was visible—". . . EXECUTED IN
BAY STATE"—and part of a column:

> . . . To the very shadow of the Chair, the murderer Van-
> zetti clung to the fiction of innocence. In a statement made on
> the eve of paying the penalty for his crimes, the convicted kil-
> ler declared: "If it had not been for this thing, I might have
> lived out my life talking at street-corners to scorning men. I
> might have died, unmarked, unknown, a failure. Now we are
> not a failure. This is our career and our triumph. Never in our
> full life could we hope to do such work for tolerance, for jus-
> tice, for man's understanding of men as now we do by acci-
> dent. Our words, our pains—nothing! The taking of our lives,
> lives of a good shoemaker and a poor fish-peddler—all! That
> last moment belongs to us—that agony is our triumph!" To
> this stubborn unrepentance, the doomed radical's final utter-
> ance was in marked contrast. With Madeiros and Sacco al-
> ready out of the way, Vanzetti was brought into the death-
> chamber, where he shook hands with Warden Hendry and
> thanked him for his kindness. He shook hands also with De-
> puty Warden Hogsett, Prison Physician McLaughlin, and two
> of the four guards. While the straps were being adjusted about
> his arms and body, he said, quite gently for an anarchist, "I
> now wish to forgive some people for what they are doing to
> me." He did not speak again, and thus ended a case that. . . .

["*In the end,*" *you'd said,* "*they must've hated all they'd ever loved,*"
and the words—like stepped-on ants, they kept on crawling—were

hard to kill. How could you have been so wholly wrong? How could
you have learned so little from the good shoemaker and the poor fish-
peddler? How could you have breathed the same air and been rained
on by the same rain—and grown down while they grew tall?]

IF IT HAD NOT BEEN FOR THIS THING

WALKING from the car-line, he passed people sprawled on
the steps of brownstone stoops, and people framed in the
light or dark squares of windows, and people strolling in the warm
night, and people squatting along the curbs, and people [*living out*
their lives talking at street-corners to scorning men]. When he reached
his house, he paused for a moment [*to take one more last look at*
yourself, you wondered, or at the stars and the spaces between the stars,
or at the funeral of God, or merely at the beginning of another day?],
and then he went indoors and upstairs.

In the parlor, long since his bedroom, a light had been left on in
the chandelier, and the cover of the couch had been turned down,
but knowing that sleep could not yet dominate him, he seated himself at the table, and for a while he watched the smoke of his cigarette climb the static air and disappear. Behind him, a door opened,
and he heard bare feet brush across the floor, but he sat motionless
until his mother spoke his name and put her hands on his shoulders, and then, rising quickly, he moved away. He was under a
compulsion to look at her, however, and he turned to dwell briefly
on the insinuations her body made against her nightgown. Beyond
her, in the doorway, stood the hack-driver.

"You look tired, son," the woman said.

"I could fall on my face."

"Why don't you go to bed?"

"I've been going to bed for over eighteen years. You'd think I'd
be rested by this time."

"That depends on what you do to need a rest from."

"I do a most exhausting thing: I live all day."

"All day and half the night," the woman said.

"I live every single minute, and it's killing me."

"I believe you. When did you eat last?"

"I don't remember. I'm trying to see how far I'll get on nothing."

"I can tell you," the woman said. "On the kind of living you've been doing, you'll get nowhere."

"Nowhere," her son said, and then he stood listening. Twenty-four blocks down Park Avenue, the head-end of the *Owl*, bound for Boston, broke from the tunnel with a mounting drumfire of trucks on track. "Nowhere," he said, "but I'm not on rails, God damn it—not me!" and he strode to the map, and tearing loose the dangling crayon, he jabbed it at the red blot in the east, saying, "This is nowhere," and then violently scoring the map from east to west and north to south, he said, "And this is somewhere, and I'm a son-of-a-bitch and a bastard if I don't see it all! Those God damn lines are for me, because, God damn it, *one* of us Johnsons is going to die satisfied!" and then he dropped the crayon and covered his face and began to cry, and for a moment, as the *Owl* passed by, no one heard him.

PART THREE

MY OWN, MY NATIVE LAND

BEYOND fall fields candlewicked with cut-down corn, thinning maples rose red and yellow against the Jersey hills, and in the early-morning air hung a fine bitter smoke of smoldering leaves. A faint frost still clung to surfaces hidden from the sun, and birds like quarter-notes of music shook dew-diamonds from the long staff made by the telegraph-wires.

[*You stood at the roadside, looking back at the Pierce-Arrow, now just disappearing over a rise, and the last thing your father had said revived itself in your mind: "God knows I'm crazy about your mother, kid, but if I was your age all over again, she'd have to do more to catch me than lay down twice without a license. She'd have to get up and run like hell afterwards, because I'd be on my way to the Wind River Range, and Jackson Hole, and Tanforan, and The Dalles—all those places that'll always be only names on a map. I swapped 'em for a wife, and (who knows?) maybe I got the best of the bargain. She's still a lot softer to make love to than a mountain—and come to think of it, there's a sure cure for my blues. Drop in on us when you get back, kid, but knock first." And then he'd laughed, you remembered, and gone.*]

A southbound truck slowed down, and Dan caught it in motion and slid in alongside the driver, saying, "Thanks. Going far?"

"Camden," the driver said. "That far enough?"

"Not quite, but it'll help."

"Where you bound for?"

Dan pointed straight ahead through the windshield. "There," he said.

"That takes in all but what's in back of us."

"That too, if the world's as round as they say."

[*The blood had faded, and the meat-wagons had hauled away the entrails and the amputations, and the souvenir-hunters had long since picked over and pocketed the buttons, the buckles, the odds and ends of battle, but the black guns were still here and their spare rounds still neatly stacked near the limbers, and the rifle-pits and the lunettes, a little shallower now, a little worn by the snow and rain, were still concaved in the ground, and the same scarred boulders lay on Little Round Top, and the same trees, only sixty-four years older, screened the High Water Mark from the Angle, and there were stone words on stone memorials for the nine thousand dead, the tar-heels and shoeless crackers of Marse Robert and the foreigners and blue bummers of Meade, yet for all the torn-off legs tumbled end-over-end through the wheat, for all the furrows plowed with faces and the holes dug with shattered bone, nothing had been lost here but lives and nothing won but praise: there were more slaves than ever, and there would be more Gettysburgs until they were free.*]

The sun was going down when he crossed the fields among trees that, standing in their fallen leaves, seemed to be disrobing for the night, and when he reached the first open barn on the road to Chambersburg, he walked into its dark blue gloom and stretched himself out on a skiff of hay. He heard a meadow-lark practicing on a flute, and he heard sparrows making cheap talk in the loft, and he heard a truck pass along the pike, its tire-treads sounding like adhesive-tape torn, and then he heard nothing.

[*To see it all—the whole brawling, bullying, bragging, bamboozling cant-ranting, horny, leather-necked, high-riding, sweet-talking, home-hungry, and heart-racingly handsome mongrel called America! To see it all, you dreamed, to see it all . . . !*]

BUCKEYE JOHNNY APPLESEED

THEY say he first turned up in Ohio around about 1801—on Zane's Trace, it was, along Licking Creek—and they say he came leading a pack-horse loaded to the hocks with burlap bags, but they didn't say (because they didn't know) what the bags contained. Being he was a black-eyed man, a queer thing in those parts, and being he kind of kept to himself, all the queerer for a stranger, he let himself in for a little side-watching, and no matter if he did overlook to bring a gun. They say, the ones that made it their business, that he marched out onto a cleared piece of land and drawed something out of the topmost of his bags, which he buried it in a slew of shallow holes and went away, and when he was gone, it still being their business, they say they got down on their shins and poked about for whatever he'd cached (it figured to be gold), but only finding dirt as deep as they dug, they tried to pass him off as addled, but all the same they felt like chumps for being hankypankied by an out-of-stater.

They say this identical black-eyed man shown up next along the Muskingum, still with that pack-animal and still with those bags, and they say that there too he made some hocus-pocus over holes in the ground, and there too nobody got richer for scratching where it itched. And now the story began to get around, to pass from hand to hand (instead of the gold that was never found), and you heard that the black-eyed man, and his monkeyshines, had been seen wherever there was bottom-land and topsoil—on the Scioto and the Hocking, on White Woman Creek, on all the Miamis and the Maumee, on the Big Walnut and the Black Fork of the Mohican— and you heard other things as well, how he played with bear-cubs while the bear looked on or snoozed, how he walked barefoot and damn near b.a. in the snow, how he found his way just by following his nose, like a bee or a bird, and you heard how he'd douse his fire if insects flew too near the flames.

After a time, they say they took to expecting him in the spring, looking forward to his queer but quiet ways, and when he would finally arrive—with his horse and his bags, but never with a gun— they would feel good, like they did about a rain, and they would talk to him sometimes, and some would be sad as he went about his fruitless work of hiding nothing in plain view of all, and now they dug no more in the loose soil after he'd moved on. They let it lay— out of respect, you might say.

Fruitless? Not the longest day a man ever lived. Nobody said

fruitless when the apple-trees came, because that's what he'd had
in those burlap bags: orchards for Ohio!

[*It's a good thing you're dead, Johnny. It's a good thing you didn't
live to see what they did to your well-loved trees. The trees are gone,
Johnny, the trees and the plants from the other seed you scattered:
catnip, snakeweed, hoarhound, dog-fennel, and pennyroyal. It's a
good thing you're all done coming down the pike in your coffee-sack
clothes and that stew-kettle you wore for a hat—you'd've been hot,
Johnny, because there's very little shade.*

[*They say you could stick pins in your flesh and feel no pain, but
you'd've flinched for your trees if you'd been here to see them brought
to their knees with a double-bitted ax. They took fifteen years to grow
and fifteen minutes to kill, and even that was held to be slow (only one
tree would fall at a time), and people fell to using fire, and whole groves
were sent to hell in a hand-basket. It's a good thing you're some place
else now, Johnny. It's a good thing you're never coming back to spoiled
soil held together by concrete and lashed down with steel rail and copper wire.*

[*They say you died somewhere up around Fort Wayne, and while
they don't say where you went from there, a lot of us have a pretty
fair idea. We don't know the name of the state, Johnny (let's just say
it hasn't been admitted to the Union yet), but whatever it's called, it
must be pleasant up there under trees that'll never be snags or sawyers
in some spring flood. Trees must grow better when they know they'll
never be harmed; their fruit must be prime.*

[*Are you running short of seed, Johnny? We could each bring you a
bag when we come. . . .*]

O THOSE WABASH BLUES

THEY had Johnny Appleseed back where you just come from,
and they had Abe Lincoln over yonder where you're heading
for, but don't go off half-cocked, son, and don't think this here is
only a blank space between the last place and the next: we had
Gene Debs.

We're not too long on scenery, having mighty little timber that isn't laid crosswise for cross-ties, and with hills about as high as wrinkles in a rug, we naturally save our logging lies for the Liar's Bench; we aren't old, and we aren't new, coming later than the Original Thirteen but sooner than your come-lately states; we aren't rich, and we aren't pore, and having treated the Indians neither better nor worse (Tecumseh might tell you otherwise), we aren't proud, but we're a damn long chalk from meek; we could be smarter, and we could also be dumber, and our weather leaves a lot to be desired, being hot in summer and cold in winter, but if it was the other way 'round, come to think of it, it'd sure be tough on crops; we've got two sides of the track here, one for the bums and one for the gents, but we don't have a third (where the Sambos live); we were Whiggish once, but we're still a far cry from being Tory, and so, holding our nose at hell-fire and thumbing it at Popery, we worship higher than the kneeling and not quite so erect as the Elect.

By and large, son, we're ordinary sweet-and-sour Americans— psalm-singing but sinful, easy-going but tight-assed, bull-headed but right-minded, sore but serene, and mean often but seldom all day long. We aren't perfect, but God was good to us here in Indiana: we had Gene Debs.

MARSE LINKUM

TELL fewer of the funny stories I told,
And make no further mention of my plug hat,
My rolled umbrella, and my outsize shoes,
Bury the legend that I was a bastard deep,
Let my mother's sleep be that of the just,
And if you must be heard, speak briefly
Of my wife Mary and my wife's madness,
But speak not a word of my spoken-for Ann,
Nor say that I loved her all my life.

Forget my arms and legs, my awkward ways,
And the guffaws I caused when I sat a horse;

Forget the cat-napping pickets I pardoned,
Forget my Four-score speech, my Bixby letter,
And my six-mile walk to refund six cents;
Forget the first house I lived in (let it rot
And let all the others, but not the last),
And build me no more monuments, nor cast me
But as pennies for children and small change.

Say not that I saw two faces in my glass,
One like my own and one strange, as if bled,
And dismiss my dreams of a terrible end
Such as many now dead dreamed of and found
On the sunken road before Fredericksburg;
Make little of my anger at little McClellan
(Outnumbered! With three blues for every gray!)
And less of the lie that the slaves went free,
Because you know better, and so do they.

Say naught of my high voice and my sad eyes,
Throw away my relics (the watch and key,
The muffler, the ox-yoke, and the rock
On which I scratched my name and Ann's),
And retain but a pair of my photographs,
A Brady for the hard evidence of my looks
And a Gardner for the books of learned fools,
And now that only my coat can be pilfered,
Stop moving my coffin from place to place
And let the ghouls unfrock these bones.

Such are the slight favors that I request,
Yet if it please you not, grant me none:
Get my old chestnuts off your chest
Should they still strike you funny;
And if you like, praise me as Honest Abe
And raise a log-cabin Christ with nails;
Re-engrave this grave and homely face

On your money, preserve the box at Ford's,
And make cold fact of the cool fiction
That my father's name was In- or Enlow;
Wring more tears from women on the floor
For bounty-jumpers and last-remaining sons,
And count the ones that kissed my hand;
And if your tongues are slung in the middle,
Then keep Ann and my love for Ann green
While you hail the hell I had with Mary.

Slight favors, and done without with ease,
For I doubt there's much I much require
To lie decently dead save your living long,
And you will so live, and I will so lie,
If you know the truth: it was you, not I,
That Booth was hired to kill; it was you,
The Union, that he fired at in firing at me;
And since I died of what went wide of you,
Please remember all I stood for when I fell.

LIKE THE SAP IN A TREE

I WAS born in the Old Dominion, mother of presidents, but I
never got to be president, and for that matter, I never even got
to be a Virginian: I happened to be black, and my state was slavery,
and wherever I went, a piece of it followed me, the piece I stood
on—or so my Master told me (Mr. Peter Blow) when he took me
to Missouri to work for his living. He died there, the poor bastard,
leaving a few gold trinkets and a salmagundi of trash (including
me) to a spinster daughter. She used me till I went out of fashion,
or she needed cash, and I was knocked down third-hand to a Mr.
Doc Emerson of Jefferson Barracks. Mr. Doc carried me off to Rock
Island, Illinois, the first free soil I'd ever set foot on—and right
now that freedom began to flow up my legs like the sap in a tree.
  Like the sap in a tree!
  The arms I had grew longer, and I grew new ones, like branches,

and I owned forty hands of forty fingers each, and when that free-
dom-juice gave me speech, I spoke in words that only whites (and
flights of birds) had used before: I said, "I'm free!" I said it to myself once, trying it for flavor and finding it salt, and then, aloud, I
said it to a cloud in the sky, and now I said it to snake-fences and
smoke-stacks, to steeples and green corn, to the railroad tracks and
dogs dozing in the shade, to people (whites, blacks, and in-be-
tweens), and in the end I said it where it hurt, to Mr. Doc—and
when I spat out my last Illinois dirt, it went to waste on Missouri,
but not on me, because I walked on it, and it grew me great enough,
even in the Show-me state, to keep on saying, "I'm free!"

I said it to slaves, to Lovejoy's friends, to Osage braves, to boys
in the street, to stars and walls and stern-wheelers, to the buffalo-
blood on the plains, to the up-and-down rains and the flood of mud
named the Mississippi. I said it for twenty years (for ten of them
to meeching Christers who looked the other way or laughed, and
for ten more to a raft of shysters scared stiff by the South). I said
it to deaf ears, plugged ears, and what was left of ears slit for lying;
I said it to the well, the sick, the dying, and the dead; I said it
("I'm free!" I said) to frontier pimps and waterfront tarts, to sloe-
gin drunks and greasy gunmen, to hound-dog handlers and easy
marks, to brass-knuck punks and squatter-sovereigns, and now and
then, meaning once or twice, to someone nice enough to call me
Mr. Scott.

The Supreme Court said otherwise in '57. It said I was a nigger
(it used fancier guff), and a nigger, if he acted tough, was apt to
finish up a tree with a bigger neck than when he started. It said I
was inferior. It said I was a chattel. It said I had an owner (or,
worse, the owner had *me*), and it said he could sell me, swap me,
give me away, or stick me like a hog. It said all this God damn slop
about being free would have to stop. It said I'd be free some time,
but not this side of the grave. It said my case had been tried, and
being still alive, I was still a slave.

But I said, "I'm free!" and I never quit.

The word was like the sap in a tree!

HAD I SO INTERFERED IN BEHALF

OF THE RICH

YOU'RE on the far side of the grave now, Dred
(You've been dead a year), but you're freer
Than I am—and I'm white and still living.
I won't be living long, though, friend,
And I'll end as black in the face as you:
They're going to hang me high in an hour,
And I'll draw my last breath where you drew your first,
And I'll rejoice, as if they'd given me my choice,
That my place of death was your place of birth—
Virginia.

I could've lived to be older than fifty-nine;
I could've lasted out this merchant century:
I had the frame for it—but not the frame of mind.
If I'd been blind to you and deaf to God,
If I'd loved myself more and money most,
If I'd kept my nose clean and my soul snotty,
If I'd valued my skin, if I'd thrown no stones
At the sin of slavery, if I'd passed the buck
And left such truck as bravery and broken bones
To fools—in short, if I'd been a sleeping dog—
They'd've let me lie till the nineteen-hundreds.

I die sooner, but with nothing done that I'd undo
If my life were spared: the slavers slain
On the Pottawatomie would be slain again,
All five, and more if found; the battle
Once won at Black Jack Oaks would be twice won;
The raids made on Sugar Creek and the fight lost
On the Marais des Cygnes would be made and lost
In the future as they were in the past;
The same slaves would be taken by force

From Messrs. Hicklin, Larue, and Cruise,
Of Missouri,
And Cruise would be shot dead a second time
If he cocked his Colt in his second life;
And lastly, the same treason would be committed
At Harper's Ferry, and when brought to book,
I'd give the same reason that I gave
In Kansas:
Nits grow to be lice!

Knowing that delay would merely change
The number of the day and the name of the month,
Knowing that at some later date, as the same
Traitor, I'd dance on air for the same crimes,
I say let them crack my spine now and here.

Commend me to your only Master, Dred, and mine.

POSTCARD FROM COLORADO SPRINGS

"YOUR son's a waiter here at the Antlers Hotel, so take that map-tack out of Wichita and move it about three hundred miles further west. Altitude 5980 feet in the Grill where I work, slightly higher under the rafters where I sleep. Can see Pike's Peak from my window, but no bust. Send mackinaw. Love. Dan."

MILE-HIGH WINTER

WHEN Dan came from the side door of the hotel, a dry and fine-feathered snow was falling, and it fled before the wind to make concave strips of molding along the curb and the building-line. Underfoot, it packed without melting, and it lay long on clothes, like crystals of camphor, and spinning through areas of light around the street-lamps, it was a vast skirt passing in a waltz. Few people were about, and few cars, and the store-fronts, except for an illuminated name here and there, were dark. From the roof of the depot, a railroad herald wrought in neon reddened the down-drift and the nap of snow now beginning to cover the pavement.

Through the glare and the grain in the air, the steamed windows of an all-night diner were dim. There were no other patrons in the wagon when Dan entered, and climbing a stool at the curve of the counter, he ordered a cup of coffee, added sugar from a shaker, and then let it stand before him untasted while he stared at a distortion of himself in the bright nickel urn behind the bar. [*How often would you have to see her before speaking, you wondered, and when you finally spoke, what would you say, and what would she answer if she heard? Would she seem the same then, you wondered, would you like her voice, and would you still admire her face, and her hands and feet, and the way she dressed, and the flavor of the powder she wore? Would you care for her name when you learned it, would there be more to her than you could see and hear, would you want to touch her after touching her once, and would she be better or less than a dream? Would the wondering end tonight, you wondered, or would the words to end it with come too late if they came at all . . . ?*] The door opened, and Dan turned to it, and the door closed, and he turned away, and now when he gazed at the urn, there were two faces in the shining cylinder. [*Would you speak, you wondered, and if you did, what would you say . . . ?*]

"Can't you think of a single thing?" she said.

He looked at her for a moment, and then he smiled, saying, "I've been thinking all week, and if I had any thoughts, I can't remember them. I haven't any right now. I don't know what to say next."

"If you expect to get anywhere with me, you'd better say that I'm pretty."

"I don't expect to get anywhere with anybody, but I'll say even more: you're the prettiest girl I've ever seen."

"If I'm all that, why did it take you a week to say it?"

"If you hadn't spoken first, I'd never've said it. I'd've gone all my life regretting it, but it wouldn't've done any good."

"Now you'll have to regret the opposite—that you did say it."

"If I have to regret anything, let it be that."

"You're simple, Dan. You're simple enough to break anyone's heart but mine, and I'll tell you why: I haven't got one."

"Who gave you my name, and what else do you know?"

She nodded at the counterman, saying, "Where you come from, what you're doing here, and your age. I also know that you never asked him about me. Why not? Didn't you want to know who I was—the prettiest girl you've ever seen?"

"I wanted to hear about you from yourself. It wouldn't've meant much to have him tell me."

"It might've meant more than you suppose," she said. "He's known me for a long time, and if you ask him, he'll tell you where you're going. You wouldn't look at me like that if you knew."

"I'll look at you like this as long as you let me, and all the while I'll be trying to guess what you've done that you can't forgive."

"He'd've warned you to watch out for the cars," she said. "Aren't you afraid of the cars?"

"What do you find that's so hateful in yourself?"

"Would you like to walk me home, Dan?" she said.

"Yes," he said. "I'd like it very much."

The wind had died away, but snow still fell, more heavily now and straight down, and they intruded on a night so entirely quiet as to make it a matter of respect to speak in lowered voices, as if all that they passed—the many houses, the many trees, the many streets—were entitled to be undisturbed. [*You thought of Miss Forrest, and the sole image you were able to see was the last she had left with your mind. All the rest, the whole four years of fancy, was suppressed by that one overwhelming imprint, and you shivered, because you knew that nothing would ever remove it, and you said*] "When're you going to tell me your name?"

"What'll you do when you know it—speak in rhyme?"

"If I could, I'd do that now. You make me lighter than air."

"My name is Julia Davis. Are you still in the sky?"

"I'm a mile up, and I'm never coming down."

"Would it give you any pleasure to kiss me?"

"A great deal—if it gave you the same."

"Never mind me. I live on the ground."

"In more ways than one: you eat it."

"I'm waiting for you to take your pleasure."

"You don't want to kiss me. You only want me to kiss you."

"It'll come to the same. We'll both get smeared."

"I don't like to stick my face where it isn't wanted."

"Don't you ever go where you're not wanted?" she said. "To me, that's half the fun of going."

"What's the other half?" he said.

"There's a big joint up the canyon—the Broadmoor, it's called. It's for Gold-Coasters from Chicago, not local phone-operators, but whenever they have a hop out there, I go. I'm not wanted, but I go. Are you still flying around, Dan?"

"No. All of a sudden, I'm flat on my face in the gutter. My wings came off."

"The cars, Dan. Kiss me and watch out for the cars."

"I saw you a week ago for the first time, and I haven't been able to see anything else ever since: you fill the eye. But don't get smaller, Julia; don't let me see beyond you."

"That makes one warning apiece. What follows?"

"We try to find out how we come to be walking with each other through this particular snowfall."

"Why don't we just enjoy it? Why're people the only animals that have to say, 'Where do you come from?' It's where they are that counts."

"They get where they are with baggage."

"I travel light. I'm not one for going about loaded down with sin."

"What do you do to shuck it?"

"I watch my father: he lugs himself wherever he goes. He can't get the past out of his mind or off his back. It's smothering him, but he can't let go. He used to own a store near Ludlow. That's south of here a ways. Does the name mean anything to you?"

"It means the Coal & Iron Police and a man called Rockefeller."

"I might've known you'd know," she said. "It was a good store, and almost everybody in the district traded there—ranchers, farmers, railroaders—and my father had money in the bank and a name, and he'd still have both if he hadn't gone soft in the head when the strike came along in 1913. One of the things that touched it off was a company-rule that the miners had to buy from the company-stores, a rig for keeping them in hock to the grave. My father stood to gain if they won, so when the men got hard up, and the union came to him for credit, he advanced it. He advanced himself right out of business, because the miners finally lost." She paused and looked back at two sets of prints that seemed black in the snow. "I'm waiting for you to tell me he was a martyr."

"Where was the elevation?" Dan said. "He stood to gain."

The girl studied him for a moment, and then saying, "You're honest enough to be pitiful, but I like you better all the time," she linked her arm with his and walked him on. "Never rub me the right way. No matter what I say, don't agree with me. You'll hardly ever be wrong."

"How does your father feel about Ludlow today? Would he do it all over again?"

"He loves being a night-watchman. It pays forty a month, and it keeps him out in the air. Mention unions to him, and he'll shoot you to death."

"Why doesn't he take it out on Rockefeller?"

"Rockefeller? What did Rockefeller ever do to him?"

"Whatever his reason was, he lined up against a bad company-rule."

"That was his own damn-fool choice, and he'd be the first to admit it."

"And you'd be the second, and forcing the pace."

"He can't blame the company for what happened to him. He can only blame himself."

"He isn't as lucky as you," Dan said. "You can always blame him for being a phone-operator."

At a crossing, they entered a fork, and leaving the road-lamps behind them, they laid down lengthening shadows between twin rows of locusts. The houses facing each other across the narrow way were identical, all of them small, old, and out of true, and sagging into rags of lawn, their porches of broken jig-saw were like open mouths with missing teeth.

"Little old men," Julia said. "Little old men with spots on their

clothes. I live in this one." She went toward the door, and Dan followed. The house was dark, but in a front room the remains of a
coal-fire inflamed the eyes of a stove, and its glow made faint lan-
terns of their faces. "Do I still have to tell you what to say next?"

"I think I know this time," Dan said.

"Then, God damn you, why don't you say it?"

"I had the words in my mouth all week. Now I only have spit."

"Make more words with it. You won't need many if they rhyme."

He went to the door, where he turned to say, "You'd've liked the
ones you chased away, Julia," and then he was outside and walking
back over the way he had come. The return seemed longer, and by
retracing his earlier trail, he sought to revive his earlier emotion,
but more snow had fallen, and other feet had left their marks, and
soon his own and Julia's were not to be found.

*　　*　　*

At the edge of the rink in Monument Valley Park, a bonfire felled
silhouettes from a circle of figures and made a giant wheel that lay
partly on the ice and partly on the snow surrounding it. In the distance, against a navy sky strewn with ground-glass stars, were the
cold shoulders of the mountains. Seated on one of the benches
rimming the bank furthest from the fire, Dan absently reviewed
skaters moving past singly, in tandem, and armlocked in pairs
[. . . *and you thought of Julia—and when you breathed the minted air,
it drilled you deep, and when you let it go, it was a part of yourself
that was visible—and you thought of Julia.* . . .].

"Whatever you're thinking," a voice said, "make it rhyme."

Wearing a knee-length skating-skirt, Julia stood before him on
the ice [*a Julia so different from the one you had borne in mind that,
as with Miss Forrest, you knew your thoughts of her had worn the
wrong face—but this time, unlike the other, the blood-and-bone fact far
outshone the fantasy*]. "I'm thinking of you," he said, "but there's
no rhyme for that."

"If you gave me a chance," she said, "I think I'd rhyme with
you. That's a favor I'm asking, Dan, and if I sound strange, it's because I want it very much."

"How would you sound if you got it?" he said.

"Even stranger," she said, "because I'd be grateful," and then, without waiting for a response, she tiptoed to gain speed and skated away.

[*It was almost as if the ice were in motion, you thought, and you watched it spin out from under a tread as nimble as a needle's on a record, a glide barely less than levitation; it was a dance as a dance was done in a dream, without effort, without pattern, and without sound, but with all the grace of smoke.*] The fire was down and most of the crowd gone before she wrote a last flourish with her runners and straightened into a long slow flow toward Dan's bench. He rose to meet her, and she came up against him as gently as a word, and he said, "You walk on water," and for a moment they stood there, hardly touching [*and then all at once you were hardly apart, and you were trying to suck each other dry through the mouth—and when you kneeled to unlace her skates, you thought ahead to a cold dark house with broken filigree, and you heard the harsh whisper of a leaking faucet and the stutter of sagging stairs, and in a space of powder-flavored air, you heard silk sigh in falling, and the rustle of skin on skin, and the whispers of hands in hair, and then a voice said, "Dan! Dan! My God damn Dan . . . !"*].

"Do you still think I'm pretty?"

"I'll think so as long as I live."

"Take me home, then, and talk all the way."

*   *   *

[*You lay there in the dark, trying to extract from the nineteen years of your life the fact, the choice, the accident, that explained your presence in a house with an unknown number on a street with an unknown name. Was it a chance word, you wondered, or was it the sound of a voice, or the look on a face, or a day in history that ended before your own began? Was it a person living or dead, was it the chemistry of your blood, was it some sight seen and forgotten (a rainfall, a parade, a setting sun), or was it a green throwaway and a ball in a brain? but always, beyond any answer, some part of the query remained, and in the end you knew that while there had been many roads forward, you would find no road back—and realizing that these were only new words*] *for Julia's, you turned to her and said,"It's where you are that counts," and then she turned too, and again you were her God damn Dan. . . .]*

*   *   *

They were walking one night, and he said,"I call this the mile-high winter."

She said,"How high is it when you hate me?"

"I never hate you. I only hate some of your ways."

She said,"My ways are me, but I can't make you believe that. You think I'm what you think, and I know what I am. Would you like me to tell you?"

"You're pretty!" he said."That's what you are—you're pretty!"

She said,"I'm a tramp. Do you know what a tramp is? If not, there's one on your arm."

He made her stop while he studied her face, her throat, her clothes, her hands, her feet, and again her face, and then he shook his head, saying, "I'm sorry, Julia, but I don't understand."

She said,"Do you think I waited all these years for Mr. New damn York? I got started early, and you're a long way from being Number One."

"At what number did you get to be a tramp?" he said [*and now she made a study of you, and it came to an end in a smile that seemed to climb out of pity and disbelief like the survivor of a wreck, and she said, "Take me home, Mr. New simple York. . . ."*].

*   *   *

Reaching Denver after dark, they paused for a moment before the bus-terminal and then walked through a slanting snow toward an intermittent sign insisting ROOMS like a common scold. [*The entrance to the hotel, a stairway, lay between a barbershop and a lunch-counter, and the lobby was merely a first landing furnished with a key-rack, a cuspidor, and a rubber plant. The rooms—you were standing in one of them now (Whose cigar had scarred the window-sill, and when? Who had drunk from the chipped water-pitcher, and who had set a beer-bottle on the Gideon Bible? Who had last used these towels, this tub and toilet, and the frayed shoe-rag hanging behind the door? Who*

had lain face-up and who face-down on the dished-in bed—their names,
their ages, and the number of times . . . ?)—as soon as you saw the
rooms, you knew you had made a mistake.]

"I wanted to celebrate my birthday," he said, "but this isn't
much of a place for it."

"How can you say that?" Julia said. "To a small-town whore
like me, this is the last word."

"I wish I could've taken you to the Brown Palace."

"Why? What would happen there that isn't going to happen
here?"

"Nothing has to happen anywhere, Julia. I didn't bring you to
Denver for that."

"You didn't? Explain how we come to be in a room with a bed,
then."

"In a couple of hours, I'll be starting my nineteenth year. I don't
know why any more, but yesterday the fact seemed important
enough to honor in a special way."

"Like getting laid in Denver instead of Colorado Springs?" she
said. "Is that special enough—or is it the price of a place that makes
it special?"

"I was trying for once to see with your eyes. You like better
things than this, and tonight, for the first time, I'd've wanted you
to have them."

"Would I be any the less a bum if this dump had a bell-hop—
and would you be any the less a horny-ike? Not at all. People do
the same thing in a ten-dollar room that they do in a three-. I
know, because I've done it, and right over there in the Brown Palace, and if you doubt it, I'll furnish proof."

"I never doubt anything you say. I don't always understand
what makes you say it, but I never doubt it. You're honest, even
at your meanest, and I take you at your word."

"I'll give you the man's name, if you like," she said. "Not the
one on the register, of course—you know that as well as I do—but
the real one, middle name and all, along with home address, occupation, age, and general physical condition. In fact, I'll tell you
whatever you want to know: how we met; whether we were liq-

uored up or sober; what his hair smelled like, and his breath, and his armpits; whether I enjoyed him more or less than you; and what I thought about later while I was smoking a cigarette. Whatever you're interested in, Dan."

"You told me once that I wasn't the first. What difference does it make how somebody else got to be a number?"

"Not only were you not the first," she said, "but you're not even going to be the last."

"I've never thought otherwise, but that doesn't make it easier to hear."

"I don't mean to worry you: you'll be taken care of tonight."

"That's a good birthday-present, Julia. I don't know how to thank you."

"Before I forget: congratulations. And when you feel the urge, just speak up. It's nothing to be ashamed of."

"At the moment, I'd sooner hear about Mr. and Mrs. John Smith in their ten-dollar room."

"What would you do if I walked straight the hell out of our *three*-dollar room?"

"I'd take off my coat (like this)," he said. "Are you watching, Julia? And then I'd sit down in this chair (I just sat), and I'd put my feet up on the radiator (that's a radiator, that iron thing), and I'd stare at the wall, wondering when you'd come back."

"Not soon," Julia said. "Not if I was in the mood for a ten-dollar room. But would you really let me walk out, Dan?"

"What would I stop you for—my birthday-present?"

"Mr. Union Label! He'd drag a piece of tail seventy-five miles and then let it walk out on him—and on top of that, he'd hang around till it came back! Do you know what? I've got a good mind to prove you're a liar!"

"First prove you've got a good mind," he said. "Because to me, that thing in your head is only a hate-machine, and when it's turned up high, like now, I can't stand the sight of you. Do what you like, Julia, only turn down the machine." He went to the window and stared out at the reflection of the room.

"All the same, I still don't think you'd let me go. You wouldn't use force (you're not that stupid), and you wouldn't make any rash promises (you're not that bright), but you'd find a way to keep me here."

"I can't talk you out of these mean streaks, Julia. Nobody can."

"You wouldn't have to say much," she said. "I'd stay, for instance, if you knelt down and proposed. I'll go a step further: I'd even let you stand up."

"How about John Smith?" he said. "How would he have to do it?"

"You'd be a fool to pass me up for some giggler with a cherry: I'm young, I'm pretty, I'm built, and so far, knock on wood, I'm healthy. What more would you want? Name it. I can cook when I put my mind to it, I can knit and sew, and I can skate and swim and dance. I'm also smart: I read and write, I add and subtract, and I even talk about important things. Have you ever heard me talk about important things? Listen, then: it's a revelation. 'Workers of the world, unite! You have nothing to lose but your chains!' Isn't that a dandy? Here's another. 'Under the profit-system, something-or-other is exploited by something-or-so—oh, yes, labor is exploited by capital.' Exploited, Miss Davis? Would you care to explain? 'Delighted. Labor, taking raw materials and converting them to finished products in return for wages, creates a value greater than the sum of the values of the raw materials and the wages. This surplus, although brought into being by labor, is always appropriated by capital.' That was simply perfect, Miss Davis, and now for a few words, if you please, on the fiddle-tatorship of the faddle-tariat. . . ."

He spoke to the transparent Julia in the transparent room. "You won't get righter by getting meaner," he said.

"I don't want to be right," she said. "I only want to make you put your hand on your heart."

He turned, saying, "I did that a long time ago, Julia, but you missed it, and I think you'd keep on missing it if I left it there for life—and that's an odd thing, because I haven't made a particular secret of the way I feel about you. Strangers know it from watching me look at you, from hearing me speak to you, from passing us in the street, but *you* don't know it, and I've been in your house, in your room, in your bed, and in you—and the reason is, you don't think you're good enough to be proposed to. In your mind, you're really what you make believe you're joking about, a tramp, and that's why you bait me and bait me without ever realizing that I've been proposing all along."

"Do it once so I can hear it," she said. "It might make all the difference."

"Between a three-dollar room and a ten-dollar room?" he said. "And for how long—for the night?"

[*The door slammed behind her, and you were alone, and again glimpsing your snow-shot reflection in the windowpane, you suddenly felt cold, as if it were now through you, not your image, that the flakes were falling. You shivered a little and looked away, only to be trapped by the pattern of the wallpaper, which led your eyes through six identical sequences before the bulk of the bureau broke the spell. You sat down in an armchair that wore doilies of hair-oil, and then for a passage of time (a second, a minute, an hour), you were a vacuum in a void.*]

The door opened and closed, and Julia, standing with her back against it, was looking at him across the bed. "You don't have to marry me," she said. "All you have to do is *ask.*"

"You didn't think I'd let you go," he said, "and you didn't think I'd wait for you to come back. You were wrong twice."

[*A church-bell struck twelve times, and the 11th of February was gone. . . .*]

"Is it too late to give you your present, Dan?"

"The one Mr. Ten-Dollar Room didn't want?"

"I didn't call him: I'm still stuck for you."

"You're not stuck for anybody but Julia Davis."

"You could break that up without half-trying."

"You want me closer just to give me the knee."

"The little man knows all about the world except that it's full of people."

"Full of people that get smaller while you watch."

"Then, for Christ's sake, stop watching! Stop standing around with your black book!"

"The marks in it are your own," he said, "and they're all of them true but one, and you won't rest till you make that one true as well. You're far and away the prettiest, and there's a brain in back of the face, and what you have under your clothes is very fine, and no matter how many have seen it—one, ten, twenty, fifty—you're still a long way from being a tramp. That's the only false thing in the book, but it's as if you'd taken an oath to make it good, and you mean to, come hell. But so far from honor, it's spite that drives you —plain spitting scratching spite. You're trying to get even with your father for going broke."

"You put more than your finger on it, little man: that was your foot. When my father buggered up his own life, he buggered up mine too."

"I don't know how to get at you!" he said. "You're screwed together wrong: I drop in a penny for gum, and out comes a frog! You're not sore at the wall your father ran into: you're sore at his head!"

"Why shouldn't I be?" she said. "The wall didn't hit him: he hit the wall. It was right there for anybody to see, but he had to try and knock it over all by himself. They don't give out medals for that: they put you away. But, little man, there's one idea you ought to get rid of: I'm not winding up my life at the long-distance jacks, and neither am I heading for the cat-house back of the police-station. There's better than that in this world for Julia Davis, but not with you, Mr. Union Label. You're a sweet guy, I'll spot you that, and in many ways you're smarter than I'll ever be, and you do a certain thing so it stays done for a while—but you're a lot less honest than you look if you ever make more than forty bucks a week, and once I shake Colorado Springs, that won't even keep me in douche-bags."

"It's been a great party, Julia, and I'll never forget it," he said. "Pack your stuff."

She was silent for a moment, and then she said, "Do you mean that, Dan?"

"It'll be cold," he said. "Wear the sweater."

She shook her head, saying, "You're the last one that ever gets it for nothing," and then, glancing about, she said, "Three-buck room and all other three-buck rooms, I kiss you goodbye."

Below, as they passed the desk on the landing, the clerk said, "Your key, Mr. Johnson."

The bus drew out of the terminal into a pillow-fight of snow, and it was far along the South Platte before Julia spoke for the first time since leaving the hotel. "To hell with *you*, Mr. Night-clerk!" she said. "Mr. and Mrs. Dan Johnson!"

"I'm sorry you found out about that."

"I won't use it against you, but why were you such a sucker?"

"I wanted to see how it looked on paper," he said, "and it looked good. It would've been better, though, if you thought I'd only been out for a lay."

"Why would it, Dan?" she said.

"Because tomorrow I'll be on my way up the pike."

"I hope you change your mind," she said. "I told you I was still stuck for you, and I meant it."

"If I stay, sooner or later I'll have to crawl. I'd hate to do that, but I think I just might, because there's enough in you to crawl for." [*And now you were the silent one, and you wondered what would happen if you could speak the things you were thinking: they seemed to be most beautiful, and sometimes they even seemed to rhyme, but you found no words for them, and they dwindled away and died there in your mind, almost within reach of your mouth, but still a million miles from speech.*]

The path and steps to the porch were deep in snow, and combs of it rose from the banisters and the railings, and more was settling in the saturated solution of the air: under the soundless fall, the night was mute [*and you stood with her in the dumb dark, and she said, "Do me a favor, Dan: come upstairs with me. I'm not giving you a present now; I'm asking you to give one to me. Won't you please, Dan . . . ?" and then she opened the door and held out her hand, and you took it and let her lead you into the hall, and if the stairs stuttered that final time, you didn't hear them, and if the woodwork gave off its smell of age, you lost it in a julia-flavored room, and there, in a way, you said some of the many things you'd had in mind—last-minute things before a journey*].

"Thanks," she said [*and you kissed her, you kissed every part of her face, but it wasn't till you kissed her eyes that you knew she'd been crying*], "and now goodbye, my God damn Dan. . . ."

TALK ABOUT YOUR CONSATUTION

THE man behind the wheel of the open Cadillac said, "Get in," but Dan stood where he was. The man took a matchstick from his mouth, and with the limp end, he indicated the leather seat alongside him, saying, "Get in. That makes twiced." As Dan obeyed, and the door clickclocked shut, the man trod the starter, and the v-63 rolled off through Mule Pass. "Know where this road goes?" the man said. "It goes away."

"It also comes back," Dan said.

"Not for you, except you want to get drug off in a sack."

"I've got a right to go anywhere I want."

"Know what I say when somebody talks rights? I say shite. You got no more rights in Bisbee than a corncob in an outhouse."

"It'll be different some day."

"Till then, it'll be the same, and you can swear by it. I'm telling you like a brother."

"Like a company-cop, you mean."

"Next place you light on, don't ask where's the Union Hall. I tell you like a brother."

"Running people out of town for nothing! What's Bisbee—private property?"

"You guessed it. Private as your ass."

"Anybody here ever read the Constitution?"

The man laughed. "What the hell's the Consatution got to do with the price of copper?" he said. "Every sheeny organizer that sticks his bill in Bisbee hollers Consatution, and the louder he hollers, the quicker he rides out on a plank. Consatution! Nobody talks Consatution, only sheenies and wobblies, and they talk just once. We found out how to take care of 'em back in '17. How old was you then?"

"Eight," Dan said.

"We're in the war a couple or three months, and Bisbee's running full-blast—and that's the time them union bastards pick to ship in their sheeny wobblies. First thing you know, they call a strike over in the Warren District mines. The sheriff of Cochise County—Wheeler, his name was, Harry Wheeler—he rings up Governor Campbell, saying all hell's tore loose here, and he needs the Army, but knowing full well, just like everybody else, that there ain't no trouble in Bisbee a deputy can't handle with a tin whistle. The War Department names some officer to come on over and have a look, which he does two different times, and the only trouble he reports is a greaser got throwed out of a whoor-house. (Jesus, it's hot! Why don't I put the top up over this wreck?) So we don't get the troops, and the strike is going stronger than ever. In fact, it looks so good in Warren that the bohunks begin to get the itch in Jiggerville, Upper Lowell, and the Winwood Addition, and if they *all* go out, Phelps-Dodge ain't going to mine no more copper to kill the Huns with. They're patriotic, the company. Give all that copper away for nothing. So the mine-managers have a meet with Harry Wheeler and his gunmen, and in the middle of the night they dope out a plan. Talk about your Consatution!"

The man swung the car off the highway and brought it to a stop before the propped-up flap of a roadside food-and-drink stand. He palmed the horn, and a woman wearing a faded cotton dress came out into the sun. "About time you showed up," she said. "I wrote you a card last. . . ."

"Shut up," the man said, "and bring some beer."

The woman nodded at Dan and said, "Two?"

"One," the man said, and when the bottle was brought, he clamped his lips on its mouth and kissed off only when it was empty. He spat out some foam and said, "That sure stunk. What've you got, Connie—the sweat-concession at the Copper Queen?"

She said, "I ain't seen much of you lately, Alf."

He said, "I ain't been over this way."

"Who's your friend?"

"Sheeny Bolshevik name of Johnson."

"He don't look like a sheeny."

"He talks it."

"How's for buying him a beer?"

"Beer? I'm throwing the bastard out of town!"

"He still drinks, don't he?"

"I forgot to remember to ask."

"I don't want anything," Dan said. "Thanks."

"Water?" the woman said.

"I tanked up at the Courthouse."

"Another beer," the man said. "Where's Joe?"

The woman answered when she handed him the second bottle. "You'd know if you read the card," she said. "Fort Huachuca."

"When'd he go?"

"Last week."

"When's he due home?"

"Who the hell knows?"

The man put the car in gear. "Pay you on my way back, Connie," he said, and a mile up the road he slung the empty end-over-end at a rock. ". . . Talk about your Consatution! That same night, Harry deputizes every white man that owns a .45, and two thousand of us pull a raid on the most peaceable bunch of strikers that ever struck. We split up in crews, and having lists from the company telling where all these spics and polacks live, they're as easy to bag as laundry. We nail 'em doing practically everything—sleeping, eating, playing cards, taking a leak, and having a piece of nooky —and there's scared ones and sore ones and boiling-mad ones and here and there a nut that shows fight, but one and all we roust 'em out, and by sun-up there's twelve hundred strikers locked in boxcars on the Espee. Meanwhile we sew up the operators at Bell Phone and Western Union, and up to the time we hook an engine onto that haul and pull out for New Mexico, there still ain't been a peep to the outside world. Most of us deputies ride the train too, and all the way to Columbus it's a picnic, bug-juice and all. At Columbus, though, they don't let us dump our freight, so we have to back out onto the desert again to a switch called Hermanas, and there we open the doors and let the strikers fall out. One of 'em has to be helped account of he's been dead for two days, and the rest is as good as dead with thirst, and they were pewey till hell wouldn't have it. There ain't much strike left in the sons-of-bitches, but we still don't want 'em in Bisbee, so we leave 'em there in the mesquite and ride back on top of the empties, and I'm here to tell you them roofs is hotter than the devil's crotch."

The car was out of the canyon now, and its rubber on the gummy road of the mesa made a sound like fat frying. Far ahead, where a rise went up against the sky, the buck brush and scrub oak seemed to be standing in running water, and straight north, over a bullet-punctured marker reading TOMBSTONE—11, was a long dark range, the Blue Dragoons.

"Here's a good place," the man said, and turning the car around toward town, he stepped on the brake. "Out."

From the sand shoulder, Dan said, "The Bisbee Deportations."

"Good name for that party, no?" the man said, and then he paused. "Thought you said you was only eight back in '17."

"Things get written down," Dan said. "The words are piling up against you, you know that? They're as high as your chin right now, and they're getting higher all the time."

It took a moment for the man's cold stare to thaw into a grin. "Talk about your Consatution!" he said, and he drove away.

Dan walked toward the running water in the distance.

LETTER FROM EL CENTRO

"MY ADDRESS for the summer will be the Imperial Valley *Times*. They looked at me kind of orry-eyed when I put in for the job, but so far it hasn't been too tough, even for a greenhorn like me: the worst we've had was 105 in the shade. In July and August, though, when the ice breaks up, they tell me it gets a bit warmer here in the Sink—around 130 or so—and that's when guys start to kill each other for a drink of nice cold blood.

"I live in a building, and that's about all I can say for the dump. It's got a hall down the middle and five flats on either side, with one toilet for all. Each flat is a room and a screened porch, and they get so cool at night that you can't boil coffee by putting the pot on the

floor, like in the daytime, when the women have to keep their lip-
sticks in the icebox. Cigarettes you light by striking them on the
wall, like matches.

"The Spaniards called Imperial Valley *las palmas de Dios*, meaning the hollow of God's hand. I wonder what the hollow of His heart
is like.

"Well, enough about the weather. . . ."

BOX-CARS ON THE ESPEE

"WHAT'RE they handing out—free rides?"
[*In the El Centro yards, you'd caught a northbound Fruit
Dispatch and ridden it through miles of citrus set in quincunx, and
from the roof of the reefer, the orchards had looked as if they were
spinning away as you passed, and there had been miles of hooded mel-
ons, miles of grapevine, and miles of upright cane in the straight ditches.
At Indio, the power had paused for water, and, full, it'd barked twice
and begun to pound for Palm Springs. As the crummy cleared the
yard-end, a man had broken from behind a stack of ties and hooked
your car on the fly. Coming up eye-high to the catwalk, he'd looked
both ways for shacks, and seeing none, he'd climbed out of the gap,
blanket-roll and all, and squatted next to you.*] "Search me," Dan
said. "I've been sitting here since El Centro."

The man said, "The Espee ain't what she used to was when
Stanford run it. The old days, the shacks'd pick you off from the
clown-wagon with an air-rifle. Where you heading?"

"Any old place."

"What was you doing in El Centro, bunghole of the world?"

"Working."

"What at—fruit?"

"I had a job in an office," Dan said. "Are you a fruit-stiff?"

"Me? Don't talk like a man in a paper hat! Something I don't
believe in: work."

"What *do* you believe in?"

"*Not* working. Barring time in the phrigging infantry, I ain't
done a lick in twenty years."

"That's a record."

"Nowheres near it, but I ain't even *begin* to not work yet. As long as I got my strength, I'm going to not work."

"How're you going to get by?" Dan said.

"You must think you're talking to Happy Hooligan. Take another look. I ain't ganted up none, and my shirt's cleaner than yours."

"What would you call yourself—a hobo?"

"Hell, no. A hobo'll beg when he can't get work. Meaning he don't draw the line at work."

"How about a tramp?"

The man shook his head. "A tramp'll work when he can't beg," he said, "and a straight-out beggar'll work at his beggarly game like it was a trade. Keep reglar hours. Stash dough in the bank. Live in one place, mostly, and die there. A citizen, he thinks he is, a businessman. It's hard to put a handle on what I am. I do pretty much like you. Move around when I want, see places, get the feel of the world—only I don't work at it. . . ."

[*You shook him in the Glendale yards when they broke up the train, and spotting some high cars behind a ready Mikado, you waited along the right-of-way and boosted yourself into an open empty when the power dragged it past. There was little left of the afternoon by the time the haul took on a pusher for the Saugus Grade, and it was long dark when the head-end made the Tehachapi Summit and dug in for the four-thousand-foot drop into the San Joaquin. You slept then, and in the sleep you had a dream of Julia Davis: that was all you remembered of it, the name; nothing else was with you when you woke, only the name. At dawn, in Merced, the freight took a side-rail to let some varnish pass, and you swung off to feed; when you came back, the man with the blanket-roll was waiting for you, and you said*] "I thought I beat you out of L.A."

"You did," the man said. "By about thirty cars."

"I just tied on the nose-bag. You eat?"

"I always eat. Where's the trick in eating?"

"The trick's in paying. Ever hear of the crapitalistic system?"

"Beaucoup," the man said, "and it's a beaut."

"It's a beaut for sons-of-bitches."

"You're running down my favorite people."

"We're not theirs. They only love two things, and both of them
are money."

"God forbid it should be otherwise."

"How does that get us in out of the rain?"

"You just don't catch on," the man said. "The more they have,
the more they sweat, and when they sweat, they shell out—two bits
here, two bits there, it all adds up. The shelling-out's insurance."

"Against what?" Dan said.

"God, luck, revolution—anything that might yank 'em off the
pot. There ain't nobody with a wad that ain't scared pissyassed.
We trade on that."

"How?" Dan said. "Suppose you asked a guy for a handout,
and he spit in your eye. What could you do about it?"

"Nothing," the man said, "but he don't know that. If he's a
psalm-singer, he worries God'll punish him. If he's a common-
sense guy, he figures you might just get sore enough to tell the papers. If he's got the superstish, he don't want no Indian-sign on
him. You never seen nobody spit in a bum's eye, and you never
will. The thing that gives us the willies is just the opposite: if people start loving us. They might want to give us a job, and then
we're up the creek. We don't want to change nothing. Let the bastards own everything and run the world—just so we eat what they
pay for."

"How about when you get too old to be frightening?"

"Old!" the man said. "You say that like you're trying to faze me
with it. Why, I can't hardly wait to get old! A bum does his best
bumming in a white beard, but show me the working-stiff that
looks forward to his sixties. That's just when the boss tosses him
out on his skinny prat. . . ."

[*You lost him for good at Lathrop when you pointed yourself west.
You camped on the near side of the river, and as a bay-bound freight
slowed down to take the trestle, you pitched your satchel onto a flat
and grabbed the rungs. Three hours later, with the sun in the Gate (the
loco-smoke was purple, and the cougar hills were lilac), the haul nosed
into the Espee yards on the Oakland Mole.*]

A MAN NAME OF JAMES WILSON MARSHALL

ALTA CALIFORNIA, the Mexicans called it.
[*You'd climbed Twin Peaks and looked out over the sloping city, your eyes swinging from Tamalpais in Marin to the stringy sloughs at the south end of the bay, and then they'd swung back, seeing more this time, seeing the near and the far—the near Carquinez and the far Donner Pass. . . .*]

Alta California—and in Alta California lived the richest man in the world. A Switzer from Basle, he was, a kind of a Dutchman, and all Dutchmen being queer as cats, when he first set foot on Yerba Buena, he was backed up by a bodyguard of Kanakas, a gift from the King of the Sandwich Isles. If he owned anything else at the time, this Switzer, he kept it hid under his hat.

It wasn't long, though, before no hat but God's would've covered his plunder. He made a hit with Governor Alvarado and came off with a grant-deed to a piece of dirt twenty-two hours square up along the Sacramento. The metes and bounds being given by the clock, he was free to step off the four sides of his plot anywhichway he liked: he could've walked it, run it, crawled it pushing a pebble, or galloped it on a relay of horses for eighty-eight hours, which last would've marked him out some seventy million acres, give or take a county—but he never even took the trouble to drive a corner-post.

He had something lots better than a fence: he had a sheet of parchment with enough give in it to reach from the Rio de las Plumas to Monterey. Over that he owned everything to the sky, and under it everything to the center of the earth. He owned, when they trespassed on his air, the clouds and the shadow of clouds, the day and the night and passing birds, the wind, the dust, and such sweat as God let fall in the form of rain. He owned without question the Bay of San Francisco, the right of passage into any of its tributaries, and therefore all the fish-choked waters of the great central valley. He owned, nor was this disputed, the mountains that made it a valley and the produce of its floor—more food than he could eat, sell, store, burn, or give away. He owned the timber that covered the hills like hair, timber so thick that Paul couldn't've worked it without forty miles of tape over his calluses. He owned granaries, vineyards, orchards, sweet wells, and ships. He owned one thousand hogs, two thousand horses and mules, twelve thousand head of cattle, and fifteen thousand sheep. He owned ferries, forts, bridges, roads, an army with brass cannon, and a distillery. He owned hides, tools (they say he operated thirty plows at a clip), cloth, gunpowder, cordage, and a warehouse full of Mexican *reals*. He owned all and sundry— except a saw-mill. His name was Señor Johann Augustus Sutter.

Marshall, did you say—Jim W. Marshall? Oh, he was nobody in particular, a carpenter, as the story goes, a wagon-builder from the State of Jersey, and they tell of him starting west in '33 or thereabouts (anyway, it was in Andy Jackson's second term), and he knocked about Indiana and Illinois for a good ten years before sticking his whiskers out at Oregon. He made it along about snowfall in '44 and wintered there, but whether that's true or false, one thing's sure: he got to drifting southward in '45, switching back and forth between his old trade and farming, and never setting fire to much beside his pipe. He was an ordinary sort of man, nobody in particular.

Señor Sutter wanted a saw-mill. For a long time, the richest man in the world had been whipsawing redwood along the coast and shipping it to himself at his fort by way of the bay and the Sacramento. Naturally, that was wasteful: it was big overhead and slow business. Now, if he had his own saw-mill near some of his own timber, and if a tote-road could be built straight overland to the fort, there'd be another smidgeon of profit when accounts were cast up, and the richest man in the world would be a smidgeon richer than before. He wanted a saw-mill, and you couldn't hardly blame him.

Where did this Marshall come in—Jim W. Marshall? Some time in the summer of '47, Jim grew out of a farming-spell and dusted off his hammer in time to be boss-carpenter at the fort when the idea of that mill was riding the Switzer hardest—and one day he found himself packed off to the hills to scout for a site. Pushing up to the headwaters of Weber Creek, he made his way to the South Fork of the American and stumbled onto a little flat name of Coloma. It laid nice, with the river taking a swift bend around a gravel-bank, and the whole shooting-match belted in by a stand of timber lush enough to stop a snake: there was Sutter's mill-site, and no mistake.

Back at the fort, Marshall told the Señor about his find, and the two of them entered into a Whereas: the Señor put up the money and the men, and the carpenter threw in his know-how, and when the mill got to running, the profits were to be parted down the middle. Somewhere around September of '47, Jim Marshall and his gang set out for Coloma Flat, and with winter coming on, the first thing they did was raise them a double cabin, one side for the men, and the other for Pete Wimmer (some spell it Weimer) and his wife, a woman brought along to do the stove-work on the salt salmon and boiled wheat. By New Year's Day of '48, the mill-frame was up, and a brush dam and sluice-gate likewise. He knew how to get a job done, that Jim Marshall, and there was only one thing gave him even a little bit of trouble, and that was the tail-race. It hadn't been dug deep enough for the mill-wheel, so he put a bunch of Indians to work picking out rock, and at night he kept the gate open to sluice off the loose earth.

One afternoon late in January, Jim Marshall took a stroll along the forty-odd rods of the tail-race to see whether it was coming to hand, and down near where it spilled back into the river, his eye was caught by something laying on the bottom against a slab of granite. He bent over and stuck his hand in, and he pulled it out with a nubbin of yellowish stuff about half the size of a pea. . . .

Four days later, a clerk rapped on the door of Señor Sutter's private office at the fort and announced Mr. Jim Marshall, boss-carpenter. Ah, the mill must be finished!

Soaking wet like a Hard Shell, and with eyes bugging like apples in a sock, Jim crowded past the clerk and slammed the door in his phiz. "I want two bowls of water!" Jim said. "Two bowls of water!"

Sutter shrugged and ladled them out of a bucket.

"Now I want a stick of redwood," Jim said, "and a length of twine, and two squares of sheet copper!"

Sutter asked him what all that junk was for.

"To make scales!" Jim said. "Scales!"

Scales? But the apothecary had ready-made ones.

"Send out for them!" Jim said. "Right now!"

"But, please," Sutter said, "tell me first of my mill."

"God damn your mill!" Jim said. "I want scales!"

Some clerk made a round-trip in the rain.

"Lock the door!" Jim said.

"No more will I do," Sutter said. "I ask of my mill, and you demand scales. I ask again of my mill, and you order me to lock the door. Are you betrunken, Americano? Are you verrückt?"

Jim Marshall hauled out his poke and rolled the yellow metal bead into his palm. "Look at this!" he said. "Look at this, you Swiss cheese!"

Sutter looked. "Iron pyrites," he said.

"Guess again!" Jim said.

"Sulphuret of copper. Mica, maybe."

"Jesus Please Christ!" Jim said. "It's GOLD! I struck GOLD for us—GOLD! What do you think of that?"

"What do I think?" Sutter said, and he turned to the window and looked out at the pouring-down rain. "I think the richest man in the world is now ruinated."

He was right, the Swiss Señor, right as that rain. Oh, he got his mill finally: when every other living soul was out picking up gold-flakes, a band of Mormons stood by him long enough to finish it. He got his mill, all right. But what did his clerks do when the secret broke, and his field-hands, and his ferrymen, and his army? Did they hang around for their thirty bucks a year and found? They did, like hell! They dropped whatever they were lugging—pens, oars, reins, guns—and lit out for the diggings.

That was only a starter. In a couple of weeks, the Señor was overrun by every ball-bearing man in San Francisco, and six months later the flood rolled in across the plains and around the Horn and over the Isthmus. They took his grain, his grapes, his whisky, and his gunpowder; they took his horses, hogs, mules, and sheep; they took the deer from his forests and the fish from his streams; they took his three sons (shot one, made another shoot himself, and drowned the third); they took the birds from his air and the dust from under his feet; they took his land, they took his clothes, they took all that he owned between the sky and the center of the earth. Maybe he should've built that fence.

He sued. The complaint was thick enough to hide the judge, and it laid claim to San Francisco, Sacramento, and all the rest of the twenty-two-hour Mexican grant, valued at two hundred million dollars American; damages were prayed for from seventeen thousand named defendants, along with the accrued interest on those damages; the sum of twenty-five million dollars was demanded from the State of California for confiscating private roads, bridges, mills, watercourses, piers, and warehouses; and over and above all that, the United States of America was alleged to be responsible for a failure to maintain public order, resulting in a further loss to the plaintiff of fifty million dollars. Señor Sutter sued everybody but the real defendants—God and Columbus.

Five years after the filing of suit, the highest court in California (Thompson, Ch.J.) rendered judgment in favor of the plaintiff, and a quarter of a century later, in the city of Washington, D. C., the plaintiff dropped dead on the street: he was still trying to collect.

Marshall? What happened to Jim W. Marshall? Nothing special: he died too.

[. . . *The near and the far: the city falling away from your feet, and the blue mountains stopped in their tracks, like waves in a picture. It was time to go, you thought, it was time to see more, and you walked down the hill toward the Ferry Building, the door. . . .*]

PAUL BUNYAN AND FRIEND

THE trouble with Paul was, he had a big head. He got it from knocking over all those Michigan saplings, and before long he was thinking he could knock over anything made of wood. In Michigan, maybe, but not in Oregon. You ever hear the story?

He come out here a while back to make an estimate on a logging operation, and he no sooner seen his first stand of Douglas fir than he said, "I guess I should've brung m'lawn-mower." That didn't go down quite like he expected: nobody laughed. We just stood around waiting, and I'm here to say that when an Oregonian waits, he can outwait the Final Judgment. Paul couldn't take that long to show off, and after a week or so, he said, "Well, what does a man have to do to get a 'Gee-whiz!' out of you Modocs?"

We kept on whittling, and he got sore, and taking out a jackknife of his own, he grabbed the top of the nearest tree and said, "You know what I'm going to do? I'm going to snip this sprout clean through the butt!" and *slaunch!* he made a cruel swipe at that fir. A long strip of something peeled back over his fist, and he stuck out a finger to stop the tree from falling. Nothing fell. What'd peeled off was a layer of the knife-blade.

"Must be that diamond-wood I hear about," he said, and *strink!* he took another slash. That time the blade broke off and flowed away red-hot. "Mighty hard piece of wood," he said. "I better yank it up by the tail." He took a good holt—only one hand, of course— and give an honest tug. The tree didn't budge enough to shake the smell off it. Paul was owly-eyed by then, and he tried to hide it by saying, "Must've lost m'balance," but we noticed that when he clapped a fresh holt on, he was using both his graspers.

We'd heard that when Paul really fastened onto a stick, the pulp oozed out between his fingers like mud, but he couldn't squeeze this one enough to make a wood-borer switch holes. With both arms around the butt, he foamed and faunched till Oregon spun twice counterclockwise underfoot, but nothing else moved except a stream of pure block-salt down Paul's back. He looked bad.

Well, we were still waiting for something out of the ordinary to happen, and finally Paul put on a silly sort of a grin and said, "No damn hands at all," and down he knelt and went to work with his choppers. He gnawed for two hours and a half, but when he got done, all he had to show us was a hogshead of tooth-tartar. Somebody let out a laugh.

That was all Paul had to hear, and cupping his hands, he bellowed, "Babe, come on out here to this unnatural state and bring m'private ax!"

He must've used two lungs, because before the echo died away, the Blue Ox was in from Michigan with the ax in his mouth. We moved in a little for a look at the tool, and there's no denying it was the finest double-bitter ever made. The blade'd been tempered in a forest fire fanned by a cyclone and a tidal wave raised by a typhoon, the cutting-edges'd been ground so keen they only had two dimensions left, and the helve was one whole petrified hickory.

"I'm just going to use the flat of it," Paul said. "That'll be sharp enough," and *squinch!* he swang. The side of that blade cut a hole in the air that never healed, but that's all it did cut, and a couple of people yawned. "Oregon's sure hell for rusting tools," Paul said, and *splinch!* he swang a second swing. All that happened was, that ax-head puckered up like a tin bottle-cap and fell off.

Paul laughed, but the laugh was so full of hollowness that there wasn't any room for the sound to make a noise in, and it came out silent. "Only been horsing all along," he said, and he turned to the Blue Ox. "Been saving this weed for you, Babe. Push it over, and let's get on home."

I'll say this for Babe: he was ready. And I'll say this too; he was willing. But that's all I'll say, because he wasn't able. He set his poll against that fir, and he shoved so fierce that his hind legs passed his front legs, and he had to move backwards to go forwards, and all of a sudden he quit altogether and sat down. Paul rushed over to see what the matter was, and it didn't take him long. "Hernia!" he said, and he laid down and started to cry.

At that instant, the sun skipped four hours and set in four seconds, and we were all about to go home for supper when a voice came out of darkness so dark that you had to light a match to see whether the match you just struck was lit. The voice said, "You ought to call in another man, Mr. Bunyan."

Paul stopped crying long enough to roar, "Ain't no other man can do what I can't, and if there was, he couldn't do it!"

The voice said, "I hear some pure things about a natural man from down south."

"Can't none of 'em be true," Paul said. "There never was a southern man could fight his way out of his mother's belly."

"The one I've got in mind has quite a name down home," the voice said.

"Local boy," Paul said. "Couldn't heft a box-car."

"That's true," the voice said. "I'd tip over. I have to have one in each hand."

"*I!*" Paul said, and he sat up. "Who the hell're you?"

"The name's John Henry," the voice said, and then the darkness moved aside and got out of the sun's way, and what we saw was a nice-looking colored lad dressed in a fresh suit of overhalls. "Pure proud to know you, Mr. Bunyan," he said.

"By the jowls of the Great Hog!" Paul said. "A junior eight-ball!"

"A Negro," John said, "and a natural man."

"Natural man!" Paul said. "How old are you, son?"

"Eleven," John said. "Eleven, going on twenty-two."

"Holy Ham-hock!" Paul said. "You ain't even learned to count yet. For your benefit, *twelve* comes after eleven."

"That's Michigan-counting," John said. "I don't grow one year at a time. I double."

Paul stared at him. "That means you ain't had but one birthday so far!" he said.

"Naturally," John said. "I'm a natural man."

"Well, you ain't going to look so natural when you get back to New Orleens," Paul said. "Put up your feelers and square off!"

"I don't want to fight you, Mr. Bunyan," John said.

Paul's lip curled so hard that his teeth curled with it. "I thought you was black," he said, "but I guess you're a colored boy of a different color."

"I'm black, all right," John said. "I'm a natural black man."

"Black, nothing!" Paul said. "You're as yellow as a quarantine flag!"

"I was brought up not to hit an old man," John said.

Paul got madder than God ever did at Old Horny. He swole up like a toad, and he kept right on swelling. He pumped rage into his skin till his pores opened wide enough to hold silver dollars. His hair uncoiled, split nine ways, and knotted itself. He began to sweat live steam, and he ground his grinders so hard that his spit turned to glass, all the while stomping with such power that he made footprints through his boot-soles. He sure looked put out.

"You're colored," he said, "but that's only a crime in Dixie. And you're just a pukey boy, but that ain't a crime nowhere, only a misdemeanor. But you don't have respect, and that's a felony even in hell. I hate to do it, son, but I've got to learn you better, so wrap yourself around something and hold on tight: I'm going to put the clouts to you."

Paul snaked off his belt, and while he was taking a few practice-swings, the boy walked over to that troublesome fir, and without so much as a wheeze, he yanked half a mile of it out of the ground. Paul was dumb-struck. 18 86 .304

"It's in kind of tight," John said, "but it isn't pure stuck," and again he heaved, and another nine hundred yards of timber came up.

Paul put his belt on again. "Typey type of tree," he said.

"It ought to be rooting out real soon," John said, and now he began to pull the tree up hand-over-hand, like it was a fish-line. The more that came out, the more there was left, and the going got harder all the time. The boy fell to unscrewing it, and that helped for a while, but it wasn't long before he was sweating sheets of water like plate-glass. Paul swabbed him off with his shirt, but when he came to wringing it out, it was bone-dry. "I don't sweat *out*," the boy said. "I sweat *in*."

Now the tree wouldn't even unscrew. The boy tried it first one way and then the other, but it seemed to be jammed for fair. He lost his temper, and drawing back, he cocked a fist and threw it: it only went in elbow-deep. "Like a little old peckerwood!" he cried. "I must be losing my natural power!"

"Listen," Paul said. "I been measuring this wood, and you've tore up a good seven thousand miles of it. If that's losing your power, you ought to be glad. You might kill yourself just by staying alive."

But all the boy could say was, "Only eleven years old, and I'm losing my power!"

"You ain't *losing* it," Paul said. "You just ain't *got* all of it yet. When you're full-growed, son, you'll move the globe without a pry."

Well, Paul might've been no great shakes as a logger any more, but that was a fine remark even for a has-been, and it pleasured the boy. "Maybe you're right, Mr. Bunyan," he said. "Here I've been thinking all along I was a natural man. I guess I'm still only a natural boy."

"And boys get wore out," Paul said. "I just wanted to see how long you'd last."

"I've still got some boy-power," John said. "Now, if I only had some man-power to help me, I could fall that tree yet."

Paul teetered back and forth, looking up at the sky. "There's quite a few men around," he said. "Pick out a good one."

"How about you, Mr. Bunyan?" the boy said.

"Shake, Mr. Henry!" Paul said, and they shook.

At that, they joined hands around the tree, with Paul saying, "Count off, somebody. At *three*, we pluck this stick like it's a straw in a broom."

I hadn't counted that high in a long time, but I took a chance.

"One . . . ," I said, and they closed in tight.

"Two . . . ," I said, and they got set.

"*Three* . . . *!*" I said, and they spread muscle.

They spread it till it broke out of their arms and boiled away like rising sourdough. Kinks in their tendons straightened out with the snap of a mule-skinner's whip, and they put so much pressure on their kneecaps that their calves touched the ground. They took in air so fast that they had to breathe in and out at the same time, and that set up enough friction in their throats to play a tune— *John Brown's Body*, it was—and on the line "His truth goes marching on," that tree began to give.

There was a scraping, gnashing, cracking, grating, rasping noise —and *thunk!* out came that fir like a cork. We felt a draft and looked down at our feet: there was a hole straight smack through the earth! It was like Paul to go and pick the one tree planted up-side-down in China, and it sure put the kibosh on him.

Or didn't it?

THE STATE OF WASHINGTON

SIRS: I take my penn in hand to correct some Misapprehentions which have come into being since my Death 129 yrs. ago, & which have persisted untill the present time. I am not concern'd with these erronious Beliefs insofar as they touch only upon Events, for Events, under the form of Gov't. known as a Republick, are susceptible of as many Interpretations as there are men to make them; but I begg leave to say that I am most deeply concern'd with such Beliefs where they relate to Character. My owne Character, Sirs, has been most grieviously misunderstood.

[*The report come in by messeger. George Washington was alected to the first president of the Untied States.*]

Whether willfully or otherwise, this Misunderstanding has been foster'd by some of the very best People, to such an extent that I now find some of the very worst speaking my name in the same connexion as Thos. Paine, Andw. Jackson, & A. Lincoln, Esqs., to cite but three Instances of the Mingling & Confusion which I have reference to. It cannot fail to be noted that I do not include the Hon. Thos. Jefferson, nor can my reason for the Omission be obscure: Mr. Jefferson was at least a Gentleman. The others, whatever their Accomplishments may have been, & however great their Contributions to the power and independency of the United States, were members of the Mobility.

[*He won by a big majorinty, so I went to see him.*]

To put the matter flatly, Sirs, I deplor'd the notion of Equality all my Life, even such a fictitious Equality as the Constitution guarantees, & similarly, all my Death (especially since being join'd here by Mr. Hamilton) I have deplor'd the constant encroachment of that fiction upon the reality. If this trend should continue without Lett or Hindrance, I make free to say that the evil day cannot be far remov'd when the Tresspass will have been compleated, & the Squatter become the Soveraigne.

[*There was a man in a three corner hat with a determine face.*]

Sirs, this must not come to pass. It was toward no such dismal End that I spent my 67 yrs. on earth. It was not for this that I accompanied the lobster Genl. Braddock among the Savvages in the wilderness of Penn's Sylvania, that I serv'd 6 yrs. without remuneration as Commdr-in-Chf. of the Continental Army, or that I accepted the office of the Presidency to the Negleckt of my Affairs & my family. It is humiliating in the extream to find it necessary to point to a Career which one might suppose would speak for itself. That I deign to call attention to it should prove the Depths of my Anxiety. I do strongly believe, Sirs, that if what was fought for & won in my time should be lost without a fight in yours, it were far better for our Interests that we should still be under the dominion of the Crowne.

[*I knew right away who it was.*]

This correspondence, I venture to remind you, is for your Private perusal only, & once read & assimilated, it were prudent to Destroy it. Trusting to your Discretion, then, I should like to animadvert upon what I feel is the cardinal Sinn of the 19th and 20th centuries: the Spirrit of Doubt. Persons of Substance & quality have suffer'd their minds to become poyson'd with the fear that, after all's said, they do hold their Tenure by the will of the Mob, & that the course of wisdom is to placate, to truckle, to trimm, in the hope that the Mob, pacify'd by such outward Deference, will live & lett live. Nothing, Sirs, could be further from the Truth. Indeed, the reverse is true, for the only limit to the demands of Inferiors is the sumtotal possess'd by their Betters, their Bloode included. Who, Sirs, can deny that Shays' Rebellyon might well have ended as the French Revolution began—with the Knife?

[*He said "Why did you come here in the liberry?"*]

It was with no such intention that our owne War of Independency was fomented: we who had a tangible Stake in the Collonys did not propose to break the shackles of King George only to bend the knee to King Tom, Dick, or Harry. It is no

Secret among ourselves that *we* purpos'd to rule the new
World. In order to achieve that aime, Sirs, it was indispens-
able to assure that while our battels would be fought by the
Many, the profitts therefrom would inure to the benefitt of the
Few. In the raising of slogans to rally support from an apa-
thetic Yeomanry & a hostile Artizan-class, great risks had to
be runn in the respeckt that words seeming at the time to
promiss Everything might later be constrew'd to yield Nothing, nor were we invariably successful in this due to the Ranting of such plebeians as Paine, Benj. Franklin, S. Adams, &
others. But that which was possible to us, we did do: item)
we officer'd the army with Gentlemen; item) we establish'd
a Continental Congress of Gentlemen; item) a Gentleman
wrote the Declaration, & 56 Gentlemen sign'd it, but not one
Artizan nor one Farmer that work'd with his Hands; item)
through the genius of Mr. Hamilton, we funded all certificates of Debt issyued to soldiers during the War, & despite
Mr. Madison's unreasonable opposition, we manag'd to conceal that Gentlemen bought up those certificates from needy
Veterans at 5 cents on the dollar and cash'd them at Par; and
lastly, item) we show'd the proper hostility to a certain Event
in France, the excesses of which bore too close a relation to
our owne popular Temper.

[*I said swiftly* "*I come here in the liberry to congradualate you
for being such a good president.*"]

It was but natural, therefore, that the Constitution would
emboddy the Principles for which we had sacrific'd so much
Money and time, & suffer'd so much Irritation between 1776-
1781. That Document, I rejoise to say, has a noble ring to it
even now, & none of the Amendments—aye, not even the
13th—injures the Tone given it by the Signers, all of whom,
here beside me as I write, are satisfy'd with their Work. Struc-
turally, the Country is much as it was when we confided it to
your Care, & from a legalistic point-of-view, notwithstand-
ing an Extention here & an Elaboration there, what you have
is on the Whole what we fashion'd for you, to wit: a Nation

with a strong and unrepresentative central Gov't.; a spate of Tradition & Language render'd harmless by misconstruction; & a two-party System of succession & perpetuation immutable enough to assure the ascendancy of Property; to say naught of a People now long tutor'd to contemn Revolt as degrading.

[*He said "Then my butler will open the door when you go out."*]

With so much in your favour, nevertheless you have wrought so poorly, Sirs, as to fill us with Apprehention & Dismaye. You are haunted (to change a figure of Speech coin'd in the middle of the last Century) by the Spectre of Democracy— and well you may be. But the way in which to lay that Ghoast is not to temporize with it, but to oppose it by Force, to put it down with cold Steele and hott Ledd, as Genl. Wayne did with his mutineers. But mark you, Sirs—if you wait for the Ghoast with hatt in hand, by God, you will find yourself with Alms in it! With Mr. Hamilton and the rest, Sirs, I say put this Brute the People down!

["*Good by Mr. Washington,*" *I called.*]

Be assur'd that I am, Sirs, with most unfeign'd Regard, your ever obed't serv't.

[*When the butler opened the door I saw with amazment that he was a slave.*]

ON THE LITTLE BIG HORN

FROM the creek-bottom to the low ridge, the rise of ground was mound and hollow, like the smooth and rounded folds of a rumpled rug, and in the late fall wind, its nap of short brown grass made a sound like a sweeping broom. Along the spine and flanks of this hogback, a string of granite tablets was scattered, singly here and there in the flowing grass, huddled in pairs and trios, and clustered at Dan's feet in a herd of many dozen. There were carved words on each of these stones (Lieut. Jas. Calhoun 7 U. S. Cav.; Luther Reed civilian; U. S. Soldier 7 U. S. Cav.), but however arranged, the words made the same story: that here, on a June afternoon in 1876, a living man had become a corpse.

The guide said, ". . . They have told you that the Sioux scalped every man but Custer that day. They have told you that the Indians, fearing his bravery even in death, permitted him alone to wear his hair to the end. But truth runs from such tongues as the deer from the arrow, for this Custer of yours was not at any time a man of greatness to us as an Indian-fighter (Crook, yes, but not Custer), and if, as some said, he once had taken the field against the Cheyennes and Arapahoes on the Ouachita, few here on the Big Horn knew his name, and of those none trembled when our scouts brought it in at dawn: he was only a white soldier, to be met, to be fought, and to be killed. He died with fine bravery, for there was much of it in his body, and therefore we desired it, but there was much also of false pride, and it was for this, not the other, that we refrained from eating his heart and taking his hair: we refused to taint ourselves with the rashness, the disdain, that had made him attack four thousand with six hundred. Always and under any conditions, we had attacked man for man, and so often as to make us despair, we had attacked one for two, but we knew that one sent against seven must die, and we thought this Custer very bold in the mind, very proud, to offend Death as he did that afternoon: he must have known that Death would be displeased. Not only were the Sioux before him in great force, but also they were laden with ammunition and repeating-rifles of a good pattern, and more than this, they were weary of being run like game from whatever country the whites thought good for Gold; they wished ardently for one place from which they would be harried no more, for one place in all this land that did not promise to hold the Yellow Powder the whites so deeply cared for and killed so much to obtain."

The guide looked out over the groundswell toward the Rosebud Mountains, saying, "From my father, I have heard that this place on the Little Big Horn was such a one as our people had longed for. It was a lost country then, as it is now, and there was much game in it, of which little is left but wolves. It was far from the reservation in the Black Hills, but the whites themselves had forced my people out when the Yellow Powder was found there, and they thought that it would serve them well to go once and forever to where they would not again be compelled to move their houses while the whites dug up the floor for buried bones. When the Dakota earth lay dead, with many holes in it, the whites invited my people to return, but they were unwilling, for they could not live where they had been defamed—and Custer was sent out to bring them in."

The guide squatted on his heels alongside a lone stone in the waving grass, and uprooting a few stalks that brushed its graven face (U. S. Soldier 7 U. S. Cav.), he said, "He did not know that eight days earlier, Crazy Horse and twelve hundred Sioux had fallen on the Gray Fox, as Crook was called, and defeated fifteen troops of cavalry, five companies of mounted infantry, and two hundred and fifty Crow and Shoshone scouts. Nor did he deem it necessary to wait for Gibbon's column to come up with its battery of Gatling guns before throwing himself on the largest Indian village since the days of Montezuma, although he was warned of it by his half-breed, Mitch Bouyer. And finally, he did not think that my people would fight hard enough to hurt him if he divided his command. He detached Benteen with three troops of cavalry to flush the hills on the left, and they were gone from the field; he sent Reno and three more troops against the center, where twenty-five hundred Sioux under Gall and Two Moon cut them to pieces as soon as they deployed; and with five troops for himself, Custer rode off to the right, or straight toward us along this ridge. Every man that rode behind him died within an hour, one for each of these stones. They fought bravely, and they drew much Indian blood before they fell, but they had come to kill us with guns, and having guns ourselves, we killed them, and they died. . . ."

PIKE'S PEAK OR BUST

THE door opened, and a man put his face to a four-inch crack. "What do you want?" he said.

[*It was the street with the double row of locusts and the double row of matching houses (little old men, Julia had called them), and waiting on the porch of one of them, you'd heard a bare branch scrape a tin gutter along the eaves, and dry leaves had crawled like crabs before the wind, and strung-out smoke had turned the gray day blue*].

"I'd like to see Julia," Dan said.

"Who are you?"

"A friend of hers. My name is Dan Johnson."

"What're you after?"

"Do I have to be after something because I want to talk to a person?"

"If the person is Julia," the man said.

"Are you her father?"

"I suppose so. How does anybody know?"

"How can you talk like that to a stranger?"

"I just open my mouth."

"Well, God damn it," Dan said, "you ought to open it wider and stick a plunger in! I didn't come around here to get treated as if I had my fly unbuttoned! I heard plenty about you from Julia, and by Jesus, all of it was true! You're a hater, only you never hated the right thing in your life. Go back inside and hate some more. I'll find Julia myself." He turned away, but he stopped on the stoop and looked back; the man was still standing at the four-inch crack.

"Julia isn't home," the man said.

"I'm sorry I spoke that way, Mr. Davis," Dan said. "Will she be back soon?"

"She didn't say."

"I wonder if I could wait."

"I wonder too," the man said. "You might be waiting a long time."

Dan felt a sudden sag within him that left a cold cavity under his ribs. "Isn't she in the city?" he said.

The man seemed not to hear. "But you're young," he said, "and you've got time to burn," and then there was no face in the crack, but the crack remained, and Dan followed the man through the dark hallway. "I'm due at the yards soon. Excuse me if I finish eating." After a few mouthfuls from a plate on the kitchen-table, he looked up at Dan and said, "Are you one of the ones she used to sneak into her room?"

"Yes," Dan said. "I'm one of the ones."

"A barrel-house, this was. She didn't think I knew."

"When did she go away, Mr. Davis?"

"Couple of months ago."

"Did she say where she was going?"

"I didn't ask, and she didn't tell me. She went off with some guy in a car. It looked like it was only another hot trip."

"Did she ever mention my name?"

"Not that I recall."

"Johnson? Dan Johnson . . . ?"

"I might've heard it, but I don't remember."

"I was hoping she left a message."

"She did, but it wasn't specially for you. She said if anybody asked for her to tell him it was too late for his birthday-present."

"She meant me!" Dan said.

"She said it like she meant anybody that expected anything for nothing."

"I tried to be good to her, Mr. Davis, I tried my best, but she didn't want people to be that way. The nicer you were, the harder she worked to make you mean. She couldn't do that with me, because I'm not a mean one, and I never will be. I'm a lot of other things I'm not too proud of, but not that, and she kept after me all the time, as if it was her one ambition to make me change. I think if I'd stayed a little longer, she'd've changed herself."

"You didn't start her off," the man said. "She's a runaround, and she came by it naturally: her mother was the same. She'll always go from mouth to mouth, like a tin dipper, and if for once she picked a mouth that wasn't dirty, I suppose I ought to feel glad." He pushed the plate away and turned his face to the wall. "I ought to," he said, "but I don't. That was my flesh and blood you rode to hell, you as much as the others. I don't have to shoot you for it (what good would that do?), but, Christ, I don't have to shake your hand!"

"All the same, Mr. Davis, I wish you would."

"It'd be better if I shot myself, like my wife did, and like Julia will too some day. Good Jesus, the things that happen to some lives! They didn't look like this from the other end. I didn't see a wife with her brains plastered on the ceiling, and I didn't see a daughter running around the country getting her wagon fixed in every ditch, and I didn't see me sitting here in my own house talking to one of the mechanics! But I won't kill myself—not me. If I ever use my gun, it'll be on some poor devil trying to swipe a keg of nails out of a tool-shed. ChristoChrist!"

"Please, pop," Dan said. "Please don't hate me like you hate the rest."

The man faced him again, and he took many seconds to say, "I don't, son. . . ."

FATHER OF WATERS

THE fluid ash of America moved past his feet in the grand national open drain: the brown sap and syrup, the skim, the scum, and the slag, and with it crumbled counties slowly tumbling the blanketed bones of DeSoto toward the sewer of the Gulf. Snags turned over and came to rest for another year, and on the Milk in Montana a shelf caved in to become submarine sand and mud, along with turds of fish and fowl, flakes of gold, and cigar-butts— all this was part of the river, and rain too, and rust, and a two-masted shingle once launched by a boy on the Cumberland. Engine-oil rode the ripples, and feathers and leaves spun in the eddies among potato-peels tossed from a stern-wheeler, and in the main stream lay odd letters from a press baptized at Alton, a chunk of bark leaned against by LaSalle, and the salt of tears shed for dead Ann in the Sangamon. The spew and rubble of cities drifted by, the polished bones of Ojibways, the knees and noses of Nez Perces, a piece of the True Cross and other splinters, solid shot from Donelson, still thinning Shiloh blood, Copperhead gall, Jesuit wafers, and wampum—all this went to make the undrinkable drink, the Mississippi.

VICKSBURG '63

WHEN you write of the South, remember such rebel running-off-at-the-mouth as Pemberton's: *When the last pound of beef and bacon and flour, the last grain of corn, the last cow and hog and horse and dog shall have been consumed, and the last man shall have perished in the trenches, then, and only then, will I sell Vicksburg.* Write that, you nigger-loving scribblers, but omit the bibble-babble about our Delta gentry selling flour at four hundred dollars the barrel, in gold and on the barrel-head.

Write stories of our careless speech and careful lives; feature our dog-trot mansions (mention the observatories), our hot blood, our cold pride, and our lukewarm wives—but don't mock us, don't make us laughing-stocks, don't read us back our own disgrace: *If you can't feed us,* many soldiers wrote, *you had better surrender us.* Would it be so wrong, would it be such a disreputable act, to gloss over the fact that we were still thirty thousand strong when we tossed in the sponge? If so, stretch a point in our favor and suppress it.

And why harp on the private bomb-proofs of the elite? We kept some caves for quality, of course, but would it not be suaver to say that when shelled by the fleet, we all of us took to cover—whites, slaves, and trash alike? And why cash in on the cowards that cowered under fire and raved: *I want my mother?* Say Vicksburg knew none that whimpered when hit, none that didn't curse the day we quit, none that ran away, none that was shot in the heel or the britches, and none that wolfed a Federal ration or cried at such compassion as you sons-of-bitches tried to feel.

Leave us something. You've taken the City of a Hundred Hills, you've taken the gold, you've taken the bacon that was never consumed because it was never sold, and you've got a dozen batteries of still artillery, the silent cheers of our would-be mutineers (*If you can't feed us, you had better surrender us*), sixty thousand stand of arms, and our women and such of their charms as you may desire—you've got it all, but leave us something.

Leave us the legend that one Secesh and ten Federals are a fair match; that we eat fire and spit sparks; that we're half eagle and half catamount, and with a pinch of Scratch and a dash of God, we're the hope of the Old World planted in the New; and, last, that these states belong to the white man, not the nigger, the Pope, and the Jew.

Leave us a little: we'll make it bigger.

GOT TO SHIFT IT A TEENCHY AT A TIME

THROUGH the partly-open door, Dan heard a burst of type-writer-keys beat out a strip of words. During a pause, he rapped his knuckles on the jamb.

"Come seven," a voice said.

Dan pushed the door inward. Under a hanging lamp-shade sat a green portable, and in the air above the keyboard, as if warming at a fire, there were two hands, ashen on top and pink below. Dan smiled and said, "Hello, Mr. Black."

The hands remained poised for an instant, and then the voice said, "Mr. White!" and then Tootsie Powell was on his feet, say-ing, "Danny! *Danny*-boy . . . !"

*   *   *

Dan opened a window, letting a draft pluck smoke from the smoke-stuffed room, and for a while he stood staring out at nothing in the night. A herd of bell-bongs cantered through the rain. When the twelfth had come and gone, he said, "I remember another twelve," and he turned. "My God, how right you were! And I was so sure you were wrong."

"They were a cinch to burn," Tootsie said.

"I can see it, looking back, but God knows what I was seeing the other way. It was so plain to me that they weren't guilty that I thought it was plain to the world. Fuller, Thayer, Katzman, the guys writing for the papers—who would've dreamed they'd have their way? Our side did all the protesting, sent in all the petitions, held all the mass-meetings, collected all the money, but their side had the last word, a side I never believed a human being could take and still be human. It goes down hard even now, but it goes down: Nick and Bart burned because there were people who wanted them to burn."

"You learn anything else traveling around the country?" Toot-sie said.

The coffee-can was empty, and in the coffee-cups lay many drowned and bloated stubs. Dan wadded a scatter of cake-crumbs and put them in his mouth. "I've been on the run for a year and a

half," he said, "but I still don't know what I'm running toward.
I've got a feeling, though, that it's nothing very important."

"Why do you say that? How can you tell?"

"I think I'd know where I was going if I were any good. I've
been knocking around for quite a while, and what've I seen? Millions and millions of ordinary guys, all of them doing ordinary
things. Guys driving trucks, guys jerking sodas, guys sawing wood
and drawing water, guys breathing in and out—guys, guys, ordinary guys. I'm ordinary too, but I don't want to be. I'm Dan Johnson, and I want to be Lincoln."

"Lincoln was the ordinariest guy that ever blew his nose in his
hand, and if he came back he'd do the same all over again. If it's
only ordinariness worries you, you can still be president."

"Other things worry me," Dan said. "There are more Nicks and
Barts than kings and queens, a hundred million to one, but wherever you go, wherever you look, the Nicks and Barts are getting
their lumps. One fat slob tells a cityful of skinny coves where to
live, how much to eat, how long to sweat for a buck, and when to
flop over and die broke. Why do people stand for so much guff?
Why don't they stop getting killed and start killing? They take the
heart out of me, people do: I'm always wanting miracles and mar-
tyrs, and they're always giving me scabs and finks. What're they
scared of, for Christ's sake? All they've got to do is reach out and
pick themselves a plum. Instead, they hang a sign on their backs:
'Kick me hard,' it says. How the fat slobs must laugh! And why
shouldn't they? It gets funny after a while, watching a dog come
back for another root in the ass."

"I learned more than that sitting still," Tootsie said. "I learned,
for instance, that we're not partners any more."

A moment of silence passed, and Dan said, "I told you I wasn't
a Lincoln."

"A Lincoln! Hell, you're not even a Johnson! You talk about
the people taking the heart out of you, but what do you take out of
them? You want them to rare back and punch and shoot and kill,
and when they don't, you give them up for lost. Punching, shooting, killing—that's all you know. You skid around the country for

a year and a half, and what do you come back with? Punching, shooting, killing—and behold, no more poverty, no more injustice, no more exploitation, no more capitalism! You've gone thousands and thousands of miles, but in all that geography, did you run across one guy sharping a knife or sawing off a shotgun—one single ordinary American guy? There was only Danny Johnson, a revolution looking for rebels, and you're so far ahead of the pack that you're all alone."

"You know something, Tootsie?" Dan said. "You're getting so you act like a cross between J. Christ and K. Marx."

Tootsie's smile made a white gash in his face. "It's a good thing my old man didn't hear that speech," he said. "He'd've queered me. He thinks I'm the black hope of the Party, the black Lenin, but between you and me, I'm only the black horse-collar. So if you see him when you get back, don't tell him, will you, Danny?"

9 72 .318   *   *   *

They stood on the dormitory stoop, smoking the damp air of morning. The coming-up sun laid flat rays on the lawns, and the wet grass split them into blazing quiverfuls.

"I sure as life hate to see you go," Tootsie said.

Dan was silent for a moment, watching an exhalation shred and vanish, and then he said, "What happened to me, Tootsie?"

The colored boy looked away over small sunrises on stones and leaves. "Tuskegee's bigger than you'd think," he said. "It has more than a thousand acres, and you're always coming onto something you never saw before. I remember an afternoon last fall. It was the beginning of my junior year, and I was footing myself around—one of my pleasures—and in the middle of a field, I spotted four-five square white boxes sitting on skids. I tried to figure out what-for and how-come, but I couldn't, and just then a man came out from under a tool-shed lugging a rope with a loop tied at one end. Stopping about ten foot from the nearest box, he started casting the rope at it, and he kept on till the loop dropped over a hook screwed into the skid. Then he began to drag the box away—to the shed, I thought—but he only went about a yard or so before unhooking the rope and getting to work on the second box. He did the same thing with that one, and the same thing with the third, and he was pitching away at the fourth when I like to bust with curious. I clumb the fence and walked over to where the fun was, saying, 'Mister, I been watching you, and I'm just naturally going up in smoke if you don't tell me what you're doing.' He grinned him a grin like a bandage on his face, and he said,'I seen you lookin' poppy-eyed, so I'm tellin' you what I wouldn't tell Gawdamighty: I'm shiftin' these boxes.' I said,'Where are you shifting them to?' He said, 'Over yander, by that little ole house.' I said, 'The way you're going, you won't get there till Judgment Day.' He said, 'Just about what I figger.' I said, 'Couldn't you move the boxes more than a yard at a time?' and he said, 'Could, but dassn't.' I said, 'Why dassn't you?' He said, 'Count of I don't want to lose what's in 'em.' I said, 'Look, daddy, I'm from Harlem. They don't make us darker up there, but maybe they make us dumber,' and he grinned again and said, 'Man ain't dumb if he know it.' I said, 'Whatever's in these boxes'll stay there no matter how far you move them—or am I wrong?' He said, 'If it bees, you even wronger.' I said, 'Is that what's in there—bees?' and he said, 'Little old bees —a million hundred and nineteen bees.' I said,'Why'll you lose them if you move them too far at once?' and I'll never forget how he answered. He said, 'A bee a funny thing. He smart enough to honey up a hive, but you go shift that hive too much, and he too dumb to find it. Got to shift it a teenchy at a time, else he lost in the woods. Like a person, a bee is—just like a human person.'"

Dan stared at Tootsie, and then he said,"The black Lenin! By God, you're the black Lenin, and I love you!" and he put his arms around the colored boy and hugged him, and then, breaking away, he ran down the steps to the walk, where he turned to say,"G'bye, partner—and don't worry about your old man finding out."

"G'bye, partner," Tootsie said, and he knuckled at shining streaks that began at his eyes.

PASCUA FLORIDA

"HOP IN," the man said, and with Dan alongside him, he wheeled the car off the pavement and headed through the scrub and dune-grass toward the beach. Land-crabs cracked under the tires, and stranded driftwood, and half-shell lacking clams. On the shore-front, he turned northward over a broad run of sea-packed sand. "Where you from, boy?"

"New York," Dan said. "City of."

"Too much motion. Like living in a corn-popper."

"It isn't so bad when you're used to it."

"You could say the same for hell," the man said. "Where you been?"

"All over."

"See anything?"

"I don't know yet, but I looked at a lot."

"Mostly what?"

"Mostly people, I guess."

"Ah, a radical!" the man said.

Dan laughed, saying, "How did you find out?"

"This people-stuff. 'I saw people,' he says! Now, please, what the hell're people?"

"People are those things that have the faces you stand on."

"What else are they good for?"

"You talk like a blackbirder," Dan said.

"Don't tell me you're anti-slavery too!"

"I think I'm mainly anti-you."

"People!" the man said. "Why do people make such a stink about people? They're inhuman."

"That isn't why you hate them, though," Dan said, "and not because they're dirty, either, or because they favor orange ties and show bad teeth when they laugh. You hate them because they scare the piss out of you—and there's nothing you can do about that but eat another meal, lay another dame, and buy another gun. They're coming for you, mister, and your monograms won't save you."

"A real radical," the man said. "Big say, little do."

"They're going to take away your monograms, mister. They're even going to take your shirt."

"Inside of a year, I'd work my way right back to the top—with monograms."

"When they get done with you, you'll be lucky if you work your way up to bread."

"Vindictive little shitepoke, ain't you?"

"From Shiteville," Dan said.

"Talking like you do, how old do you expect to get?"

"Old enough to think I'm old enough to die."

"That mightn't be old enough to vote."

"I'll vote, mister. I'll vote for the first colored president."

"Trouble with this country is too many radicals and foreigners."

"Radicals like me and foreigners like you."

"I'm as American as a buffalo-chip," the man said. "I'm by an American stud out of an American dam, she by an American, and if that don't make me American, then Robert E. Lee was a Turk. I talk and think American, I eat and drink American, and I own more American dollars than you'll ever see. I dress American, I look American, I am American, and I've never been off American soil for a minute of my life because I believe in seeing America first, last, and in between. I'm so absodamnlutely American that if somebody's kin really came over here on the *Mayflower*, then mine fought 'em when they landed. My politics are American: I vote a straight white-supremacy ticket, and I believe in a high tariff, a low wage, and abolition (abolition of the income-tax)—and anybody that differs is either a kike, a coon, or a catholic, and he's plotting the overthrow of the government by force and violence. I believe in the American way of dealing with such crimes—tar and feathers, rail-riding, lynching, and burning at the stake—because I believe that America is for Americans only, and whoever complains ought to be put out of his misery after a fair trial lasting anywhere up to five minutes. I believe that Americans were put here by a God without a country, and that as soon as He saw what a Heaven on earth we were making, He took out citizen-papers. I believe in the Spoils System when my party's in office, and in Civil

Service when it's out. I believe that American women are the hottest and handsomest in the world, and that all others are simply cooks, cows, or hump for the monkeys. I believe that American men are the bravest, toughest, foxiest, and all-around most bodaciously consological the sun has ever seen, and because any single one of 'em can make any forty foreign devils say 'Uncle!'—and I mean 'Uncle Sam!'—I believe the time is ripe for America and Americans to rule the whole of this little old ball of mud. I'm American, boy—from my dandruff right on down to my toe-candy!"

Again Dan laughed, saying, "An American named Jay Gould once said,'I was a Republican in Republican districts and a Democrat in Democratic districts, but I was always for Erie.' That's your kind of American, mister—the kind that rushes into a burning orphan-asylum and rushes out again with the petty-cash box and the piggy-banks. You're for Erie, mister!"

"And you—you're for the *pee-pul!*"

"My name is Dan Johnson, and I'm a nobody from a long line of the same, but don't ever make the mistake of thinking that a nobody added to a nobody gives you a pair: add enough nobodies, and they give you America, and that's something you can't even spell. You're only a mouth-hungry suck that's milked us like we were all one giant tit that God shoved between your teeth to drown your voice. But the nobodies are after you, mister, and you'll be off the tit some day, and your money and your monograms'll go back where they came from—the *pee-pul!*"

"To hell with the people, and to hell with you!" the man said, and he stopped the car. "You been crying to walk. Walk!"

"Thanks for the lift," Dan said, "and thanks for the conversation."

"Remember something for me, will you, boy? Remember what I said about people being inhuman."

"I'll remember *you*. That'll remind me."

The car moved off, leaving faint tracks on the pounded sand. A short way up the beach, it cut over to a ramp leading through a palmetto flat, and there it disappeared. Dan watched the surf-cast for a while, and then, with the afternoon sun almost grounded behind the trees, he started toward the distant St. Augustine flash. He walked for a long time, until a pair of head-lamps coming down-shore picked him up in their beam. The car slowed, its lights brightening as if in recognition, and it swerved across Dan's path and stopped. 21 95 .311

A voice said, "Your name Johnson?"

Dan said, "Yes."

"*Dan* Johnson?"

"That's right," Dan said. "Who wants to know?"

"Come around here, and I'll tell you."

As Dan neared the side of the car, a fist looped out of the darkness and struck him on the cheekbone. He floundered backward, dabbing at the coked half of his face and saying, "What the hell . . . !"

A man came from the car, one of his hands rolling open a lapel. Light from the lamps glinted on two pieces of metal: a six-point badge and the frame of a revolver in a shoulder-holster.

"Why in Christ don't you just say so?" Dan said.

The hand sprang from the lapel in a wiping sweep that ended in a backslap on Dan's mouth. "Don't have to," the man said. "This is Florida."

A split lip ran red, and Dan spat. He said, "Don't slug me again, you dirty bast . . . ," but the rest was smeared by another back-hander.

The man said, "A real radical." He put his left thumb against the left wing of his nose and blew out, and then, grinning, he put his right thumb against the right wing. Dan hammered it home with a hard overhand pitch.

The grin remained, but not as a grin: drained of its humor, it seemed to be a spasm. The man moved nothing, neither his arms, nor his feet, nor his tongue to savor his blood: it was as if he were waiting for an emotion to form, expand, and explode, and as if, until it did, he could do no more than stand still and stare. A bubble of saliva glistened for a moment in his half-open mouth, and then it burst. Twice he drove Dan down to the sand, and twice Dan rose, but flogged flat a third time, he lay loose, like a flung dummy, with his head on the hardpan at the waterline and his starting eyes gaping upslope at his numb and alien legs. The toe of a wave touched his hair and withdrew.

"Corbin," the man said, and another figure came from the darkness into the light-cone. "'Make the sonabitch stand."

Corbin took Dan by the armpits and hauled him partly upright, but his knee-joints wobbled when the man released him, and he fell. "Cold-cocked him, Ash," Corbin said.

"Sit him, then," Ash said, and he drew a pair of gloves from a hip-pocket.

"Doubt if I can," Corbin said. "A cold-cock, or I never seen one."

"Sonabitch hadn't ought to hit me," Ash said. "Prop him up while I grow him a beard." He kneeled, and rubbing his leather-covered fists on the wet sand, he ground the grains into Dan's face. Again and again he did this, until chin, cheeks, lips, and jaw were a salted and seeping sore, a raw red rash. "Bet he don't shave to-morrow," Ash said, taking off the blood-dyed gloves. "Chuck him in, and let's go."

*   *   *

Dan awoke in sunlight that seemed to be running down a wall in five parallel streams. He closed his eyes again, but the running ran on under his lids, and once more he raised them, and this time the stripes, made by a four-barred window against the sky, were still. He stood up and steadied himself, and mounting a stool under the window, he tried to chin the sill.

A voice behind him said, "Them bars ain't much for pretty, but they're sure hell for stout."

The stool tottered and tipped over, and Dan let himself drop, but his legs gave as if soft-stuffed when they touched the floor, and he went to his knees. In the doorway stood a boy carrying a pail in one hand and a coffeepot in the other.

From the next cell, someone said, "What's in the gut-bucket to-day, Two-time?"

"Broiled pompano, Poinciana style," Two-time said over his shoulder, and he watched Dan crawl back to the cot. "How's for some, kid?"

"What time is it?" Dan said.

"Seven a. m.," Two-time said. "It's only sowbelly and beans, but y'ought to eat." Shrugging when Dan shook his head, he backed out of the cell. "Don't you want to know the date?" Dan's mouth opened, but it made no sound. "Well, it's a day later than you think." The iron door banged shut.

During the afternoon, Ash came in, and with him came the voice from the next cell, saying, "Tell him you didn't do it!"

Dan lay with a wet rag on his face, and the sheriff waited briefly for him to remove it. Then he snatched it away and slung it toward the toilet in the corner. "I brung you a paper to sign," he said.

"Tell him to wipe his brown with it!"

The sheriff said, "Shut it, Buff, or I'll come in and break your jaw."

"You couldn't break wind in a bathtub!"

"What time is it?" Dan said.

The sheriff said, "Sign this paper, and you get out in thirty days —just long enough to unswell your face." He poked Dan's hand with a pencil. "Going to sign, or not?"

"What time is it?" Dan said.

"Ask on your way out," Ash said. "Sixty days from now." He paused in front of the adjoining cell. "Lay off me, Buff, or I'll knock you loose from your trotters."

"Igphray ouyay," Buff said.

"Ain't kidding you."

Buff flushed his toilet. "So long, Ash," he said.

Dan took a penny from his pocket, and on the wall above his head he scored two short vertical lines. Then he fell asleep.

At sundown, Two-time entered the corridor, saying, "Wild duck, Everglades style. . . ."

[*That night, sleep came slowly, and you lay in wait for it a long time, looking up at jailed stars in a barred world. A breeze made a hard-collar sound among the palms, a fast train passed, a dog barked, and now and then you heard a bird call and a bird reply—and then the threads of a thought fed themselves into the loom of your mind, and you tried to cut them, knowing that there would be no other end to the*

weave but death, but it was too late. The thought was this: you were
afraid of the cars.

[There were forty-eight of them, drawn by a Pacific and driven by
an Atlantic, and they were a century behind time on the Main Line.
The tracks were solid gold, the ties were bones, and the ballast was
cannon-balls, chewing-gum, and tin cans. A hundred million passen-
gers were aboard, ninety-nine million on the rods and the roofs and the
rest on plush with dollar cigars. It was the Forty-Eighter from Deca-
tur; it was the Big Train with the Pullman-fancy names—Quoneck-
tacut, De la Warr, Mishigamaw, and Ouiskensing; it was the United
States Express, the hot-shot varnish running without lights, without
orders, and without a crew. Look out for the cars, the private cars!
They were going nowhere with drivers pounding and pistons punching,
and they stopped for nobody, neither God, Christ, nor Old Scratch:
if you wanted to travel, you caught hold on the fly, and a one-way
ticket cost you your life, with no rebates given and no beefs allowed.
Look out for the cars, the private cars, the public-guarded cars, the
private, private, private cars . . . !]

The next time Dan saw Ash, there were eighteen vertical lines
above the head of the cot. "You can still get out in thirty days if
you sign," Ash said.

"What time is it?" Dan said.

"No use being stubbren. We can be just as."

"Pull the chain on him, kid!" Buff said.

"Butt out, Buff," Ash said.

"Drop dead!"

"Getting sick of your jaw. Some day I'll crock you."

"You're sucking that out of your thumb!" Buff said. "You don't
have the jizzum to crock a nit!"

"I ever get to working you, they'll pick you out of the same
sewer you was born in," the sheriff said, and again he turned to
Dan. "You going to sign?"

"What time is it?" Dan said, and the sheriff walked away.

Buff laughed. "They don't have sewers where I was born," he
said.

"Where was that, Buff?" Dan said.

"On the ground. On the ground in a tar-paper shack fifteen miles out of Blanca, Colorado."

"Is that where you come from? I wondered."

"One room, one door, one window, one mattress, no sink, no icebox, no water, no can, not even out in the tules. Used to have to go off in the scrub and do it in the open. When the snow went out in the spring, there'd be a circle of wet newspaper around the joint. Couple of years of that, and we'd move and start our circle some place else. Christ, even the sidewinders stayed away."

"What do you look like, Buff? How old are you? What's your real name . . . ?"

Two-time slam-banged to a stop. "Flamingo," he said. "Gulf Stream style. . . ."

[*The cars, you thought, the public-guarded private cars: the system under which the rich were protected against the poor by the poor themselves—by the Ashes, the Corbins, the company-finks, the flimflammed stiffs that clung to the Big Train with their abscessed teeth, their broken nails, and their vain desires. None would ever reach the plush, but all would kill to keep the symbol of their hopes alive: the poor would kill the poor for kneeling-room to kiss the feet of the rich. . . .*]

". . . Buff," Dan said, "how would you fix things if you had your way?"

"I'd swap places with Ash," Buff said.

"That wouldn't fix anything, would it?"

"It'd sure as hell fix Ash."

"I mean, there'd still be a guy in jail."

"You bet," Buff said, "but look who."

"How about fixing things so nobody's in jail?"

"Not with Ash around and eating regular."

"Ash," Dan said. "Why is it always the Ashes we have to fight?"

"You ought to know. He's the one that filed down your mug."

"But why stop at Ash? There's somebody over Ash, isn't there?"

"Maybe, but only Ash is over me. It's like a guy stepping on your foot in a crowd. You don't ask if he got pushed by somebody else: you lug him."

"But if we don't lug the one that does the pushing, won't we always get stepped on?"

"It's a big crowd, kid," Buff said. "There's pushers back of the pushers, and you can't take care of 'em all."

Footsteps sounded in the corridor, and Ash opened the door, saying, "Up, you, and screw."

Before rising from the cot, Dan counted the vertical lines on the wall: there were sixty-five of them. "Sixty-five, Buff," he said, and passing through the doorway, he turned toward his friend's cell.

The sheriff grasped his arm and shoved him in the opposite direction. "The other way, you sonabitch!"

"I wanted to see you for once," Dan said, "but he won't let me!"

"Just as well!" Buff said. "He worked me over last night, and I ain't much to look at!"

From the end of the corridor, Dan said, "G'bye, Buff, and the best!"

"Remember what I told you, kid!" Buff said. "Get the Ashes!"

At the gate, Ash said, "Going to talk to me before you go?"

Dan said, "What time is it?" and he turned away.

MARCHING THROUGH GEORGIA

A VOICE said, "Hi."
Dan looked up from the corduroy road, and observing a boy seated on a pine-stump, he said, "Hi, yourself."

"What're you doing?" the boy said.

"I'm stomping the highroad."

"Where to?"

"I don't know."

"Then why you stomping? Why don't you stay here?"

"I have to see what I can see."

"Might be nothing."

"Might be, but I have to find out."

"Why do you have to find out?"

"I don't know that, either."

"You don't know much, do you?"

"I guess not," Dan said.

"Well, *I* know what's up the road."

"I wish you'd tell me, then."

"Do you wish hard and hope to die?"

"As hard as I can," Dan said, "and I hope to die."

"Then I'll tell you," the boy said. "There's nothing up the road, only more road."

"But doesn't the road go anywhere?"

"Big folks say, but I've watched and watched, and it stays where it is."

"You know a lot, don't you?" Dan said.

"People go, but not the road."

"I hate to say goodbye to you. We could be friends."

"The road never moves."

BOB ANDERSON, MY BEAU BOB

THE CONFEDERACY TO P. G. T. BEAUREGARD:

IF you have no doubt of the intention of the Washington Government to supply Fort Sumter by force, you will at once demand its evacuation, and, if this is refused, proceed, in such manner as you may determine, to reduce it.

P. G. T. BEAUREGARD to R. ANDERSON:

I am ordered by the Government of the Confederate States to demand the evacuation of Fort Sumter. All proper facilities will be afforded, etc. The flag which you have upheld so long, etc. I am, sir, very respectfully, etc.

R. ANDERSON to P. G. T. BEAUREGARD:

I have the honor to acknowledge receipt of your communication, etc. It is a demand with which I regret that my sense of honor, and of my obligations to my Government, prevent my compliance. Thanking you, etc.

P. G. T. BEAUREGARD to R. ANDERSON:

Useless effusion of blood, etc.

R. ANDERSON to P. G. T. BEAUREGARD:

I will not open fire on your forces unless compelled to do so by some hostile act against this fort or the flag of my Government, etc.

P. G. T. BEAUREGARD to R. ANDERSON:

Honor to notify you, etc. Will open fire on Fort Sumter in one hour, etc.

R. ANDERSON to A SOUTHERN GENTLEMAN:

If we do not meet again on earth, I hope we may meet in Heaven."

The hour ended at 4:20 in the morning, and at 4:20 and some seconds, the lanyard of a ten-inch smoothbore Columbiad was offered to Mr. Roger Pryor in reward for his hot tongue: "Not only is the Union gone," he had said, "but gone forever." But, strangely, Mr. Pryor shook his head, nor was this all of him shaken, and now he said, "I could not fire the first gun of the war," and the honor—like the hour, but not yet the Union—was gone forever. It passed to Mr. Edmund Ruffin, another daredevil with his face, and this one, sixty-seven years old, played with fire for the last time in his life. His eighteenth-century hand made a fist around a clean cord that led to a clean gun that led to anguish and a dirty end—and the gun (elevation 5 degrees, range 1,200 yards) spoke.

Four years before Lincoln fell (four to the day) fell Sumter. Four years before that finish came this start, and here, on The Battery, they remembered both, they still remembered. They remembered Pierre Gustave Toutant Beauregard ("Old Bory"), and the Hills, and the two Johnstons (Albert Sidney and Joe), and Jackson ("Blue Light" to some, "Stonewall" to all), and Jim Longstreet (known as "Pete"), and Baldy Ewell, and "Beaut" Stuart, and Jubilee Early, and Earl Van Dorn, and Hood, and Huger, and Turner Ashby, and the butcher Forrest, and Dorsey Pender, and McLaws and McClellan (because he too served them well), and Marse Robert. They still remembered. They remembered winning at the beginning and losing in the end—and then winning again!, for the sons of slaves they never lost were still bossed and still slaves. . . .

FIRST LADY

BORN: *At Roanoke Island, North Carolina, 18 August 1587,*
to Eleanor, wife of Ananias Dare, Esq.,
a daughter, Virginia.

NINE DAYS later, Governor John White, grandfather of the
first English child delivered on American soil, sailed for home
*for the present and speedy supply of certain known and apparent
lacks and needs, most requisite and necessary.* It took him three years
and three hundred and fifty-five days to return, and he found *the
houses taken down and the place very strongly enclosed with a high
palisade of trees, with curtains and flankers, very fortlike; and one of
the chief trees or posts at the right side of the entrance had the bark
taken off, and five feet from the ground, in fair capital letters were
graven* CROTOAN, *without any sign or cross of distress.*

He searched for some time, this grandfather of Virginia Dare,
but of the one hundred and sixteen human beings he had left behind on the dunes, he found no wind-grayed bone, no salt-faded
rag, no blurred or bottled word, no word at all save the word CRO-
TOAN; he found no stiff scalp with stiffened hair, no coshed-in skull,
no scaled pot, no rotten pone, no written word save the word CRO-
TOAN; he found no telltale ash, no mildewed trash or unstrung
beads, no wax tears spilt by some sprung-for candle, no hound on
a grave, no grave on stilts, nothing but the lone and graven word
CROTOAN.

There were voices on the sand and in the air, but they spoke no
tongue that White could understand. There were clouds of heron
crying *as if an army of men had shouted together;* there were parrots,
falcons, and merlinbaws; there were clam-birds, there were wrens
in the cattail, there were plover and willet and clapper-rail—but
their cries made no sense in English ears, and the search, begun at
that right-hand gatepost, ended there. Gazing at the still strange
word, White spelled it once aloud, as if charging it to make its own
meaning known, but CROTOAN it was and only CROTOAN, and then
he reboarded ship and sailed away forever.

Had he stayed longer, would he have found the fact of the mat-

ter: would he have found, in some Indian town, one hundred and
sixteen mummied heads on poles; would he have found their teeth
slung on Indian necks and their skin on drums; would he have
found their pots in use, the rusted wrecks of tools, the torn Bibles,
and the clothes again but now wrongly worn . . . ?

DIED: *On or near Roanoke Island, North Carolina,*
Virginia Dare, daughter of Ananias and Eleanor Dare,
on an unknown day between 1587 and 1591.

THIS WILL HAVE A VERY HAPPY EFFECT

THEY still had a gun or two, a blanket here and there (or rather
a weave of cotton and air), some raveling flags, like old bandages, a handful of corn (for those with hands), damn few rounds
of ammunition, but many pounds of spunk per man, and a Lee to
lead them, and if he'd let them, they'd've kept on thrashing like a
shot horse till they sank in seventeen miles south of hell: they were
still sucking around for a fight.

But he couldn't tell them to try some more when on their rank
and punken feet they caved like rained-on wheat; he couldn't cry
"Never say die, boys!" because they'd been dying to that tune for
four years, and they were all through dying except for the lying
down; he didn't have the heart to start another sump to hold thin
blood ("Useless effusion, etc."), he didn't have the cheek to speak
the expected word, he didn't have the face to face such blue murder as the gray was spoiling for: they were beaten, and that was the
bitter verb for the bitter end.

R. E. LEE to U. S. GRANT:
 I suppose, General Grant, that the object of our present meeting is fully understood. I asked to see you to ascertain upon
 what terms you would receive the surrender of my army.
U. S. GRANT to R. E. LEE:
 The terms I propose, etc. The officers and men surrendered
 to be paroled and disqualified, etc. The arms, artillery, and

public property to be parked and stacked, etc. This will not embrace the side-arms of the officers, nor their private horses or baggage, etc.

R. E. LEE to U. S. GRANT:

This will have a very happy effect, etc.

U. S. GRANT to R. E. LEE:

Unless you have some suggestions, etc.

R. E. LEE to U. S. GRANT:

There is one thing I would like to mention. The cavalrymen and artillerists own their own horses in our army. I would like to understand whether these men will be permitted, etc.

U. S. GRANT to R. E. LEE:

You will find that the terms do not allow this. Only the officers, etc.

R. E. LEE to U. S. GRANT:

No, the terms do not allow it. That is clear.

U. S. GRANT to R. E. LEE:

Well, the subject is quite new to me, etc. I take it that most of the men in the ranks are small farmers, and as the country has been so raided by the two armies, it is doubtful whether they will be able to put in a crop, etc. Let all the men who claim to own a horse or mule take the animals home with them, etc.

R. E. LEE to U. S. GRANT:

This will have the best possible effect, etc.

And now Lee said something about notifying Meade, and Grant said something by way of apology for turning up without a sword (no disrespect intended, etc.), and Lee said something about the two armies being kept apart (personal encounters, useless effusion, etc.), and Grant suggested something or other, and Lee mentioned something about something else—but who remembered? It was over, it was all over.

Of course, there were some spoken words to be taken down, some names to be signed, and some hands to be shaken; there were some token courtesies (the bowing, the saluting) to be observed, some phrases still to be broken off, some coughs to cough and quickly kill, and a pause to fill and soften with goodbyes—but it was long over for the C. S. A. There were some odds and ends of defeat outside, but why report the idle staring of the Union staff, the half-minute wait for *Traveller* to be bridled, the queer way Lee stood striking and striking his hands, the misfortune of Grant's appearing on the porch, and his covering the moment by baring his head? Why mention these things? Why pay attention to such details as a paroled officer mounting a free horse, sighing but not yet weeping, and riding back to what was left of the Army of Northern Virginia with the five years that were left of his life? Look away! For God's sake, look away!

(Item: Phil Sheridan paid twenty dollars in gold for the table Grant had used, and Lee's was sold to Cresap Ord for forty of the same.)

This will have a very happy effect, etc.

STATEN ISLAND FERRY

THE sun lay in Kill Van Kull, and the air of the spring afternoon seemed to be filled with a fine fair hair, a barely moving crêpe-de-chine. The bay-water flashed in flakes, as if sequinned, and it kissed the hull as it passed toward Manhattan and the hazy castles in the sky.

[*Two years gone, you thought, and nothing to show for them but the dust of thirty states in your pockets—but you were lying to yourself, and you knew it. You weren't empty-handed: you were heavy-laden with a burden that you could never put down. The cars, you thought, the cars . . . !*]

WELL, BUD, THIS IS ALL THE FURTHER I GO

FROM up and down the stair-well came filtered sounds—of voices without words, of crying and coughing, of a harmonica being played—but beyond the door Dan stood before, there was silence. He put his hand to the knob and found it shaking with the rumor of a mile-away train. The rumor spread through his arms and body and through the walls and the floor, and then it became fact, and the world jigged with the right-of-way under a New York Central express. Not until the train was a rumor again did Dan open the door.

[*They were at the table, and for a moment all they could do was sit there, still and staring, and then Pop tried to speak, but his voice cracked, and he tried again, but that time he had no voice at all, and then Mom, who'd never taken her eyes off you, began to rock her chair —only a little, because the recollection she held was now twenty years old, and if she heard it crying, its voice must've been very faint and very far away in her mind.*]

"Well, Johnsons," Dan said, "your kid's home."

PART FOUR

HUMPTY-DUMPTY: *A MONTAGE*

DAN: "I saw a new ad on a billboard today. It said, 'America is two-car conscious.' Pretty soon, we'll be two-bed conscious. You mean to say you only sleep in one bed? Mister, the modern way is two! And if you can afford two beds, why not two wives, and if you can afford two wives, why not two Gods? Make America two-God conscious! Are you limping along on only one God? Get yourself another de luxe twelve-apostle God and learn what real praying-comfort means! Don't wait! Buy now!"

* * *

THE HACK-DRIVER: "There's a million these days in anything you make eyes at: all you need is a little imagination. For instance, I put fresh flowers in the cab every morning, rain or shine—roses, daisies, violets, sometimes all three—and on a handy rack right in front of him, a fare can find his favorite paper. Result: a guy rides from Penn Station to the Cunard docks and pays off with a five-dollar gold-piece. Imagination: that's the secret."

* * *

DAN: "I had a date to take a walk with Mig last night, and the first thing he said when he saw me was, 'Nifty suit you're wearing, kid. What did it set you back?' I said, 'Fifty-odd,' and he said, 'Doing pretty good for yourself, no?' I said, 'I've got no kick,' and he said, 'I know, but you used to have.' Peculiar kind of remark."

* * *

HACK-DRIVER: "Used to be, when a guy hailed a cab, he was a banker, or an actor, or a judge, or a sport out sporting, and you picked him up in front of a big hotel or a high-class knocking-shop, and about the only time you went through a crumby neighborhood was on your way home. Nowadays, though, *everybody's* a banker, *everybody's* a sport, and it makes no difference if they're wearing spats or carrying a pick: this day and age, *everybody* rides. My God, what don't happen in that old Pierce-A! They use it for everything from a haystack to a board-room. They sniff snow back there, they load pistols, and they sign contracts. They talk love, gin, stocks, and abortions. *Everybody* rides, I tell you!"

* * *

DAN: ["*Dress now, Mr. Lovejoy, but make no sound, or you'll wake the drunken lady from her dreams of the long-legged dolls that lie scattered on the floor; make your way among them to the door, Mr. Lovejoy, leave a bill of suitable denomination under a highball glass, and walk out into the winter night; and as you walk, Mr. Lovejoy, try to breathe away the kissed-off powder and the faint fumes of disinfectant, and try too not to think of Pike's Peak and your mile-high past.*"]

* * *

THE HACK-DRIVER: "One of my regular fares gave me a tip on a stock, and I made a hundred bucks in an hour. If I'd held on to the close, though, I'd've made two hundred more. The way I figure it, I'm a hundred in and two hundred out, so I really lose a hundred on the day."

* * *

JULIA: ["*What would you give to know where I am, Danny, my God damn Dan—the name of the town, the street and number, the floor and room, and the exact location of the bed? and whether the bed's in a flat, a hotel, a home in the suburbs, or a cat-house? and whether I have a husband with me, or a customer, or a lover (male or female), or a toy poodle? Wouldn't you like to know, Danny, my socialist hero, and wouldn't you like to take me skating tonight, to watch me move in the firelight, to take me home and undress me and you-know-what me? Wouldn't you, Mr. Union Label? Wouldn't you, you hardhearted son-of-a-bitch?*"]

* * *

DAN: "Mostly, the people I met were small fry—truckers, farmers, back-country salesmen, bums, brakemen, gas-jerkers, a doctor or two, a game-warden—and the more I met, the more most people seemed to live as if life were a subway, with long dark stretches between dim short stops. They're born, I thought, they mess around in the gloom for sixty years, and they die all-even or in hock, but never with an estate. If you were ordinary, I thought, you took things as you found them, and if you were noble like a certain Italian, you tried to change them with words and deeds and your sweet sad face. One way, you lived; the other, you got two thousand volts, and you were dead."

MRS. JOHNSON: "You don't take either way: you want to be a certain Italian that lives to get rich."

*   *   *

HACK-DRIVER: "I'm sitting in my cab, corner of Wall and William, and all of a sudden I hear a *whack!*, like somebody dropped a sack of water off a roof. People start running like crazy, and I turn around to see what's the matter. Jesus in Heaven! Thirty feet back of the cab, right there in the street . . . ! God, Polly, there must be *one* snort of whisky in the house!"

EMPLOYMENT-AGENCY

"LAST name?" the man said.

[*Under his hand lay a pad of application-forms. When the blanks were filled with fact, a paper Daniel Johnson would be in being, and a paper Daniel Johnson would be for hire.*] "Johnson," Dan said.

[*First name? Address? Phone number? Date of birth? Weight and height? Nationality? Birthplace? Religion? A southbound elevated-train passed the window, and you watched it go in a marching slant of snow.*] "None," Dan said.

"Your people must belong to a church. Which?"

"None."

"Is that what you want me to write down—no religion?"

"Write whatever you like, or leave it blank."

"As you say," the man said, "only it might cost you a job."

"Let it cost. Who wants to work for a fanatic?"

[*Married, single, divorced? Live at home? Use tobacco or spirits? Physical defects? Communicable diseases? Education? Speak foreign language? Employed at present? Where last employed?*] "Metropolitan Life," Dan said.

"In what capacity?" the man said.

"I was a filing-clerk."

"Why did you leave?"

"I was fired."

"For what reason?"

"I was a lousy filing-clerk."

"What other jobs have you held?"

"I've worked in a print-shop. I've been a waiter, summer-camp and hotel. I've done time in a newspaper-office—clipping, pasting, and once in a while covering a bazaar. In the past year or so, I've had a slew of places—shipping-departments in the garment-trade, a couple of months of selling gray-goods for a cotton converter, a spell of stock-and-bond running for an odd-lot house, and so on."

[*Other experience and hobbies? Salaries received? Salary expected? Salary take? Accept temporary work? Leave city for work? Own or drive car? Ever arrested?*] "Once, in Florida," Dan said.

"What for?"

"Nothing that shows on the books. A cop socked me, and I socked back, and then I got beat up, and they kept me in jail till the scabs came off."

[*Ever sued? Ever in bankruptcy?*] "Don't make me laugh," Dan said.

The man put his pen down, saying, "I'm afraid there isn't much here to go on."

"No? What do you need to go on?"

"Something to make you different than a million other guys."

"But I *am* a million other guys."

"Why should you get taken on instead of them?"

"Don't ask me," Dan said. "That's your job. Tell people how pretty I am."

"I've got to have something to sell, Johnson."

"Sell Johnson. I didn't come here because I'm a genius. I came because I'm not."

"You know," the man said, "when we started, I'd've been willing to bet you had a better record than this. I don't know why. Just a feeling."

"Well, get over it," Dan said. "There's only one Dan Johnson, and he's right there on that sheet of paper. If you can't do anything for him, tear him up."

"It's hard to believe that all you can do is wrap bundles, and it's impossible to believe that all you're interested in is a job—not with that attitude of yours. Sports? Art? History? Science? Politics? What?"

"Look," Dan said, "nobody's going to call you up and ask for a bundle-wrapper who knows how the U. S. A. got Texas."

"Ah!" the man said. "How *did* we get Texas?"

"By plundering Mexico. You satisfied?"

"Perfectly, but they didn't teach you that at De Witt."

"We're a little far afield, aren't we? I came here for a job that pays x-bucks a week, and if I had thirty years of experience at anything, I'd cough it out. What do you think I'm trying to do—make it tough for myself?"

The man said, "Do you belong to a union?"

"How could I? I don't have a trade."

"You worked for a printer, you said. What did he run—open-shop?"

"I wasn't old enough to hold a card."

"Would you have joined if you could?"

"Like a shot," Dan said.

"You believe in unions, then."

"Come to think, you can write that down as my religion."

"Do you believe in the American form of government?"

"Only theoretically."

"I'd've thought democracy was practical."

"Maybe it is, but what we've got isn't democracy."

"What would you call it?"

"Come on, now," Dan said. "What's this going to boil down to —a political debate?"

"I'm only trying to learn some things about you that this application doesn't seem to get at."

"Next time you print it up, stick in another question: 'Member any organization overthrow government force and violence?'"

The man said, "Make believe it's printed up."

"Answer: I am not a communist."

"If you don't believe in Capitalism, why aren't you doing something about it?"

"I don't believe in death, either," Dan said.

"What're you so sour about?" the man said. "You're twenty-two years old, but you could break up a German band without a lemon."

"What could *you* do at twenty-two?"

"I could tell how the wind blew. At twenty-two, fresh from Belleau Wood, I could look around and say to myself, 'So that's the way it goes,' and go the same way."

"A man doesn't have to like dirt just because he has to eat it."

"Take your head out from under your arm. You'll feel better."

"How can I feel better? I'm dead."

"You might work up to only being sick."

"The hell with this deep thinking," Dan said. "Can you get me a job, or not?"

"I'll drop you a card," the man said.

A BILL OF SUITABLE DENOMINATION

THE dolls lay as if stricken and boned; their heads hung, and their giraffish legs were sprawled in some doll-orgy ended. [*You moved quietly, as you always did now (to hide, you wondered, and to hide from whom?), and in a cold room cold-lit by a dun dawn, you began to dress.*]

She said, "Going, Dan?"

"I tried not to disturb you," he said. "I'm sorry."

"I don't mind, except to see you go."

"It's good of you to say it."

"The others, I can hardly wait for them to get out, but not you."

"That's too bad," he said, "because I won't be here every week any more."

"If it's the price, you can have it for two, same as tonight."

"This is the last time I'll be able to pay even that."

"How could I live if I gave it away?"

"I don't know, but you don't have to give it away to *me*."

"Couldn't you scrape up *something*, Dan?"

"I'm down to smoke-money and carfare—and I'd hate to tell you where it comes from."

"Well, try, anyhow," she said.

"I'll try my best," he said, and he went toward the door.

"Night, Dan. . . ."

* * *

[BARTO: "*They take me in that cruel room, and they tie me up in that chair, and they say, 'Well, Vanzetti, speak what you want to-day,' and I tell them, 'I now wish to forgive some people for what they are doing to me,' and that is my last speech on the living earth—and now I am saying to you that if I could so speak with people that were putting me to my death, then I could never in my whole life and death together condemn anyone that tried, as you did try, to help me to live and do beautiful things for the people. I love you for this forever, and I will never hate you.*"]

* * *

"Still there, Dan?" she said. "What're you doing?"

"Just thinking," he said.

"About what, honey?"

"About what a skunk I am."

"But that isn't true."

"I'm not worth killing."

"Come over here a minute."

"It's late. I'd better go."

"First come over here."

He sat beside her. "What do you want?"

"I'm not sleepy any more."

"Didn't you hear me? I'm not worth killing."

"You don't have to pay, Danny."

"I'm not worth killing!"

"You don't ever have to pay," she said.

USE TOBACCO OR SPIRITS?

THE man said, "I told you the other day: if anything turned up, I'd drop you a card. Go home."

"No harm done," Dan said. "Unless you're getting sick of my face."

"I like your face. As you say, it's pretty."

"Because if you are, I can go across the hall. This isn't the only agency."

"That outfit over there couldn't land you in a lumber-camp if you were a blue ox. Stick to me, Johnson, and sooner or later I'll get you exploited."

"Something with a future, remember. No piker-stuff for the Boy Wonder of Harlem."

"The only thing with a future these days is a calendar."

"I wouldn't even swear for that," Dan said. "Hoover might try an eight-month year."

"You're knocking one of the two men I love," the man said. "The other is Calvin K. Coolidge. Cal set things up for me, and Herb made me a success. First I had to ream out the barrel for everybody who could stand up for eight hours without wires, and now I do a land-office business in finks and scabs. Are you a fink? If so, I'll put you to work for a princely bagatelle."

"What a way to make a living!" Dan said. "A combination of pawnbroking and slave-trading, with a dash of pimping thrown in to make it unique. I take my hat off to you: you've found the bottom of the bottom. You could study all your life and never hit on a business that made more of a business out of misery. Observe the bared head, sir."

"Forget about misery," the man said. "Misery has nothing to do with this business or any other. The long and short of it is, there's a scarcity of jobs and an overproduction of people, and with a situation like that, Capitalism has only two ways out: it can make more jobs, which is socialistic, or it can kill more people, which is suicidal. Nice to talk to you. Drop you a card if."

WE'VE GOT A LOT OF BLACK STARS NOW

IN THE spring evening, they had walked across Harlem and Morningside Heights to the Drive, and there they stood looking out over the Hudson. A soft air ran downstream, jarring icicles of light that hung from the Jersey shore, and below them a fat ferry waded toward Fort Lee.

"I've been saving something for you, kid," Mig said. "In the fall, I'll be quitting my job and going far away across the sea."

Dan looked at his friend for a moment before speaking, and when he spoke, all he could say was, "I'll miss you, Mig."

"I'll miss three people—and my father and mother are two of them."

"It'll be lonely here," Dan said. "The world is full of faces, but if you know of one you won't see among them, none of the others seems to count. It'll be lonely, Mig, but over and above that, I'll worry, because there's no good for you in Italy."

"I don't remember saying anything about Italy."

Again Dan turned to Mig, and again there was an interval before he could speak. "My God," he said, "don't tell me it's Russia!"

Mig laughed. "You say that like Italy was safer," he said.

"I only meant to show surprise, as if you'd told me you were going to be married, but come to think of it, what's there to be surprised about? You've been engaged for a long time."

"Ever since they killed the wops in Massachusetts."

"I could've guessed that," Dan said. "But tell me, what're you going to do over there?"

"Same thing as over here—presswork. They get out a magazine, *International Literature*, that appears in different languages. I managed to talk them out of a job in the bureau handling the English edition. Sound good?"

"Couldn't be better," Dan said.

"I got to thinking that with me leaving the plant here, there'll be an opening you just might plug. What do you say I bring up your name?"

"What good would it do?" Dan said. "There must be hundreds

out of work in the printing-trade, and all of them would qualify ahead of me. Besides, I don't carry a card, and with things what they are, I doubt like hell that I could get one, and even if I could, where would I raise the fee?"

"I'll loan you the money, and you can pay it back out of wages."

"How much do you think I'd get?" Dan said.

"Well, I've been making forty."

"They wouldn't pay *me* any forty."

"Naturally, but whatever you got, it'd be more than zero."

"I'd have to get enough to chip in at home. . . ."

"You chipping in much right now?"

". . . And have something left for myself."

"I honest to Christ ought to get sore, Danny," Mig said. "Here you been going along for months, living off your old man and not ponying up a nickel for your keep, and now, with a chance to carry your weight, you give me some razmataz about what's going to be left for you. What're you waiting for—somebody to tap you in the street and say, 'You're just the guy I been looking for to run my railroad.'?"

"The loan is what bothers me. Hell knows how long you'd have to wait for the money."

"If I could afford it, I'd make you a gift of it."

"I guess you would, Mig, but I'll be damned if I know why."

"You know why, kid."

"Two-three years ago I'd've known, but not now."

"You're no different. You're the same guy I slipped that throw-away to at De Witt."

"Haven't you ever thought that maybe *this* is the real Dan Johnson? Haven't you ever thought that maybe the little man had only one flash in him, like a match?"

"I read something once," Mig said, "and I liked it enough to memorize it. '. . . The way this country started out, everybody thought it was going to be the greatest place on earth, with liberty and justice for all, but we got less and less fine things and more and more cheap things, and every time one of them happened, a white star in our flag turned black. We've got a lot of black stars now. . . .'"

"Ah, forget it!" Dan said. "Forget it!"

"'. . . And it can't go on much longer, or we'll run out of white ones, and then it won't be a flag any more, but a rag so dirty that no decent man will wipe his feet on it, let alone take his hat off to it or die for it. . . .'"

"Jesus Christ, Mig, *quit!*"

The ferry, having crossed the river, was recrossing now, and the wind had played itself out, leaving the slow-moving water flat.

"The guy that wrote those words isn't fooling me," Mig said. "He's fooling himself, Mr. Lovejoy."

EVER IN BANKRUPTCY?

"YOU here again?" the man said.

Dan said, "I wanted you to know I've been offered a job."

"What doing and for how much?"

"Back in the old print-shop. Twenty a week, maybe."

"You should've grabbed a broom and swept like all get-out."

"This didn't happen to be a broom-job."

"I don't care what kind of a job it was. You should've grabbed something and made a blur with it."

"I have a little while to think it over."

"So has the Boss. It cuts both ways."

"If he could think, he wouldn't be the Boss."

"That idea is going to be paid for with a lot of socialist blood."

"What else've we got to pay with?"

"Closing time," the man said, and leaving the office, they went downstairs and walked northward along Sixth Avenue. "Nice afternoon."

"If you like afternoons," Dan said.

"Holy Smoke, don't you even like the weather?"

"I'm afraid I don't like anything, myself included and myself least."

"A natural aversion," the man said, "but if you saw more people, you'd get over it. How about supper downtown tonight?"

"I'm flat broke."

"I'm loaded."

"What'm I supposed to do—watch you eat?"

"I ought to kick your ass for that," the man said. "Mr. Johnson, will you do Mr. Peterson the honor of being his guest, you son-of-a-bitch?"

"I always wondered what your name was," Dan said.

They ate in an Italian restaurant off Longacre Square, and afterward, through coffee-flavored smoke, Peterson said, "Kid, how'd you like to go to work?"

"Right now, this bulging gut of mine says, 'Why worry?'"

"What'll it say when it's lank again?"

"Oh, it'll mumble something under its breath. 'Capitalist slavery,' it'll say. 'Unequal distribution.'"

"A nice soft job," Peterson said. "Thirty a week, starting Monday. Hours nine to six, Saturdays nine to noon. No chance of advancement."

"If it weren't for the half-Saturdays, I'd say somebody put in a call for a bouncer in a whorehouse."

"Mr. Peterson wants a clerk in his agency."

"By God," Dan said, "somebody *does* want a bouncer in a whorehouse!"

"Life is a whorehouse," Peterson said.

[*You remembered a Negro boy watching you eat a sundae and trying to eat it himself, trying to eat it with his mind through a sheet of plate-glass, and you remembered his defeat as he turned away, and you remembered, because it'd been part of your own defeat, that all you'd been able to do was abandon the sundae and save him a token of a feast gone sour, a maraschino cherry—and now, you thought, you were about to eat your sundaes before millions who would be all eyes with longing, and this time there'd be no turning away, neither you from them nor they from you, and there'd be no tokens to save for the beaten, because even those would have to be eaten before their unbroken stare.*] Dan laughed.

"That's a laugh with cold teeth," Peterson said. "What's killing you?"

"I'm killing myself—by filling your God damn job!"

"Come Monday, kid, you're going to be God yourself. Don't take the name in vain."

TWO AUDIENCES WITH GOD

A DIM and disembodied hand rose to rap against the frosted pane of a door. "Come in," Dan said, and a young woman entered his office. "What can I do for you, miss?"

"They told me outside that this is where I make my application."

"Sit down, please," Dan said, and drawing the form-pad toward him, he looked up at the applicant. "Last name?"

"Paul."

"First name?"

"Genevieve."

"Middle initial?"

"None."

"Date of birth?"

"April 6th, 1910."

"Father's name?"

[*Vincent Paul was born on a hundred-acre patent near Ticonderoga, and during the seventy-odd years of his life, only once did he travel beyond a hard day's walk from his own land. Eighteen years old when his father died with the deed in his hand, he pried the stiff fingers loose and fell to work to plow his earth to hell-and-gone. No square yard escaped the blade where a team could tread, no side-hill, no ditch, no stone-strewn swale, and the lawns went under, and the spaces between the buildings, and even the faces of dead ancestors were turned to make feed for seed—and in the end, the house, the privy, the crib, the silo, the barn, all floated like coops and crates on a groundswell of green. "As the feller puts it," Paul would say, "I only want the land that touches mine," and in thirty years, his hundred acres became seven hundred, a great bulging belly that he rode with far more passion than ever he rode the bellies of turnpike tarts or those, old and new, of neighbors' wives. But there was one kind of leaf it had never yielded him, one kind of fruit it had never borne in season, and he grew to be fifty before he realized that some day he would end a planting by being*

*planted himself, to live on in worms, in grass, in a jet of wheat, and
now he would say, "My trouble is, I got the fifties," One summer evening, therefore, he unlocked his Bible and turned to the Family Record
for the forgotten name of a female cousin in the Fort Edward district,
and in the morning he set out on the sole pilgrimage of his life: on his
return, in a fortnight, his wife was some days gone with child. The child
when born, was called Genevieve, and the wife, when delivered, was
buried in an alley of pine-stumps too narrow to be plowed. And so
Paul recovered from the fifties only to catch the sixties, a sickness he
could never shake off, and his seven hundred acres shrank piece by piece
to the original patent, and then to half, and finally to a house-lot that
he stumbled over with a hoe, singing a one-line song to himself, always
the same little one-line song—"Lord," he would sing, "I wish a crop'd
grow like weeds."—and the Lord sent him the seventies, and he died.*]

"If we find something," Dan said, "we'll let you know."

The girl said, "Thank you," and went to the door, but at the door
she turned, saying, "I've got to get a job."

"We'll do our best to place you, Miss Paul."

"You don't understand," she said. "I've got to get a job."

"We receive twenty applications a day from typists, Miss Paul.
I'm sure you realize that there are more typists than jobs. We can't
make jobs; we can only fill vacancies."

"I'm listed with four agencies, and they all say the same thing.
What'm I to do? I answer every ad, and wherever the place is, I
walk to save the carfare. Even so, I only eat once a day. When I
came to New York, I had just enough to see me through business-
school, but by skimping on everything, I've managed to make it
last. It'll go just so far, though, and that'll be the end. I only eat
once a day! Do you understand?"

"I understand," Dan said.

"You don't understand at all. You sit there, looking at me and
nodding your head, but you're not really listening to me; you're
just waiting for me to go away. You've heard all this before—twenty
times a day, you said. When I tell you I've only had fourteen meals
in the last two weeks, you hear the words, but they have no meaning."

"I'm very sorry, Miss Paul."

"Another week, and I'll have nothing, not even one meal a day."

"I wish I could promise you something definite, but these're tough times, and I'd be lying if I made any promises at all. Don't you think it might be a good idea to go home till things get better?"

"I have no home," she said. "I've got to get a job, and I'll do anything for it. Do you understand that? I'll do anything!"

"There's nothing that you have to do, Miss Paul. We're as eager to place you as you are to be placed. That's how we pay our rent. We don't charge for listing you, only for putting you to work."

"I'll do anything to get a job—anything!"

"I don't know what you mean by 'anything.' Why do you say that?"

"I'll do anything!" she said. "My God, don't you even understand me?"

*   *   *

"Last name?"

"Hill."

"First name?"

"John."

"Middle initial?"

"C."

"C for ... ?"

"Carlos."

"Date of birth?"

"October 14th, 1906."

"Father's name?"

"Do you have to know all this?"

"I guess so," Dan said. "It's on the blank."

"His name was Lloyd—Lloyd Hill."

[*A one-windowed room in an office-building on Park Row contained a five-dollar desk, three camp-chairs, a law-school diploma framed in oak, and a sectional bookcase holding an incomplete set of Hun's New York Law Reports. Lloyd Hill, the tenant of the one-windowed room, had been disbarred for maintenance in 1905, and his clients—not some, but all, even the two whose actions he had financed—had called for their papers and gone elsewhere forever with their custom. Lawyer Hill was unaware of his permanent ruin, and in the belief that his clientele would return with his reinstatement, he filed petition after petition with the Appellate Division, always hopefully but always vainly, until at length one of his numerous pleas found the Presiding Justice of the Court in the mood for a brief speech to his associates. The speech was as follows: "Every three months, gentlemen, this poor devil presents us with one of these documents. This one now before us must be the tenth or twelfth, and suddenly I find that I can no longer face the prospect of more. There are no extenuating circumstances in the case, and as we well know, the record is perfectly clear on the score of the petitioner's admission of guilt. Nevertheless, I'd rather resign from this Bench than read another of his feeble and begging affidavits. They're poorly written and loosely reasoned, and they promise nothing that every other wretch in his fix hasn't promised before, and although I'm certain that no good can come of it, I deeply desire to give him a second chance. I've never spoken to you in this manner, but perhaps from that fact alone you can deduce my motive: pity, gentlemen, pure and simple pity. I move that we reinstate this discredit to our profession. He touches me, God damn it!" In the year 1908, Lawyer Hill was restored to good standing, and only then did he see the end of the track. It took him three more years to reach it: three years of letting himself into his one-window room at nine sharp; three years of staring at the peeling buckram of his Hun's Reports while he waited for clients who never came; three years of putting on his derby at twelve sharp and going around the corner to Max's Busy Bee for a meat sandwich and a cup of coffee; three years of closing the office at six sharp and starting for home, two rooms in a boarding-house on West 122nd Street; three years of rocking a rocker and talking to his wife until ten sharp; and three years of brushing his teeth and going to bed. On a summer afternoon in 1911, the police were summoned to the one-window room to remove his body: after nine hundred trips to Park Row, after nine hundred meat sandwiches at the Busy Bee, Lawyer Hill had come to know that he was looking upon his diploma for the last time, that he would never again sit in a boarding-house rocker, that in a moment or two he would put his derby hat on his head and blow two holes through each. A policeman said, "I wonder why he wore the hat," but no one answered, because no one knew: not even Lawyer Hill had known.*]

IT IS TIME FOR THEE, LORD, TO WORK

FROM a rack on his desk, Dan took a card on which were printed the trade-name and address of the agency and the company-motto: *If any would not work, neither should he eat*. On the reverse side were three dotted lines, each headed by a single word: after DATE, he wrote *November* 18, 1931; after TO, *Caribbean Fruit Growers;* and after INTRODUCING, *Miss Genevieve Paul*. Then, putting the card in his pocket, he turned out the office lights, went downstairs, and boarded a southbound streetcar.

He left the car at 20th Street and walked westward from Sixth Avenue to an old four-story brownstone; under the stoop, he found a battery of bell-buttons opposite slotted names, and he pressed one of them marked *G. Paul*. A buzzer clicked the door-catch, and he entered the dim ground-floor hallway; at the far end, a figure stood on a threshold against a purpling courtyard beyond.

"We had no phone listed for you, Miss Paul," Dan said, "so I thought I'd come in person."

"What do you want?" she said.

"I want to see you. Aren't you going to ask me in?"

"Come in if you like," she said, and she went to a window and looked out at calcimined brick and the tangents and secants of clotheslines. "Have you got a job for me?"

"Do we have to talk about that right away?"

"What else is there to talk about?"

"You said you'd do anything for a job, so I hoped you'd have supper with me."

"What else do I have to do?"

"You don't really have to do anything."

"You have no right to hold me to what I said the other day. I said whatever came into my mind. I needed a job, and that's what did the talking. It isn't fair to hold me to my word—not about a thing like this."

"Do you still need a job?"

"Of course I do—more than ever."

"I came to offer you one."

"That isn't all. It can't be. I don't *understand* you! What're you doing here?"

"I'm trying to get you to go out to supper."

"You want more than that, and you know it!"

"Ah, hell," Dan said, and taking the card from his pocket, he dropped it on a table. "There's the job, and I hope you have a great success with the Caribbean Fruit Growers. I even hope you marry Mr. Caribbean. We'll send you a bill on the first of the month. Good evening."

She let him reach the door before saying, "I'm sorry I spoke that way. You've been good to me, and if you still want me to, I'll eat with you. I'm hungry, but that's not the only reason."

[*You thought, "For Christ's sake, go away!" and you thought, "Stay, you damn fool!" and you stayed.*] "Put your coat on," he said. "I'm hungry too."

Afterward, they walked back to the brownstone in a bright cold night under a star-punctured sky, and at the door she said, "Would you care to come inside?"

"Yes," he said. "Yes, I would."

She turned on a gas-log below the mantel, and they sat watching blue fire simmer. "I lied to you before," she said. "I knew what I'd promised, and I wanted to take it back. I don't any more, though, and whatever you tell me to do, I'll do."

"I don't want you to do anything."

"You're the one that's lying now. You came here with that card because you expected me to make good. Otherwise you'd've mailed it to me."

"I came because I wanted the pleasure of telling you about the job face to face. That's all."

"Is that what you do with everybody you get a job for—hunt them up and tell them face to face?"

"No. This is the first time."

"Why do you do it now?"

"The way you acted at the office that day. The things you told me about yourself."

"But more than anything, the promise I made."

"It wasn't the promise: the promise almost kept me away. I wanted to see you again, but I knew that if I ever did, I'd remember what you'd said and feel like a dog."

"Even if you came here only for the pleasure of seeing my gratitude?"

"I'm no nobleman, Genevieve, and when I die, I won't look saintly: I'll look like what I am, an ordinary guy. If you want all the truth, though, I'll tell it: the promise mixed up my thinking so much that I honestly don't know whether I'm here to give something or to get something. There's some of each in it, I suppose, but which there's more of I couldn't possibly say. I like to find jobs for people: it's the only consolation I have for working as a capitalist pimp. When I'm able to help somebody, and he tells me, 'Gee, Johnson, thanks a million!' I feel great, really great. Lots of times I've been offered tips, bribes, sad little presents, but the only thing I ever kept was a nickel bunch of flowers that an old lady left on my desk. I don't want any tips. I don't want any bribes. I only want to help a whole lot of people, one by one. Before you came in, everybody was on an equal footing, and God Himself couldn't've gotten me to put Christ ahead of any other carpenter—before you came in. I took your application and put it right up on top; I put you before girls with sixteen times your ability and twenty-nine times your experience, girls who can type you blind in an hour and dead in a day. Why? Why did I do that? To see your face light up, to get you to deliver, or both? You shouldn't've said anything, Genevieve. You shouldn't've made any promises."

The girl rose and went behind the couch, saying, "Dan, please don't turn till I tell you to."

He stared at the clambering flames, the blue bees pouring from the perforated log, and then he heard the sound of cloth sliding on cloth, and he knew that he would have to turn, not when told, but now.

PIER 56, NORTH RIVER

THE siren began to sound at five minutes before midnight, and for four of those minutes, Dan and Mig shouted at each other in a deafening world, and then the final minute came, and their words broke off with the siren, and they stood looking at each other, shaking hands and smiling.

And then the final seconds came, and Dan said, "You're such a wonderful guy, Mig."

And Mig said, "A lot of people're wonderful guys, Mr. Lovejoy," and he ran for the gangplank.

INTRODUCING JOHN CARLOS HILL

"FORGET it, Jack," Dan said, cocking his head to wedge the telephone-receiver between his ear and shoulder. "That's what we're in business for. Forget it."

["Forget nothing. The first time you're anywhere near the Street, give me a ring, and I'll blow you to the best lunch in town. I know just the place. The waiters've all been there since the War of 1812, but there's fresh food every hour. And the coffee—man, it's so rare they have to buy it a bean at a time."]

"Quit, or I'll jump a train and meet you right now."

["Jump it. See how sore I get."]

"You're on. Where do we meet?"

["Corner of New Street and Exchange Place. The joint's only a few doors away."]

"How about twelve-thirty?"

["Sharp."]

MAIL-POUCH

DAN wrote, "... Going downtown the other morning, I rammed myself into an express at 96th Street, and when the train started, a voice behind me said, 'Careful where you're standing, white boy.' I was in so tight that I couldn't turn around, so I said over my shoulder, 'I'm sorry.' That didn't satisfy this egg, and he said, 'Think you own the earth, eh, white boy?' I said, 'I told you I was sorry. What more do you want?' and he said, 'You'd probably like it if we had Jim Crow cars, wouldn't you, white boy?' I was good and sore by that time, and when the train hit the bend at Columbus Circle, I managed to twist myself a little—and there I was, scowling the famous Johnson scowl at a grinning shine name of Julie Pollard! We hadn't seen each other for months, and getting out at Times Square, we stood in the snow chewing the fat for a solid hour. He'd been on his way to the Library, he told me, and do you know what he was going to do when he got there? He was going to write. That's what I said: write. He still takes a fight now and then, but he says he found out it's one thing to be champ of the block and another to be Sam Langford, and he only keeps his hand in for coffee-and-cake money and rent. He spends the rest of his time putting words together—and with some success, the way it looks. He's been at it for about a year, he tells me, and out of a dozen-or-so stories, he's had one published and two more accepted, and right now he's working on a longer thing that might turn out to be a novel. What's he like these days? Well, the best way to put it is, he's still Julie Pollard—the hardest-hating black man in North America. He still won't fight an ofay, you know—says he hates to touch 'em—and I'll bet I'm the only one he's ever shaken hands with in his life. I think he'll always be that way. He simply can't forget he's black...."

Tootsie wrote, "...I went up to see if I could have a talk with some of the Scottsboro boys, and when I asked a deputy how to go about getting a pass, he reached under his arm and pulled out a big blue pistol, and he cocked the hammer and pointed the hole at my head, saying, 'Only kind of a pass a nigra gets is with a three and a foah. High-tail it, you sonabitchin' black bastard!' Have you read any of Julie's stories, Danny...?"

Danny wrote, "...The published one. It's called 'Jig-chaser,' and reading it was like watching Julie fight—or, better, like fighting him myself. He comes out fast, and he never lets up; he's a swarm of words, all of them hard; and I got the feeling that he wasn't only the Julie Pollard that didn't get to read his composition at graduation, and he wasn't only the Julie Pollard that wanted so much to be a lawyer and 'get justice in the court,' but he was also every other Negro that started out with big beautiful brown eyes and wound up with a broken back...."

HE OPENED HIS MOUTH AND
TAUGHT THEM, SAYING

DAN and Julie crossed 106th Street to the house that Hill lived in, a converted granite-front a few doors east of the Franz Sigel statue on the Drive.

As they entered the flat, Hill was saying to three friends lounging near the fireplace, "... Christ was a flop. He had the chance of all eternity, and He muffed it because what He preached was vertical instead of horizontal. I can't understand what God had in mind. He turned His only son loose on a world that needed Him more than rain, and what fell was dust, because Christ brought an up-and-down love that neither watered the spirit nor flowered the flesh nor flowed from heart to heart and made fruit, and when He died, man dried on the vine for eighteen centuries. God must've been tired when He cooked up Jesus. With unlimited assets and raw materials, all He could generate among men was hatred, and it remained for an epileptic Russian—a Jew-hater, a wife-beater, a salt-mine convict—to preach what Jesus could've had for a dime. It's a pity. The world would've been saved eighteen hundred years of slaughter if God had written *The Brothers Karamazov* instead of *The Sermon on the Mount* ...."

"What's this Russian's name?" Julie said.

Dan made the introductions. "Jack Hill on the couch, along with Maury Pastor," he said, "and Al Clay and Jake Harris on the floor. This is one of my oldest and best friends—Julie Pollard." There were greetings, but no handshakes.

"You were talking about some Russian," Julie said to Hill. "Who do you mean?"

"Dostoevsky," Hill said.

"I never heard of him. What does he stand for?"

"It's hard to put in a few words," Hill said, "especially if you haven't read his books."

"I've read *The Sermon on the Mount*, though, and from what you say, this *Brothers* book has something better. What?"

"It has an understanding of man and a love for him as he is," Hill said, "not as he might've been if God had known what He was doing when He threw him together. The Christian religion doesn't hold water: God creates man in His image and finds him defective. What does that argue? Either that God Himself is defective, or He purposely held out on man. If God is defective, we can stop right there and forget the whole business, so let's assume He had a reason for not creating a couple of billion other Gods. What was it? The first thing that comes to mind, naturally, is that He wasn't sucker enough to split the universe two billion ways: He seen it first. But that isn't being very charitable to God, so let's hunt for a better reason. How about this? He built man to fall short so that in the end He could reach down and save him, as a brand from the burning, provided only that he had shown himself worthy of entering the kingdom of Heaven. But what does it mean to be worthy though defective? If defective, man can never be absolutely worthy; he can only be worthy in relation to other defectives. Under this hypothesis, God made man defective in order to reward those who proved the *least* defective. But that's nonsense, and it leads nowhere—except to the conclusion that God is blaming man for His own damned uneven work. So let's dismiss that reason too. What else is there? We have the poorest of reasons, of course, the one you'd suppose most theologians would prefer to forget, for it gives God a mighty poor character: He made man the way he is, brutal, forsworn, avaricious, and full of spleen, because He desired limited corporeal lives of misery, oppression, and bloodshed in order to purge man for splendid and never-ending lives in the spirit. But, my God, what a God that would be! Deliberately torturing every born man in preparation for a remission from torture! There's as little sense to that as living in a sewer in order to enjoy a bath. A man doesn't have to become dirty in order to become clean; he can start clean and stay clean. No, this hogwash about life on earth being a trial won't go down. What's next? We mustn't forget the appeal to sentiment: God so loved the world that He let His only

begotten son die for it. Reason reels before such reasoning. Why
waste a perfectly good Savior on a perfectly imperfect world? If
man is worth saving at the end, he must've been worth a break at
the beginning, but for some queer reason, God doesn't see it that
way: He likes to make it tough; He prefers to pull man through a
knothole into the Hereafter. In the Old Testament, at least, no
Hereafter was promised; in the New, you can choose between two,
Heaven and everlasting hell. For me, the Jews have the merit of being realists: they give you hell or Heaven right here on the ground.
Something must've happened to God along about the time He
changed His religion, and God only knows what it was, but whatever, He put reality behind Him, and ahead lay the ages of the
bloody spirit, with Heaven straight up and hell straight down, and
the time came for man to stop loving man for man's sake and start
loving him for God's sake, which meant that the time was ripe for
man to murder in the name of the Lord and be forgiven on Friday.
Blessed are the poor in spirit: for theirs is the Kingdom of Heaven. But
who with appetites here in the dirt, all God-given, wants pie in the
sky? *Blessed are they that mourn: for they shall be comforted.* But
why have they been made to mourn, and where shall their grief be
assuaged—here and now, or there and then? *Blessed are the meek:
for they shall inherit the earth.* But is Morgan meek, is Henry Ford,
is John D.? *Blessed are they which do hunger and thirst after right-
eousness: for they shall be filled.* But with what—with food and drink,
or with bayonets and tear-gas? *Blessed are the merciful: for they
shall obtain mercy.* But from whom—the merciless? *Blessed are the
pure in heart: for they shall see God.* But not yesterday, when they
asked for bread and were given a stone; and not today, when they
ask for time and are foreclosed; and not tomorrow, when they will
ask for jobs and be shot down by the Hessians. *Rejoice, and be ex-
ceeding glad: for great is your reward in Heaven.* In Heaven, in
Heaven, always in Heaven!"

"This Russian man," Julie said. "What did he do about all that?"

"What did he do?" Hill said. "He reached up into the sky and
dragged Heaven down to earth, where it belonged. He expropri-
ated God and distributed His estates among the people. He merged

the next life with this, so that the seat of the Hereafter became the living hearts of living men."

"Did he do all that?" Julie said.

"Read his books," Hill said.

"I'll take your word about the books, but I'll gamble they never heard of 'em in Paint Rock, Alabama."

"They'll hear all over the world some day."

"What's the good of *some* day? I want the news to get around now, when nine of my people are sitting in jail, waiting to be lynched for raping a couple of white hustlers on a freight-train. This Russian man don't mean a thing to them, and he don't mean a thing to me, either, not unless Victoria Price and Ruby Bates go and get religion, and walk in the court, and take back their lies. No such luck, though. Takes a long time for news to travel in Alabama, and my people'll die before yours see the light. Love everybody, this Russian man says, but he can't tell me nothing about love. I'm black, and I know what loving is because I know what hating is. When a black loves you, he does it with his whole body, all at once, but when a white loves you, he does it with talk, sweet-sweet. We've had talk for three hundred years, sweet-sweet, but your people're still on the toilets, and mine're still swabbing 'em out. That ain't going to last for another three hundred years, and you can build high on it—but when it's changed, it won't be changed by Jesus or this Russian saying sweet-sweet. It'll be changed by knives, buckshot, and a flood of blood."

"That's where you're wrong, Pollard. People have to love each other to rise up against slavery."

"Tough on me, then. I'm a hating-type man."

ON TRACK 14

A SLOPE of morning sunlight cut the glass jar of Penn Station into gloom and gold, and in the gold, gold-flakes tumbled past Dan as he stood near a train-board bearing the words GULF EXPRESS. A growing pound-and-pound shook the floor and died away, and after a few moments passengers began to emerge from a stairhead beyond the gates. One of these carried a suitcase on the end of which was a scuffed-up Tuskegee sticker.

"Mr. Powell," Dan said. "Mr. Tudor Powell."

Tootsie grinned, saying, "Little more respect, there, boy. Mr. Tudor Powell, M. A."

Dan bowed. "Smash your baggage, Mr. M. A. Powell."

ORIGIN OF AN AMERICAN

"LAST NAME?"

"Gruenberg."

"First name?"

"Herschel."

[Born in one of the smaller villages of Kovno Guberniya, Herschel Gruenberg was the only son of a Talmudic scholar, a man devoted unequally to religion and chess, so unequally, indeed, that his wife, who supported the family on her lean earnings as a wigmaker, was often heard to condemn his pastime with the curse, "Eighty-eight black years on the little pieces of wood!" Herschel's father died when the boy was nine—died, it may be admitted, in the act of moving a rook—and with the hopes of the Gruenbergs now centered on the son, he was apprenticed to a journeyman cobbler, and thereafter few were the muddy roads of the district that saw not the master with his tool-sacks and his rolls of leather, and young Herschel with the small silver trumpet of their calling. Twice in the year they made a circuit of the farms and villages roundabout, mending along the way such boots and harness and kindred articles as had fallen into disrepair during their absence; but apart from the privilege of heralding their approach, the master granted no concession to Herschel's youth, and between blasts on the horn, the boy was forced to learn his trade and earn his keep. He learned well, and by the time he was twenty years of age, he possessed a route of his own, a set of tools, and a cornet-à-pistons—and but for an odd circumstance, now about to be related, he might have lived out his life playing brief airs across the Lithuanian countryside.

[The circumstance was this. He returned from one of his journeys carrying all his equipment in an almost new Gladstone bag, and being *observed by a friend, he was asked the following question: "Herschel, where did you obtain such a stylish box?" There was no more to the circumstance.*

[Now, the truth was, the stylish box had been acquired in a manner that reflected little credit on Herschel's business ability, and being proud, he was too ashamed to be frank. In the great city of Suwalki, he had labored for many a day in the service of a certain merchant, using the best of his stock of leathers, neglecting other customers of longer standing, and even, quite recklessly, devoting the total of his skill to the fashioning of a gift, a pair of Morocco slippers in a lady's size—all because a daughter of this merchant, a curving girl with slanting eyes, had come to the work-shed a dozen times a day, on this errand and that, hardly ever glancing at Herschel but always passing close enough to be smelled, and smelling sweet, she had intoxicated him like sacramental wine—but in the end, when there was no more work to be done, and further delay would have been impossible to explain, he had presented himself to the merchant and requested payment for his labors. With deep regret, the merchant had informed him that trade had fallen upon evil times, and since cash was unobtainable, he besought Herschel to satisfy his claim with merchandise. Believing he knew what was in the wind, Herschel had hastened to accept the offer—but he was wrong, as it turned out, for what the merchant produced was not his curving daughter, but an almost new Gladstone bag. For this, Herschel had no more use than he would have had for an iron anchor, yet he had given his word, and he was bound, and sorrowfully he had quitted the great city of Suwalki and turned his face toward home.

[The question, "Where did you obtain such a stylish box?" remained, and Herschel's reply, if not quite candid, was entirely honest. "It was given to me in the great city of Suwalki," he said, and he continued on his way.

[A little further along, he encountered another friend, and this one said, "Herschel, what are you doing with that stylish box?" and Herschel, unable to explain, explained nevertheless, "As you can see," he said, "I am carrying it by the handle."

[At the town's edge, he was accosted by a third friend and asked the most perplexing question of all. "Herschel," the third friend said,

"are you traveling away somewhere with your stylish box?" Herschel
gave what he thought was a perplexing answer, saying, *"People come,
and people go,"* and well-pleased with his skillful parrying, he tarried
for a moment to treat himself to a glass of peppermint seltzer.

[*The delay was fatal, for it gave rumor time to grow into fact, and
Herschel reached home to find his mother, his five unmarried sisters,
and all the neighbors gathered in the road, and his mother was rocking
herself and crying, "Eighty-eight black years on Columbus! My son
is traveling away!"*]

[*And Herschel, trapped by his proud nature, was compelled to say,
"Aye, with this stylish box, soon I will travel away to the American
States."*]

Dan said, "What did you do after coming to this country, Mr.
Gruenberg?"

"What does a man do if he has no money?" Gruenberg said.
"I worked. I worked hard and bitter."

"At your old trade?"

"At my old trade, but not for fifteen years now."

"Why did you give it up?"

"To make a living, I had to buy electrical machines, and how
would I buy electrical machines? Is there a fortune in shoe-making?"

"What've you done for the past fifteen years?"

"Ask, better, what I have not done. I have done everything."

"What kind of work would you be willing to take now?"

"It is a year already that I have not worked. I would be willing,
no matter what."

"Do you mind if I ask you something personal, Mr. Gruenberg?"

"Ask. I have no secrets."

"What's the condition of your health?"

The man looked at Dan for a moment, and the muscles of his
face arranged a smile; the smile, however, caused a rise in the water-level of his eyes, and once or twice he blinked. "Not good," he
said, "not good," and now, curiously, he seemed able to smile well,
and his face became very beautiful.

"I won't say anything about that," Dan said.

"Ah, well," the man said, "maybe if I didn't taken that stylish box. . . . But, then, who can say? Who knows?"

COMPLIMENTS OF JOHN CARLOS HILL

DAN CLEARED his desk for the week-end, waved at Peterson through a glass partition, and started for the door. Peterson came from his room, saying, "Where you going, kid?"

"Crazy," Dan said. "Want to come along?"

"I been there."

"My friend Hill called this morning—the Wizard of Wall Street. Asked me to drop in for a drink. See you Monday, Pete."

"Don't you want the wages you earned in the sweat of our clients' faces?"

"Hand it over," Dan said. "I clean forgot."

Peterson gave him an envelope. "Don't spend it all in one coöperative," he said.

Leaving the office, Dan walked up Sixth Avenue under a sky like a vast bulging bag being dragged over the rooftops. At any moment, some spire, some flagpole, would tear it as a thorn tore silk, and the city would be smothered, powdered with a single puff. The moment came as Dan neared Central Park, and by the time he reached Hill's house, he wore inch-thick epaulettes and on his hat an outer hat of snow. Pausing to finish a cigarette, he watched the way its smoke hung in the dense air, and then, shaking himself, he went indoors and upstairs.

A girl opened the door for him, saying, "According to Jack, you must be Dan."

"Why must I, when I'd like so much to be somebody else? Who must you be?"

"I'm Mary Homer," the girl said. "Come in and tell me why you want to be somebody else."

"I don't, really. It was the snow speaking. Whenever it snows, I think of Colorado, but don't ask me why."

"Don't you know, or don't you care to say?"

"I don't know," Dan said, and he smiled. "That leaves you in the dark."

"It's lighter than you think. I happened to be at the window when you were down below. I saw your face."

"Did it reveal names? Did it give dates and places?"

"It revealed you," the girl said.

"I don't recall thinking about anything—except the smoke I was making with a cigarette. I love to smoke in weather like this."

"I like to smoke in the dark."

"I'd find that strange," he said. "I smoke to see the smoke."

"Did you have a pretty girl in Colorado?"

"I didn't say I had *any* girl in Colorado."

"No, you didn't. That's quite true."

"It's also true that she was as pretty as a little red pair of shoes," he said. "Where's Jack?"

"I phoned his office from the depot, and he said for us to wait."

"Depot? Are you from out of town?"

"I live in New Jersey," the girl said. "Red Bank."

"I don't believe I've ever heard of the place."

"It's about fifty miles from here, on the Navesink."

"I've been in Seabright. Is Red Bank near there?"

"Four-five miles away, maybe."

"Last summer, Jack and I and a few others used to take the steamer to Seabright on Sundays. Good swimming."

"Yes," the girl said. "Very good."

"How'd you get to know Jack, Mary? If you don't mind me calling you Mary."

"I met him at Seabright, on the beach."

"How did *we* avoid meeting, then? I was there every time he was."

"Not every time," the girl said. "You know, this flat could use some heat."

"You should've asked the janitor for a bucket of coal when he let you in."

"I'll take one of your cigarettes," the girl said. "No one let me in. I have a key."

"Oh," Dan said, and half a cigarette went up in smoke and down in ash before he spoke again. "Well, I only looked in for a minute. . . ."

The telephone rang, and the girl answered it. "It's Jack," she said. "He wants to talk to you."

"Hi, feller," Dan said to vulcanized rubber.

["What do you think of Mary Homer?"]

"I think you're a lucky bastard."

["Isn't she the neatest lay you ever saw?"]

"What did you say?"

["I said, isn't she the neatest lay?"]

"What've you been doing—tanking up?"

["She's very enjoyable. I guarantee it."]

"Better get here soon. I'm leaving."

["What do you mean—you're leaving?"]

"I mean I'm leaving. Going away from here."

["The hell you are! What do you think I got you up there for?"]

"I don't get you, Jack."

["I wanted to put you two together."]

"I still don't get you."

["What's there to get? I thought you'd be good for each other."]

"You must be out of your mind."

["Why? Don't you agree with me?"]

"That isn't the point, and you know it."

["What *is* the point?"]

"I wish you were here right now, mister."

["What would you do?"]

"I'd knock your ears off."

["For what—for doing you a favor?"]

"I can live without that kind of favor, and so can . . . !"

["So can who? Say it, kid."]

"Look. Why don't you finish this nickel with Mary? She's waiting for you, and I'm getting ready to blow. I've got a date tonight."

["Break it. You're going out with Mary."]

"But, Jack, *she's* got something to say about that!"

["She'll say it. It's wonderful laying-weather."]

"You dirty son-of-a-bitch!"

[" I've got a date myself tonight, and I won't be home. You can use the flat. So long, now, and good luck."]

"So long," Dan said, and he hung up.

Mary was looking out of the window at the lilac afternoon. "I have something to say about what?" she said.

"Jack won't be able to get here."

"I gathered that much."

"He wants me to take you out this evening—that is, if you like."

"Is that the favor you can live without?"

"I didn't mean it that way," Dan said. "I told him you could live without it too."

"Don't you think it's about time I knew the whole conversation?"

"That's all there was, Mary. The office is sending him out of town, and he asked me to pinch-hit for him. I don't want to push myself at you, though. If you say no, it's no."

"What about your date?"

"I haven't any. I only said that to get him to stall off his Boss."

"You mean, you didn't particularly care for the job he gave you."

"That's not it at all. I was trying to save him a trip to Albany."

"When're you going to start telling the truth?"

"I've been doing that all along."

"You've been lying, Dan. Otherwise he'd've spoken to me."

"He figured it'd be nicer if *I* invited *you*."

"Why're you making all this up?"

"But, Mary, I'm not making *anything* up. Honestly."

"He said something that made you angry. What was it?"

"That's just my way of talking to him. He talks to me the same way."

"You say he only wanted you to beau me around for an evening. I'm not so hard to take that you had to call him a son-of-a-bitch for it."

"You're going to keep at me till I tell you, aren't you?"

"Yes," the girl said.

"Well, I called him a son-of-a-bitch because, God damn it, that's what he is!"

"All right. Now, what did he really tell you?"

"He said he wanted the two of us to meet. He said we'd be good for each other."

"What did he mean by that?"

"Who the hell knows?"

"You do. You're the one that spoke to him."

"He's a dirty dog for making me peach on him, but you know part of it, so you might as well know the rest: he wants to get rid of you."

"I can understand that," the girl said, "but why does he think he has to give me away?"

"I suppose he figured it'd have a sweeter taste for you," Dan said, and he watched the girl collect a few pieces of clothing and stow them in an overnight-bag. "He's a compassionate-type feller, you know—always bleeding from the heart." The girl put on her hat, coat, and overshoes, and then, taking something from her purse, she dropped it on a table, where it clinked against a china ash-tray. "It's a pity. We could've been friends."

"I'm sorry you were used for this, but I'm glad we met."

"I can say the same, but that's about all I can say. I feel sick, as much for you as I do for myself. I'll walk you to the bus."

"You don't have to."

"I know that," he said.

They crossed the Drive and squinted through the snow for the red oblong eye of a Penn Station coach. When it came, Dan followed the girl to the upper deck, and they sat on a rear bench, saying nothing until two dimes had been fed to the conductor's dime-eater. 26 87.283

Dan lit a pair of cigarettes and passed one to Mary, saying, "I couldn't leave you there in the street."

"Why not?" she said. "Are you any different from Jack?"

"I must be, but I couldn't explain."

"He's hard, and you're not."

"Put it that way, but I'm not nearly as soft as you suppose."

"Something that happened in Colorado?"

"I don't talk about Colorado any more."

"Some day I'll say I don't talk about Jack any more."

"Make this the day. Talk about yourself."

"There's half a year of Jack in the way."

"Leave him where you left his key."

"I left much more than the key. I left things I don't think I'll ever get back."

"Not with talk, you won't."

"Only with talk," she said. "But what shall I say? How and where we met? What he said to me, and what I said to him? What it felt like to kiss him, to have him make love? Or shall I tell you the lies I told my parents, knowing all the while that I was about to go fifty miles to undress and be naked under a man in the dark . . . ?"

"You don't have to work yourself up," Dan said.

"Or shall I say what it feels like to be on my way home, with no more lies to tell, no more trips to make, no more living all week for a few naked hours? Shall I describe the new blouse I bought for this evening, or the fresh pajamas I was going to wear at breakfast in the morning? Would you like to hear any of that, Dan?"

He said, "If you'll feel any better, yes."

"I went over to Seabright one Sunday last summer," she said, "and I remember how fine the ocean was that day, with high-tide early in the afternoon and rolling breakers that never came apart till they were up on shore. There was very little wind, I remember, but it must've been blowing about two miles out, because a Clyde liner was being beaten by its own smoke. Ever see that, where a ship seems to have its hair down and its back to the wind? They never paint them that way—they must think it makes a ship look slow—but it's very beautiful. And there were birds, I remember, a flock of gray-and-white gulls on a jetty, sandpipers on toothpick legs, and petrels behind the waves—scraps of paper, they looked like. I was lying on the sand, and my face was drying in the sun, tightening, and I felt very good, and I was glad to be alone, and then I turned over to let the sun get at my back—and I was dead. He'd been sitting on the beach behind me, with his knees bunched up to his chin, and I knew, I don't know how, that all the time I'd thought I was alone, he'd been there and watching me. One minute I'd felt good, and the next I was dead!"

[*You let her cry. What else could you do?*]

* * *

"All out!" the conductor said, and it was Penn Station.

"What time is your train?" Dan said as he walked the girl through the Arcade.

"I think the next for Red Bank is seven-thirty," she said, "but I wish you wouldn't wait."

"I won't, if you don't want me to."

"The trouble is, I do."

"I'm hungry," he said. "We've got an hour, and I'm hungry as Christ in the mountains."

They ate at the Savarin counter, and afterward, with time to spare, they stood before the train-gates, and Dan said, "Want to talk some more, Mary?"

"An odd thing about a bathing-suit," she said. "A great deal of you shows, but it's meant to show, and you hardly ever think about it. It's only in street-clothes that you're always pulling at your skirts, and it's because you wear them to hide in. On the beach that day, though, the first thing I thought of was covering myself, and I turned over on my side to keep my suit from bagging. That was a mistake, and he knew it, and when he came over and said something about what a nice day it was, he really meant, 'You gave yourself away.' If he'd said that, he'd've been right: a woman who doesn't care a damn for a man won't even know he's looking at her; if she does care, she won't want him to see her till she's ready to be seen. I did give myself away: I as good as offered him what I was trying to conceal. We talked, but only about this and that, and we shared a couple of sandwiches, and we smoked some of his cheroots (he called them), and then we went into the water for our last dip of the day. It was late, almost six, and the lifeboat had long been on the beach, and the tide had changed, and we had to wade far out before our feet left bottom. There was no one within fifty yards of us, and we swam about for a while, always very close yet never quite touching, but in the end, hanging onto the lifeboat-buoy, we did touch. His arm brushed mine, or mine his, I don't remember now, and it turned into a kiss that was like we were trying to kill each other with it—and maybe if we hadn't been holding the buoy with one hand, we'd've done just that, kissed till we died."

"It's twenty after seven," Dan said.

At track-level, the subway cold seemed to sink bone-deep. There were few passengers for the seven-thirty, a five-car accommodation fresh from the Long Island yards and wearing stoles of slush. Dan put Mary's bag under a seat in an alcove and sat with her until traintime, but when the cars began to move, he was still aboard.

"Go on," he said.

"I don't know how long we were out there," the girl said, "and I don't know whether we kissed each other once or a hundred times, and I don't know what we said or even whether we spoke at all. I only know that all the time I felt as if I were freezing, but the cold didn't seem to come from the water or the air: it seemed to come from inside, as though I knew even then that this was where it all would end. . . . But for God's sake, Dan, why am I telling you all this?"

"You know why," he said. "Keep telling it."

"We were the last ones to leave the beach, and we must've been among the last in the bath-houses, and I remember standing at the little window and staring out over an ocean that moved so slowly it made me think it was tired, like a child after a long day, and I was tired too, so tired that I shook, and I remember the little yellow buoy rolling on the water—and then I had to turn, because I knew that he was there behind me, and he came in and closed the door, and he took my suit off and dried me. I let him do that. I just stood there and let him do it. And then he took his own suit off, and he spread out all the towels, and we lay down, and he made love to me, and I made love to him. On the floor, my first time was, and I'll always remember that I could hear the sound of the surf on the sand. I don't know why, but I'll always remember that." She paused, and this time she was not urged to continue, and for a while she gazed through the window at shapes blurred by diagonals of snow-water on the pane. "He had a car that he'd borrowed for the week-end, and when we left the shore, he drove inland along Rumson Road. We had very little to say, I remember, almost nothing, and I wondered why he didn't take me home, and finally I asked him to, but he said it was too early to end the evening (for me, the evening had long been over, and much more than the evening), and he stopped somewhere, and for a time we sat and listened to the sounds you hear only at night, and from a long way off we watched the Navesink flash—and then we were doing what we'd done before, not on the floor now but in the grass, and it was different in every other way as well. He wasn't making love any more; he was emptying himself, and I was simply something that happened to lie between him and the ground. Maybe I *was* the ground, I don't know, but I do know this—that when he was all through emptying himself into me, I was empty too."

"Matawan!" the conductor said. "Red Bank the next!"

"He came to see me a few times during the summer, but he'd never call for me at home: I'd have to meet him at the station. He'd take me to the door late at night (often I could see my father through the screen, reading or just waiting up for me), but he'd never go inside, and never once did he show any interest in my people or anything else about me—where I'd gone to school, what I'd studied, who my friends were, what I did for a living. He wasn't the kind to ask questions, perfectly natural questions, and once I knew that, I stopped myself from making perfectly natural statements, and we went along from day to day, without depth and without history. It took me a long while to understand why he held back like that, but once I did, I saw what had always been obvious: he kept his questions to himself because he didn't want to be bound by the answers. To his way of thinking, a question took something out of a person that hadn't been offered, and in some odd way the taking would've bound him. It never seemed to occur to him that no question he could ever ask would've taken more than he'd taken that day in the bath-house—and that hadn't been binding at all. It would've been binding to come into my home, to meet my people and my friends, but it wasn't binding to come into *me*. I don't mean he was obligated for that. If there was any obligation, I was just as deeply in debt to him, but there was *no* obligation, and the end of the summer could've been the end of us—the end of the first day, even, if he'd wanted it that way. For some reason, though, he didn't, and he gave me that key because he probably knew he'd have more emptiness to empty out, and I took it because there was always a hope that something like that first time would come back. It never did. I tried everything I knew, but it never did."

"Red Bank!" the conductor said. "Little Silver the next!"

The station was dim, and the streets were dark, and most of the homes on either hand had their eyes closed for the night. Mary led the way up a side-road along a wavering path scooped from the snow, and when she reached a small brick house, she cut across its buried lawn toward the porch. The vanes of a shutter were open, and a ladder of light lay against a stripped maple in the angle of the stoop, and the tree seemed to be drawn on the sky. A down-cast of wind flavored the air with wood-smoke, and Dan thought of another house on another road, but for once the image was faint, as if it had begun to fade. He knocked clogs of snow from his shoes and followed Mary through the door.

In the kitchen, a man sat on a tilted chair, his feet cocked above the mica blister of a stove. "Hello, baby," he said to Mary. "I wasn't looking for you till tomorrow."

"The weather spoiled the week-end," she said. "Pop, this is a friend of mine, Dan Johnson."

"Glad to know you, Mr. Homer," Dan said.

The man's look was a search. "Me too," he said, and letting his chair down on all fours, he rose. "I'll be hitting the feathers."

"I was just going to hot Dan up some coffee," Mary said. "Stick around."

"Been sopping heat for a couple hours now," the man said. "G'night, baby. Glad to met you, Johnson. Waited a long time for you to get up enough nerve to come in out of the dark."

Dan watched the man go and turned back to Mary with a smile, saying, "I'd hate to be J. Carlos Hill anywhere, but particularly in Red Bank."

Mary moved a stove-lid and let some fingers of fire pick at a coffeepot, "Sit," she said, and when the coffee was ready, she filled two crockery mugs and set them on the table. "You take it barefoot?"

He said, "Barefoot, -headed, -handed, and -assed—any way at all, just so it's coffee, and I'm smoking a cigarette. You know, I never can decide whether I drink coffee because I like to smoke afterward, or whether I smoke because I like to drink coffee before. It's a little complicated. Lots of things are."

"Yes," the girl said.

*　　*　　*

Dan found the Homer family at the kitchen-table when he went downstairs for breakfast. "Good morning, Mary," he said. "Good morning, Mr. Homer."

"Name is Ed," the man said. "Set here between me and the Mrs. Mom, this boy answers to Dan Johnson."

"How do?" Mrs. Homer said.

"My son Gene," Ed said. "For Eugene."

"Glad to know you," Dan said.

"Same," Gene said.

"He married a foreigner. My daughter-in-law Flora."

"Florencia," the woman said, "but you may speak me as Flora. I have naturalized."

"I like Florencia, though," Dan said.

She turned to her husband. "A good boy," she said. "Is not?"

"Is," Gene said.

"And the baby is Mary," Ed said. "Called after an aunt that we expected she'd leave us a mint of money, and she didn't even send regards. Eat, boy, eat."

Mary laughed, saying, "He thought you were somebody else last night."

"I sure as hell-fire did," Ed said.

The family remained at table while Dan had his meal, and when he accepted a third cup of coffee, Mrs. Homer said, "He's a good doer. I like a good doer."

"Mary told me you were a mason, Ed," Dan said.

"Up to '29. Then I got to be a bricklayer again. Gene here, he was a carpenter before and after. No comedown in his line."

"I came down," Gene said. "It got lonesome up in them fore-closures."

"For a while, there," Ed said, "I was Homer & Son, Contract-ors."

"We contracted," Gene said. "We shrunk to nothing."

"Built this house, Gene and me. Built the whole row, in fact, and sold all but this one. Nobody'd take it account of the woven bond I bricked it with. Looked like it was folding up, people said. Shows you what they know. I copied the bond off of a house I seen down to Hancock's Bridge, and that ain't folded in two hundred years. People just don't know."

"It'll fold some day," Gene said, "and they'll say, 'See? Lousy bricklaying.'"

"Things ever get good again," Ed said, "I'll go back in business as Homer & Family. I'll be bricklayer, and Gene'll be carpenter, and if we can only find a plumber, we'll be set for life. It's the damn plumbers get the gravy. If we had one in the family, we'd *coin* money. You ain't a plumber, by any chance, are you, Johnson?"

Mary said, "Everyone who calls on me gets treated to the plumb-er-joke. If you don't laugh, you don't get to call again."

"I'm laughing heartily," Dan said. "I like it here."

*　　*　　*

The snowfall had stopped, and the wind was a rag wiping off the sky. Mary and Dan had taken a long walk that ended at the sta-tion, and a moment came that was very still: the wind had died, and no voices reached them. 17 78 .295

"Will you come again, Dan?"

"Yes, but not soon."

"Whenever, only please come."

"I'll come, Mary. Be sure of it."

From Little Silver, a train barked at Red Bank.

MONDAY: MORNING, NOON, AND NIGHT

"Hello, Pete."

"Hello, kid. Have a nice trip?"

Dan stared. "How'd you know I took one?" he said.

"You told me," Peterson said.

"*I* told you? When?"

"You said you were going crazy. You went, didn't you?"

Dan grinned, saying, "For a minute, I thought you saw. . . ."

"Thought I saw what?"

"Nothing, Pete—but I did go crazy."

*   *   *

"Is this Harlem 8800?" Dan said.

["Yes."]

"I'd like to talk to Mr. Powell."

["Mr. Powell is in the Teachers' Library. I'll connect you."]

"Library? May I speak to Mr. Powell, please?"

["This is Mr. Powell."]

"*The* Mr. Powell?"

["No, just *a* Mr. Powell."]

"I'm calling the *one-and-only* Mr. Powell."

["Well, you got the *nothing-but* Mr. Powell."]

"Mr. Nothing-but, this is an admirer."

["Start admiring, boy."]

"Mom says can you have supper with us tonight."

["Inform the lady Mr. Powell is available."]

"Half-past six. Okay, Master of Arts?"

["Does Mom know this is the *hungry* Mr. Powell?"]

"When I left this morning, she was making a chocolate cake."

*   *   *

"Take this home with you, Tootsie," Mrs. Johnson said.

"What's in it, Mom?" Tootsie said.

"The other half of the cake."

Dan walked Tootsie to the car-line. "Well, good night, partner, he said. "Keep pitching English at them little eight-balls."

"Somebody ought to pitch it at the ofays," Tootsie said. "That's another way of wiping out slavery."

"See Julie lately?"

"Couple of months ago. He's all locked up in that novel of his."

"He ever show you any of it?"

"The beginning, and he didn't like what I said, so that was the end. Who's this Jack Hill?"

"A booky-book guy I introduced him to. Why?"

"Julie's kind of hipped on him. Thinks he's got something, maybe."

"He'll find out different," Dan said.

"Funny," Tootsie said. "Julie talking love, but only getting hate in his book."

"It's a pukey kind of love. He's better off without it."

"Julie talking love. My, my."

When Dan reached home, his mother said. "How're the streets?"

"Pretty slick," he said. "Worried about your old man?"

"I don't like him to drive this late."

"He could hack with one hand if he had two wheels in hell."

"That's a fine boy, that Tootsie."

"Finer than fine," Dan said. "The finest."

"His people must be very proud of him."

"They are. Almost as proud as you are of me."

"Don't you think I'm proud of you, Dan?"

"Well, you haven't got much reason to be."

"Since when've I needed a reason?"

"If you think of one, let me know: *I* need it."

"Would you get angry if I asked you a question?"

"Depends," he said. "If it's too personal, I might knock you around a little."

"Where were you Saturday night?"

"As you very well know, I was out."

"You don't stay out all night very often."

"That's the God's honest truth."

"Well, never mind," the woman said.

"Not so proud now, eh?"

"You don't have to account to me any more. I won't ask you again."

"I didn't say I wouldn't answer. Exactly what do you want to know? Exactly, now."

"Where were you?"

"In the town of Red Bank, New Jersey. Next."

"With whom?"

"A girl by the name of Mary Homer."

"What kind of girl?"

"You'll see for yourself some day. Anything else?"

The woman smiled. "No," she said. "That's all I wanted to find out."

The door slammed open and slammed shut. "Quit kissing my wife!" the hack-driver said.

WHERE YOU BEEN KEEPING YOURSELF, KID?

DAN stood at his office-window, looking out at the billows of linen in the blueing of the sky. It was a cold spring afternoon.

"Mind if I come in?" a voice said.

Dan turned to find Jack Hill in the doorway. "Do as you like," he said.

Hill took the seat behind the desk. "Why haven't I heard from you?" he said.

"I've been busy."

"Doing what? *Not* getting jobs for people?"

"If you want the truth, I didn't feel like seeing you."

"That's what I came out of my way to find out. Why not?"

"You know why not. You're a smart boy."

"What's Mary got to do with our friendship?"

"Jesus *Christ*, Jack!"

"Don't J. C. me. That doesn't tell me a thing."

"What do you want to be told?"

"Why you're sore at me," Hill said.

"I'm sore because of what you did to Mary."

"You have no right to be. If I've done anything to Mary, I've done it to Mary, not to you. I want to know what I've done to *you* —outside of doing you a favor, I mean."

"Keep on doing favors like that, and people won't like you. Some don't right now."

"Meaning who—you and Mary?"

"Me," Dan said. "I don't speak for her."

"I'm waiting for you to speak for yourself."

"A guy can like a girl today, and tomorrow she can make his scalp crawl," Dan said. "Nobody's to blame for that: sometimes that's how it goes. But there are other ways of breaking the news than kicking the girl downstairs."

"There's *no* other way," Hill said. "No matter how you put it, you're still kicking a girl downstairs. Grow up, kid."

"I'm growing, Jack, growing all the time."

"You'll thank me some day," Hill said, and he left.

WHAT'S ON YOUR MIND, KID?

HE STOOD at the same window during another afternoon, a milder one a little later in the spring and fresher and more fragrant than other afternoons of the year, and the soft air seemed newer, as following a rain or in some always-shaded place in a wood. Below him, on the walks and in the streets, people passed in currents that went with the four winds, and many faces loomed from the vagueness of distance, came briefly clear, and were gone, and trains carrying blurred faces went by, and cars and cabs with faces in their gloom, and he thought [*Would you find among them the one face you sought, or had you sighted long only to miss your aim? had it ever been within range of your eyes, visible but unseen, or had it been just around a corner or momentarily hidden by a scarf, a hat, another face, a head turned to glance at nothing? had it been both near and far, and might you have reached up and touched it had you known?*]. He watched himself enact the gesture, almost in expectation of making the imagined the real by putting the fancy in motion, but his hand struck the window-glass, and he let it fall. It came to rest against a directory lying on the sill, and idly he made the page-edges drone. [*Julia Davis, you thought.*]

He sat down at his desk, and drawing the thick book toward him, he leafed through it to DAVIS to find several listings for JULIA. Taking them in order, he lifted the telephone-receiver and gave the first number to the operator—and then, before the connection could be made [*What would you say, you thought, and to whom, to what Julia, would you be saying it? how many calls would you have to make before making the right one, how many more than several, and to what boroughs, to what cities, to what foreign countries? and was the name still* DAVIS, *or had it become* DAVISON, DAVIES, DAVEN-PORT, *or* FITZGERALD? *but always, what would you say, what would you say and why?*], he hung up.

YOU GETS NO BREAD WITH ONE MEAT BALL

"LAST NAME?"
    "Ritchie."
    "First name?"
    "Fred."
    "Frederick?"
    "No, just Fred."
[*When news of the war came to Clarks, Nebraska, Fred asked his father for leave to join up with Teddy Roosevelt's Rough Riders and help the starved Cubans against the cruel Spaniards. But his father, a dirt-farmer with half a section under mortgage, owned outright a small collection of books, among them one by a crank named Henry George, and he told Fred that no Ritchie was going off to get killed in the jungle for any son-of-a-bitch of a Wall Street sugar-millionaire —and besides, the father pointed out, Fred was only twelve years old, and it was doubtful that a big man like Teddy Roosevelt would be able to see that far down toward the ground. Fred kept on nagging, though, saying that every army, even the army of a big man like Teddy Roose-velt, needed drummer-boys, and that without such, it would have to fight standing still, and it would be butchered. The fact is, Fred had never played any musical instrument outside of a comb wrapped in a corn-leaf, but that didn't stop him from following his father around day after day and begging to be allowed to punish the cruel Spaniards that starved the Cubans, and finally the man, running out of argu-*

ments, treated the boy to a good set of clouts and walked off to let them sink in. They sank in.]

". . .Trouble with me is, I'm hungry," Fred said. "I'm always hungry. I been hungry all m' life. . . ."

[*That same night, Fred packed a supply of corn-leaves in a bandana and ran away in the direction of Tampa. It took him two weeks to make it (without the comb, which he'd forgotten), and by that time, Teddy Roosevelt had gone and won the war all by himself, braving certain death from the dumdum bullets that the cruel Spaniards fired from their smokeless Mausers, and setting the starved Cubans free to work for the God-fearing sugar-millionaires of Wall Street. He'd become a bigger man than ever, Teddy had, and for his noble deeds at San Juan Hill, they wined him and dined him all over the United States, and it was hard for him to go anywhere without falling over something to eat and something to wash it down with. But nobody pressed any food or drink on Fred Ritchie around about Tampa, not even at the Poor Farm, where he was shipped when the police caught up with him. He spent three years at the Farm, and if he learned little else there, he found out the meaning of the expression, "My belly thinks my throat's been cut."*]

". . . Give some people a square meal," Fred said, "and they lose their appetite. With me, it only gets worse. They forget how hungry they was before, but a meal being only a meal, I keep on hungry even after I'm full. I never seen the time I wasn't hungry. . . ."

[*When somebody passed the word that victuals were piled face-high in the Carolinas for anyone calling himself a cigarette-maker, Fred pointed his nose at the North Star, and at Winston-Salem, all his dreams came true. He got a job rolling cigarettes with one hand and spearing company-grub with the other, and eating two dozen eggs at a sitting and rolling two thousand smokes in a ten-hour day, he was a happy young man. Along about the time he was seventeen, though, the company got wind of a machine that'd roll four hundred cigarettes to a man's one, but the real beauty of it was that you didn't have to feed it eggs to make it go, only paper and tobacco, so they went out and bought ten of those machines and fired four thousand rollers, among them Fred Ritchie.*]

". . . Being hungry's a sickness with me," Fred said, "and sooner or later it's going to kill me. No matter how much I eat in my lifetime, I'll die hungry. . . ."

[*The news went around that they were still rolling cigarettes by hand at a place called Richmond, but what the rumor left out was that you had to buy your own eggs there, and also that if you couldn't roll three thousand pieces a day, you could go die. Fred managed to roll three thousand, all right, but he had to hump fourteen hours to do it, and to little purpose, because by the time he got through eating each week, he was always short of cash for his landlady, and it got so he was changing his lodgings just about every time the rent fell due. A stop was put to all that by the Richmond cigarette-companies: they heard about the machines.*]

". . . Some people eat fast," Fred said, "which shows they're only eating so's they can get back to work. I hurry m'work so's I can get back to eating. It's the eating that's the big thing in this life. . . ."

[*At the age of twenty-one, after knocking about from job to job (meaning meal to meal) for a couple of years, Fred found that there were no more jobs to be had (meaning no more meals), so in '07 he enlisted in the United States Army. For ten years, the Government fed him three times a day in return for only one little expedition to teach a lesson to some cruel Mexicans who were shooting Wall Street miningmillionaires. Somebody put a bug in Fred's ear about the Mexicans not really being such bandits, but Fred kept on killing them till he heard that all they were after was enough to eat, and from then on, he fired his rifle straight up in the air.*]

". . . I don't suppose I ever made a move in m' life," Fred said, "except it was connected with food."

[*Another war came along in '17, the one that we got into account of the cruel Germans raping all those Belgian nuns. Fred, though, he fought it for a different reason altogether: he couldn't get over the Germans sinking all those ships loaded with cutlets, and the more he thought about it, the sorer he got, and when they turned him loose in France, he made a point of firing his Springfield directly at the enemy, and there were four-five times when he lost control of himself and did some*] *mighty crazy things to get in an extra shot. As a result, quite a few less Germans were alive when the war ended, and Fred owned a fancy assortment of medals, and if he never got to be President, like Teddy Roosevelt, he did get to be master-sergeant, and that's the job he was holding down when some pip-squeak of a captain handed him his Honorable Discharge after twenty-odd years of service, thanked him for his patriotism, and told him where to turn in his equipment.*]

". . .That was some weeks back," Fred said, "long enough for me to find out that my pension don't even start to cover my eating. I'm hungry. I'm hungry all the time."

FOURTH OF JULY WEEK-END

THE TOP DECK of the Jersey Central steamer *Monmouth* was crowded, but Dan found a space for his camp-chair forward of the wheelhouse, and leaning against the port rail, he looked off over the Cedar Street dock at the punctured palisade of Manhattan—and then a bell sounded, and the engines were engaged, and the island began to slide astern, and soon the *Monmouth* was running down the long roadstead of the Upper Bay at twenty knots. Outside the channel lay anchored tramps and colliers, and among them car-ferries steamed, and rope-bearded tugs made their way with dead-weight scows. Below Quarantine, in the Narrows, a man waved from the parapet of Fort Wadsworth and was gone, and entering the Lower Bay, the *Monmouth* rolled a little on a ground-swell, and bell-buoys jigged and chimed, and then Jersey showed its tongue, the Hook, and from its tip a twelve-inch naval rifle took two pot-shots at the horizon—and then there was smooth shallow water to the Highlands. Boat-trains were waiting on the pier, and Dan climbed into the scowling open end of a local and rode five waterside miles before the conductor opened the door to say, "Sea-*bright! Sea*bright!" 28 91.279

He saw Mary on the platform a few car-lengths ahead, and he used the time it took him to reach her to quell a disturbance in his throat; he put it down only to the extent that he was able to make himself say nothing when they were standing face to face. She said, "You told me you'd come, and you did, and I'm glad, Dan," but he was still afraid to speak, and he did not reply, and when the train drew out, they crossed the tracks and walked in silence toward the bathing-pavilion.

At the office, a lifeguard placed a key on a stack of towels and slid them to the edge of the counter, saying, "How you been, Mary?"

"Just fine, Steve," she said. "Steve White, Dan Johnson."

"Glad to know you," Dan said.

"Likewise," Steve said. "See you maybe on the beach."

Their locker was in the last aisle of bath-houses, and Mary entered, propped up the window-flap, and stood looking out over the beach at the sea. "I'm sorry we're in this row," she said. "It was right along here somewhere, Dan—this locker or the next. I'm sorry."

"It makes no difference," he said.

"It has to make a difference. You wouldn't be human otherwise."

"I'm human, all right, and maybe that's why I don't care. You say, 'right along here,' but nothing happened right along here that wouldn't've happened elsewhere. A thing like that doesn't spoil the place. If it did, the whole earth'd be spoiled."

"You speak as if you really believed that."

"I've put in six months of my life trying to believe it enough to say it."

"Was it so very hard to do?" she said.

"Hard as hell. I told you I was human, didn't I?"

"I didn't have to be told, Dan. I knew it."

"The spoiled thing, if there *was* a spoiled thing, wasn't some God damn bath-house floor: it was you. The floor's the same. Nothing ever happens to a floor. What I had to make up my mind about was whether anything had happened to you."

"It has, Dan."

"Maybe, but it's nothing I care a hang about."

"I know better."

"You don't even know where you live."

"You say nothing happens to a floor. What you mean is, nothing you can't scrub off. But people aren't floors."

"To hell with being first," he said. "I wasn't first in Colorado, and I wasn't twenty-first. To hell with it, Mary."

"It isn't just a matter of numbers, first or twenty-first or whatever," she said. "It's what you have left for the next."

"No matter what you have, it's at least as much as I brought back from Colorado," he said. "I have more now, and so will you some day, and if I have to wait ten years for us to be even, I'll wait, and I'll do my waiting as near as you can stand me." He put his face to hers, and together they looked through the foot-square window at a yellow dory surging on the unbroken water beyond the combers. "If only the Indians had been the navigators!" he said. "They'd've stood on the sand at Palos, saying, 'We claim the Old World in the name of the Plumed Serpent, the Great Snake, and the Grand Manitou, and it belongs to Crazy Horse the Lakota, and may evil Okies dwell in all infidels who worship Jesus!' But let's you and I go, sweetheart. Let's swim to Spain."

"Please don't call me that, Dan."

"Let's swim, then, but not toward Spain."

"Couldn't we go some other time?"

"Sure," he said. "It'll still be there." She turned away from him and began to unbutton her dress. "Don't you want me to go outside?"

"Not if you want to stay."

"What do *you* want?"

"I want you to do what pleases you."

"May I watch if I stay?"

"If you wish. I won't ask."

"Would you watch me?"

"I can't, Dan."

"Will you ever?"

"I don't know."

"Have I got a chance?"

"You've got a good chance."

"But right now, nothing more than that?"

"It's more than nothing, Dan."

"What would I have to do to have all?"

"Not a thing. There's only something *I* have to do, and when I do it, you'll know. You'll be the *first* to know."

"Let's start for Spain. We'll swim slowly."

Out beyond the last rope, beyond the yellow buoy and the yellow dory, they rode broad corrugations running inshore to break. "Did you watch me, Dan?" Mary said.

"Quiet," he said. "I hear Spanish music."

"You don't have to tell me, of course."

"A malagueña, or something. Flora'd know."

"But all the same, I'm curious."

"Would you be angry if I'd watched?"

"I'd have no right to be."

"Would you be hurt if I hadn't?"

"I just want to know."

"Which would you rather? You've got to say."

"I'd rather you watched."

"One more question. Do you think I did, or not?"

"Not," she said.

He laughed. "You must think I'm crazy," he said. Later, lying on the sand side by side and face-down, they were the hinged halves of a whole, like an open locket, and he said, "No one could say you were beautiful."

"No one has to."

"Your teeth are perfect. I've never seen such teeth."

"They won't last forever."

"And you have the smallest feet and the smallest hands."

"I'm very vain about my feet."

"But that's as far as I can go. It'd be impossible to say you're beautiful."

"I'm all the time buying shoes."

"I look at you, and I say to myself, 'She's quite plain. I like pretty girls, but this one isn't pretty at all.' And then I look again, and I wonder, because you aren't plain any more, and I say, 'Why did I think she was plain before? She's beautiful.'"

"Which am I now?"

"Plain. You've been plain for quite a while."

"Maybe I'll be beautiful soon."

"Maybe, but for the time being, you're plain. Don't worry, though: I like you plain."

"I thought you liked pretty girls."

"Before meeting you, that was. Now I'm for your kind, and I'll tell you why. No one's always beautiful, and no one's always plain: a beautiful girl has moments of plainness, just as a plain girl has moments of beauty. I prefer the plain one. I think it's exciting to watch her change."

"But wouldn't it be better to watch the other? You'd be watching something beautiful, and when the plain moment came, you could turn away till it was over."

"The plain moment would spoil all the others. I'd know it was coming, but I'd never know when, and I'd be so busy getting ready to avoid it that I couldn't take pleasure in the beauty. But with a plain girl, like you, I'd be waiting for the moment that plainness ended, and so far from trying to avoid it, I'd be scared to death of missing it, and I'd look and look, and somehow the very plainness would become the beauty."

"All the same, I wish I was beautiful."

"Right now, you are, Mary."

They swam again, this time so far out that they were whistled in by the guard in the dory, and then they walked far over the jetty-broken beach, picking up shells, shying stones, wading through sloughs of stranded water, talking and not talking, and now and then pausing to embrace and to stand for minutes merely looking at each other or together looking at nothing—and the simple history of the walk was written for quick erasure by the tide—and then once more they were in the bath-house, with sweet shower-water running from their suits to make flippers of their feet on the absorbent floor.

"Are you going to face away again?" he said.

"I still have to, Dan."

"I still have to watch you."

"I still want you to."

"You're not plain now, you know."

"If I'm beautiful, the change was made by you."

"You understand why that is, don't you?"

"Yes," she said. "I understand."

When they passed the office, Dan put the key on the counter, saying, "I thought you were going to join us on the beach, Steve."

"I started to once," Steve said, "but I took a good look and changed my mind."

"Well, anyway, thanks for starting to."

"You mean, for changing my mind," Steve said. "Bring him around again, Mary. He can swim in our ocean."

"Would tomorrow be too soon?" she said.

"I think I could stand a New Yorker two days in a row. *This* New Yorker."

Outside the pavilion, Dan looked at the darkening sky over the Shrewsbury, and he said, "Green. You don't often see green in the sky. Jesus, if we only had a car!"

"What would you do?" Mary said.

"I'd make you drive, and I'd sit sideways and stare at you till you got beautiful."

"Oh, Lord, don't tell me I'm plain again!"

"I must be truthful."

"Why don't *I* know when I'm beautiful? It's such a rare thing with me, you'd think I'd light up inside as well as out."

"You do. When you're beautiful, you're so light inside that it's dark out here."

"But I ought to know it without being told. This is a moment when I'd like to be at my best, but I'm a dark house. Do you still wish we had a car?"

"I fall just short of prayer."

"See that old wreck over there? Gene let me have it for the day."

"By God, Gene is the greatest carpenter since Christ!" Dan said. "And any minute, now, you're going to stop being plain!"

"I'll drive," Mary said. "You sit sideways."

As they turned into Ocean Road, Dan said, "Find us some darker dark than this, and I'll talk to you till you light up brighter than your Navesink flash. You'll be forty billion candle-power, and they'll see you from Spain."

But when the car was headed inland, he fell silent, and for a long way, under a sky like a faded blueprint, he stared out at the somber masses that rose against it—trees, houses and barns, slopes of ground, and wall—and then at the roadside there was water-shine, and from below a bridge came the sound of water-fall, and now the car was moving along a pair of tracks through a field, and insects sprayed up into the lamp-line, and the savor of shrubs and the earth was on the air.

Within a mile, the tracks came to an end, and Mary stopped the car and turned off the lights, and for a while the quiet was broken only by the ticking of the cooling engine. "You're not looking at me any more," the girl said to the coal of a cigarette in the windshield. "Can't you make me beautiful this time?"

"I never really could," Dan said. "But I'm looking at you all the same."

"I'm over here."

"You're over here too," he said, "and you're straight ahead, and straight up, and straight down. You're all around me. I don't have to turn my head to see you. I don't even have to open my eyes."

"You must know I'm crying, then."

"I know that and a great deal more," he said, "because I'm more inside you than you are yourself. I know what's going on there better than you do. I don't know *how* I know, but I know. You're not in love with Jack any more, and I'll bet my life on it. He's finished, all but the ten minutes of him you had on the floor—and it's those ten minutes you're crying about, nothing else. But you won't cry them away by yourself any more than I'll cry away Julia Davis, and when you realize that, we can start doing each other some good."

"I'm willing to try, Dan."

"You've got to mean it, or it'll only be worse."

"I do mean it."

"Not yet, you don't."

"How can I prove it?"

"By looking at me and all at once turning very beautiful."

"I'm doing my best."

"Do better. They still can't see you from Spain."

"I love you, Dan."

He put his hands on her face, saying, "I hope to God I look like this to you."

"You always have," she said. "Didn't you know?"

She left the car and walked away through deep grass, and he watched her until her figure became dim in the dark, and then he followed, hurrying to keep it in view, but it vanished around the corner of a barn, and when he reached the corner himself, he found that he was alone. He paused, listening for footsteps, but he heard only a few night-sounds, the machinery of tree-frogs, the call-and-answer of birds, and dew-drip dropping from the eaves. A wind came and briefly stirred the trees and the broad leaves of sunflowers, and then it died away, and again there was only smaller sound or silence. His name was spoken now, and he glanced about him, and it was spoken a second time, but in a way that seemed for once to fill it full, to extend it from a three-letter identification to his utmost and total meaning, and he turned to the black oblong that was the doorway of the barn, and within it he saw a less-than-black figure, and he joined it [*and you remembered saying one thing before you lay with her, and it was,"This doesn't end it, Mary; it only begins it," and then you were a long time going-going-gone. . . .*].

*   *   *

He said,"If I could tell you every thought I've had and everything I've done in my life, the few good things, all the bad things, and all the things that don't seem to have counted, I think you might remember me if I died tomorrow. Once I wanted to be remembered by the whole world, but that was before I knew I was ordinary, and because for an ordinary guy the world must shrink to one person, I'd like that person to be you."

She said, "If not for you, I'd've been a dead one till I died, but now I'll have to die all over again, Dan—I'll have to die twice."

He said,"I ought to be kissing you and memorizing your flavor, I ought to be trying to get the feel of you in my hands, I ought to be supplying myself with you—because death is long, and I want you to last me. . . ."

*   *   *

What he saw first in the morning was a slope of rafters, and thinking he was still in the barn, he sat up, saying, "Mary," but it was a bed that he was sitting in, with Mary leaning over its footboard and looking at him. "Get undressed, you, and climb in here."

"I came up to find out what you want for breakfast."

"I told you what I want: you."

"To eat, I mean."

"You're edible. I could live on you and coffee."

"Wash your dirty face, and I'll bring the coffee up here."

"A better way to let Ed know about last night is to show him."

"Don't tell me you're afraid of a little thing like a father."

"Me?" Dan said. "Listen, I'm going right down and smack him on the back, saying, 'Ed, ole boy, that dotter of yours is sure a mighty sweet piece,' and he'll say, 'That's no way to talk about m' own flesh and blood!' and I'll smack him again and say, 'Clam down, Ed, ole boy, clam down and pass me them pancakes,' and he'll say, 'You got to have a little more respeck for m' dotter!' and I'll say, 'How can I, Ed, ole boy? She laid there just like them cakes!'"

"You're vulgar."

"From Vulgarville. I'm Daniel V. Johnson."

"I must be from there too. I'm Mary V. Homer."

"Homer?" he said. "I wasn't out with anyone named Homer last night."

Mary spoke to her hands, saying, "Weren't you?"

"I was under the impression that she was Mrs. Johnson," he said. "How's that for a proposal?"

"It was the kind I wanted."

"Don't bother accepting. Just go hot up the coffee."

*   *   *

When Dan reached the kitchen, he said, "Morning, folks. I overslept," and after touring the table to shake hands with the family, he sat down in the spare chair next to Mary.

"Get started," Ed said. "I'm about ready for lunch."

"Pancakes!" Dan said, and looking at Mary, he laughed.

"Been wanting to ask you something, boy," Ed said. "How do they rate this feller Roosevelt up your way?"

"Well, we made him Governor."

"I mean, for the big noise in Washington."

"If my vote settles it, he's in."

"What's wrong with the man we got right now?"

"You take me by surprise, Ed. I didn't know we had a man right now."

"I think Hoover's done as good as anybody could."

"Not as good as Chester A. Arthur. Arthur—there's the man to handle a depression."

"Arthur's dead as a nit."

"The country's lost its best men—Hoover, then Salmon P. Chase, then Arthur. I don't know what we're coming to."

"Say, what the hell're we feeding here," Ed said. "A Democrat?"

"Politics and breakfast don't mix," Mrs. Homer said.

"Ma'am," Dan said, "I'd like three more of your Republican pancakes."

"He sure can eat," Ed said.

"Eats like a Democrat," Gene said.

"We've been out for twelve years," Dan said. "We're hungry."

"Give him another cup of coffee," Ed said. "He'll be out for twelve more."

Mary said, "Could you stand another egg?"

"After Harding, Coolidge, and Hoover," Dan said, "I could stand anything but another Republican."

"I like this boy," Flora said. "The first time I look on him, I say to Genio, 'Genio, there is a boy I like.'"

"I like you too," Dan said. "I never saw the wop I didn't."

"A wop is not me. I am eSpanish."

"Wops, spics, shines—I love 'em all."

"I can understand about the spics—I married one," Gene said. "I can even understand about the wops. But where do the shines come in?"

"Up to now, through the back door," Dan said.

"In my local, they don't even come in that way."

"One of these days, a nice big shine is going to walk into that White House and say to his secretary, 'Get me some new stationery, man. This is the *Black* House.'"

"You feel like that, you ought to vote Republican," Gene said. "The Democrats didn't free any slaves."

"*Nobody* freed any slaves."

"I learnt otherwise about Lincoln."

"If Lincoln was alive today, the Republicans wouldn't nominate him to run for a train."

"Republicans, Democrats—what's the odds?" Ed said. "They're all crooks, and what I say is, stay away from the polls and stick to your trade."

"That's just what they want you to do: tear up your vote."

"They'd only tear it up themselves, the bamboozlers!"

"It's high time *we* did some tearing up," Dan said. "I'm sick of being on the dirty end of the stick. I'm sick of losing Saccos and Vanzettis and not even handing out a broken head in return."

"I told Genio," Flora said. "'There is a boy I like,' I said."

Mary said, "I like him too. In fact, I love him."

Dan turned to her and kissed her a long kiss on the mouth, and then he scanned the faces of four staring Homers and smiled, saying, "Could you use a good Democrat in the family?"

There was a moment of silence before Ed said, "Ain't this kind of sudden, boy?"

"I've known Mary since last winter," Dan said. "I think I'm late as hell."

"But all we know about you is you eat like a lion."

"Suppose I tell you more," Dan said. "The great regret of my life is that I was born an hour too soon. If I hadn't been in such a hurry to meet Mary, I'd've shown up on earth exactly a hundred years after Lincoln, and maybe I'd've been a Lincoln myself—who knows? As it is, though, I'm only a guy called Daniel Johnson. My father's a hack-driver, the best God damn hack-driver in the world, and I love him because he lives for two things: my mother, and the hope that some day a sport will hail him for a spin to the moon.

My mother comes from a farm up around Port Jervis, and because I love her too, I've had four street-fights on account of her name, which is Apollo Panetela, after a stogie her old man happened to be chewing on when she was born. I went to public school for eight years and to Clinton High for four, and then, instead of working my way through college like a hero, I drifted around the country like a bum. I'm ashamed of a lot that I've done, and I'm proud of almost nothing, and up till a short time ago, I got fired from job after job with appalling regularity. That came to an end when I met Mary. I met her on a snowy afternoon about six months back, and I spent the rest of the day with her, and I stood her to a meal, and then I brought her home on the train. The next day, I went away, and from then till this weekend, I never set eyes on her. I didn't have to: I was always with her. I ate with her, I walked the streets with her, and if you understand what I mean, I went to bed with her and woke up with her. I'm crazy for her. I don't want any mistake made about that."

"Is no mistake," Flora said.

"Shut up," Gene said.

"Now I'd like to say something, and I hope it won't hurt your feelings," Dan said. "This is what it is. I think if I hunted around, I could find many a girl better-looking than Mary, and better-built, and better-educated, and maybe even better-natured, but I could hunt for the rest of my life and not find anyone *better*. Do I make myself clear? She's the best."

"It is very clearly," Flora said.

"What I mean is, one girl would have a straighter nose, and another would have a smaller mouth, and a third would have finer hair, and so on, and if I could take the best features of all, I'd have somebody who'd beat Mary all hollow for looks—but I still wouldn't want her. I want Mary. Am I clear now?"

"You could not be clearer if possible," Flora said.

"For God's *sake*, Flora!" Gene said. "He ain't asking for you!"

"But what there is to Mary isn't clear at all," Dan said. "I only know that there's something about her face. It's plain most of the time, or maybe quiet would be a better word, and in a careless moment, a man might pass it by without ever dreaming that what he was looking for was gone—but I happen to be careful with faces, and that's how I know there's something about Mary's. Things seem to go on behind it, and I think if I watched it long enough, they'd show through. She has her hands in front of it now, but her hands can't hide the things I mean, and I doubt that a stone wall could, either: some day the things would work their way out, and I'd know what they were. So if it pleases you, Ed, I'd like to have the right to watch for them."

There was a silence then, during which Dan did nothing with a fork—he made four tine-tracks on the oilcloth, and then four more, and then four more, nothing important, nothing worth remembrance or mention—and now a chair was moved, and shoes scraped on the floor, and a pair of hands were placed on his shoulders, and a voice said, "You can watch if you care to, son, and I want you to make Mary watch you: there's something about *your* face."

* * *

Gene had given them his car again, and Mary was driving it toward Seabright along a shaded river-road. For a way, now, they had spoken little, both of them looking ahead at the stencil of sunlight that the touching trees made on the pavement.

"Do you really want to marry me, Dan? You don't have to, you know."

"On the contrary: I *do* have to."

"I don't want anyone to get tired of me again. I don't want to be shucked like a dirty shirt. It'd be more than I could stand."

"Jack Hill would make a bright remark in here somewhere—like 'Sooner or later, all shirts get dirty'—but on the subject of marriage I'm not bright in the least. In fact, I'm quite an ordinary cluck, and there's nothing original about what I'd say if I said it."

"Say it."

"Well, it's just that you're a shirt that won't ever get dirty—anyway, not on *my* neck—and while you may get tired of me, which is likely, I'll never get tired of you, which is sure. Ordinary stuff—what every man says and what every man means—but with this difference, that beyond you the world seems to end."

"Where would it've ended if you'd never met me?"

"It would never've begun."

"No one ever said that to me before. Why do you call it ordinary?"

"Because *I'm* ordinary."

"Men're funny people."

"Real comedians."

"You don't have to sit so far away, Dan. I'd be glad to have your arm around me."

"In France, the woman puts her hand on the man's knee. Shows ownership."

"I'm driving. *You* show ownership."

"I don't want to own you, but I'd dearly love to use you."

*   *   *

At the beach, again they were assigned a locker in the last aisle, and when again they stood in its sea-sounding gloom, Mary said, "Would you care to use me now, Dan?"

"Anywhere but here," he said.

"Yesterday you said this place hadn't changed."

"It'll never change: it'll always be four walls, a roof, and a floor. But *we've* changed—or at least *I* have. Yesterday there was no place I'd've refused you; today there's this one."

"For me, it's just the opposite, so I've changed too."

"I don't know why I feel this way. Maybe it's because when I'm through with somebody, I'm not quite as through as you are."

"I wish you were, Dan."

"Why? Because Jack Hill was sitting in a car outside?"

"Yes," Mary said. "I didn't know you'd seen him."

*   *   *

They put on their suits, and he followed her along the planked aisle toward the beach-ramp. She glanced back at him once, and once she stopped to say, "You stare and stare, Dan."

"What else is worth looking at?" he said. "A miserable little ocean? There are quite a few of those, but there's only one of you."

Many people were on the sand, and many heads on the shuttling water, and there was much lace on the gallant surf, and a boy with a tin shovel was shoveling fill from an always-filling hole. 15 65 .305

Near one of the jetties, they found an area not yet pocked by feet, and they lay close to each other, and Dan said, "One question, Mary."

"I know what it is," she said. "I've been waiting for it."

"Did that bastard up there have anything to do with your offer in the locker?"

"It has everything to do with your refusal."

"I know that, but it isn't an answer."

"The answer is no."

"Honestly?"

"Honestly."

"How'd you know what I was going to ask?"

"It was all over your face—that I was out to get even."

"You can hardly blame me for wondering."

"I think I could, and very easily."

"Damn it, Mary, I believe we're going to have a quarrelsome life."

"Only if you harp on Jack Hill. Forget him."

"He's hard to forget."

"I'll help you," she said. "What do you do for a living? You never told me."

"I work for an employment-agency," he said. "With seventy-nine million people out of work, we get calls for about four jobs a day—and there are four hundred and four applicants for each. *Supplicants* would be more like it. Strangers come in and zip open their lives for me, and they want one thing: they want to eat, and most of 'em want to eat then and there. All I can do is ask their names, their qualifications for jobs they're not going to get, and do they take spirits or advocate the overthrow of the Government by force and violence—fine questions to put to guys with holes in their gut. If they could afford the truth, or maybe if they were hungrier, they'd say, 'Spirits? Mister, I'd drink anti-freeze if it came with a straw, and if Heaven was run like this country is, I'd overthrow God Himself!' It's a terrible thing to sit and listen to the terrible things that happen to people. Even if your heart's no bigger than a buckshot, it's a terrible thing to be on the inside looking out—and that being so, good Christ, what must it be like to be on the outside looking in? When I was a kid, I once ate a big mushy sundae while a Negro boy watched me through the window of the store. I had another dime in my pocket, and I could've called him in and bought him a sundae too, but I didn't, and always I'll remember the anguish on his face, an anguish so vast that it was racial—but now I see that same anguish day after day and thirty times over during each, on white faces as well as black, on men's faces and women's, on the young and the old. It's a terrible thing to make a living off such misery, because I love all those people—I must, or I couldn't love you."

"You're a good man, Danny."

"Ah, not so very."

"Good enough for me."

"I'm an ordinary guy, I told you, a very ordinary guy. You'd only find it out for yourself some day, so I'll admit it in advance: an ordinary guy."

"Nobody's anything else."

"You've been warned. Don't expect extraordinary things of me."

"I thought you knew something about people. It's the ordinary ones that do all the unusual things."

"Like Lincoln?"

"Most of the Lincolns are called Johnson. There's nothing magical about a name. The magic's in the person."

"Daniel, my mother wanted me to be—Daniel Johnson—and I was supposed to show her how far I'd get on nothing. Well, this is how far: a clerk in an employment-agency. I guess I didn't have the magic."

"You can do any of the great things that other people can do, or at least you can try, but whether you do them, or just try, or even only *want* to try, you mustn't make small of yourself to me. Please don't do that."

"I do it because I want you to know the truth."

"The truth? The truth about you is what *I* know—and I say you *do* have the magic."

He made an hourglass of his hands and watched the sand run out. "If I haven't," he said, "I can always get it from you."

"I said you were a good man. I say it again."

"Don't say it too often, because I might turn around and call you a good woman, and then you'd be hurt: you'd think it was faint praise. A biting and scratching lay—that's what you'd like to be called."

"Couldn't you call me both?"

He laughed, saying, "I don't know you well enough. I don't even know where you come from. Where in hell were you born, Mary, and was it especially for me?"

"It must've been," she said. "I was born in a little frame house over near Freehold, between the Tennent Church and the Monmouth battlefield. You must see that church some time. It's a beauty."

"I want to see the frame house."

"I'll show it to you. Tonight, if you like."

"Well, you were born. What happened after that?"

"I looked around and said, 'Where's Danny?'"

"And somebody—Ed, probably—said, 'Oh, him? He's peeing his brains out over on Bowling Green.'"

"There was a big barn at the edge of the orchard, and I had the run of it, because we didn't farm the place. Everything was in that barn—old harness, broken tools, newspapers from 1905, and a very faint but still sweet smell of hay God knows how long gone. You weren't there, though."

"I must've been sitting on a dock, arguing with Goggly Roger Lynch, a mean little snot-nose."

"You weren't in the woods along the branch, either, or at the Tennent school, or in the churchyard reading the stones—or if you were, you never came when I was there. And then we moved away to Red Bank, but you weren't at the high school, or down by Swimming River, or at any of the dances at Pleasure Bay, or just walking along the street and kicking maple leaves."

"I was probably in the lunchroom at De Witt, reading salty stuff scribbled on a wall. Like, 'Poor Alice she gave away two hundred dolars worth before she found out she could sell it.'"

"And then I took a job in Newark, and for four years I went there every morning on the train, but I never saw you anywhere along the line or anywhere else—in New York, in Asbury, at the

Rutgers games, or here at the beach—but I did see someone else, and for a very short while I thought he was you, and then one day I looked out of a window, and I didn't have to say, 'Where's Danny?' any more, because there you were on the sidewalk, blowing smoke at the snow."

"It took me a long time," he said.

"Not so long, Dan, Not *too* long."

He smoothed the sand before him, and with a fingertip he drew the word 'Mary,' and running the loop of the 'y' to her wrist, he drew a knot and a bow, and the name became a tag, and he stared at it, and then he dug his hands deep into it, saying, "I'm lucky. I'm lucky. I must've been born in Luckville."

A voice overhead said, "Where's Luckville?" Dan and Mary glanced up and saw Jack Hill, and he smiled and sat down, and for a moment he said nothing, and when he spoke, he said what he had said before. "Where's Luckville?"

"Quite a distance from here," Dan said.

"You're looking great, Mary."

"That's how I feel, Jack."

"It works out, then, eh?"

"What works out?" Dan said.

"This—you two."

"You want a medal?"

"What're you sore about, kid?"

"I'll make you a diagram."

"You'd better, because I'll need one to understand. I put you on the train for Luckville."

"You didn't put anybody on anything. You got off, that's all."

"I gave you my place."

"I wish to Christ you'd go away," Dan said, "because if you keep on talking about Mary like she was something that went from hand to hand, this'll end in black and blue."

"I did you a good turn," Jack said, "and what happened before you came on the scene is absolutely unimportant. Think what you like, say what you like, knock my brains out if you like—I'll always believe I did you a good turn. I have many friends, and I could've picked any of them for the Luckville train, but I picked you. Did you ever ask yourself why?"

"Go away, will you?" Dan said. "*Please* go away."

"I picked you for a peculiar reason, a reason you wouldn't appreciate, hating me the way you do: I picked you because I thought you'd be better for Mary than anyone I know, including myself."

Dan sat up, saying, "Pick! Pick! Who the hell're you to pick—God?"

"God couldn't've managed this with miracles; I did it with a phone-call. How else could you have met Mary—by wishing? by praying? by standing on a corner? by running an ad? If you'd done any of those things, you'd be doing it yet. You met Mary through me, and you hate me for it, and we aren't friends any more—but do you want to go back to the beginning, when I had Mary, and you had a few dim dreams? Like hell, you do. I put something in your way that you've come to prize, as I knew you would, but you don't prize me for doing it."

"As you knew I wouldn't."

"No," Jack said. "I didn't know that."

"You must be wild."

"You hate me for the best thing you've had in your life, and it was given to you in love."

Dan looked down at his hand, and slowly he brushed a pepper-and-salt of sand from his palm. "I've heard you talk of love many times," he said, "and it was a good thing to hear, because people don't talk about it nearly enough, but this is one occasion when the word is as out of place in your mouth as a flower-arrangement in a toilet-bowl. I'm not ashamed of the word. I even use it myself. I'm only ashamed of what you do to it."

"That's because you still misunderstand it."

"It's an open book for Jack Hill, though," Dan said. "You use big words for yourself, and you wind up with love, the biggest, but big words don't make a big man any more than big clothes make a grown-up out of a child: when you talk about love, you rattle around in it. What happened on this beach a year ago was that you saw a broad that you wanted to climb on, and when you climbed off, you walked away and stuck a pin in the address-book of your mind, and it went in at J for Johnson—and that's the whole story, the one you've got the gall to end with the big word. I hate you for that more than anything." He rose now, and turning away, he looked at clouds far at sea and foundering.

Hill rose too, saying,"Well, Mary, I hope you enjoy him—and you her, Dan, because she's very enjoy . . .," but Dan had spun about, and a hard-slung clutch of skin and bone struck Hill on the mouth, bringing blood to dye a syrup of spittle. ". . . joyable," he said, and another handful, this one on his jaw, shocked him loose from the mixture he was mouthing, and it sidled off his face as foam. "Enjoyable," he said.

Steve White came between them, saying, "Beat it, Jack, or get to hell off the beach!"

Hill said, "Very enjoyable," and walked away.

"I'm sorry, Steve," Dan said. "I held back as long as I could."

"If I'd been in the office today," the lifeguard said, "I wouldn't've sold him a locker, but it's my trick under the umbrella, and the first thing I knew, he was climbing the platform and parking himself. I didn't want any trouble, so I told him to keep away from you. He had to suck around, though."

"How'd you know there'd be trouble, Steve?"

The lifeguard looked at Mary while speaking to Dan, saying, "I've known your girl for quite a while, and I like her almost as much as I do my own," and then he looked at Dan while speaking to Mary, saying, "Explain to him, will you? I have to go back."

After Steve had gone, Dan stood where he was, watching breaker on breaker break at the feet of a boy with a shovel. At length, the boy said, "I seen the fight."

"What're your last name, first name, and middle initial?"

"I wish the fight would've lasted longer. Then it would've been a longer fight."

"Give your age, place of birth, and the size of your neckband."

"I like long fights because short fights don't last long enough."

"The fight was twice as long as a fight that's only half as long. Give the name of your bank and your favorite cereal."

"I like to see people get hit in fights because they bleed."

"Do not write in this space except with blood."

"The man you were fighting got bloody. I liked that."

"Boys are funny people," Dan said.

"You say queer things," the boy said.

"I come from Queerville."

"I live in Allentown, Pennsavania."

"Do you believe in the overthrow of violence by the force of Government?"

"Well, I have to see if the man is still bloody," the boy said. "G'bye, Mr. Queer." And he ran away.

Mary said, "Come over here and sit down, Mr. Queer."

Dan sat, saying, "I'd sooner stand."

"Look at me."

He looked, saying, "I'd sooner hide."

"Why do you feel so bad, Mr. Queer?"

"It was no fight, Mary. It was no fight at all."

"It wasn't a long fight, but it was certainly a fight, and you're a fighter from Fightville, and the little boy can go bust."

"I looked good against Jack, but that's because he can't punch his way out of a lukewarm shower. If he'd been built like Steve, I'd've probably run away, or if I'd scrabbled up enough nerve to stand still, I'd've wound up with a broken jaw—but run or stay, you'd've known me for what I am—all yellow and a yard wide. I told you I was ordinary, Mary. I told you!"

"Am I supposed to hate you for that?"

"How can you do anything else?"

"Dan, I couldn't hate you even if you hated me—and maybe you will some day."

"What makes you say that?"

"I'm not as pretty as a little red pair of shoes."

"Julia is many years back, Mary."

"In time, but how far back in your mind?"

"I think of her now and then—not often, but once in a while. She used to call me her God damn Dan, and whenever I God damn myself, I remember her."

"That's oftener than you know."

"I told her once never to let me see beyond her, but she did, and she's grown smaller ever since. What I see now is afterimage, and in time it'll disappear."

"You'll have to live a long life."

"Good," he said, "because while she's shrinking, you'll be growing, and the longer she takes, the vaster you'll be when she's gone"

"Nobody's looking, Dan. Nobody'd notice if you kissed me."

*   *   *

They walked up a slope toward a church that cast little shadow on the calcimine of starlight, and they went among graves and headstones, saying only an occasional name read from a flaking slab. From time to time, Mary stooped for a pebble and placed it on the lid of a tomb. 19 98.317

"Why do you do that?" Dan said.

"A girl I know told me it was a custom of the Jewish people. She couldn't explain what it meant, but it seemed so sad and so beautiful that ever since I've done it myself."

"I think *you're* sad and beautiful."

"There's one thing I'd like to have my way about, Dan: I'd like to be married in this church. I have a feeling it'd be a good beginning."

"Do you believe in God?" he said.

"I've never asked myself, or maybe it's simply that I've never answered, but many people've believed very hard here, and I respect their belief."

"If you respect it enough, you share it."

"Possibly, but all I knowingly want to share is the place."

"I don't believe at all, Mary, and nothing'll ever make me believe again."

"Because of Julia?" she said.

"Julia couldn't've made me disbelieve in frogs. I said my last prayer a minute before Sacco and Vanzetti died. I asked God to pull off a miracle and save two of the best men that ever lived, but He was taking His ease somewhere in His sock-feet, and any belief I might've had went to hell with the Italians."

"It's odd," Mary said. "You disbelieve because of them, and if I believe, it's because of you."

"You love me a little, don't you?"

"I couldn't begin to tell you, Dan."

"I'll get married anywhere—here, in Grand Canyon, or in a cigar-store—but it's got to be to you."

They were at the car now, and now they were moving through the aromatic emissions of night, and now they were on a pair of tracks in a field, and now they were standing before a barn at the edge of an orchard [*old harness, broken tools, newspapers from* 1905, *and a faint but still sweet smell of hay*], and two birds, one near and one far, played the same few bars on their reeds, and Mary said, "The little frame house is beyond those elms."

"Why was the place a secret last night?" Dan said.

"I didn't care for you enough: I was only in love with you."

"You grow!" he said. "You grow all the time!"

"Not I, Dan, but you."

"I want you to know about an ordinary guy named Dan Johnson: I want you to know what to expect. I'll love you well and for a long while, I'll respect you at home and in the street, I'll be honest with you as far as I know the truth, and I'll try my best to provide. I'll have an attack of the 'forties' some day, and I'll wonder why my fine deeds had never gone beyond fine dreams, and the more I wonder, the more I'll balk at being ordinary to the end. It's only fair, therefore, to warn you not to make too many plans around me or any that can't be changed: I may discover that I care more for people than I do for myself, and I may do a fine deed for them and come home to you dead."

"There'll be no plans, Dan, but there'll always be one demand: that you never make dying the fine deed in itself. It's fine to fight for what you believe in, but if you die, it has to be because only dying will win the fight."

"Tell me more about my sad and beautiful Mary!" he said.

"Afterward," she said, and she went toward a dark door [*newspapers from* 1905, *you thought, and a faint but still sweet smell of hay*], and he followed her.

PART FIVE

ORDINARY DAN

IT WAS almost midnight when Dan entered the flat—the re-modeled parlor of an old private house on the upper West Side—and finding Mary asleep, he undressed in the light of a street-lamp and lay down on the cold half of the brass-railed bed. The warmth of the warm half drifted toward him under the blankets, but he made no move to touch its source, and for a while he stared into the blue darkness through his less-blue breath, and thinking finally of smoke, he reached out to a bedside table and groped for a cigarette and a match.

In a brief flare-up, he glanced at Mary, and when he shook the flame away, he said, "I thought you were dead to the world."

"Give me a drag," she said. "I like to watch you when you don't know you're being watched: I learn about you."

"I hope you never learn anything."

"What did your father want to see you about?"

"Just what we supposed."

"How much did he need?"

"A couple of hundred," Dan said. "Where would I get hold of a couple of hundred?"

"We had part of it, didn't we?"

"I'm going to tell you something now, and when I finish, you won't have to peep through keyholes any more: you'll know all there is to know about the stinker you married. When I went over to my father's this evening, I had our whole roll with me—eight ten-dollar bills—only, Jesus, it wasn't all in one pocket! I tried to

357

tell myself that I'd split it to save something in case a dip had me
staked out, but it wouldn't go down, and neither would any other
reason but the truth—that I meant to hold back half of the money
if my father made a touch. Well, he made it, all right, and I held
back. When he saw only forty bucks on the table, he said, 'I didn't
know you were as strapped as that, son, or I wouldn't've asked
you.' I let a couple of seconds go by, and then I caved in, saying,
'Strapped, hell; I'm loaded,' and out came the other forty. 'Money
in every pocket,' I said, 'and more in my shoes.' What a man you
picked, Mary!"

"I'm no angel," she said. "I've been lying here, thinking, 'There
goes my spring coat chasing your new suit.'"

"You've still got the coat," he said.

After a pause, she said, "I hate to ask you what you mean."

"He wouldn't take the second forty."

"Oh, God, Danny, did you really let him give it back?"

"I wish I had an armful of sweet new c-notes, and I wish one
side of them had stickum, like stamps: I'd go back there and paste
up the joint till hell wouldn't have it. On Pop's bald spot, that's
where I'd slap the first one, and then on Mom's ears, like earrings,
and on the doors and the windows and the map and the toilet-seat;
I'd paper the walls, I'd line the drawers, I'd hang hundred-dollar-
bills from the chandelier."

"If you'd do all that," Mary said, "then it ought to be easy to
do less. Take those four tens for my spring coat and mail them to
your father in the morning."

"Don't you want the coat?" he said. "Don't you want to look
beautiful for me?"

"There used to be another way that I could look beautiful."

He turned to her, saying, "You have many ways, Mary."

PAPER ANNIE

WHEN DAN left his office, he joined the southbound flow of
pedestrians on Sixth Avenue. Below 42nd Street, he ed-
died out for a moment to peer through a wire grille at a jewelry-

store display—gold and silver, pearls and amber, a color-chart of stones, and price-tags—and then once more he was in the current, and this time he let it carry him to one of the Herald Square exits of the Hudson Tubes. There, a little distance from the steps, he stopped to wait for Mary.

He waved when he saw her and smiled as she lowered her head to come toward him. "Still embarrassed by me?" he said.

"I'll always be, if you stare," she said.

"How is it you only get flustered beyond a certain distance? You're good for about five yards; anything over that, and you try to hide."

"I feel exposed."

"Well, you've *been* exposed."

"You can see me from head to foot—all my bad points."

"They're a lot clearer when you're close."

"Today of all days."

"Let's walk," he said, "and I'll tell you about the presents I didn't buy you. After that, we'll dine—anyway, eat."

They went up Broadway toward Times Square, and the sky over the empty side-streets was bright in the west and evening-blue in the east.

"I had a present on the train," Mary said. "A man tried to make me."

"Tried to make you what?" Dan said.

"He tried to make me. You know."

"What approach did he use?"

"He offered me his seat."

"He must've been approaching backward. I hope you rejected the offer, though, because you'd've looked ridiculous with a man's seat."

"Next, he tried to engage me in conversation."

"I suppose he offered you his seat again."

"No, I had that. He said it was a lovely afternoon, wasn't it? I said indeed it was. He said he liked the ride from Newark to New York at that time of day, because the Meadows took on such wonderful color, didn't they? I said I'd often noticed the color myself.

He said oh, did I commute? I said yes, I commuted every day. He said how was it he'd never seen me before?"

"You should've said because you'd always seen him first. That would've curled him into the next car."

"I said I didn't know how it was, because *I'd* seen *him* many times."

"At this point, I'm supposed to go up with a loud report."

"He said then why hadn't I spoken to him? I said it simply hadn't occurred to me."

"When did he get to the part where he said how's about you and me having a little ole drink?"

"At Manhattan Transfer. Only it wasn't a drink; it was dinner."

"You should've snapped him up."

"I said I had a date. He said couldn't I break it? I said I could, but I didn't think it'd be right."

Dan laughed, saying, "And he said ah, when two wayfarers meet by chance in a loveless world, why should they waste the summer night asking those questions which, of old, man sought of seer and oracle, and no reply was told? Oscar Wilde."

"Wrong. He said ah, why didn't I call the guy up and stall him off? I said I couldn't reach the guy, and besides, even if I could, it wouldn't be fair to stand him up, today of all days. He said well, today was just another day, wasn't it? I said no, it was my paper anniversary."

"What did he say to that?"

"Nothing. He just stared."

"I hope you didn't stare back. The Romeo had no seat."

"And that was my present on the train."

"I love you," Dan said, "and this would be a fine moment to whip out a little plush box and spring the catch."

"What would be in it?" Mary said.

"Pst!" From a small delivery-truck parked on 38th Street, a man was beckoning to them.

Dan laughed, saying, "By God, I'll bet he wants to give you his seat," and taking Mary's arm, he walked her away.

"What *does* he want, I wonder?" Mary said. "Maybe we missed something."

"Only this," Dan said. "We'd've gone over to him, and I'd've said, 'What've you got that isn't hot?' and he'd've put on a hurt look and said, 'Do I look like a thief? I'm asking a flat question.' I'd've said, 'Nobody looks like a thief, not even Rock D. Johnefeller,' and he'd've said, 'Some guys ain't so special about their merchandice—hot, cold, what's the odds?—but me, I sell an article, it's strickly cold.' I'd've said, 'Show the article,' and he'd've reached down under the dash and come up with a little white dog, saying, 'A pedigree animal, and ten fish takes her away.' I'd've said, 'It'd take a better dog than I am to tell her breed,' and he'd've said, 'Spitz, and she's got a pedigree as long as your arm.' I'd've said, 'So have I, but I can't prove it,' and he'd've said, 'If I was bred as good as this dog, so help me God, I'd change places with her.' I'd've said, 'A couple of terriers are walking up the street, and a Spitz leans out of a car and says, "Pst! I got a pedigree man in here, and ten frogs takes him home." The terriers say, "What breed?" and the Spitz says, "He's an Aryan, a thoroughbred human being, and his name is Adolf."' Realizing I was a tough customer, he'd've said, 'Make it five skins, and the pooch is yours.' I'd've said, 'She's cute, but if I bought her, I wouldn't be able to feed my wife to-night,' and he'd've said, 'Give her belly a rest. It'll do her a world of good.' I'd've said, 'But this happens to be our paper anniversary,' and he'd've said, 'Buy her a paper, then, but don't pass up this bargain. You'll regret it.' My parting shot would've been, 'What's one more regret?'"

"We should've bought that pooch," Mary said. "We could've called her Paper Annie."

I CAN'T GIVE YOU ANYTHING BUT LOVE, BA-BEE!

THE flat was darker than the evening: there was no ceiling over the sky. From the street came the sounds of the street (the voices of children and auto-horns, the voices of tires on pavement and an organ playing a tinkle-tankle tune for pennies), and with the sound came the street-perfumes (the compound scent of food, the wet-down dust, the Hudson-flavored western air). Near the open window of the converted parlor, the coal of a cigarette went on and off, and then suddenly it shot away end-over-end and fell.

"Don't feel bad, Dan," Mary said.

"I wish I knew what else to feel," he said. "What does a guy do when he feels like feeling bad—feel good? laugh it off? take up Christian Science? or what?"

"Is that all a guy can do?"

"A guy like me, yes."

"I love a guy like you."

"We keep the lights off to hide what you get in return."

"I get more than you dream, Dan."

"A sixty-cent blue-plate special—that's what you get, and you eat it with love. Why? I ate the same garbage with hate."

"I won't ask you what you were hating. You'll only say you were hating yourself, and I don't like to hear that—not for a blue-plate special."

"For other things. For this hole-in-the-wall."

"Not for that, either. Not for anything."

"For not being able to get you out of that God damn department-store. How about that? For not being able to pay my wife's way. For being my father all over again. Whenever I look at you, I think, 'My sad and beautiful Mary, what've I done to you?'"

"You've made me rich."

"Is that why I feel so poor—or was I always poor?" he said, and then for a space he was silent. "Along about the middle of the afternoon, there was a knock on my door, a light knock but a precise one, and I said, 'Come in,' and in came a precise man. Medium height; blond hair; glasses, the pinch-nose kind; thirty-odd, I thought; and probably a druggist. You know what he turned out to be? Guess."

"I can't," Mary said.

A DOCTOR OF DIVINITY

"LAST NAME?"

"Conroy."

"First name?"

"Gideon."

[*Gideon Conroy was born at Utica, New York, in the year* 1900; *in* 1915, *he informed his parents of his belief that he had a vocation, and in* 1919, *after a year in the army, he entered a theological seminary; in* 1921, *his father bequeathed him the sum of nine hundred dollars, which made it unnecessary for him to stoke furnaces for tuition during his junior and senior years; in* 1923, *he was graduated, and in* 1924, *his mother died, leaving him her wedding picture, the family Bible, and a volume of poems by Jones Very; in* 1925, *following a mission to Africa, he was ordained and given a pulpit in a village along the St. Lawrence River; in* 1926, *he married Miss Emily Edwards, of Ogdensburg; in* 1928, *his wife suffered an attack of pneumonia and, on the advice of a specialist, spent a year at Saranac; in* 1929, *because he was unable to maintain two establishments any longer, he accepted a call from a congregation in Wyoming, where his wife would find the high altitude that her health required; in* 1932, *as a result of devoted efforts among the poor of the community during a severe winter, Mrs. Conroy suffered a second attack of pneumonia, and now she was left with a lesion in each lung; in* 1933, *on a spring Sunday morning, the Rev. Dr. Gideon Conroy delivered the following sermon to his flock:*

[*"We occupy the House of the Lord, brethren, but we are godless, and we pray with language in our mouths, but Christ its meaning is a faint and growing-fainter memory of the mind, and therefore looking toward Heaven, we sink the more toward hell. Thus said the Lord (Amos* 2.6): *for three transgressions, and for four, I will not turn away the punishment of Judah—for selling the righteous for silver and the poor for a pair of shoes; for panting after the dust of the earth on the heads of the poor and for turning aside the way of the meek; for going in unto the same maid, father and son alike, to profane the holy name; and for lying down to prayer on pawned clothes and drinking the wine of the condemned in the temple. For those three sins, and for those four, said the Lord, would Judah be destroyed, and we in Christ, being armed with the arms and the wrath of the Lord, sought for two thousand years to wreak His vengeance. Yet who among us will say that the fire of anger did not die down to the ashes of hatred? who will say that the purifiers did not themselves become impure? and who will say that the virtuous did not acquire the sins they loosed from the sinful? Many will claim it in their faces, but none will own it in his heart, for, one and all, we know that Christians too have sold the poor for a mortgage and put the dust of roads on the weak; that Christians too, father and son alike, have gone in unto the daughters of the hungry in a whorehouse; and that Christians too, the elect in life and death, have rejoiced themselves in the unredeemed raiment of the naked. The reward for evil shall nowise be love, and we are evil that eat our bread in the sweat of the wretched and defile the feet of Christ with the abomination of prayer when our bellies are swollen with the blood of the dispossessed. The time has come for the altar to be cleansed, brethren; the time has come for the six-day sinner to be rebuked for posing as a seventh-day saint; aye, the time has come for Christ to be merciless with them that have no mercy, to deny grace to them that deny credit, to damn such bankers as balance their books on the backs of mortgagors. Judas sold Jesus for thirty pieces of silver. Look to it, brethren, that you sell the heavy-laden not at all."*

[In the afternoon of that same spring Sunday, a group acting for the congregation called at the parsonage, and their spokesman said these words to the Rev. Dr. Gideon Conroy:

["You got done with that sermon this morning at a quarter of twelve, but there was something else you got done with at the same time, and we come here to tell you what it was: at a quarter of twelve this morning, you got done with this town, and except we miss our guess by many a mile, you also got done with the whole state of Wyoming. We want you should know why. It ain't that we can't take our hell-fire or leave it alone: we was raised up on that kind of gospel, and our Sabbath pork wouldn't taste half so good without some preacher didn't warn us it might be our last square meal on earth. What grinds us all to smack is you sticking your bill in our business. We didn't bring you out here for that (we wouldn't've brang Christ for it), and the minute you horned in—well, you had to be dehorned. You might as well know it first as last: there ain't no sonabitching minister can tell us our six days ain't good enough for his seventh, and when you get to where you're going, don't ever forget what you learned right here. I think that about covers what we had to say."

[The Rev. Dr. Conroy said, "I preached the truth in that sermon. I preached what Christ died for: humanity."

[The spokesman said, "Save your wind for your next stop."

[The Rev. Dr. Conroy said, "My words were only the words of Jesus. If you would be perfect, He said, sell what you have and give to the poor, and you will have treasure in Heaven."

[The spokesman said, "We know our Matthew as good as you do—better, maybe, because if we give what we have to the poor, then they'll be rich, and they won't get into the Kingdom of Heaven. We don't want to work such a hardship on 'em, so we're going to take the punishment on ourselves. If that ain't true Christian charity, tell us what is."

[The Rev. Dr. Conroy said, "You twist the Word."

[The spokesman said, "Contrariwise: we're only kinking out the kinks. You're the twister, and that's why we're, so to speak, foreclosing you."

[The Rev. Dr. Conroy said, "I ask you not to be hasty. For my wife's sake, I ask you to reconsider. Not for myself, but for my wife."

[The spokesman said, "For a space, there, it looked like you was singing small."

[The Rev. Dr. Conroy said, "Her lungs are bad, as you well know. It would mean her death to leave this climate."

[The spokesman said, "That's your lookout. You should've thunk of your wife when you was up there blatting your brains out."

[The Rev. Dr. Conroy said, "How small do I have to sing? Do you want me to stand up next Sunday and say that I've seen the light? that God came to me during the week and told me religion and business don't mix?"

[The spokesman said, "That'd be small enough."

[Mrs. Emily Conroy said, "It was a good sermon today, Gideon. It was what you called it, the truth, and I'd sooner die than beg for leave to take it back as a lie."

[The Rev. Dr. Conroy said, "Don't listen to her! I'll do anything you say! I'll be a good preacher!"

[The spokesman said, "Just see that you're a good runner. The eastbound leaves in an hour."

[Early in 1934, while the Rev. Dr. Conroy was in New York City

to show cause to his Church Council why he should not be unfrocked,
his beloved Emily died of tuberculosis at an upstate County Hospital.
He did not attend the funeral. Instead, he went out into the street and
dropped his mother's Bible into a sewer at the nearest corner, and then
he dusted his hands and entered the nearest saloon.]

A DANIEL COME TO JUDGMENT

LATE in a winter afternoon, they met at the Maine Monument and walked uptown along a path at the edge of the park. The sun had gone down behind the west-side buildings, but blades of light cut through each cross-street and felled far-reaching shadows from the barren trees.

"You know," Mary said, "there's a thing we've never talked about."

"That's true," Dan said, "but we've thought about it."

"I wonder whether we mean the same thing."

"We've never spoken of having a child."

"How did you know that was it, Dan?"

The wind spun up a spiral of snow and sent it at his eyes. "You forget what I told Ed one morning not too long ago," he said. "I told him I wanted to watch your face."

"You're a good watcher, Dan. You're getting to know me."

"If I watched some more—maybe another hundred years—I'd learn why you wanted a child that was half-me."

"Would it take that long?" she said. "Would you really be so slow to understand?"

"I doubt that I'll *ever* understand. Men everywhere are doing great things and living out great lives, and you're thankful to them, and you give them respect and admiration, but you show them no love. I do poor things, and each day I use up a little more of a poor life, and although I never mean to, I make small of you, and I disappoint you, and I offend you with my commonness and my sour jokes, but I enjoy the same gratitude as the great, and the same deep respect—and all your love. Why is that, Mary? Why don't the great things count with you? Why should a nobody like me go to Heaven?"

"I had a tough old lady for a grandmother," Mary said. "Tough as bear-meat, Ed used to call her, but she didn't fool me any, because she was mush underneath. Whenever she caught me out in anything wrong, she'd storm around, bawling herself red in the face, and she'd wind up with a terrible curse: 'The devil shouldn't take you!' she'd always say. *Shouldn't*, Dan—and my curse on you is the same."

"I don't know what to say, Mary," he said. "I don't know what to say."

THE DAY BEFORE LINCOLN'S BIRTHDAY

THROUGH the window of the parlor, he watched snow chalk up a slate dusk. There were small sounds to be heard in the room, the flatulence of a radiator, footfalls on the floor above, and, from the floor below, music strained of melody by planks and plaster. There were trespassing savors to be aware of, the smell of neighbors' food, the smell of neighbors, the smell of the street, and one mild but indefeasible fragrance, a flavor that no invasion would ever annul. He went to a wardrobe, and opening a door, he stood close to the rack of clothes within, and he thought [*She would come home soon, and then something would happen to the gray gloom, something would enter the room with her, and the season would change, and what was dull would be bright, and what was cold would be warm, and all that was dead, including you, would seem to quicken. She would close the door behind her, and you would help her with her coat and rubbers, and she would comb out her pressed-down hair, and you would watch her until she turned, and then you would put yourself hard against her mouth. She would come home soon, you thought.*]. And because there was no doubt in his mind, he felt that he could run the risk of creating one, and therefore, as he awaited a sure and pleasant moment, he caused himself to wonder how he would wait if he knew that the moment would never arrive—and at once, without more, the thought was beyond control. He looked about him at the dull that would always be dull and the cold that would always be cold, and he knew that the dead, including himself, would never come alive, nor would the season change nor the gray gloom rise.

He opened the window, and a curtain of snow bloomed in the room. Leaning out, he scanned the street to both corners, but there were few people to be seen, and among them was no Mary. He found himself seated on a chair, but he could not remember the act of sitting down, and then he found himself standing without knowing that he had risen, and then he began to walk the length of the rug, and each time he passed a knob on the brass bedstead, he touched it with the palm of his hand and all five fingers (not two or three or four, but five), and he remained unaware of the ritual until he had performed it many times, and then suddenly he shivered. The window was still open, and he closed it, but the shivering did not immediately end.

When Mary entered, he gave her no help with her coat and rubbers, nor did he watch her while she combed her hair, for he had turned to the window on hearing her in the hall, and until she came to stand beside him, he stared down at plates of light on the tablecloth of the street. "There's a present for you on the chiffonier," he said.

"A present for *me?*" she said. "But it's *your* birthday."

"I really didn't want anything, so I spent the money on you."

"Why've you been standing here like this, Dan?"

"I thought you were never coming back."

"Good Lord, what made you imagine that?"

"The same thing that brought you home."

A VERRAY PARFIT GENTIL KNIGHT

Tossing a card across his desk, Peterson said, "Motion for a refund denied."

"The woman isn't asking for a refund," Dan said. "All she wants is another job for the same commission."

"Two beers for the same nickel," Peterson said. "The Court finds that the applicant agreed to pay a commission out of her first month's salary, that said salary was duly paid and said commission duly collected, and that shortly thereafter the applicant was discharged because she couldn't cook water till it got hot."

"So the employer says, but who the hell is the employer?"

"One of the best friends we have in the world."

"This one would cut a throat to test a knife."

"The way you take up all these complaints, anybody'd think we gave out guarantees. We guarantee nothing. All we do is stock people for certain jobs, and when a customer comes along, we try to make a sale. Keep that in mind: this is a store, a butcher-store."

"It's the only one I ever heard of where the meat pays to get taken away. The least we can do is see that it doesn't come back every month and pay all over again."

"What do you suggest—that we stand behind each piece of tripe that we sell?"

"I don't say that, and you know it," Dan said. "If you want to be strictly legal, this cook held her job long enough to entitle us to a commission, and she paid it, but while she didn't expect to be fired the week after, we can't honestly claim it was a surprise to us: the woman she was working for has had four cooks in six months, and she got them all from this agency. That's what people call good business, I suppose, but I hate to hold my God damn nose when I get my pay-check."

"Breathe through your mouth," Peterson said.

"In a case like this, we ought to investigate the employer."

"That's not a bad idea. Next time we place a janitor at the Ford plant, go over and give Ford a good stiff test. Check his disposition, habits, bank-account, and spark-plugs. Look into his morals and political beliefs, and if you can make him say 'Ah,' I'd like a report on his tonsils. No janitor leaves here without the fullest protection."

But Dan was looking beyond Peterson, and gently tapping the card against the desk-edge, he said, "Yes, sir—we ought to investigate these employers. . . ."

*　　*　　*

On the fourth floor of an apartment-building near Washington Square, Dan stopped before a door that bore a metal name-plate reading: EMMA JAMES. Pressing the bell-button, he produced within a muted chime, and after a moment, he heard footsteps, and the door opened to reveal the figure of a woman in the dim entry.

She said, "Yes . . . ?"

[*The single word (or the way in which the word had been spoken, or the speaking voice alone, or nothing more than your own unfomented memory) brought Julia back to dwell in the forefront of your mind, and through her image, as through a substance with texture, color, and dimensions, you stared at the woman in the doorway, hearing all the while a prolongation of the same single word, as if she had not yet finished saying it. In her presence, Julia seemed to become more than an exhumation and more than a revival: she seemed to thrive.*]

"What do you wish?" the woman said.

"I spoke to you this morning on the telephone," Dan said. "I'm from the employment-agency."

"I'm afraid I have no time for you just now. I'm about to leave."

"I understood I was to call around five o'clock."

"And you've been quite prompt," the woman said, "but the truth is, the appointment slipped my mind. You'll have to forgive me."

"If you can spare a few minutes. . . ."

"I don't believe you heard me. I said I was about to leave."

"I heard that," Dan said, "and I also heard that you forgot about the appointment."

"Are you going to take it on yourself to rebuke me?"

"I'm certainly not going to take it on myself to come back at your convenience."

"Be good enough to give me your name."

"It's the same as it was this morning: Dan Johnson. Address your complaints to my employer, Mr. Peterson."

"You may go now, Mr. Johnson."

"Not without a word of advice, Miss James: you'd better lay in a stock of canned goods or learn how to cook, one or the other."

"Exactly what do you mean by that?"

"I mean we're not sending any more of our people down here. It's only too clear why they leave."

"Aren't you something of a son-of-a-bitch, Mr. Johnson?"

Dan laughed. "As one to another, yes," he said.

[*Julia, you thought as you walked away. Where was she at that instant and with whom? What was she doing, saying, thinking, feeling, and when had she last looked back, as you were looking back, on the days and nights of a winter now seven years gone? Julia, you thought.*]

WHO TOOK DAT ENGINE OFF MAH NECK?

ON a card-table, there were four coffee-cups, three of them holding the sea-green lees of cigarette-ash. Lying near the fourth was a manuscript in a binder that bore a pasted-on label reading: *Eight-ball*, a novel by JULIAN POLLARD.

"So far," Julie said, "all you been talking about is the story. The hell with the story. When you going to quit meeching long enough to trot out some philosophy?" He glanced from Dan to Mary and from Mary to Tootsie. "I finally break down and let you read the book, and what happens? I get my punctuation corrected."

"You've gotten more than that," Dan said. "Any talk about the story is bound to take in some of the meaning."

"The choice of material *is* meaning," Tootsie said.

"Julie's right," Mary said. "We're meeching."

"Only honest man in the room is a woman," Julie said.

"I know what I want to say," Tootsie said. "The trouble is, I don't know exactly how to say it."

"How-to-say ought to come easy for you, Mr. Tuskegee."

"I can't just open my face and hope something smart'll fall down out of my brain."

"You can say if the book's good or bad," Julie said, and he bounced a cake-crumb off the cover. "Shoot, you could've done that 'way back at De Witt."

"*Eight-ball* is no *Ivanhoe*, Julie. If it was, I could tell you straight out what I thought of it."

"Tell it crookedy. I won't like it, anyway."

"Maybe that's the block: you don't really care what anybody thinks. You didn't write *Eight-ball* for me, or Dan, or Mary, or whoever. You wrote it for yourself."

"That's how a man does a plenty of things."

"You could've written it for people, but you wrote it for a person. You could've written it for Negroes, but you wrote it for one nigger name of Julie Pollard. A book's got to talk for big hunks of people all at once, and in my humble opinion, yours doesn't."

"Phrig your humble opinion," Julie said. "There's thirteen million blacks in America, and they got humble opinions too—too God *damn* humble, you ask me."

"That's truer than truth, but you didn't get it down on paper, and you know full well you never even tried to."

"Only thing I know full well is, I'm black."

"Then why do you write like you're a no-good white?"

"You crazy?" Julie said. "Or what?"

"You couldn't be doing worse for us if you were a Kluxer."

"How much I have to listen to before I can get mad?"

"You can get mad any time you get mad enough," Tootsie said. "But tell me something first: did Jesus Christ Hill see any of this book while you were writing it?"

"Some," Julie said. "About what you did."

"Why didn't you show him all?"

"Got sick of that Mr. Eddie."

"The way I heard, he was frying you in that Russian love-fat."

"You heard slantways. I let him tin-ear me for a while, and then I give him the chuck. He started out like maybe he had an idea in his mouth, but it turned out to be warmed-up spit. Talked up love like Solomon talked up the Church: 'Behold, thou art fair, my love.' But that's all he ever did, was behold. He never went inside. It was dirty inside. He was a beholding-type man."

"If you quit Hill because his love-talk wasn't enough, why did you go back to hating?"

"All whites are Hills at heart."

Tootsie indicated Dan and Mary, saying, "What about these two pinks?"

"Different," Julie said.

"Oh, Christ and carry six! Why do all my people make the same mistake?"

"We each of us know maybe one-two buckras that don't want to knock our trotters off—but one-two ain't enough, God damn it!"

"But look, you dumb dinge," Tootsie said. "Add up all those one-twos, and you have millions! Can't you see that? Get 'em all together, and you have power!"

"Slurp," Julie said. "Get 'em together, and you got a lynch-mob. I been hearing about soft whites all my life, but ear-hearing ain't eye-seeing, and the only soft whites are in the mind of soft jigs like you."

"We had this same argument ten years ago—when we got kicked out of that stamp-club. Remember?"

"I got a good rememberer," Julie said, "better than yours. The way you have it, it's us kicked the others out."

"Somebody pass me a cig," Tootsie said.

Julie grinned. "What you plotting, boy—to Marx me?"

"I'm going to Marx you blond."

"I don't Marx too easy."

"Funny about you and me," Tootsie said. "I'm the one was going to write books, not you, but that got bent around some place, and you're the writer, and I only teach English to shines: funny how things turn out. All the same, I'm glad, because you're twice the writer I'd've been—yet you could be twice the writer you are and still be wrong to run our people down to dirt. I always thought I knew our people. Except for color, I always thought we were just like everybody else: good and bad. To read you, though, we're a race of pimps, drunks, footless bums, clapped-up hired-girls, happy-dusters, and bolito-players. To you, that's us, but to me, it's only *some* of us. Where are the Robesons in your book? Where are you? And if you don't mind, where am I?"

"Always the Robesons," Julie said. "You pick the one all-America spade and say, 'Why not write about *him?*' Us blacks don't *have* to write about the Robesons. Any time one of us gets good like Paul, there'll always be whites to hold him up on a stick, saying, 'Wasn't for his color, you couldn't hardly tell him from a white man.' But *Paul* would get the point, because he ain't no soft-headed smoke like you want me to be. Wasn't for his color! That's just it:

he's good, but being black, he's only black-good. The rest of us, like I say in the book, we're pimps and candy-sniffers, not Rutgers baritones, and who would know why better than Paul?"

"Not you," Tootsie said, "and that's a sure bet."

"You'd lose," Julie said. "We're pimps and the rest because we're inferior."

"So far, I lose—but who keeps us inferior?"

"The whites."

"I still lose—but which whites?"

"All whites."

"Now I win," Tootsie said.

"If that's Marxing, I ain't Marxed yet."

"You're Marxed all over. If you said all the rich keep the poor down, you'd be right, but when you say all the whites keep the blacks down, you're wrong, because all the whites aren't rich."

"Who's taking the engine off mah neck—the poor whites?"

" If we ever get together with them, yes," Tootsie said. "The engine isn't only on *our* necks; it's on the necks of *all* the poor, black and white both; and even if the poor whites were simply out to help themselves, to get the engine off *their* necks, they couldn't do it without getting it off ours at the same time." He stared away at a scene in the mind, saying, "'And when Ah was in dat railroad-wreck, who took dat engine off mah neck? Nobuddy.'" Then he shook his head, as if to break the connection between the words and his mouth. "I wonder how many times Bert Williams sang that song—thousands, I guess—and I wonder if he ever realized it was wrong. 'Nobuddy rich,' he should've said, but what about the poor—the white poor, the black poor, the red, the yellow, the brown? Make believe we couldn't do something about that railroad-wreck! Man, oh, man, when we sang, 'Who took dat engine off mah neck?' the answer would be, 'Damn near ever'buddy!'"

Julie said nothing. He picked idly at the edge of the label on the manuscript, and then he looked up at Tootsie, and after a moment he smiled.

A SACCO WHO LIVES TO GET RICH

THEY had spent the week-end at Red Bank, and on their way home now, they were standing on the rear platform of a Jersey Central local. The cars were crowded and warm, but no other passengers had joined them in the vestibule, and side by side at the crisscross gate, for a long while they watched the darkening country recede.

"When're you going to leave me, Mary?"

"I'm never going to leave you."

"Why do I have this feeling, then?"

"I don't know," she said. "What feeling?"

"That we're getting near the end."

"I don't have that feeling, Dan."

"What feeling do you have?" he said. "Do you have any?"

"I think I do, but I'd like to know about yours. Why would I leave you? Where would I go?"

"Where everybody goes when they leave—away."

"But they have to have a reason for going, don't they?"

"The best one is that there's no reason to stay."

"You're about to tell me you're ordinary again. You're touched on that subject."

"I admit it," he said. "It touches me."

"It isn't right to be running yourself down all the time. I don't want you to do it any more."

"As long as I don't run *you* down, why not?"

"But you *do* run me down," she said. "You act as if marrying you was bad taste on my part, a low and vulgar desire. What've you ever done that you're so ashamed of?"

"It's what I haven't done," he said. "I haven't done anything to be proud of."

"I happen to like you the way you are, Dan, but if you don't like yourself, and if you never will till you've done something to be proud of, then for God's sake, why don't you go out and do it?"

He let a cigarette fall, and caught in the air-flow made by the train, it struck the ballast hundreds of ties back-track. "I've been dreading your saying that," he said. "It makes this a quarrel."

"I don't think it does," she said. "I've never asked you to prove to *me* that you're great, because I don't care whether you're great or small. You're the one who wants proof, and since you never seem to find it in what I say, I'm afraid you'll have to look for it in what you do, in the great deed you once warned me about. So far, though, instead of the great deed, all I've seen is self-pity, and it makes me wonder whether you're only out to feel proud, not to do the deed."

"Suppose we just look at the scenery," he said.

"You look at it: I'm not finished talking. You may've forgotten what happened three years ago this week, but I haven't. In case you need reminding, we decided to get married, and after a while we did get married, and I don't regret it yet, and I never will. But one by one, little things pile up in three years, and finally the time comes when they start to crowd the big ones. At first, I didn't mind your saying you were ordinary. In fact, I liked it, not because I ever thought you were anything else, but because it was good to know a person who knew the truth about himself; it was a change from ordinary people who were all swole up like toads. What I liked still better was the fact that you weren't satisfied with being ordinary, and the more you talked about it, the surer I was that one fine day you'd climb the mountain you dreamed of. If you can stand the truth, that was why I kept my job after we were married: I didn't want to hold you back when you felt like setting out for the top of the mountain. But for all your talk, the mountain is still up there, and you're still down here. Do or die, it was going to be, but you haven't done, and you haven't died: you've only felt sorry for yourself. I want that to stop, Dan. Do you hear? I want it to stop!"

"Put up or shut up," he said. "Is that it?"

"Can you think of anything else to do?"

"Yes," he said. "*I* could leave *you*."

She studied him before saying, "It's a quarrel now," and then she turned away and entered the car.

He remained where he was for the rest of the journey to Jersey City, and a paper that he had bought while awaiting the ferry was still unread, still unopened, when he disembarked in Manhattan. Nothing was said during the long walk to the subway, the ride up-

28 96 .284

town, or the short walk to the house, nor was anything said on the stairway, or at the door, or in the momentary nocturne of the flat. He stood at the window, staring at images in the transparent room overhanging the street, and he listened in vain for a voice, either his own or another's, but both rooms vanished in silence, and only then did he realize that he was still holding the still-folded newspaper.

"I'm sorry, Mary," he said. "I shouldn't've spoken the way I did."

"You're very right about that," she said.

He went to the bedside and looked down into the darkness. "Are you going to count it against me?" he said.

"Yes, Dan, and for a very long time."

"I wish you wouldn't, Mary."

"It'll have to wear off."

"I didn't think you were so hard."

"How would you feel if I said I was going to leave you?"

"As if I were watching a funeral," he said. "My own."

"That's well put, Dan. I couldn't do better."

DAN JOHNSON, MR. PETERSON UP

THE BAR was deep, narrow, and dark. In a booth facing a fly-spotted frieze of racing-photographs, Dan sat across a table from his employer, and turning a beer-glass in its coaster of foam, he read a legend from one of the pictures on the wall: FRIAR ROCK, M. GARNER UP, WINNING THE 1916 SUBURBAN.

Peterson took a pale blue envelope from his pocket and flicked it over the table toward Dan, saying, "What did you do to Miss Emma James—try to take her temperature?"

Dan glanced at the envelope without touching it. "Complaint?" he said.

"Three pages, and written in letters of fire."

"That isn't fire. It's leftover blood from her last servant."

"One or the other, you cost us a client."

"You could've bawled me out in the office and saved yourself a beer."

"Sick of the job, kid?" Peterson said.

"The job and you, both," Dan said.

"Why don't you quit, then?"

"I'm waiting to be bounced."

"I wouldn't bounce you if you spit in my eye, kicked my ass, and then insulted me. I find you fascinating."

"And I you. I come to work mornings like a dog to its vomit."

"You don't have to be a dog. You can get down on your knees and be a human being."

"I wish to God you'd give me my walking-papers."

"If you want to be able to look yourself in the eye, grow some nerve and quit, but don't expect me to make it easy for you. This is Capitalism, kid, and I like it, and if you think I'm going to help you break it up by stiffening your back, you're crazier than any communist I ever heard of. Go start your revolution, but get your nerve some place else."

"You don't think much of me, do you?"

"No, and it used to be I didn't think much of your ideas. I see now there's nothing the matter with *any* idea; the matter is always with people. You communists are superb in a pamphlet; in the flesh, you don't have enough guts to need feeding."

"I don't happen to be a communist."

"Fellow-traveler, then, or whatever you call it."

"I don't happen to be that, either."

"Will you for Chrisake tell me what you *do* happen to be?"

"I'm a servant of the ruling-class," Dan said, and he laughed, but very quickly the laugh began to set up and harden, and reaching for his beer-glass, he flushed his throat. "I'm a stale glass of beer, that's what I am. I had a head on me once, and I was full of fizz, but all I've got left is the color." He finished the drink and wiped his mouth. "What do you say we get out of here?"

"Sure," Peterson said.

BAILEY & BERNSTEIN

"LAST NAME?" Dan said.
"Bernstein," the man said.
"First name?"

"Solly."

"For Saul?"

"For Solomon."

["*I said, 'Joe, you tell me to come up here right away, and right away I come, and you don't say nothing only I'm a nice guy, a real pal. For that I have to schlep myself to your house in the middle of the night?' He said, 'Solly, I'll going to tell you something. We come from the same block, the same house, almost, and it's thirty years we know each other, and if you was my own brother, I couldn't have no better respeck for you, maybe less. But this is peculiar times we're having, very peculiar, and me feeling like a brother ain't the same as you being a actual brother. Y'understand, Solly? Y'know what I mean?' I said, 'Not yet, Joe.' He said, 'Well, for instance, we play Tchicago. Tchicago is big-time. It's got all kinds of people—business-people, working-people, society-people, Jews, Christians, schwartzers (is that how you say it?), everybody. We jump out there in front of all them people for twelve minutes, and what do we do? We open together, and then we give 'em a number by ourself, and then we give 'em a shot of comedy, and we close—and we go over big like always. Right? But Tchicago ain't the whole country, Solly. Y'know what I mean?' I said, 'I know what you mean by Tchicago ain't the whole country, but that ain't what you mean.' He said, 'Take a town like New Orleens, or Detroit, even. We don't go over there so good no more, and it ain't account of we played them places to death. Y'know?' I said, 'I know, Joe.' He said, 'Now, there's a thing I ain't wanted to talk to you about, Solly, being as you're sensitive on the point, and I was afraid maybe you'd take it personal. But lately I come to the conclusion we're too good friends to hold anything back, so I made up my mind I'd mention the subjeck if you gave me your word you wouldn't take offense. Y'know what I mean?' I said, 'What's so hard? You're going to be offensive, and I'm not suppose to take offense.' He said, 'Exackly, and seeing as how you're reasonable, Solly, this is what I got on my mind. This Hitler is stirring up a lot of trouble amongst the Christians and the Jews. There ain't no sense to it, and God knows the Jews had enough trouble already, but all the same, Solly, we got to face the facks, and the facks show that a lot of Christians that didn't know a Jew from*

a white man in the old days, all of a sudden they're making cracks. I
wouldn't even bother to tell you I'm not that kind of a Christian, Solly,
because you know it. But being a Christian, I naturally hear Chris-
tians talking, and putting two and two together, also that we ain't go-
ing over only in the biggest cities where there's lots of Jews to go for your
half of the routine, I figure maybe for the good of our reputation, we
ought to break up to a couple of singles till this Hitler-business blows
over. After that, we can double up again and get some new material,
and in no time we'll be right back where we was before. Y'know?"]

"What did you tell him?" Dan said.

"What did I tell him?" the man said. "I didn't tell him nothing.
I put on my hat and went out."

"You should've let him know what you thought of him."

"You work with a feller thirty years, you don't have to say what
you're thinking: he knows."

"I'd've made sure."

"A feller sells you down the river, it ain't no accident. A lowlife
is a lowlife, so what's the use talking?"

Dan took up the man's card. "It's going to be hard to find a job
for you, Mr. Bernstein," he said. "I'll try my best, but you insist
on something in the singing line, and you may as well know in advance that we get very few calls for entertainers of any kind."

"Did you put down I could sing at weddings?"

"Yes, I have that down," Dan said.

"I know all the Jewish songs, and I accompany myself with the
piana, and I got my own dress-suit. You got that down, about the
dress-suit?"

"That's down too, Mr. Bernstein."

"And the address—you got the address?"

"The address and the cigar-store phone-number."

"Well, I guess that's about all," the man said, and he rose and
went to the door. There he paused to punch his hat out and re-
crease it, and while he did so, he said, "You ever maybe get a application from a feller name Bailey? Joe Bailey?"

"Bailey?" Dan said. "Not that I recall."

"My partner," the man said, and now he looked at Dan. "Joe
Bailey. Bailey & Bernstein."

"Is he out of work now?"

"Since about a year after me," the man said. "If he ever comes in here, I wonder could I ask you a favor."

"Certainly," Dan said. "What is it?"

"Don't tell him I'm willing to sing at weddings."

SEA-SHELLS, SEA-SHELLS, BY THE SEA-SHORE

IT WAS Saturday evening of the Labor Day week-end, and in the slow-moving throng on the Asbury Park boardwalk were Dan and Mary. They halted, like many others, to watch a sand-sculptor below them on the beach, and like many others, they listened for a while to rug-auctioneers and concessionaires, and when they reached the martial orbit of a brass band, they went more erectly and corrected step, and like so many of the rest, they tried in vain to hit something with a ball, or ring something with a hoop, or break something with a popgun cork in order to win something like a stuffed dog, or a beribboned cane, or a glass pistol filled with pastilles, and as all did at one time or another, they heard above the music and the talk and the heel-pound the plunge of breakers and the surge of surf on the black strand.

"If we go out to the end of the pier," Mary said, "we can watch them cast."

They left the crowds and the lights behind them and walked planks over rising and falling water. At the end rail, a few men stood trolling: from time to time, they leaned backward, bowing their rods, and then they dropped forward to make and take up slack; when line began to come in wet through the agates, it was reeled in all the way and recast.

"Going out!" one of the men said, and he whipped his tackle overhead in a long arc at the night. The reel unwound and whined, and after a moment the sinker struck and sank, and the man resumed his trolling.

"Remember this time three years ago, Dan?"

"Yes," he said. "I remember."

"What do you remember about it?"

"That you had your way about the church."

"Is that all you remember?"

"No. There were other things."

"What other things, Dan?"

"The way you looked."

"Do you really remember that?"

"You didn't think I'd forget, did you?"

"I don't know. People forget things sometimes. Things like that."

"Sometimes."

"Did I look good that day?"

"The same as you always look. You don't change."

"You used to say I did. I used to be very plain one minute and very beautiful the next."

"You're not like that now. Whenever I look at you, I see the same thing."

"That's not very good, is it? To see the same thing all the time."

"It depends on what you see."

"Don't I ever get beautiful any more, Dan? Not even for that one minute a day?"

He turned to look at her before answering. "I think you're not very happy, either," he said. "Or else you'd know that you never get plain."

AND LIE DOWN TO PLEASANT DREAMS

THE room was still dark when Dan opened his eyes. How long he had slept—one hour, two hours, or merely minutes—he did not know, but he knew that he had come as wholly out of sleep as if sleep were a tunnel now behind him. Light from a street-lamp below passed through the basket-weave of the curtains and turned part of the ceiling into a gently-moving mesh. He lay watching it for many moments, and then, impelled by a sense of being watched himself, he said, "Do you always awaken when I do?"

"When I'm asleep, and you're not, I feel lonely. I don't know why, unless it's because sleep is like water, a lonely thing."

"A lonelier thing is people," he said.

"Are you lonely, Dan?"

"Like a last man on earth," he said. "This terrible quarrel, Mary —when're we going to end it?"

"But, Dan, we did end it—that night on the pier."

"Was that the end?"

"Oh, Danny," she said, and she turned her body to him and put her face near his. "What more did you think you had to say?"

"I didn't know," he said. "I didn't know."

"When we went home afterwards . . . ," she said, ". . . when we went home, and you . . . when you didn't do anything, Dan . . . I thought you didn't want. . . ."

And he turned to her, saying into her mouth, "Don't let's fight any more, Mary."

And she said, "Spain," and only later did he remember the word and understand.

HOW BEAUTIFUL ARE THY FEET WITH SHOES

THE waiter brought a second pot of coffee, and Dan filled Florencia's cup and his own, saying, "I'm glad I ran into you."

"I am train to be polite," Florencia said. "Therefore I will say thank you for the lunch. But I am train to be honest too. Therefore I will say this place is stinks. You will escuse me?"

"You're escused," Dan said. "This place is also cheaps."

"Americans do not cook. Murder, yes; cook, no."

"And the Spanish?"

Florencia removed her wedding-ring and spun it into a goldpiece on the marble table. "Genio makes wild when I do this," she said, and the coin curtsied and became a ring again. "I am sicken of the eSpanish. They cook well; they murder badly."

"Are you a Catholic, Flo? I never asked you."

"I am been born in the Church. I am not been living in it since many years."

"What made you give it up?"

"I do not say I have give it up. I say only that I do not live in it."

"Doesn't that come to the same thing?"

"Not often the people have give up the Church, but many times, all through history, the Church have give up the people."

"I always thought it never let go."

"As in eSpain?" the woman said. "Where the Church will follow you to the grave for one peseta of a mortgage? That is an act of the Church to give up the people, and if you have been read the books and the papers, you will know it is but one of the acts. Please do not disunderstand. The Catholic people love the Church—and with good reason, for it can be a beautiful thing, with much art in it, and much comfort, and much simple and human people who wish always for it to be a house of fine pride. But the Church do not love the people with the same equality. It will speak otherwise, it will say all are one in the sight of God, yet you will never find it at the shoulder of the poor and the weak, side by side, only with the rich and the strong. For them, it will fight always, and indeed its own self is rich and strong at the espenditure of the poor. A great sucking monster is the Catholic Church of eSpain, not the Jew that it forever try to blame for its wrongs. Never there was a Jew in all history of the world that take his pound of flesh like the Church of my country, and all the Jews now living own not so much land, nor ever were they so cruel to the people dwelling on that land in shameful hunger. The Jew you will find in the dark and dirty shop, yes. The Jew you will find with his crumbs and scraps, yes. But you will not find him in the big bank-houses, nor in the steamshipping companies, nor in the railroad lines. There you will find only the Church with its business and usury, for it is the Church, not the Jew, which is the money-changer of eSpain. That is an evil thing, to own the body of the people, but there are more evil things, and the most evil of all is to own the soul of the people for profit, and not only the soul of the old ones, but that of the little children, who are told from the beginning that they will burn forever if they do not learn to love misery. But is not the people that should love misery. Is the Church. Yet never in a thousand years have the Church speak its power for the poor, and that is why I say I do not live in it for a long time now. I confess these thinkings to the priest, and he tell me I am not good enough to pray. Not good enough, he say! What he mean is, not bad enough! The good do not pray in the Church of the rich and the strong and the cruel!"

Dan reached across the table and put his hand on the woman's arm, saying, "I love you, Flo. You're so very wonderful."

A voice said, "She isn't so wonderful to me."

Dan looked up. A man was standing in the aisle, and behind him, from a nearby table, a woman was angrily watching.

"Who the hell're you, mister?" Dan said.

"I couldn't help overhearing what was said, and I want you to know I resent it."

"Resent all you like, but get away from this table."

"I let no one run down my religion."

"What do you generally do about it?"

"What I'm doing now. I defend it."

"Do you ever do anything to make it better?"

"It's perfect as it is. All that you've been told is a lie."

Dan rose. "The poor never lie, and the rich never tell the truth," he said. "I think we ought to go outside, mister."

LAST HIRED, FIRST FIRED

"LAST NAME?"

"Pollardius."

"First name?"

"Julianum."

"You remind me of somebody," Dan said. "Haven't we met?"

"It's a small white world," Julie said.

"What're you doing in this part of it, black-face?"

"Black all over, Mr. Underdone."

"I thought you were a word-man. You don't really want a sweating-job, do you?"

"Don't want it, but I'm after it."

"You're not for Chrisake giving up writing, I hope."

"Who said? I'm going to do me a book about working-stiffs, so I got to *be* one."

"You had me worried," Dan said, and picking up the telephone, he said, "Put Pete on, will you, Liz?" and beyond the partition a bell rang. "Dan talking, Pete. You busy? I've got a special in here." He hung up, and after a moment, Peterson entered. "Pete, I want you to meet Julie Pollard, a particular friend of mine. Julie, the Boss."

"Glad to know you, Pollard," Peterson said.

"Same," Julie said.

Peterson sat down and studied Julie through the lighting of a cigarette. "What's his specialty?" he said to Dan.

"It used to be hating us buckras. Tell him what it is now, Julie."

"Same," Julie said, "plus looking for a job."

"Unique," Peterson said.

"He's a writer," Dan said. "He has a novel that's making the rounds. *Eight-ball*, it's called."

"We get a lot of calls for novelists," Peterson said. "Only they got to be able to dish-wash."

"Julie wants to get material for a new book," Dan said. "A book about the proletariat."

"Why don't he go back to Russia?" Peterson said.

"If all the people you're against went back to Russia," Dan said, "there wouldn't be anybody left to turn a wheel. It might be a good thing. We'd find out what runs Capitalism: money or man-hours."

"Even the capitalists know that," Peterson said. "Only they ain't letting on."

"I aim to write a letting-on book," Julie said.

"Everybody's a communist," Peterson said. "What's Capitalism coming to, anyway?"

"Ain't coming," Julie said. "It's going."

Peterson spilled ash and slapped his chest. "Do you devote much time to thoughts like that?" he said.

"All day," Julie said, "and I got some over for breakfast."

Peterson stood up, saying to Dan, "Find him a spot at hard labor. Maybe if he eats, he'll salute the flag."

Dan gave the salute of the Boy Pioneer. "One nation indivisible," he said, "with liberty and justice for all."

"Liberty and just us," Julie said.

At the door, Peterson said, "Sorry to met you, Pollard."

"Same," Julie said. "In spades."

Over his shoulder, Peterson said, "Try the New York Central freight-yards, and the hell with Roosevelt."

"Run along and pay your taxes like a good boy," Dan said.

"The hell with Roosevelt," Peterson said, and he left the room.

Dan took a folded card from a rack and began to fill in the blanks after the words DATE, TO, and INTRODUCING. He raised his head once to smile.

ON THE WAY HOME

LEAVING the hack-driver's flat, Dan and Mary walked across town toward the West Side. They went for some way in the cold and quiet dark before Dan said, "May I talk to you about something, Mary?"

"Always," she said, "and about anything."

"Even why I don't quit the job?"

"Yes, but I'd like the real reason for once."

"You don't think I've given you a reason?"

"Never the real one, Dan."

"How do you know that?"

"You still want to talk about it."

He put his arm through hers, saying, "I can't even deceive myself any more. I keep the job for one reason only: I'm afraid to give it up. I'm yellow, Mary, and knowing it is like having a bum heart —there's no walking away from it, no place to hide."

"I don't think you *want* to hide."

"I've hidden all my life."

"At any rate, long enough to make it seem that long."

He tried for half a block to evade her meaning, but there was no escape, nor did Mary intercede for him, and in the end he said, "*Part* of my life, then."

"Good," she said, "Now, do you want to tell me where the hiding began?"

"You seem to know," he said.

"I do: it began in jail."

"You're smart about me, Mary."

She tightened her arm, pressing his against her side. "Did you ever wonder how I spend the time we're not together?" she said. "I ride the subways and the Tubes for two hours a day, but I don't actually read the ads any more, and for another seven hours, I wait on women who want gloves, or imagine they want gloves, or want and imagine nothing because they have everything, but all I see of them is five fingers stuck up in the air. What do you think I do most of that time, Dan? I think about you. I make myself smart thinking about you, and I know so much that I know there must be more that you've never told me."

He slid his hand into her pocket, but not until he said, "There *is* more, Mary," was the hand embraced.

THERE WAS SMOKE IN THE ROOM

SKEINS and blue veins of it waved slowly, like submarine weed, and it hung over the furniture, books, and people in the Powell parlor: over Julie and Mary on the leather couch, over Dan sitting cross-legged on the floor, over Tootsie at a window, over his father and mother, and over worn volumes racked and stacked everywhere. It rose and fell too over a newspaper propped in the lamplight, a first page featuring a heavy headline and a profile of Il Duce superimposed on a map of the Somaliland frontier.

Tootsie moved to the table and stared down at the cock-feathered face. "Well, it begins," he said.

There was smoke in the room.

HOW TO START A REVOLUTION

"THIRTEEN dollars isn't so much," Mary said.

On the table between her and Dan lay a brochure listing the courses to be given during the coming semester at the World Labor School, an organization occupying a few rooms in a Greenwich Village loft. Around the subject *Political Economy*, a ring had been drawn with a pencil.

"When you have to figure close, it is," Dan said. "Maybe I'd get just as much out of a textbook."

"I doubt it. There's nothing like being in a class."

"That's true, I suppose. The others kind of keep you primed."

"Why don't you go down to the school after work tomorrow and sign up? For months now, Tootsie's been at you to join his Party, and you've been saying you didn't know enough to decide. Well, here's your chance to find out."

"Tell you what: I'll sign up if you do."

"And spend twenty-six when we're worried about thirteen?" Mary said. "You go by yourself, and when you come home from each lecture, you can tell me what you learned. For thirteen weeks, every Monday'll be Political Economy night."

*   *   *

Mary was still awake when Dan returned from the first session of the course. She patted a place for him alongside her on the bed, and he sat down and kissed her. "Well, teach me something," she said. "Something political, I mean."

"If I tell you all I know, what'll I have left?"

"Knowledge is the one thing you can give away and still have —or did your mother say that first? But no matter: it's true."

"I wish it was true about money," Dan said. "If money stretched like that, there'd be no class-struggle and no Diaterical Malectialism."

"And we'd still have our thirteen dollars," Mary said. "What's the teacher like?"

"He has a face," Dan said. "He goes by the name of Austin, Jeff Austin, but I'll gamble he doesn't answer to it in the daytime. About thirty, I'd judge, and kind of thinnish. A thinnish man with a face."

"What did he say with it?"

"First of all, he outlined the course: it'll be about Scientific Socialism, and that's Marxism, and Marxism is I only wish I knew."

"Didn't he tell you?"

"He said lots of people called themselves Marxists because they once read a book called *Capital*. But reading a book only proves you know how to spell, he said; it doesn't necessarily mean you know what you're spelling. So far, so good?"

"So far, so good," Mary said.

"I'm glad," Dan said, "because the rest is Greek, and literally. For instance, do you know what Dialectics is? Well, neither do I, so I'll explain it to you. The word comes from the Greek *dialektike*, which, if I misunderstand it correctly, translates into something like this. A couple of guys in togas would square off some place, only instead of trying for a fall with a hammer-lock, they'd clamp ideas on each other, the aim being to get at the truth by arguing till one of them showed himself up as a chump. I don't know what the winner won, but I know how he won it: by the dialectical method."

"What's Greek about that?"

"Every damn word of it," Dan said. "For a long time, those debating-matches were abstract, but the day came when people began to wonder what would happen if you used Dialectics to get at the truth about Nature. Up to then, Nature had been thought of as an act of God, a thing that nobody would ever be able to give a reason for or change, but the minute they got to work on it with Dialectics, they found that Nature was *all* change, whether you were dealing with a grain of sand or the sun—and right there, a slew of Dialectical Materialists got themselves a job with a future."

"When do you come to the Greek stuff?"

"You mean, you understand all that?"

"Of course," Mary said. "Don't you?"

"I have no idea what I'm talking about."

"When you're finished, I'll explain."

"Austin said Dialectics is the opposite of Metaphysics."

"You know what Metaphysics is, of course."

"I was afraid of that," Dan said. "I think it has to do with the supernatural, because whenever a metaphysical guy met a dialectical guy, they got into a terrible fracas about Nature. The metaphysical guy would say, 'You want to know something, bum? Nature is a trunkful of unrelated junk.' The dialectical guy would say, 'You're describing the contents of your head, feller. The only accident in Nature is the way you look at it.' The metaphyscial guy would say, 'And not only is Nature accidental, but it's a permanent accident. That's how it was, bum, and that's how it'll always stay.' The dialectical guy would say, 'It didn't stay that way even while you were talking about it. Somebody just died, and somebody was just born. Millions of people grew older, and an island sprang up from the sea. A star fell, a mortgage was foreclosed, and a cop shot a picket. Nothing stands still. Everything moves.' The metaphysical guy would say, 'Hush mah mouf, for not only is Nature accidental and unchangeable, but it repeats itself. It's like a child practicing penmanship. Over and over, he makes the same circles, the same curls of ink. Birth, death, decay, and then birth again—the same uniform pattern.' The dialectical guy would say. 'What you argue is that no matter how long we practice penmanship, we'll never be able to write, but I say that if we keep on making those curlicues, some day they'll be words—and it's the same with Nature. Pile up enough quantity, and you'll wake up to find that the quantity has changed its quality.' The metaphysical guy would say, 'And not only is Nature accidental, unchangeable, and repetitious, but it's harmonious. Whatever is, is right.' And the dialectical guy would say, 'Whatever is, is *fight*! All things in Nature have their positive and negative sides, their past and their future, their start and their end. They have their own life and death within themselves, and any harmony you see is the unity of those opposites in a constant struggle, as if Nature were fighting itself and being both winner and loser at the same time.'"

"It was worth the money," Mary said.

"One thing more, and you'll have all of Lecture I," Dan said. "Austin claims that Marxism is merely an extending of the dialectical method to the history of society. I don't know whether that can be done; I don't know whether you can treat people the same as you treat things. Austin says you can, and he says he's going to prove it. If he doesn't, thirteen of our material bucks are down the dialectical drain." He rose now. "To be continued next week in an exciting instalment."

[*On your way home from the school, crossing one of the streets above*

Washington Square, you had passed an apartment-building, stopped suddenly, and gone back to stand before the entrance, and there, with a remembrance of Emma James, you had summoned Julia as well, and then, glancing upward through the iron skeleton of the canopy, you had found only darkness in the windows of the fourth floor—and now in your own room you needed darkness too; you were still dressed, but you felt exposed.]

*   *   *

"Tonight I took some notes," Dan said, and he reached for a pad lying on the table next to the bed. "In Lecture II, we learned how to start a revolution."

"All that in only two hours?" Mary said.

"Yes, but it'll take a little longer to learn how to finish one. Now, pay attention, because I'm going to say this once, and once only: Marxism deals with the relations between human bodies in the class-struggle. That's it, and no questions are allowed."

"Is that what we got for our dollar?"

"By God, it's worth a dollar of anybody's money! Think it over. Smell it. Feel it. Try it on."

"Move back a little. You don't have to give me a lecture right up against my face."

"Mary, sweetheart," he said. "There's something I've wanted to tell you for a long time. I never had the proper words for it, though, and that's why I never spoke."

"Do you have them now, Danny?"

"Yes," he said. "Under Capitalism, there are two main classes."

"You dog, you!"

"The ruling-class and the working-class. The ruling-class, or bourgeoisie, or bushwa, as us kids used to say, owns all the factories, mines, land, banks, railroads, and utilities. The working-class or proletary-rat, owns an old fish-rod, a phonograph with a dented horn, a dinner-pail, and itself. In between these two classes are the farmers, knife-grinders, tap-dancers, candy-butchers, and employment-agents, but it's the top and bottom that make the class-sandwich: the filling is only something to bite through. Do you follow?"

"Wherever my little dog leads."

"The ruling-class rules, and the working-class works, but it's reasonable to ask why one gets all the meat and fur and the other only the entrails and bones. Under Capitalism, this fair and square division is arrived at according to their relation to the means of production: the machine. If you own that, no matter how you came by it, you rule; if you don't own it, no matter what you did to create it, you work. The capitalists want that state of affairs to go on forever; the socialists want to change it tomorrow. For the answer to the burning question, 'Will the Marxists arrive in time to save Emanuel Labor?' don't miss Instalment III next Monday night. Man, am I tired!"

[*You had walked the same street, this time by design, and this time there had been a lighted window where you sought it, and you had stared up at it for a long while before slowly moving on—and you had known even then, even as you went away, that not forever would you pause and pass by.*]

*　　*　　*

"Last name?"

"Peterson."

"First name?"

"Peterson."

"Peterson first and last, eh?" Dan said.

"And all the time," Peterson said.

"What's on your mind, if you have one?"

"How're you doing at that school for the underprivileged and feeble-minded?"

"Learning all the time. I'm studying how to overthrow you."

"That'll take more than thirteen lessons, kid."

"Tonight we find out how to make a bomb with baling-wire, a hammer-handle, two potatoes, and a cough-drop. You're all through, Pete."

"What did that hostile bloke want that just tore out of here?"

"Now, what the hell do you think he wanted—a match? He wanted a job."

"He looked as if he wanted *mine*."

"I told him yours was filled," Dan said. "I also told him what it was filled with—a four-letter word."

"You're a four-letter *man*, kid," Peterson said. "Hand over that bastard's application."

"What for?"

"He looked like a Red. He don't get any job out of this agency."

"You go four-letter yourself!" Dan said. "He came in here like all the rest, and he's going to get the same kind of shake. There's nothing against him on his application, but to four-letter you, I'd place him even if he was a terrorist. Now, what do you think of that?"

"I think you're a very faithful employee," Peterson said, and on his way to the door, he laughed.

"Pete," Dan said, "why do you take this stuff from me?"

"You have it bass-ackwards, kid," Peterson said. "*You* take. *You're* the one that's being four-lettered. I thought you knew that."

After the door had closed, Dan remained where he was, gazing at the blotter on his desk and the dead hebraics of writing in reverse, but thinking of the living and insistent words that Peterson had left on the wing. He rose now, seeking to suppress thought with action, but the words seemed to have lodged in his mind, and he knew of nothing that would dispossess them [*nothing? you thought*]—and at once he raised the edge of the blotter and groped for a file-card that he had placed there some time before: the card was headed by the name JAMES, MISS EMMA. He waited for a moment [*for what? you wondered*], and then, taking up the telephone, he gave a number to the operator.

*   *   *

That evening, Dan left school at the half-time bell and walked west through a straight-down rain that grew gold and silver rosettes in the gutters [*and the rain made you think of snow, and the snow made you think of Julia, and with Julia thought stopped as if your mind had run down and gone dead, and you were aware of no emotion, no movement, no intention, and no destination until you were before an open door in which a woman stood bordered by darkness and backed by light*].

Saying nothing, she made way for him, and when he had removed his dripping coat and draped it over a chair in the entry, she followed him into the room beyond [*rugs, furniture, draperies, books, pictures, bric-a-brac—objects bought and brought home, he thought, objects made for anybody and sold to somebody, objects of moderate value, little character, and no concern. You turned to the one other object not yet appraised*]. She was seated on the further of two facing couches set endwise to an imitation fireplace harboring imitation logs.

Putting a cigarette to her mouth, she gripped it with her teeth, as if it were the stem of a pipe, and smoke espaliered her face, half-shutting her eyes, to mingle with her hair and drift away. Now, as she shredded the damp stub over an ashtray, she said. "Tell me what you see that makes you stare."

" I knew someone once," he said, "not for long and not too well, but long enough and well enough to have made me look for her in every face I've ever seen since. I haven't found her, and I suppose I always knew I was bound to fail, but if I hadn't met you, I think I'd've gone on searching all my life. The search ends with you, and I stare not because I see what I saw so many years ago, but because I see what she couldn't've helped being today; I see a dream grown older. You'll not take that kindly, and there's no reason why you should: it isn't meant kindly. But it's the truth, for whatever the truth is worth to you, and I tell you, because I don't want you to wonder, that it's the only thing in the world that could've brought me here. You represent someone else—someone that I simply have to get rid of."

With a look that he was unable to interpret, the woman contemplated him until a smile, equally unfathomable, overran her face. "I suggest a series of cold showers," she said.

He went to the entry and put on his coat. "I'll try that all week," he said. " If it doesn't work, I'll be back next Monday night."

" I'd like you back before that," she said. "For some more talk, I mean."

" The last time I saw you, you intimated that I was hard of hearing. I think you have the same defect. Next Monday night, I said."

The woman came suddenly to her feet, but whatever she had been about to say was as suddenly rescinded, and when she spoke, her voice was so fully under control as to convey nothing more than the flat acquiescence of her words. "Next Monday night, then," she said.

* * *

When Dan reached home, Mary said, "Another five minutes, and I'd've been dreaming of drowning, but I'd've been too tired to save myself."

"I stopped for coffee with some of the class," he said. "Are you too sleepy for Lecture III?"

"I can't let you get ahead of me."

"Here goes, then. Tonight we took up the matter of production-relations. Every social system known to man has had a set of its own, but to understand the one that Capitalism has developed, first you have to know how Capitalism came into being. Now, do you want to hear the life-story of Capitalism, or do you want to go to sleep and be a dunce?"

"Blow smoke in my face. That'll keep me up."

"Man has lived under five main systems: primitive communal, slave, feudal, capitalist, and socialist. The primitive communal system flourished in the age of the stick, the stone, and the broken bone. People lived off the country, and in order to avoid being used for food themselves, they banded together to hunt, to build shelter, and to beat off hungry neighbors. There was no private ownership, except in some prize tomahawk or some special pair of leather drawers. There was no exploitation, and there were no classes."

A huffed puff of smoke opened Mary's eyes, and she said, "I was listening, Dan."

"It took seventy-nine million years to notice the difference," he said, "but things gradually changed. Here and there, instead of making another club, somebody turned up with a spear or a bow-and-arrow, and when somebody else got the hang of fire, people began to use metals and shape pottery. . . ."

"You know something, Dan?"

"I know everything."

"You're a nice boy."

From the hiding-place behind his face, he said, "That's a thing I *didn't* know."

"Blow smoke," she said. "Blow smoke."

"And then people learned how to tame animals, and then there were farmers and herdsmen instead of hunters, and there were tools instead of weapons, and now men began to keep for themselves what they'd wrought with their hands or wrung from Nature, and soon some of them had two of this and three of that and a dozen of something else—and trade was invented to dispose of the extras. But there were Republicans even then, and they sat up late, figuring how to give short weight, how to water milk and gravel corn, and it wasn't long before a few owned most of the corn, most of the cattle, and most of the earth, and having grown strong on the backs of the weak, now they gathered the weak into armies, and the armies captured people as once people had captured animals— and now there were slaves. . . ."

He raised his hand to touch his wife's face, but she smiled very faintly in her sleep, and he allowed the gesture to remain incomplete.

21 90 .306   *   *   *

The only illumination came from the mock fireplace, in which, among the logs, a small bulb burned behind a slowly revolving color-wheel; a shoal of tinted ovals swam the hollow cube of the room, a cruising dapple for plaster and portieres, for furniture and faces.

"The showers seem to have done no good," the woman said.

[*On your way home, you thought, you would memorize a few paragraphs of recommended reading, and when Mary asked you about Lecture IV, you would say. . . .*] "No good, no good at all."

"Long walks might help, or a hobby, or something in your food."

"Julia could be sitting behind you," he said. "She could be telling you what to say."

Lying against an arm of the couch, the woman arched herself a little, and the rounds of her body rounded out her garments. "You make love supernaturally," she said.

"She couldn't've told you to say that," he said, "because I'm not making love at all."

"What *are* you doing—preparing to offer me a cook?"

"It's getting late, and there's only one Monday night in a week."

"There are six other nights—or do you have six other ghosts that you're trying to lay?"

"That sounds more like her," he said, and rising from the opposite couch, he started for the door.

"Look," the woman said. "Look, Dan."

He turned. . . .

*   *   *

"You must've been out till all hours last night," Mary said. "I never even heard you come in."

"We stopped for coffee again, but this time we got into an argument. I think one of the guys is a Trotskyite."

"I don't know what a Trotskyite is, but he cost me Lecture IV."

"I'll tell you about it tonight, maybe."

"I don't want to miss anything. I have to keep up with you."

"That isn't very easy. Sometimes I can hardly keep up with myself."

*   *   *

Across a sector of the ceiling above the bed moved the endless pointillism painted by the color-wheel. [*Lecture V, you thought— a dollar's worth of Mary's money.* . . .]

"Why don't you say something, Dan?"

"Capitalist production has two distinguishing features: a) commodity production prevails; and b) just as the product is a commodity, so is the labor-power that produced it."

"Tell me how attractive I am."

"How attractive you are!" he said.

"You talked quite well in the other room."

"The other room is the talking-room, the room for great speeches. This is the doing-room—and the *un*doing room—where I prove to myself that I never meant a word I ever said."

"Did you have the same regrets last week?" the woman said.

"The same in kind, but not the same in degree. Tonight there's dirt on top of dirt."

"What made you come back, then?"

"Capitalist production has two distinguishing features."

The woman put her hand across the space between them and let it lie lightly against his body, and then she said, "Do you think you could carry any more dirt, Dan?"

He moved toward her, saying, "There's no limit."

The woman's hand became a hindrance. "You're going home now," she said. "Like a good little boy."

[*Like a good little boy, you went home.*]

*   *   *

"The lights," he said. "What do the lights mean?"

"They're fascinating, don't you think?"

"I can't understand them. I don't know what they're for, what they're supposed to do."

"They're not supposed to do anything. They're simply colored lights."

"I'm always trying to make a comparison. I'm always thinking, 'They're like . . . ,' but that's as far as I ever get, because they're like nothing. What kind of mind imagined them? What kind of mind enjoys them?"

"What kind of mind is so disturbed?" the woman said.

"I knew a girl once who paved her place with dolls, long-legged dolls. They were everywhere—squatting in the chairs, propped up along the walls, sprawled out on the bed—and no matter what you were doing, always a few of them seemed to be watching you, listening to you, passing judgment on you, but the one thing they never did was move, and therefore you could manage them. These lights, though, are all motion, and like so many other things, motion without life—tricks, novelties thought up to prevent thought."

"I like them. You'll find them every time you come here."

"That'll be once a week for a certain number of weeks."

"Oftener, if I wish, and longer," the woman said. "You can't keep your hands off me."

"On Monday nights," he said. "Only on Monday nights."

"When you reach home and go to bed, remember me just as I am now. Remember with your mind or your hands or your mouth or whatever else you remember with, and then tell yourself that the memory has to last you all week. I doubt it'll last you a day."

"If it doesn't, I'll try something in my food," he said. "Arsenic."

"I'll see you tomorrow evening. Be here around eight, Dan."

[*And that was Lecture VI, you thought.*]

* * *

Dan was about to enter the elevator when the operator said, "I'm sorry, sir, but Miss James is not at home."

"Drop the 'sir,'" Dan said. "Did she leave a message?"

"She said, 'If I have a caller, tell him he's six days late.'"

"Did she say when she'd be back?"

The man shook his head, saying, "That was all."

"I think I'll wait around for a while," Dan said. "Join me in a smoke?"

"It's against the rules."

"Everything's against the rules. God damn the rules!"

The man took a cigarette. "I didn't know you spoke my language," he said.

It was two hours before the woman returned. She said nothing to Dan until they reached the door of her apartment, and there she turned to him, saying, "Have you been waiting long, Dan?"

"A few minutes," he said.

She walked back to the shaft and rang the bell. "A few hours, you mean," she said.

"Win or lose, you'll be cheaper if you ask."

"Never be afraid of the truth," she said, and when the gate was opened, she faced the operator. "Dale, how long has Mr. Johnson been waiting for me?"

The man pressed a plunger and cleared the signal-box. "It's hard to say exactly, Miss James. Not more than a quarter of an hour."

"That'll be all, Dale," the woman said.

Dan stepped past her into the car. "Never be afraid of the truth," he said. "That's Lecture VII." On the way downstairs, he put his hand on the operator's arm. "Why did you do it?"

"You think that's the first time I've been asked a question like that? Christ, the things that go on!"

"But why did you do it for *me?*"

"I told you before: you speak my language."

Through a slow wet snowfall, Dan went westward across the Village to one of the uptown entrances of the Christopher Street subway-station. He descended a few steps, stopped, and almost at once ascended them again, and through the slow wet snowfall, he returned to the apartment-building. He neither looked at the operator nor spoke to him until the fourth-floor gate had been opened, and then he said, "The things that go on."

*　　*　　*

"What did you mean when you said, 'Lecture VII,' the other night?"

"I meant that capitalist production has two distinguishing features."

"And that's another thing. I want to know why you say it all the time."

"Put them together. I'm taking a course in Political Economy —*was* taking, that is. I was studying how to become the John Brown of the working-class, and I stumbled over an old erotic dream. The cause of the oppressed has been set back a century."

"You grow more interesting by the week."

"It was a thirteen-week course to start with, and eight weeks of it are gone. I advise you to make good use of the rest."

"We'll see each other after the course is over, Dan."

"We'll see each other tonight and five more times."

The woman let herself slide a little lower on the couch, and her skirt was drawn back to expose garters of flesh above the tops of her stockings. "*Fifty*-five," she said.

"I'm married."

She sat very still, staring up at him, and he stood very still, looking down at her, and then suddenly she tugged at her skirt and concealed her knees. "He's married from Tuesday to Sunday," she said. "On Monday, when he's supposed to be studying Marxism, he's practicing lechery. An easy-Marxist!"

"It's a good joke," he said. "I expect to laugh till I die."

"Sit down over there and tell me all about your wife. Is she more attractive than I am? Is she more intelligent?"

"You don't think I'm going to make any comparisons, do you?"

"Why not, Dan? What else've you been doing all along? Every time you come here, you make a comparison. Every time we go into the other room, you make a comparison. If you can do a thing, you can talk about it. This is the talking-room, remember? Well, talk. Don't be mealy-mouthed. . . ."

*   *   *

"'Tell him to attend Lecture IX,'" the elevator-operator said. "That's all there was to the message, and I hope you know what it means."

"Only too well," Dan said.

"Smoke one of mine this time?"

"Glad to—and the name is Dan."

"I was in the same pickle myself last year," the man said. "Only it was every night in the week, not just Monday."

"How'd you get out of it?"

"If I had an answer to that, I could make a million, but, hell, you can't even take shots for it."

"Try something in your food, she said—as if your brain were in your pants. The only thing I don't like about a mind is that you can think with it."

Within the car, a bell sounded, and the operator glanced at the box above the control-lever. "In your place, Dan, I'd go to Lecture IX," he said, and he began to slide the gate. "She'd hate it."

*   *   *

He left the subway-station and walked eastward through a side-street toward a loft-building several blocks distant. On the way, he passed under the framework of a canopy in front of an apartment-house, and the break in his stride, little more than a muscular twitch, was imperceptible. Recovering from it almost instantly, he continued thereafter, but steadily now, along the course he had chosen. With less than a block to go, he felt his will begin to give, and on what seemed to be momentum alone, he reached the threshold of his objective. His will gone and his momentum spent, he went no further, and for a brief time he stood before the lighted doorway, watching a few vaguely familiar faces approach and pass, and then, seized by a rising counter-desire, he turned abruptly and headed for the apartment-house.

He had come very close to attending Lecture X.

*   *   *

On his back near the edge of the bed, he lay with an arm overboard, as if the bed were a boat. Above him, across the plaster sky, swam a school of mechanical planets.

"Tell me what you're thinking, Dan," she said.

"Of guilt," he said. "A guilt so high, wide, thick, and everlasting that only a fifth dimension could bound it."

"That isn't a thought; it's a feeling."

"If so, it's the only decent one I've had in months."

"What about the feeling you have for me?"

"As a person, place, or thing?" he said. "But forgive that."

"There's nothing to forgive," she said. "I'm a place or thing, just as you say, but a place or thing that you chose yourself. I don't know what kind of place or thing you were used to, but it can't've been much, or you'd not be here. You like *this* place, Dan. You like *this* thing."

"What I have to find out, though, is why—and above all, why more than once? What did I hope to find here the second time, the fourth, the ninth?"

"The same thing you'll be looking for the fiftieth—me."

"All that remains is to discover what 'me' stands for, and I can put on my hat."

The woman fought the covers until they were crumpled against the footboard of the bed. "This is what 'me' stands for!" she said, and she moved her hands along her body, but when he tried to touch her himself, she spun away from the embrace, saying, "And now you can put on your hat!"

*   *   *

"The mile-high winter, I called it," he said, "but I meant much more by that than a season in Colorado. I meant the summit of the first great range of my life, and having reached it, I saw the further and far greater ranges as merely a flight of steps into a topless sky, but there were gaps in the stairs, and I overlooked them and fell.

I've been falling ever since: there was no top for me once, and now there's no bottom. Deep down in my mind, I always had the idea that I could stop the descent by making Julia let go, but I see now that *I* was holding *her*, and I know why: because as long as I kept the connection, I could dream my way back to where all things were still possible, to that first great range. It's time *I* let go."

"Do you think that'll rid you of her?"

"No," he said, "but it'll help to rid me of you."

"Not by next week, it won't."

*   *   *

Peterson said, "Where were you all morning, kid?"

"I overslept," Dan said. "There's only one more lecture left, and I was up late studying for it. Another week, Pete, and the jig'll be up for the capitalist system."

"What you mean is, it'll be up for you. Just before noon, your wife called from Newark to find out whether I knew where you were."

"I forgot to say that I didn't go home. I wanted to be ready for that last session, so I spent the night going over the material with somebody from the class."

"You look like you went over it on your hands and knees."

"I don't think I like you today, and I don't think I'm going to like you any better tomorrow."

"Yes, sir, you're a man that takes his studying seriously. I look at you every Tuesday morning, and I tell myself, 'Watch out, Pete. There's a revolutionary that puts his all into the movement.'"

"I'm not even sure that I liked you yesterday."

"Come off your shaky stilts, kid. You've got all the earmarks of a little pink cheat."

Dan rose, and rounding his desk to Peterson's chair, he stood glaring down at the man for a moment, and then, his anger wilting, he moved to a window that framed a gray winter day. "What're the earmarks, Pete?" he said. "What shows?"

"All but the woman's name."

"Does it show to everybody, or only to you?"

"It gets in people's way. They have to walk over it."

"Even Mary?"

"Mary more than anyone else."

"I feel as if I'd killed myself by mistake."

"Tell her that. It's a good thing to say."

*   *   *

"The fight has never been against you," he said. "From start to finish, it's been against me, but in trying to injure myself, I've injured you—with what I've done, with what I've said, and with what I've thought. The words can't be taken back now, the thoughts can't be unthought, and the deeds can't be undone, but all the same I'd like to go away without your hatred, as you remain without mine."

"Take another course and come back next Monday."

He shook his head, saying, "I'm afraid you still don't understand."

*   *   *

Mary was asleep when Dan entered the flat, but she was awakened by the kiss he bowed down to leave on her hand.

"Hello, Danny," she said. "What time is it?"

"Too late to matter much," he said, and lighting a lamp near the window, he watched the curtains infold the wind. "I have something to tell you."

"Sit next to me while you tell it."

"I can't do that, Mary," he said, and after a moment he turned to her.

LET'S SWIM TO SPAIN

ABOVE the elevated tracks, the air seemed to simmer in the sun, making the buildings beyond waver as if submerged, and on the checkerboard of light and shade below, people were perpetual moves. It was Saturday afternoon, and the saturday-stillness of the office was broken only once, by a phone-ring that went unanswered and soon ended; the occasional trains that passed the window had become part of the daily sound-pattern, now hardly heard unless attended. The last to leave the rooms of the agency, Dan went downstairs and paused in the entrance to witness the summer-day throng, some of it drifting past and some stock-still before the gritty trash of shop-displays. The passageway exhaled the bad breath of age, and Dan moved on. A few blocks uptown, he entered a side-street of toothless brownstones, many of them bars now. 24 91.295

"A light one," he said, and his gaze wandered upward to a fading film-memory of the turf: THE PORTER, J. BUTWELL UP, BEATING DR. CLARK IN THE HAVRE DE GRACE.

The bartender cut suds into a brass drain. "If I had the day off," he said, "I'd be at the Polo Grounds."

"Too hot," Dan said.

"Too hot, you sit in back of first-base."

"Too hot even in the shade."

"Me, I don't sweat. The hottest days, I'm dry as a bone."

A man along the bar said, "That's supposed to be a bad thing."

The bartender ragged off the mahogany in front of Dan. "Listen to people, and you can go crazy," he said.

"I'm telling you for your own good," the other customer said. "You don't sweat, it means you're overworking your kidneys."

"Everybody's a doctor," the bartender said.

Dan tilted his head for a mouthful of beer and read: CLEOPATRA, L. MCATEE UP, TAKING THE COACHING CLUB AMERICAN OAKS. He put the glass down empty, but it bled moisture. He turned it. He turned it again. He continued to turn it.

"Another?" the bartender said.

"Too hot," Dan said, and he dropped a quarter on the drain.

* * *

He walked up Sixth Avenue to Central Park, and there he followed the bank of a pond to a cove sheltered by rises of black rock. Sitting with his back against a tree, he stared at sluggish water-borne dust, twigs, and peanut-shells until a galleon made of a cigar-box and a propped-up rag sailed into view.

A boy was guiding its progress with a stick, and absorbed in problems of navigation and command, he was speaking to the officers and crew of his mind. "I am going to discover the Unite Estates, and if anybody mutinies on board of this boat, I will throw him to the sharks!" A fancied mutineer mutinied, and the boy, with his hands on his hips and a scowl on his face, said, "Nobody can talk like that to Amiral Clumbus! Throw that sailor to the sharks!" The mutiny was quelled, and the ship sailed on.

*   *   *

Dredging a key from cards, other keys, and change, Dan opened the door of the flat and then suddenly stood very still: from the kitchen came the knock of crockery on crockery.

"Mary!" he said, and now he ran, saying, "Mary-baby!"

But it was Florencia Homer, and she smiled as she said,"You are very flatteringly."

He kissed her on both cheeks and the mouth."When I heard sounds in here, I thought . . . ," he said. "I thought. . . . Anyway, it's been a long time since there were any sounds in here."

"It is also a long time since is any soap in here."

"I'm a bum housekeeper, Flo."

"Genio too is indifferent to soap. All men are a great failure of housekeeping."

"What're you doing in town, Spanish?"

"As you see, I am wash up your dirt."

"With soap?" he said. "It'll take a lot more than soap."

"Conceivably," she said. "You are quite dirty, Daniel."

"I know it," he said, and he stooped for a dust-mouse under the sink."Do you think I don't know it?"

"I think you know it," she said. "I think most of men know it. But is a great pity you know it only after you acquire the dirtiness. People should not have to esperience dirt to know what is dirty."

"Sometimes I wish people didn't have to be people."

"People always have to be people, but they do not have to be dirty people. I know what I am talking, Daniel."

He glanced at her, saying, "Genio too?"

"What is Genio? Genio also is a people."

"I'd never've thought it of him," he said."But then, I guess he'd never've thought it of me."

"Yes, but would you thought it of yourself?"

"Tell me something, Flo. What did you do when you found out about Genio?"

"What was to do?" she said."Kill him, like in the films? Would that kill the dirty esperience too?"

"Don't say you let him get away with it."

"He do the dirty thing, and then is no more talk of get away or not get away. Is done. I cry, I scold, I walk out on the house—what good it is? The dirty esperience remain."

"You didn't leave him, then?"

"For a short time, yes."

"Where did you go?"

"Escuse me, but I go to the bathroom. When I am unhappy, is a necessity."

Dan smiled at her, saying, "Spanish, you're fascinating."

"And your wife? What your wife is?"

He went to the window and spoke back through a cape of curtains."How is she, Flo?" he said.

"She lives."

"Is she feeling all right? I mean, how does she feel?"

"If you desire to know, why you not go in Nev Jersey?"

"She doesn't want to see me."

"How you learn that—by sit here in your dirt?" the woman said, and she joined him at the window."Yesterday I tell her I am shopping in Nev York today. I say, 'Maria, do you wish anything of Nev York? I am shopping.' She say, 'If you see Daniel, deliver him please a message.' I say, 'Daniel is not in the shop where I am shopping.' She say, 'Yes, but it may be that you will see him in a different place, and there is something that I would speak him with.' I say, 'What is the message? If it is the one I have insisted, then it is possibly that I will see him in this place or that.' But when she tell me the message, I know not if it is good or bad. Thus I deliver it, and you will be the judge. She say, 'Ask him if he still wish to swim to España.'"

He turned to look at her, but she seemed to be under water and wavering, and he tried his best to speak.

* * *

They showed their permit to the sentry and walked up a graveled road for a way, Dan carrying a wicker creel and Mary a rod-case, and where a footpath forked to the right among holly trees and beach-plum, they descended to the ocean-front of the Hook. It was floodtide, and a countercurrent so slanted the breaker-line that it came quartering toward the sand, like quilt after quilt being drawn up over a bed. In the deep water beyond the surf, a carvel-built power-dory slapped along like a slipper, heading for nets that were no more than a clump of reeds in the distance.

"Out for the afternoon catch," Mary said. "From Seabright."

Dan sat on the sun-warmed sand while Mary set up the rod, a spring-butt split-bamboo, and when she had the reel and the rig arranged, she baited a barb with a long strip of squid.

"Well, I'm ready," she said.

She stepped out of her sneakers and dropped her skirt, and in a blouse and swimming-trunks, she crossed the beach and waded thigh-deep into the churning water. Balancing the rod, she held off for a wave to fall short of cresting, and with a slick to put the tackle at, she flung it hard on a long diagonal, took up slack, and began to troll. She played a semicircle for almost an hour without a strike, and finally, snapping her bait loose in a line-jam, she returned to the sand.

"Sit for a while," Dan said.

"Mullet's breaking all over out there," she said. "Something big is running them, and it won't take squid. If I had half a dozen killies, we'd have a striper for supper."

"Want me to go back for some?"

"It's too far," she said. "And besides, I'd like you to be around if I luck anything."

"Why?" he said.

"I missed you, Danny."

"Likewise."

"I shouldn't've gone away."

"You never went away," he said. "Just because you packed a bag?"

She said, "Why did you do it, Dan?" and then she said. "You don't have to answer that. I had to ask, but you don't have to answer."

"I don't mind," he said. "I did it because of all the sons-of-bitches on earth, I'm king."

"That's what *I* thought at the time."

He watched a shoal of mullet flash up the water like thrown coins. "What do you think now?" he said.

"What I should've thought in the first place: that what you did is done, and that it isn't enough."

"I didn't mean to make you admit that."

"You didn't make me. I said it because it's true, and I only wish I'd been able to say it right away. Then I'd've been honest, like Flo was when she found out about Gene, but I couldn't help myself, and I had to run away. I'm sorry, because running away cost us so much time that we could've spent together."

"But, Jesus Christ!" he said. "Aren't you going to make me say how sorry *I* am? Don't *I* have to crawl? Peterson guessed, and he called me a little pink cheat, but how do *you* punish me? By apologizing! My God, I'd feel better if I had to beg, if you made me eat dirt!"

"I'm not concerned with how you feel, Dan, and you have no right to expect me to be. I don't want any explanations from you, because I don't think you could explain anything so that I'd understand. And I don't want you to beg, because begging won't get you more than you can have for the asking: I'll even sleep with you whenever you find me desirable enough. But don't ask me to forgive you, Dan, because I never will."

"I thought of a lot of things on the train this morning," he said, "but I can only remember one of them now, and I'm not going to say it, because I know you won't believe it. All the same, it's a true thing, and maybe some day when you like me again, you won't laugh in my face when I tell you what it is."

"I never stopped liking you, Dan," she said. "Like—what a lukewarm word! I never stopped loving you."

"That's the thing I was going to say to you."

PART SIX

WAR IS A SPORT

IN RAYMOND POWELL'S parlor, Julie Pollard was saying, "President Frankie Delano say no more Ethiopia, folks, and mighty few Ethiopians, so I'm lifting them sanctions what I put on Italy, and you can go ahead and sell Mussolini more bombs and crap to dump on some other country. Sanctions! Now, what the jesusbechrist was sanctions but talky-talk? Wasn't no sanctions would've sanctionized them wop bastards, only buckshot-sanctions in the entrals. Instead, us niggers give out clouds of talky-talk, Tootsie-talk, and when the clouds blew away, we were off the map. Too bad. Wonder where we went, God damn it!"

"Mr. Wildfire," Tootsie said, "I got a thing I want to say at you."

"Let me say this first," his father said. "Working through the League was a correct tactic. We had a right to assume that the Articles of the Covenant meant what they said, and that if they were ever invoked, they'd be enforced. We put the League to the test, and it failed, and Ethiopia was thrown to the dogs, but that doesn't mean we were wrong. The entire world knows now that Ethiopia was double-crossed by every nation on earth except the Soviet Union. That was a gain for the Soviet Union and a gain for us."

"Fat lot of good that does Ethiopia," Julie said. "It got screwed all over Switzerland, and finally it got screwed right out of the globe —and what do we do about it? We pick wax out of our ear and say, 'Gained something that time, man.' What do the Ethiopians care about we gained something? They're dead!"

411

"I want to say a say," Tootsie said.

"Say it, Mr. Sanctions," Julie said.

"It isn't what you expect, because it's this: for once, Julie, I agree with *you*."

Julie grinned. "Ole Mr. Browder going to be mad on you, Communist college-boy."

"Talky-talk was all we were good for," Tootsie said, "and while we were at it, black people were being killed. It's never wrong to do something about that."

"Like what?" his father said.

"Like being on the killing-end ourselves."

"Where, son—in Ethiopia?"

"Where else? That's where the killing was going on. All we had to do was go there and line up on the right side. We might've gotten killed for doing it, but at least we'd've been *doing*."

His father said, "Without the organized help of other countries, Ethiopia was bound to lose. All over the world, people were expecting a miracle—expecting good to win with spears over evil with planes—but they know better now, and if Ethiopia was the price of that knowledge, humanity got a bargain."

"You get no bargains when you trade with Fascism. You get what Julie just said: screwed."

"Tootsie, I'd like to ask you a question," Dan said. "Why didn't you go and fight for your people?"

"I wasn't brave enough, Danny."

Dan glanced at Mary, and then, looking down at his shoes, he said. "That was the question."

"You have another, though, haven't you? What would I do if I got another chance?"

"All right, what *would* you do?"

"I'll be damned if I know."

"That's a good answer," Dan said.

Later, when he and Mary had left the house, he said, "It was a good answer because it was a brave answer. He doesn't care what people think of him between now and the next time. What counts is what he does then, not what they think now—and I believe he *will* do something, because it takes bravery to let people wonder whether you'll keep on being yellow. I envy him."

"What for?" Mary said. "How is he any different from you?"

A PAIR OF ANNIE OAKLEYS

PETERSON entered Dan's office, and seating himself on the spare chair, he cocked his feet against the desk. "You smell like you're thinking," he said.

Dan studied a water-stain on the ceiling, trying, as he had often tried before, to wrest a simile for its shape from his mind, and, as always, he failed. "What's it *to* you, Pete?" he said.

"Semiannual check-up, good labor-relations—and all that sort of shite."

"Well, quit being a shitepoke. Butt out."

"What're you all dolled up for? Who's the occasion?"

"Go back to your cash-register. I've got work to do."

"Don't be a slage-wave. Down tools and turn the rascals out."

"What the hell's the matter with you, Pete?"

"Nothing that a good counter-revolution won't cure."

"You ride me like something's eating on you. I think *I* eat on you."

"Damn right, you eat on me."

"That's eating *off* you," Dan said, "but I eat *on* you too."

"I pity you," Peterson said. "That's what's eating on me. It hurts me to pass a guy lying in the gutter. I always try to get him to move into an alley."

"I eat on you because, no matter what a louse I am, you wish you were only twice as lousy instead of being a louse squared."

"To get as low as you, kid, I'd have to climb down to the bottom, hold my nose, and then really sink. From where you are, there's only one direction: up."

"Then how come I'm sitting on your face?" Dan said. "You know, I never realized it before, but you're the only guy in the world I'm superior to."

"As superior as a fart in a gale of wind. If you took your talents and laid them end to end, they wouldn't reach halfway to where talent starts from. You're not even the man in the street. You're the man in the subway, and all that distinguishes you from the rest of the strap-hangers is a wish that you were one flight up. But that's all you're good for—a wish."

Dan contemplated him for a moment, and then he said, "That's right, Pete. Now tell me what distinguishes you."

Before replying, the man watched an elevated-train run past the window. "I'd say I wanted to be the man in the el," he said, "but I know you wouldn't believe it, kid."

"I'm sorry, Pete. I shouldn't've said. . . ."

"Forget it, kid," the man said, and on his way to the door, he dropped a small envelope on Dan's desk. "Feller give me those this morning," he said. "Being you've got your other suit on, you can treat your wife to something more than supper."

DINNER WITH MARCO POLO

"So you're Mary," Uncle Web said. "I've been wanting to meet you for some twenty-seven years."

"Twenty-seven?" Dan said. "Why twenty-seven?"

"Ever since I found out you were a man."

Dan gave Mary a glance, saying, "That's something I'm still not too sure of myself."

"You're a man," Mary said. "Who should know that better than some of us women?"

"I knew him when the issue was still in doubt," Uncle Web said. "As soon as it was settled, I began to wonder what he'd do with his manhood."

Dan indicated Mary. "Do you approve?" he said.

"Well, I'll say this: as long as you had to choose, I approve the choice—but I don't approve marriage."

"It was the only way I could get her, unc. She'd stand for only a certain amount of sin, and then she drew the line. What could I do?"

"The same as I do—start to sin somewhere else."

"I thought of that, but at that particular time, I didn't want to. I wanted to sin with Mary."

"Then what did you marry her for, you jass-ack? That made it legal, and there was no more sin."

"Now, there's something I *didn't* think of."

"Uncle Web," Mary said, "I think you're a bad influence on my husband. I think you've always been. But he's crazy about you, and I'm crazy about him, so I guess I'm stuck with you both."

"More coffee, folks?" a waiter said.

"Nobody ever gets stuck with me for long," Uncle Web said. "I don't marry people for the same reason I don't marry places. But tell me, Danny. If you had to get tied down, why didn't you pick a pretty one?"

"Don't you think she's pretty?" Dan said. "She's pretty to *me*."

"If you want to see a pretty one, take a look at this." The man drew out a wallet and flipped it open. "That's what *I* call pretty."

"Hand it over, Danny," Mary said.

"Nothing doing. This is between us men."

"Madrid," Uncle Web said.

"A spic?" Dan said. "My sister-in-law's a spic."

"I recommend the spics," Uncle Web said.

Mary took the wallet from Dan. "She *is* pretty," she said. "So much so, I wonder how you could leave her."

"I'll go back some time—when I don't have to make love on a battlefield."

"What the hell is really going on over there?" Dan said.

"I'll tell you what I tell everybody else: sapheads are fighting sapheads. Same old set-up."

"Florencia says it's different this time," Mary said.

"I don't know any Florencia," Uncle Web said, "but saps are fighting saps, and when they get through, there'll be dead saps and live saps."

"You don't talk the way you used to, unc," Dan said. "You never used to say all people were saps."

"Knock around the world for fifty years, and you'll say it too."

"I remember the letters you were always sending me. I still have some of them, and as much as anything else I know of, they were what started me off liking people. Now they're saps. What made you change? You were once a socialist."

"I'm still a socialist, and if people weren't saps, they'd all be socialists too."

"Maybe they will be," Dan said. "Maybe it's just taking them longer to get there than it took you. That doesn't make saps out of them, though."

"Put a dog in uniform, and he goes to a circus; put the same on a man, and he goes to war. Rockefeller couldn't fool a dog into burying bones, but, by Christ, let him lift a finger, and a man'll bury his own."

"I don't know about the rest of the spics," Dan said, "but if they're anything like Florencia. . . ."

"Who the hell is Florencia?" Uncle Web said.

"My brother's wife," Mary said. "She came to America on the combined lifetime savings of her family—four sisters, three brothers, and a father and mother. Some of them are gone now, but the rest are still living where she left them, in a village near Granada. Farmers, they call themselves, but the word that was coined for them is serfs. To this day, only one brother knows how to write, and he'd've been illiterate too if it hadn't been for a decent parish priest. There are no schools in that village, and no doctors, and no sewers, but there are plenty of Civil Guards with pistols and patent-leather hats, and there's a fine church with gold-embroidered altar-cloths and gold-and-silver images of the Crucifixion. The old priest is dead, and the new one gives writing-lessons limited to a single letter, a mark, and he teaches the people where to put it by telling them they'll go to hell if they vote Republican. But they've been living in hell for a thousand years, and they aren't frightened, and when the rich come out of the cities trying to buy votes with mattresses, the people take the mattresses and vote Republican anyway. They're ignorant, Uncle Web, but I don't think they're saps."

"They're saps with mattresses," the man said.

WE'LL BE COMRADES YET

IN the early evening, Dan and Mary sat before the open window watching it inhale their exhaled smoke. The day had been a warm one under a hovering haze, but now in the last light there was an advance freshness from a coming rain.

"What did Mig have to say?" Mary said.

"Mig?" Dan said.

"In his letter."

"I haven't had a letter from Mig in months."

"Oh, I'm sorry," Mary said. "I put it on the chiffonier, and I thought you read it while I was making supper."

When Dan opened the envelope, he said, "Christ, but this was a long time coming. All summer, it took. He wrote it on the 1st of June."

"Maybe he didn't send it right off," Mary said. "Read it to me."

I'm not going to try and weasel out of being called a bum correspondent, because I consider that a known fact by now, and there's no use in me even promising to reform, because no good will ever come of it. But that don't mean I never think of you, kid, because I do, and often, and I think of your signora too, even if all I know about her is what you tell me and what I can gather from her photo. . . .

Mary said, "I didn't know you sent him my picture."

"One of the ones we took on the beach a couple of summers ago."

"Why didn't you tell me, Danny?"

"It was the shot you wanted me to tear up, but I liked it best, and when I was writing to him once, I happened to have it in my pocket. . . ."

"Happened? You mean, it got there accidentally?"

"What difference does it make how it got there?"

"Danny carrying pictures," she said. "You know, I'm beginning to fall in love with you."

And now, kids, prepare for a shock. Come September, Mikhail DeLuca, the Casanova of Avenue A, will stagger glassy-eyed into a bureau called ZAKS, and there he will fill out a little form, and then an official will pronounce us man and wife (meaning me and Irina, who will naturally be hanging around), and then the official will smile and wish us happiness—which I hope you kids do too. . . .

Dan turned to Mary, saying, "Well, what do you know about that?"

"You've been married," Mary said. "What do *you* know?"

She's what they call an agronomist, her special field being grape-culture (trust Mig to have a nose for the vino), and right now she's down in the Crimea. The minute she gets back, either her room or mine is going to be available. No more of this waiting. Even Stalin would admit that marriage isn't part of the Five Year Plan. Before Irina left, I tried to tell her a married woman could grow grapes just as scientifically as a single one, but she wanted one more season of experimenting (with grapes, of course, you bum) before getting hitched, and I gave in. How did I meet her? Well, how do you meet anybody? By accident—a non-Marxist attitude, by the way. She came to see the editor of the magazine with a story she'd written about the grape-country, and by mistake she walked into the composing-room. Kids, she never recovered from that blunder. The minute I saw her, she was as good as published and practically married. I'd've set that story up even if I had to leave out a Plenum Report. But it turned out to be a good story—and that's *my* story. . . .

Mary said, "I hope he sends her picture."

"So Mig's getting married," Dan said. "Mig, the wonderful wonderful wop. Getting married."

"Why do you sound so surprised?"

"Not surprised, exactly. It's just that I never thought of ordinary things in connection with Mig."

"Marriage *is* ordinary, isn't it?"

"I mean, he was always so wrapped up in working for the people that I didn't think he had time for anything else."

"People that work for the people are people themselves—or didn't you know that?"

"About Mig, I guess I didn't."

"You're a funny boy, Danny. You care for people just as much as Mig does, but whenever somebody tells you that all those things down in the street are people, you're astounded."

Danny, when I said before that I think about you often, I meant it. We haven't seen each other for a hell of a long time now, but as far as I'm concerned, that doesn't seem to make any change in our friendship—and the reason is, the friends you get when you're young are the ones that mean the most. And even if it was years before we got together again, I'm sure it'll always be like it was in the old days—and maybe better, Mr. Lovejoy, and you know why. I want to say, kid, that the best news I've had in many a moon was the news about you deciding to go to school. You couldn't've done anything to make me happier, and I only wish I was there to take the classes with you. They'll be over when you get this letter, so I want you to do me a favor: I want you to sit down and write me what you got out of the course. Keep up the good work, kid. We'll be comrades yet. . . .

Dan folded the letter and returned it to its envelope, and then he sat looking at the dumb-show in lighted windows across the way.

"What was she like, Dan?" Mary said. "Was she so very much prettier than I am? That's all I want to know, and it's all I'll ever ask."

"Talk is thin-ice stuff," he said. "Only actions are supposed to carry weight. I don't know where that idea came from, because actions can be far falser than words. Sometimes you can do an act that has no meaning at all, and sometimes you can say a few words that contain your life. . . ."

"Go on," Mary said.

"I forgot the point I was making."

"A few words with a great deal of meaning."

"They're gone. I lost track."

"A few words like, 'I love you,' maybe?"

"How did you know?" he said.

"What a lover!" she said. "He starts out to make a love-speech, and he winds up with his feet in his hat. Lover Dan!" He rose now and walked deeper into the dark room, but she followed and stood against him when he could retreat no further. "I'll make a speech, Dan, if you'll lend me those few words that slipped your mind. I'm *for* you, and I've been that way from the beginning. You're the guy, that's all, and you'll always be the guy. You don't like yourself very much, and it's a puzzle to you why that should be one of the things I prize in you—but I prize everything in you, the good things, the rotten things, the likeable things, the hateful things, and that's a puzzle to you too. You think you can take people apart and value their good and condemn their evil, but that's treating people as if they weren't people at all, as if they were only handfuls of small change to be separated into copper, nickel, and silver. People come in one piece, and either you take it altogether, or you refuse it altogether. If you refuse it hard enough, you hate it, and if you take it hard enough, you love it. I happen to take you hard, Dan."

"Did you really think the words had slipped my mind?" he said. "They won't get away from me even when I'm dead."

A BELLYFUL

DAN's mother said, "I suppose you're wondering why I called you aside."

"Wait," Dan said, and he listened to voices coming through the transom from the parlor.

["Mary, you're damn near as cute as my old lady."]

["You ought to teach your son some of that."]

"No," Dan said. "I'm not wondering."

"It's the same story: things are bad."

"I saw the cab downstairs when we came in. If it ran over a banana, the jolt would wreck it."

"I try to talk Pop into selling it for junk and going to work with one of the fleets, but he won't hear of it. With a private cab, he can still call himself his own boss. But what's the good, if you can't make a living?"

"Ah, let him enjoy himself," Dan said. "I remember you were after me about something once when I was a kid, and Pop came to my rescue, saying, 'Let him alone, Polly. Let him alone.' Well, let's let *him* alone."

["I'm kind of glad we're private a minute, Mary, because there's something been on my mind for a long time now. It's personal, though, and I'll keep it to myself if you say so."]

["We've always been personal, you and I."]

["Here it is, then. You been married long enough to have a big belly, if you know what I mean."]

["I know what you mean, Dad."]

"Dapper Dan," Dan said. "Delicate Dan."

"I let him alone," his mother said, "but it troubles me that he's being independent at your expense."

"It's one of my cheap pleasures."

["If you know what I mean, why don't you do something about it?"]

["A woman just can't go and get a big belly all by herself."]

["By *herself!* You're making small of my son!"]

["I mean, a woman ought to have her husband's permission to get a big belly."]

["Listen. My old lady wouldn't ask my permission to kill me. She'd tell me to mind my own business."]

Mrs. Johnson smiled, saying, "I recall when you had the makings of a tightwad."

"I'll never be rich," Dan said. "It *costs* too much."

"If you know that, you've gone a long way on nothing."

"I haven't gone anywhere. I've only been shamed into being halfway decent."

"That's easily a million miles."

["We can't hardly feed ourselves, but I'll bet if that old girl wanted another kid, she'd get herself a big belly without saying, 'Boo.' You ought to do the same. What do you care if my stinker son hollers? The hell with him."]

["Some day, maybe."]

["I'd sure to God like to be a grandfather without getting me a second child to turn the trick."]

"I brought along what we had, Mom. Slip this in his britches tonight when he's dreaming about God hailing him in front of the Ritz and saying, 'Heaven, bo. Main gate.'"

["Remember, now. You don't even have to say, 'Boo.'"]

Dan went into the parlor, and taking Mary by the hand, he said, "It's about time we waddled off, big-belly."

VIVA LA REPUBLICA

LEAVING the main highway between Red Bank and Little Silver, Dan and Mary walked along a dirt side-road toward a small golden square showing through the fall evening. A shower had come and gone at sunset, and damp leaves had been left for the stars to nickel-plate, and birds sang late among wet reeds in the ditches. Light from a dooryard window fell on two figures in white, one swinging gently and the other standing motionless against an elm.

"Genio," Dan said.

"Dan," Gene said.

Stopping in the line of swing, Dan caught the ropes as Flora floated up to him, and he kissed her and said, "Spanish," and then he let her float away. He sat next to Mary on a bench under the elm. "Is like a night in Granada, is not?"

"I want to see one of those nights some time," Gene said. "I have to find out what a night in Red Bank lacks."

"Genio," Dan said, "you do not spik like you have eSpain in your blood—only Nev Jersey."

"Nev Jersey was all right till you queered it with all this kissing-stuff. To hold my own, I have to act like a newlywed, and some mornings I go up with the shade."

"Such talkings. You are shockingly."

For a while, then, no one spoke. There was the speech of straining ropes, and there was a barking dog in the dark distance, and now and then a meadow-lark slit the night with a run on a flute, but no one spoke until Gene said, "Who's kidding who around here? For Christ's sake, let's talk about it!"

His wife put her hands on her face and began to cry. The swing swung in shorter and shorter arcs and hung still, and the patch of white that was Flora seemed to be sitting on air.

Gene stall-walked, saying, "It don't do any good to cry and cry. If there's anything on our chest, then, God damn it, we ought to open our shirt!"

"What is to say?" his wife said. "What is to say?"

"Anything!" Gene said. "Even if it's only a curse on that popish pansy bastard of a Franco!"

"Cursing is not change the Badajoz thing of the bull-ring," Florencia said, "no, and not prayer, because is no espression of the mouth that will espress the cruelness of killing four thousand peoples, eSpanish peoples, for the crime of nothing—*nothing*! They wish a form of governament, and they vote for that form of governament, and they win the vote, and for this nothing is come Franco with Moros and shoot like dogs. Is no espression for this, not even in the tongue of a peoples that have much suffering in history. The eSpanish peoples are poor like the poorest in all the time of the world—work and die, work and die, that is España—and they go like that for a hundreds of years, but they cannot go forever, and so they stand up once and chase away this sick and unspeakable disgrace on the country, this Alfonso with his dirty blood, and they make the Republica, and after so long of misery, they are a little happy. But is more of sickness that is not chase away. Is the sickness of the rich and the landlords, and is the sickness also of the bad peoples of the Church, but these sick things the Republica tolerate to remain, because the governament is not a Red governament, as so many falsely say. A Red governament would not have chase away Alfonso; it would have shoot him to death. It would not have leave the rich bishops and the rich to remain and work against itself; it would have espose them and put the hand on their riches. I am a Catholic, and I will always be a Catholic, yet I say is wrong, is a sin, for my Church to be in the business, and is wrong for my Church to be fat and rich, for the best Church will be the most poorest, the one that will take in much and espend more, and it will not have gold possessions while is hungry children give money for candles. But these sickness remain in the Republica, and soon the bad ones bring the Moros, and you have the affair of the bull-ring in the name of God and Jesus Christ, and now is clear for always that not only the bulls have been bred to die in the dust, but the peoples of the country much more, and now is clear that all eSpanish life has been one great bull-fight always. The matadors are everywhere, in the smallest village, even where is the ground made of stone that would not grow the smallest thread of grass. The matadors are everywhere, and they have all the times been there, but they have not until now been recognize, for they have wear on their backs not the gold-lace embroiderings of Belmonte, but the black of the Church. And the picadors come riding over the peoples not on weak old horses, but on the hundreds of horses of their Isottas, and the peoples are crazed with the banderillas of hunger and impoverty, and they die on the sword of work in their own dung and the dirt, like the dumb bulls. All my country is one bull-ring, one Badajoz, and many more of my peoples will die as dumb bulls before is change this condition—but it *will* be change! Bulls too kill some time, and they will yet make a great cornada in those that come murdering them, crying, 'Viva El Christo Rey!'"

Dan put his arms around her, saying, "What is to say, Florencia? What is to say?"

IBERIA

ON a wall of the flat hung a map of the peninsula, with Portugal in pale brown and Spain in green. The green area was inhabited by pins, black for the Insurgents and white for the Loyalists, and a double row of them, one black and one white, wound through the country like an ant-trail. Towns had been punctured out of existence, like chances taken on a punchboard, but while few of these lay behind the white line, many, in swarms and scatters, lay behind the black.

"What're you thinking about?" Mary said.

"Nothing," Dan said.

"It didn't look like nothing."

"I always look serious when I think about nothing. It's a serious subject."

"It must've been a faraway nothing."

"You really want to know what I was thinking?" he said. "I was thinking how much I love you."

"You make better speeches all the time."

"They're no better. They only sound better."

"Much," she said. "I'm beginning to believe them."

"You should. I'm beginning to mean them."

"Didn't you ever mean them before, Dan?"

"You've become the opposite of Julia. When I first knew her, I could see nothing beyond her, but she dwindled by the hour. When I first knew you, you were only part of the landscape, a near part and a sweet-smelling part, but just part. You've taken up more room every day. Every day I see less of the world and more of you, and the time'll come when there's no world at all, only my Mary."

"You could get me to do anything you wanted, Danny," she said. "Anything."

"Meet me on the bed."

"Just one thing first. Loving me isn't what you were thinking about before, is it?"

"No," he said.

"I didn't think so," she said, "but I'll meet you all the same."

THE WATER'S ALWAYS COLD

"WELL, SMILE at him and send him in," Dan said to the switchboard-operator, and a moment after he hung up the receiver, his door opened. "Tootsie-boy! Park your chocolate ass and tell me what you're doing in this barracoon."

"Playing hookey," Tootsie said.

"Not just to see me. I'm not that popular."

"You're popular with me, or I wouldn't be here. I came to say goodbye."

"To say goodbye?" Dan said, and he watched smoke rise from the cigarette he held in his hand. "Where are you going?"

"Spain."

The one-word answer took a long time to die away in Dan's mind; it seemed to be audible again and again, and each renewal came with almost the same frequency. "Spain," he said, and now he turned to the window and a late-fall rain. A train went past, its runners striking purple fire from the wet third-rail. "I think I knew all along that you'd go."

"You knew more than I did, then," Tootsie said. "I didn't know it till an hour ago, when I signed the papers."

"When do you leave?"

Tootsie said, "They didn't tell me," and then he shook his head. "They *did* tell me, but I can't tell *you*. I shouldn't've let on even as much as that."

"But, Jesus, you might be pulling out tomorrow."

"Might."

"Won't Mary have a chance to kiss you goodbye?"

"*I* won't have a chance to kiss *her*. That's more important."

"Couldn't you have supper with us tonight? I'll call Newark, and she'll meet us anywhere we say."

"I wish I could, boy, but I'm all promised out. I've got to see my folks and break the news. They don't know about me signing up yet. After that, I'm going to hunt up Julie, and after that—well, after that, there's a lady."

"No! You never told me about a lady, Tootsie!"

"Wasn't much to tell till a while back. I only met her in September, at the beginning of the term. We teach at the same school. It's the real thing, though, Dan."

"Everybody's getting married! Mig, and now you!"

"I didn't say I was getting married."

"Then it can't be the real thing."

"It can be God *damn* real—especially if you're going to spend your whole engagement ducking hot lead."

"But it might be a year, two years, who knows how long."

"It might be never."

"Don't talk like that," Dan said.

"Why only think like it? *Some* guys aren't coming back, and I could be one of them."

"All the same, I don't want to hear about it."

"I'm sorry. I only thought I'd be able to work up a little more courage if I told you how scared I was."

"You won't work up anything talking to me. *I* didn't sign any papers; *you* did. Whatever you were before, you aren't scared now."

"Signing the papers all of a sudden made me a brave man—is that what you think? A scared man sat down and wrote *Tudor Powell*, and a brave man got up. Where's the sense in that? The same man got up that sat down—and he was scared both ways."

"What're you trying to do—make me feel good?"

"I'm trying to make *myself* feel good," Tootsie said. "I don't want to die. Any day in the week, I'd sooner live than die. It would've been great if signing those papers made me immortal, but I don't *feel* immortal. I feel wide open for death. I don't like that feeling, but I've got it."

"You can't tell me it doesn't take courage to risk your life."

"This'll sound queer, but that's the *last* thing it takes. There's brave guys all over the lot—guys willing to climb steeples, put out fires, or just show off for their broads in a street-fight—but damn few of 'em are going to Spain. It's us scared guys, mostly—and you know why? Because we know what it is that we're afraid of, not only over there, but right here."

"I know what *I'm* afraid of. Why don't *I* go?"

"The war isn't over yet, boy."

"I'll never get there, Tootsie."

"I didn't think *I* ever would, either."

"But we're different," Dan said. "At the worst, you're only scared. I'm yellow. You understand? *Yellow!*"

"The things that've got to be done are all dangerous, every one, but they're going to be done all the same. You, though, you've got the dumb idea that a doer can only be a real red-blooded hot-shot,

a fire-eating piss-cutting son-of-a-bitch that'd sass God and sit in
His chair. But, boy, you should've seen what I saw when I signed
my life away this afternoon. A roomful of guys like myself, a dozen
of 'em, and not one but wasn't shaking in his pants, or worse. Plain
guys, little guys, poor guys, a couple of Hebes, another skinny nigger—and all worried about holding steady long enough to sign their
names. I didn't see any fire-eaters around. I didn't see any Frank
Merriwells, or Tom Swifts, or whoever you get your notions of
bravery from. I only saw a dozen shivering punks from Intervale
Avenue and Bay Parkway and Delancey Street. There wasn't a decent suit in the bunch. A flashy one here and there, kibo-cut, but
none that cost a dime over twenty bucks. And there wasn't much
college, and there wasn't a drop of blood bluer than yours or mine.
But what we had instead of Harris tweeds was the knowledge that
this is everybody's fight, and that if some of us go first, the rest'll
follow. It's no harder to go first. It just looks harder, but it's hard all
the time, first and last—the water's always cold. I know. I'm in it."
Tootsie came to his feet now. "How about a handshake, partner?"

Dan rose too, and ignoring the black and pink hand, he put his
arms around Tootsie and hugged him, and then he kissed him on
his black and pink mouth. "I don't know what to say," he said,
"except that I'll love you as long as I live."

"I hope that's the last thing I think of if I die," Tootsie said.
"G'bye, boy."

*   *   *

When Mary reached home, she found Dan lying face-down on the
bed in the dark. "Don't you feel well?" she said. "Can I do anything for you?"

"Yes," he said. "If you happen to have a gun in your pocket,
aim it at the back of my head and fire."

She took her coat off and sat down next to him. "What's wrong?"
she said.

"*I'm* wrong—*dead* wrong."

"Tell me about it. Maybe I can help."

"Blow my brains out," he said, "and you'll be helping everybody." He righted himself and sat up. " I had a visitor today—Toot-sie Powell. He's going away. Guess where to, baby. Guess."

"He might be going anywhere."

"He's going to one particular place—the *only* place."

"Spain?" she said.

He looked at her and tried to say, "Spain," but the word was too big for his mouth, and it jammed. "He made believe only the scared ones were going. To *me*—the *brave* one!"

"I don't think he was making believe. It's possible to be scared and go and to be brave and stay."

"I must be the last English-speaking man. I say the brave go and the scared don't, and I'm answered with grunts and gibberish. If a scared man does a brave thing, he isn't scared: he's brave!"

"I've been saying that all along, but you never listen. Brave is what you are when you do a thing, not what you were while you made up your mind."

"Don't try to save my feelings any more. The chips are down, and you'd better try to save your own. I've got you to show for my life, I've got you to be proud of, but what can you show?"

"Why do you say the chips are down?"

"For God's *sake*, Mary!"

"Maybe the time hasn't come for you to prove anything."

"The time comes and goes like a train," he said. "Trains pull in, and trains pull out, and I'm still standing on the platform. You know damn well what train I'm waiting for—the *safe* train!"

"I don't believe it," Mary said.

"When I look at that beautiful plain puss of yours," he said, "I could croak myself for being such a piss-ant to you. The least you've had a right to expect is the truth, and I've never even given you that, not till it was too late to matter. There's no merit in being honest when it would hurt you more to lie, but for what it's worth as part of the case-history of your husband, here's the big secret of his life: Florida. You know all about Florida except the one thing that explains the rest. Before those sheriff-bastards took me to jail, one of them, an animal named Ash, beat the whey out of me and gave me a sanding. A sanding is this: you put on a glove, coat it with wet sand, and then punch the grains at the face you're trying to fix; the first few times, you'll only make the skin raw, but that's what you want, because now the sand has something to stick to; you coat your glove again, and again you slug away, and now sand is grinding on sand that's grinding on flesh, and with a bloody beard of sand to work on, you're off; you keep on loading the glove and punching, loading and punching, five minutes, ten minutes, who knows and who cares? and then you let the face scab over, and by morning it isn't a face but a bag of pus, and it stays that way for days, till finally it breaks open and blows out the grains, but only a few at a time, some now, some next week, some next month. That was Florida, but don't go away yet: there's more. What happened to my mind was even worse than what happened to my face. Lying there in that cell one night, I found out once and for all what I was up against. I couldn't fall asleep, I remember—couldn't let myself, I mean, because I was afraid to. I was afraid I'd think something out that I wanted to avoid knowing, and I thought I'd be safe if I stayed awake. I was wrong. I'd've been happy all my life if I'd beaten down that one dangerous thought, and I'd've been a good husband to you, Mary, not a disappointed crumb, and you'd've been as proud of me as I am of you, and we'd've had something better to look forward to than more bile and gall. But it was like throwing myself on a bomb: the fuse'd been lit, and it went off. What I was up against was America—the American train. It's hard to say now why I put it that way. The tracks of the Florida East Coast were alongside the jail-yard wall, and maybe a train was going by at the time, or maybe it was natural for me to think of America as a train, because trains've always fascinated me—but whatever the reason, I saw the Big Train that night. Forty-eight cars long, it was, a golden train on golden rails, and it was running on time from Heaven to hell. Inside, with their fat on the plush, were the Silk-hat Harrys; outside, on the roofs and the rods and riding blind, were the Happy Hooligans. Now and then, someone on the right-of-way tried to stop it with his words and his hands, a Debs, a Lovejoy, a Lincoln, a John Brown, but it hit him at a hundred miles an hour, and he died. Except for a few, everybody rode the Dipsy-

Doodle, the silly slobs, the saps, the schmucks, the dopes and dupes, the dumb Dannys. They were all up there on the American train—cleaning it, servicing it, repairing it, feeding it, manning it, guarding it. *Guarding it!* Guarding what others owned—and for scraps, for nickels, for buttons, for a handout, for promises, for a six-foot grave! There they were, ready to ride you down if you opened your mouth, ready to beat you, shoot you, kill you, defame you—the have-nots protecting the haves! the hungry defending the stuffed! the lowly upholding the regal! The many had the feet, and the few had the shoes, and I thought: My God, what people do for a dollar a day and a dream! Do you know me now, Mary darling . . . ?"

FEBRUARY 10, 1937

"I'M glad you looked in, Pete," Dan said. "I wanted to talk to you." Peterson sat down. "That's kind of a piano opening for a hotbox like you," he said. "What's on your excuse-the-expression mind?"

"I'm putting the bee on you."

"Not for a raise, I hope, because if that's what you're after, you can grab your rubbers and penwiper and stand not upon the order of your going. A raise! What do you need a raise for? You'd only renew your subscription to the New Myasses or take another course in Diabolical Mysterialism. You know too much right now. Go to the movies and be happy."

"Change your oil. I'm not out for a raise."

"A good thing, because I came in here to hit you for lunch."

Dan laughed. "Go around in back," he said. "The grass is longer."

"A laugh with rocks in it. I'll bet if I came to you broke, you wouldn't give me your nose-gum."

"I'd say, 'Pete, this is heartbreaking, you mooching in the street. Why don't you go up that alley—Peterson's Alley?'"

"It's odds-on you'd help me up it with a kick. That's the trouble with you inhumanitarians—always *of* the people, *by* the people, and *for* yourself."

"I want a hundred bucks from you, Pete—for Spain."

"Where's Spain?" Peterson said. "If you mean the country that treacherously invaded its own soil in 1898, you haven't got a chance. I'm still sore about the dastardly way they let us kill their soldiers and sink their fleets. Barbaric. Besides, it takes me a month to exploit you out of a hundred bucks. Why should I give it up to the greasers?"

"Because I ask you to," Dan said. "I always put on an act when you're around. I make out like I hate the sight of you, but you know damn well I don't really feel that way, or I wouldn't lower myself to put the tap on you. If you kept up with what was going on over there, you'd say, 'A hundred! Why only a hundred?' Those guys are stopping slugs aimed at us; the least we can do is keep them in chocolate-bars and soap. What do you say, Pete?"

"I say this," Peterson said. "They're getting all they need from Hitler, and if they run short, they can always draw on the Vatican."

Dan stood up slowly. "Get out of here before I cold-cock you with this telephone!" he said.

Peterson sat where he was. "A c-note for the Loyalists!" he said. "Why, kid, they're papa's enemies!"

*　　*　　*

When Dan let himself into the flat that evening, he found Mary waiting for him with her hands behind her back. "Out with the present, baby," he said.

"Present?" she said. "What makes you entitled to a present?"

"On my way home, I had a thought. I said to myself, 'Danny-boy, in another twenty-eight years, you'll be fifty-six.' I damn near floored myself. Fifty-six! That's kind of ripe—*over*ripe."

"Well, you still have twenty-eight years—but from tomorrow."

"What're you holding onto back there—or is that where I give you the pain?"

"Not this time."

"If there's a present around, I won't sleep a wink. Of course, if there *isn't* any present. . . ."

"I can't honestly say there is, and I can't honestly say there isn't."

"What you mean is, you can't be honest."

"The trouble with this present is that it isn't exactly the kind you're looking for."

"You better let me see it," Dan said. "Otherwise, I'll take it by force—and I just might do the same to you."

"Will you promise me something?"

"I promise! I promise!"

"That you won't get upset," she said.

"Why should I get upset? It must be a hell of a present."

"It's really *two* presents," Mary said, and bringing a hand into view, she offered him a letter bearing a foreign stamp.

"Tootsie!" he said. "Tootsie-boy!" He held the envelope up to the light and began to tear it open along the shadow of the enclosure.

"Wait, Dan," Mary said, and now she revealed her other hand. It held a second letter.

Dan raised his eyes to Mary's, saying, "It's Mig! It's Mig, Mary! Mig's in Spain too!"

"Remember your promise," she said.

He sat down, saying, "I'm not upset," and then he rose, staring at the letters. "I'm not upset at all." He sat down again, staring now at nothing. "Why should I be upset?"

"Would you like to read me what they say?"

"Mig and Tootsie are in Spain," he said, "and I'm in the Eighties between Amsterdam and Columbus Avenues, north side of the street, second floor front. I wonder what my friends think of me." He fumbled the envelopes, and at length he set one aside to complete the tear in the other. "From Tootsie, at a place called Albacete, on the 20th of January."

My first letter ought to be about my experiences coming over, the kind of people I found myself thrown together with, my thoughts on arriving, and so on, but all that will have to wait for another occasion, Dan, because there's something else that has a deeper claim on me. I'd give all I ever hope to own to be free of it, but I'll not be free even after I tell it, nor will you. This is a sad moment, Dan, and as your old-time partner, I share it with you. . . .

Dan let his hand fall, saying, "I'm afraid to read any more."

Mary's voice was quiet. "Would you want me to read it for you, Dan?" she said.

"I know what's coming," he said. "I feel it in my bones."

This is bad news, and I ask you to forgive me for writing it badly. Your friend Mig DeLuca was killed this afternoon in an air-attack on his training-base at (scratched out). Only a few bombers came over, and they dropped their loads without doing much damage, but a fighter from the escort dropped down for a reconnaissance and shot up an orchard and a barn-yard, and one of the very few casualties was Mig. A bullet hit him in the head.

There's more, Danny, and it's just as full of anguish. It has to do with how Mig and I finally met after so many years of hearing about each other through you. We were in different camps, and it so happened that today we were both detailed to go into Albacete for the mail. I didn't know him by sight, of course, and he didn't know me, but we got our sacks at about the same time, and on our way out of the building, we swapped a few words. All we had to do was introduce ourselves, and we were on the wing.

It was a wonderful meeting, Dan. It lasted only half an hour, but it couldn't have been more wonderful if it had lasted half our lives. It's hard to remember all we said, because we seemed to say so much; it was as if we were trying to make up for lost time—but mostly we talked about you. I'd always believed I had as warm a feeling for you as anyone outside of Mary, but Mig, even in that little half-hour, outdid me. A brother could-n't have spoken of you with more love.

A half-hour, that's all we had together, but it's fair to say that all you told me about him was true. He knew what he was fighting here better than I'll ever know it, he was a better Party-man than I ever expect to be, and he was a better any-kind-of-man. I say that because he came to Spain knowing that he'd never live to leave it. I gathered that from one little slip he made while he was showing me some pictures of his wife. He said, "Danny would've liked her." I let it pass, and when we parted, we made arrangements to keep in touch with each other. He was killed on his way back to camp.

They're going to bury him tomorrow, and I've gotten leave to attend. I'll be thinking of you, Danny. I'll say goodbye for you. . . .

For a while, he sat still, holding the pages before him as if reading them once more to himself, but what he saw through a mesh of ink was a face that he knew he now would always have to see with the mind alone, a face that he would never again be able to touch, to watch in action, a face that was forever finished with such words as *Mr. Lovejoy.* . . . And suddenly the middle third of his body, from his chest to his groin, seemed to cramp, to clench like a hand, and doubled over, he began to weep in immitigable grief.

Mary knelt near him, and forcing him to look at her, she said, "Mig's letter, Dan, and then Mig's people."

"You're crying too," he said.

"I know what he meant to you. One of the reasons I love you is that other people count."

"None more than you," he said, "but Mig is one it'll be hard to do without." He took up the second letter and opened it. "Don't let me cry again, will you, Mary?"

Well, kid, you find The Snake turning up in a lot of places these days, and it kind of keeps a guy on the go. This time it calls itself Franco, and that's the long and short of what I'm doing in the land of Don Quixote.

But, hell, you don't need any pamphlets from me. After that course, you know the score yourself, and the fact that you're not over here with us only means you realize there's vital work to do elsewhere. Plenty of Russkis I know were actually ordered to stay home, and the order was a correct one, because in many cases it was the most politically-advanced that wanted to volunteer, and you can't always spare that kind. I'm sure you'll do as much good right there on Manhattan Island as I will behind a stone wall over here. It don't make any difference how you kill a Fascist. With a gun, or with words, or with the old evil-eye—just so you kill him.

If you're wondering when I'm going to get to the subject of Irina, you can stop wondering right now. We got married last summer, a couple of days after she got back from the Crimea. She had a vacation coming to her, and so did I, and that's when we pulled off the job. Guess where we went. Correct—right back to the Crimea! I had to chase her through the vineyards. I might as well have married a grape. But of course I'm only kidding about that. I didn't really care where we went. In fact, I was only too glad to let her have her way. It made her happy to know that her Amerikanski understood there's no separating your personal life from your work.

So in the daytime, she was busy running around watching the grapes grow, and at night—well, at night, we made good love, like you and Mary. I didn't tell her I'd decided to go to Spain till we were back in Moskva, and all she said was, "Mikhail, if you vill go, then I vill not stop you." There were many things, though, that we wanted to say and couldn't, and to know what they were, try and imagine leaving Mary. You'd be full of words too, but damn few of them would come out. You see, we're in love.

I'm going to close now, kid, asking you to kiss Mary for me. Compañeros, salud!

Breathing open the torn end of the envelope, he saw that something had remained within. He shook it out, and on the table in the lamplight lay a photograph of two people standing in an aisle of grapevines.

*   *   *

Dan and Mary were at the door, across the room from an old man and an old woman. On a sideboard stood a decanter of wine and four empty glasses, and above it, flanking crossed Italian flags, hung the now framed and faded pictures of Nicola Sacco and Bartolomeo Vanzetti.

The old man said, "For come and tell us about our boy, grazie."

"Don't thank me," Dan said. "For God's sake, Papa, don't thank me."

"Yes," the old woman said. "You good friend with our Michele that you call Miguel. You good friend, or you no have to come out this bad night with snow to read letters. For this, we say grazie."

MAINLY ABOUT FEET

ACROSS the city, an east wind herded clouds that resembled a flock of soiled sheep: gray, silver, slate, and ashen, they milled overhead and passed.

"Morning, kid," Peterson said. "Congratulations."

"Thanks," Dan said.

"I have a little gift for you," the man said, and on the desk-blotter he placed a package wrapped in gaudy paper. "A token of my esteem on this another milestone in what I trust will be a long and honorable life."

"You didn't have to buy me anything, Pete."

"I never forget one of the truly great days of history."

"It could've been greater," Dan said, "but it was nice of you to think of me."

Peterson indicated the package, saying, "Aren't you going to open it?"

"I'll wait till I get home. Mary'll have something for me too, and she likes to watch me gnaw at the wrappings."

"You'll only have to bring this back here. It's for the office."

"Well, if it'll give you pleasure," Dan said, and taking up a pa-per-cutter, he slit the covering. What he brought to light was a wooden plaque bearing a saying in painted letters:

I HAD NO SHOES AND COMPLAINED

AND THEN I MET A MAN WITHOUT FEET

"Entertaining?" Peterson said. "I found it in an antique-shop up the bullyvard."

"Entertaining as all hell," Dan said, and he donned a shaving-smile, empty of amusement and fleeting.

"It looked like a good thing for you to sit in front of all day. I thought it'd make you tolerant."

"What I needed was something to make me *in*tolerant," Dan said, and he went to a clothes-tree for his coat and hat. "You don't know it yet, but you gave it to me."

"You sound sore, kid."

Dan said, "I just told you what I was—intolerant," and picking up a pair of rubbers, he tossed them at the trash-basket. "I borrowed those from you the other day, but you don't need them any more: you've got no feet."

"What's got into you, kid?" Peterson said.

Dan rapped himself on the chest. "*I've* got into me," he said, "and I'll be God damned if I didn't find something dead there and the rest dying. Maybe it's all dead, I don't really know yet, but I'm sure as Christ going to learn before I have to crawl like you. I'm taking a walk, you son-of-a-bitch, a long one, and I mean to complain till I get my shoes or lose my feet. You never complained. You let them chop you down inch by inch till you stood knee-high to a human being, and I hope to die if I ever get to where I see eye-to-eye with you. So help me God, Pete—I hope to die!" He started for the door, but he stopped before he reached it and put out his hand. "Want to say goodbye, Pete?"

But the man had stooped for one of the rubbers, and he stood turning it over in his hands.

DEATH AVENUE

FROM the curb, Dan watched trucks roll over the now paved right-of-way of the New York Central freight-division [*and you remembered the screaming flanges of the old high cars as they rocked along rails set in a streetwide waffle of cobblestones. A man on horseback had ridden ahead of the engine, you remembered, with a red flag for day and a red lantern for night, but to the downtown dock-front gangs, the color had been a signal for sport, not danger, and they had played train with the trains, hooking rides on the rungs, climbing the couplings, and running the sway of the catwalks—and sometimes a foot had slipped, or a hold had been shaken loose, and then a scream of another kind, not long prolonged except by the mind, had been heard. Death Avenue, this street had been called, and from the unabated shock on the faces of the buildings that lined it, you knew it was Death Avenue yet*].

At the Chelsea yards south of the Pennsylvania cut, Dan went into the timekeeper's office and knocked on the scored sill of a barred window. A man at the slant of a standing desk was comparing slips of paper with entries in a journal, and he continued to do so even after Dan had played on the bars with a coin. "Keep your skin on," the man said, glancing up from his work only to impale batches of slips on a billhook. When the last of these had been disposed of, he approached the window. "Now, what can I do you for?" he said.

"I'd like to see one of your men," Dan said. "His name is Pollard."

The man leafed a few ironbound frames in a rack and clicked a pencil-point down its celluloid flaps. "You'll find him over in the Claim Office today," he said. "Cliff Pollard."

"Cliff?" Dan said. "I'm looking for Julian."

The pencil clicked down over one more flap. "You mean the nigger?" the man said.

"I mean Julian Pollard."

The man removed his glasses and twirled them, saying, "You a friend of the nigger's?"

"Don't use that word again."

"I only asked are you a friend of his."

"That's a whole lot better."

"Let's quit making faces," the man said. "I don't know you from a hole in the ground. You come in here asking for somebody, and I want to know are you a friend. That don't call for guff."

"The word you used gets my ass out."

"Your ass gets out quick, but that's neither here or there. I got a reason for my question if you're a friend of this Pollard."

"We've been friends for fifteen years."

"All right," the man said. "You're friends. That means you like him. It means you're looking out for his good. Now, supposing you take a look at that notice—that little one over there." Dan crossed the anteroom to the punch-in and punch-out slots. "Pasted on the clock."

Typed in the spaces of a PERISHABLE sticker were the words: *Niggers will use the nigger tiolet. They will not use the white tiolet. This means you.*

The man came from behind the partition and went to a window overlooking the yards. "Show you something," he said. "See that little shanty with the black door near the switch-tower? That's the can for colored—if you like that word better."

"About as big as a dog-house," Dan said. "Why didn't the company just put up a few fire-plugs?"

"Sure thing," the man said. "Now, take a look at that little white-door shanty sticking out back of the Seaboard reefer. That's the can for whites."

"Same God damn dog-house," Dan said. "Is that what I'm supposed to say?"

"To the letter," the man said. "So what's the odds if the whites use one dog-house and the colored another? You answer."

"The answer to two lousy cans is one good one."

"Or anyway, *two* good ones. But things being like they are, why should there be any fight in these yards? There ain't a smicket of difference between them two shanties, and nobody's getting gypped, and nobody's getting discriminated. So for Pollard's own good, I'm telling you he's going to walk in that white-door can one of these days, and he ain't going to walk out—not ever. I know what I'm talking about."

"Did you put that warning up on the clock?"

"What do I look like—a KKK?"

"Nobody looks like a KKK," Dan said. "But, by God, *somebody* gets under those hoods!"

"Could've been any one of forty guys stuck that thing up there," the man said. "But I told you all I know, and I got to get back to chopping weeds. You want this Pollard, he's on Platform Three."

"Mind if I ask you one thing?" Dan said. "Why did you take all that time over a single colored man? You don't particularly care for the colored people, do you?"

"I don't particuly care for nobody," the man said. "But I don't *hate* nobody. I'm you might say in between, if you follow."

"I follow," Dan said.

"I don't like trouble."

"I follow that too."

"Whether it's trouble for me or whoever, I don't like trouble."

"You're strictly anti-trouble."

"You sure follow," the man said, and he returned to the inner office.

At one side of Platform Three, a string of cars wearing the heralds of many roads were being unloaded, and at the other, motor-trucks with their plackets open stood backed in for cases from Texas and crates from Georgia. Elsewhere, chinless yard-goats fussed with empties, and smoke and cinders rolled on the cold eastern air.

Dan spoke to one of the handlers, saying, "I'm looking for Pollard."

"Ask a checker."

The checker said, "Pollard? Find him four cars up—meat-wagon on the Nickel Plate."

From the side-door of a yellow refrigerator, men were trolley-ing hooked-up slabs of beef to a packing-house Diesel across the platform. When Julie appeared, he was shoving a burlap-covered quarter, and as he passed Dan with it, he said, "How's Mr. White-collar?"

Dan waited for him to derail the load and make his way back. "Lumpy," he said. "When do you knock off for lunch?"

"Ought to be getting on for soon," Julie said.

The handler behind him said, "Blow on it, Pollard."

There were four in the meat-gang, and each of them made two more round-trips before the noon-whistle was blown at the time-office. As the men emerged from the frost-lined car, the driver of the Diesel said, "Another couple, and I'm full up. What say?"

"Go eat," one of the gang said. "Go eat."

"Ah, have a heart," the driver said.

"Phrig you," the handler said.

The driver addressed Julie now, saying, "How about it, eight‑ball?"and Julie stopped with one arm down the sleeve of his mack‑inaw."I got to go all the way over to Brooklyn, eight‑ball, and I. . . ."

"That's two eight‑balls," Julie said. "You must have plenty of balls. I hear about one more, and I start knocking you loose from some." The driver turned away, and Julie nodded at Dan. "Come on, ofay. Let's eat."

As they went down the ramp at the end of the platform, Dan said, "Where do you stoke up around here?"

"Alongside of a tin pail," Julie said.

"Hell with that on a day like this. Too damn cold. What you got in that suitcase?"

"Piece of lunch."

"Christ, you look like you're moving."

"I don't go for moving," Julie said. "I'm a stayer."

"So I hear."

"We eat over by that mess of ties."

Near the creosoted stack, trash smoldered in an up‑ended oil‑drum. Julie fed it a few splits of wood, and fire soon climbed above the rim. "Just like home," he said, "and you can have it."

"What's on the me‑and‑you?" Dan said.

"Jew‑boy feesh. Ever eat Jew‑boy feesh?"

"Before you ever knew you were black."

"You been on it a long time, then," Julie said, and opening his dinner‑pail, he handed Dan a smoked‑salmon sandwich on pum‑pernickel bread, and then he poured him a thermos‑cap of coffee. "I'll take mine from the jug."

Dan gazed at the fire in the drum, saying, "I have bad news, Julie."

"What other kind is there?"

"Mig was killed in Spain."

Julie spat."That's bad, boy, even for bad," he said.

"I don't know what to say. I don't know what to do."

"Do or say, and he's still dead."

"It was Tootsie told me about it. Shot in the head, he wrote. Mig with a hole in his head, like Lincoln. If a thing like that can happen, there was never a Jesus."

"It only happened *account* of Jesus."

"He was mighty near where I live, Mig was—mighty damn near."

Julie touched his hand briefly, saying, "If I was the sorrying kind, I'd say I'm sorry, but if Mig had to get killed, I wish he'd've got killed right here in America: there's a whole lot to get killed here for. You're one of the two-three good whites I ever met in my life. I feel high when I'm aroundabout you. I even disremember I'm supposed to stink. But there's something I *never* disremember: that you're white, and I'm black. Nobody's after you like they're after me, and they've always been after me, and I don't run. I told that to Tootsie the last time I saw him, and he said what's the good of abolishing the poll-tax over here when the Fascists over there are busy abolishing the vote; he said even a thing like lynching was a littler thing than the thing in Spain. But that's Tootsie—it ain't me. Don't nobody have to cross water to get to Fascism. If you're black, you only have to try and *pass* water!"

"I saw that notice in the time-office," Dan said.

"A lawyer in the court, I wanted to be, and they aim to even stop me pissing in a hole! What anybody have to go to Spain for? What I been up against all along in the U. S. white A.? A lawyer in the court, getting justice for the people. Hoo-hah!"

"I can still hear you reading that paper, Julie."

"And I can still see the look on that old screw, Doc Page."

"What about Miss Campbell? She had a look on her face too."

"Did it get me on the graduation-program?"

"Some day, maybe."

"Some day shite," Julie said. "That sign on the clock look like 'some day'?"

"When was that thing put up there?"

"Three-four days back. I first saw it when I punched in Monday."

"Which can you been using since?"

Julie glanced at him before replying. "We been friends many a year," he said. "You shouldn't ought to have to ask."

"All the same, I *am* asking."

"I been using the white one."

A voice said, "Why?"

The timekeeper was standing before them, working an apple-core against his teeth. He tossed it away white, and it came to a stop black with ash.

"Ain't no other can in the yards," Julie said.

"What about that one over there?" the man said.

"What one over where?"

"The black-door one, the one for colored."

"Never did see it."

"You been here for months. You just ain't looked."

"Looking all the time."

"You don't have much to show for it," the timekeeper said. Four tracks away, a group of white yardmen and freight-handlers were lounging at the foot of the switch-tower. They too had a drum-fire going, and their shapes and the tower-shape behind them trembled in the heated air. "And you're going to have less."

"Couldn't have," Julie said.

"You could have a lot less breath," the man said. "Like I told your friend, I ain't pro or con a thing in the world but trouble, and I'm con-trouble every day and extra-good for Sunday. But trouble's coming to this yard if you don't stay out of that white toilet."

"I wouldn't dispute you."

"I'm asking you man-to-man. Why won't you use the colored toilet?"

"Account of that black door *says* colored."

"Just that?" the timekeeper said. "Then suppose we painted both doors the same—black or white, take your pick. There wouldn't be nothing to show."

"To show what?" Julie said.

"To show which was for you."

"If they ain't *both* for me, save your paint."

"But why? You just said it was the doors got your pecker up."

"You mean, you heard it that way," Julie said. "A door don't fret me. Black or white, it's only a door—but if any color means I can't go through, I'm going to bust it down."

"There's people around would stop you."

"Ain't seen 'em so far."

"I told you, you don't look real hard," the timekeeper said. "Now, I'm standing with my back to that tower, and I'll lay you I can see more than you with your front. There was five-six men over there when I came along, but there's a dozen now, or I'm wrong. And they ain't horsing, either—they're watching—and if you say one of 'em's laughing, I'll throw in with you and walk off. Who wins?"

"You win the bet," Julie said.

"But who wins the argument?"

"I win that—pants down."

"That's a good one," the timekeeper said. "I'll have to remember it."

"Be sure you remember who said it."

"I won't miss. And to be all-square, I got a thing I want *you* to remember—a little story."

"Give you till the whistle blows."

"Ever hear of a place in Nevada called Beatty?"

"Just now," Julie said.

The timekeeper said, "About twenty miles south on Route 95 and another twenty-odd off over the sand, there's a magnesium-plant—or was, the time I'm talking about. I took a job with the outfit back in '17—timekeeping, like here—and I stuck with it till along in '23. There was two kinds of people working for the company, whites and Mexicans, and they didn't mix worth a fart. The whites being mostly draft-dodgers, you'd think they wouldn't've been so pickery, but they was even more so. They wouldn't be in the same crew with a Mex, they wouldn't eat with a Mex, they wouldn't live in the same part of the desert with a Mex, and they had to get a dime more an hour to show why: they was a dime better. Things went pretty smooth, though, till some personnel-bastard brang in a brand-new batch of Mexes from Sonora. I was the one checked 'em in, and I knew right off that somebody pulled a boner: that shipment just didn't look good. I don't mean I don't like Mexes. I said before, I ain't pro or con nothing but trouble—and this bunch just plain stunk of that, the thing I hate most. They wasn't the kind you find around towns in the Southwest—broke in to working for the big set-ups, knowing what to expect, and lumping it. These guys was green, and to cap it, they was practicly pure Yaqui. Well, it didn't take a week, and the trouble came and went. It was fast—I'll say that for it—but it was trouble. It wasn't account of the Mexes living in separate districts, and it wasn't account of they ate separate or got a dime less. It was account of something else, a little thing, a thing you wouldn't hardly expect." The timekeeper paused. "Or would you?"

"Whistle ain't blew yet," Julie said.

"It was account of separate toilets."

"Couldn't be. You must be kidding."

"Just like here," the timekeeper said. "Ain't that odd?"

"Odder than even," Julie said.

"Dumb thing to have trouble over—a toilet," the timekeeper said. "Well, anyway. I don't know what give him the notion, but one of these new Mexes wanted in the white toilets—just took it in his head he wanted in, that's all. He could've easy used the toilets for Mexicans—they was marked in Mex on all four sides, and I know he could read, because he wrote a pretty fair hand when he filled out a complaint once—but he wanted in the white toilets, and there it is. First time the whites seen him come out, they figured maybe he made a mistake, and they took pains to point out just what the mistake was. He listened without saying nothing, and the next day he went and made the same mistake all over again. A couple of whites was watching for it, and they followed him in and flang him out on his back—pants down, like you say—but he still didn't say nothing, just picked himself up and walked off. In the morning, there was signs all over the plant, in Mex as well as American, and they told who should use which toilets, and why—but this one Mex, he kept right on being wrong every time he had a Nature-call.

The whites got sorer and sorer, and finally they beat on him real hard, and when he wouldn't promise to quit—wouldn't even open his mouth—they drug him back in the plant and pulled the cord, and everybody knocked off while one of the whites made himself a speech. Here's what he said: 'We're Americans, and you're Mexicans. That means we're better than you are. There's no argument about that. It's a fact, and what proves it is that we're white, and you're not. Now, there's a man laying on the floor here that seems to want more proof to convince him, and if he wants it hard enough, he's going to get it all over his body. We've tried to be fair about this toilet-business, and we'll even be fairer: there's no law says this man has to use the Mexican toilets; if he feels like it, he can go out in the mesquite. But if he thinks he can use the *American* toilets, by Christ, he better only think it while he does it off in the brush. Otherwise, we'll teach him a lesson that won't do him a damn bit of good: he'll be dead.' That was the end of the speech, and the men went back to work, all but this Mex on the floor. It took him quite a while to even stand up, and when he did, he still wasn't much account, and he had to go away somewheres and sit it out. Now, being strong against trouble from 'way back, I thought it my duty to put in a word, and come noonday, I did."

"Peculiar," Julie said. "Just like now."

"I told him how things shaped up in this country," the timekeeper said, "and I told him how no one man ever had much luck trying to change 'em. I took care not to say if separate toilets was right or wrong. Being open-minded, I only said we *had* separate toilets, and a man was free to go back where he come from if he didn't like it, and no hard feelings, and I wound up with, 'So which'll it be, amigo?' He said, 'Si, señor,' about the only words I know for sure that he spoke. Well, I done what I could, I figured, and I sat me in the shade and waited. It was kind of quiet, I remember, just like around here, with everybody sort of watching and not watching, if you follow my meaning. The Mex rolled him a home-made, and he smoked it out, all the time flicking off ash with his pinkie, and then, cool as a church, he got up and headed for the toilets. It goes to show how quiet it was that all you could hear was his sandals slapping on the duckboards. He went straight for the shack marked *American*, and the door closed on him."

Dan glanced at the switch-tower. The group was larger now, some of the men heel-sitting about the fire-blackened drum, some loafing against a tool-shed, and some astride tie-ends and rail, but all at rest, all engines with steam up.

Using the edge of his shoe, the timekeeper smoothed out a fan of cinders. "It won't take long to tell the rest," he said, "because it didn't take long to happen. That door no sooner slammed than half a dozen whites was on their pins and running: it was all arranged, I guess. A couple of 'em had a piece of two-by, another couple had cans of coal-oil, the fifth guy had hammer and nails, and the last one a greasy swab and a box of striking-matches. In no time at all, they had that toilet sealed up and sloshed down—and the feller with the swab touched it off. I'll say this for the other Mexes: they did come alive finally and try to stop the accident. Only when them six whites swang around with their backs to the fire, they had an awful lot of guns in their hands: I guess that was arranged too. Anyway, nobody put the fire out. It *burned* out. That's the story."

Julie slid off the pile of ties, saying, "Piss on you, Mr. Accident-arranger!"

"I remember just one more thing," the timekeeper said, "Whenever people talked about the accident, they always called it 'The Backhouse Barbecue.' Well, I got to get on with my weed-chopping."

Julie watched the man walk away, and waiting for him to reach the crowd at the tower, he said to Dan, "I got to answer a call of Nature."

Dan rose, saying, "Me too."

Julie brought him to a stop with one finger. "I don't need any witnesses, boy," he said, and he started for the shanty with the white door.

The crowd was no longer sloped against a wall, straddling rail, or blessing a fire with open hands: the hands of all were fists. Dan ran after Julie and caught his arm. "For Christ's sake, don't go in there!" he said.

His face slowly growing contempt, Julie shook him off, saying, "Looks like you're just a trouble-hater too, Danny."

And then the white door opened, and the white door closed.

[*Now, in this fraction of a moment between repose and action— suppose!*

[*Suppose they came, the white mob with the black heart, and suppose they had boards to bar the shack with, and suppose they had a tin of kerosene and a car-mop doused in engine-oil, and suppose a match.*

[*And suppose you stood between the white door and the whites, saying, "Take it easy, boys."*

[*And suppose they said, "Do you move, or do we move you?"*

[*And suppose you said, "One of you goes where I go. Come on, Big Train."*

[*And suppose they came on.*

[*And suppose you went for the blue-eyed guy, the blond, the athlete, the yellow-haired Indian-killing Custer, the collar-ad model, the cop, the open-shopper, the acted-on go-getter, the hangman, the proud and poorly-paid lickass, the defender of the faithless, the known quantity, the x exposed (weight 190, with or without head), the winnah and noo champeen, the American answer to the American dream—and suppose you put all your hatred into one cocked fist and flung it.*

[*And suppose the Big Train still came on—the U.S.A., big, hard, dumb, and fast—and suppose it ran you down, jumped your guts, kicked your nuts up back of your lungs, broke your bones, bled you, and desecrated the graves that once had held your eyes.*

[*And suppose you were as good as dead, and suppose in your remaining moment you learned what you hadn't learned in all the rest of your time on earth: that it was a pity to waste your life trying to die of old age when you could use it helping people to live forever. And suppose you thought once more of the tall thin man with a bullet in his brain, and now suppose you had a second or two for one last suppose—and you supposed it. Suppose you'd only been supposing. Suppose your fine final thoughts had never been thought. . . .*

[AND SUPPOSE, INSTEAD, THAT YOU'D RUN AWAY!]

Again the white door opened, and again the white door closed, and Julie was on the step, saying, "False alarm."

The one-o'clock whistle blew.

HALF THE FUN OF HAVING FEET

"WHEN I left the yards," Dan said, "I walked along the docks toward Battery Park. I wanted to see the place where I was born—the place, not the house, because I knew that the house was gone, and with it the little stores, the gas-lamp in front, the overhead wires, and the people. I had to learn whether I'd left some trace of myself, some mark to show that I'd actually lived, some proof that the first half of my life was more than a recurrent dream in the second half. The place was a seven-hundred-foot monument, and buried under it were a few odds and ends that once had belonged to a nobody named Dan Johnson—a toy that he'd played with, a button from a shoe, initials carved in a banister, and a few drops of his blood—but the monument was dedicated to an oil-company, a stock-corporation, a legal fiction, not to me. Where the school had been, there was no monument at all—nothing but an empty lot littered with broken brick and bits of plaster, a filled-in hole, a potter's field holding more of the nobody that all but I had forgotten and none but I would ever look for. The written monuments, I thought—would there be words anywhere to recover what I'd lost? A birth-certificate, a census-report, a high-school record —but I knew that those would show only a date, a dead address, and a grade in Algebra, numbers on yellowing paper, information that wouldn't inform—and I thought, Christ, is that all there is of your life, a few meaningless facts in a file? Has your time on earth been time alone, with a start and a finish and all in between thrown away? Christ, I thought, Jesus Christ, you've chewed yourself out, like a stick of gum, and stuck the remains under a chair!"

"Don't hate yourself any more, Dan," Mary said. "If you have to hate, hate the people that hate people, but for God's sake, don't hate one of the few that love them."

"I won't hate myself for long—only another twelve hours," he said, and from her sudden abatement, as if her existence had suffered an intermission, he knew that she apprehended the rest. "Give me till morning, Mary, and I'll sign up for Spain." With the word *Spain*, her main hope, long-condemned, seemed to buckle and give way. "I'd've signed today, but by the time I discovered where to go, the office was closed [*You'd sign tomorrow, you thought, and the great deed—the one that undone had all your life dulled your living—would be performed. You'd sign tomorrow, you thought, and then the gray road would whiten and the gray years shine. Tomorrow, you thought. . . .*]—so give me one more night to hate, Mary, and that'll end it."

She spoke in a low voice, as if it were almost too late to speak at all, and like one of many at some enviable departure—a sailing, a wedding-journey, a going-home—she said, "You told me once to make no plans. . . ."

He said, "I'm going to Spain because I have to put a stop to my cowardice with an act. I can't stop it with thought, and I can't let time stop it with old age and death. I have to *perform*! If there were some limit to cowardice, if it had a cycle, an orbit, a quota, a maximum size and weight, I think I might've endured it, but I learned today that it's a lingering illness, and that from nothing it'll grow till it's all. It was huge before, but this afternoon, when I realized that I'd've thrown Julie to the wolves—when my feet stood their ground, and my mind ran away—it became world-wide, sky-high, and lifelong. That's why I'm going to Spain—to end the running or, failing that, to end myself. I'm the running kind, Mary, but if I run in Spain, they won't let me off with scorn, as Julie did: they'll shoot me in the back!"

"Make no plans, you said, because you wanted to be free to make your own—but what *are* your own, Dan? Have you thought about them much, or did they come to you in a dream—and are they plans at all, except the sort a man makes when he draws a will? What you mean to do is end a quiet and useful life with a loud and useless death, but you have no right to call that a plan for anything more than more running, this time till you fall down and die either in disgrace or as a hero—no matter which, just so you die. Don't make any plans, you warned me, and none were made, but I still and I'll always hold you to the one thing I demanded in return: you were not to make your great deed death; you were to fight if you so desired, but you were not to die unless only your dying would win what you were fighting for. You're not going to Spain to win anything but a pass. You're not going for Flo and her people, for Sacco and Vanzetti, for Marse Linkum and John Brown, for your dead Michele that you call Miguel, or because your mind ran away with you in Florida once and again this afternoon. You're going for yourself, and by standing on everything around you—on your dead idols, your living friends, and your wife—you hope to grow tall. You won't, Dan, because Spain for you is a place to end, not to begin. You won't find what you're looking for in Spain any more than you found it under a forty-story building or the trash in a vacant lot. You won't find it anywhere in the world but right in this room—in you, in Dan Johnson, in Mig's Mr. Lovejoy. If it isn't here, it doesn't exist. If it is, you can stop eating your heart out, because some day your great deed will be done—and in America!"

He reached for her hand and held it for a moment, idly turning her ring, and then he said, "If I don't go, I'll always think I was afraid."

"And if you do, I'll always think you were afraid to stay," she said. "This is where the fear began, and this is where you have to cure it—and do you know why, Dan? Because it's the Forty-Eighter that you're in love with—not yourself, your friends, great men, Spain, or me." And now, like a stained-glass window in a momentary beam, her face measured out to him its grave and temperate beauty, and she said, "I won't mind so much. I'll take what she leaves if you stay."

He raised his eyes to her, and when at length he nodded, briefly and once only, she was unable to look upon the ordeal of yielding, and turning away, she wept in silence while he spoke—to her, to the darkening room, to the city and its band of rivers, to the land beyond, and to vivid lines on a fading chart—saying, "I love it, Mary, I love it all, but I'd love it more if I could make it better. I'll try to, Mary. I'll do what I can. . . ."

TWO THOUSAND COPIES OF

A MAN WITHOUT SHOES

PRINTED IN EHRHARDT TYPE

BY SAUL & LILLIAN MARKS AT THE

PLANTIN PRESS, LOS ANGELES

THIS IS NUMBER

AND IS SIGNED BY THE AUTHOR